SAMUEL BLACK

The Ground is Burning

faber and faber

K

First published in 2010
by Faber and Faber Limited
Bloomsbury House
74–77 Great Russell Street
London WC1B 3DA

Typeset by RefineCatch Limited, Bungay, Suffolk
Printed in England by CPI Mackays Chatham

A CIP record for this book
is available from the British Library

ISBN 978-0-571-26940-2

2 4 6 8 10 9 7 5 3 1

for Michiel van den Eeckhout
who made the desk on which this book was written

and as an offering to Fortune

Contents

Map of Central Italy   VIII

List of Principal Characters   IX

I
Towards the Glorious Future
(1479–1498)   1
Know Your Enemy
(1499–1502)   43

II
The Castle of Crossed Destinies
(Autumn 1502)   145
The Peak of the Mountain
(Winter 1502/03)   265

III
Where the Wind Blows
(Summer 1503–Autumn 1504)   333
Fortune's Smile
(1505–1516)   387

Afterword   404

Map of Central Italy

List of Principal Characters

LEONARDO DA VINCI (1452–1519)
NICCOLÒ MACHIAVELLI (1469–1527)
CESARE BORGIA (1475–1507)

DOROTEA CARACCIOLO, young noblewoman abducted by
Cesare Borgia
VITELLOZZO VITELLI, ruler of Città di Castello, soldier of
fortune, and one of Cesare's captains

Ser Piero da Vinci, Leonardo's father
Francesco da Vinci, his uncle
Tommaso Masini, Leonardo's assistant
Giacomo Caprotti, aka Salai, Leonardo's young lover and
assistant
Donato Bramante, aka Donnino, architect and friend of
Leonardo
Luca Pacioli, mathematician and friend of Leonardo

Bernardo Machiavelli, Niccolò's father
Totto Machiavelli, his brother
Biagio Buonaccorsi, his friend and colleague
Agostino Vespucci, his friend and colleague
Marietta Machiavelli, his wife
Francesco Soderini, his friend and colleague, later a
cardinal
Piero Soderini, Florentine ambassador, later gonfalonier
of the republic

Alamanno Salviati, Florentine politician and Niccolò's
   enemy

Rodrigo Borgia, aka Pope Alexander VI, Cesare's father
Juan Borgia, Cesare's brother
Lucrezia Borgia, his sister
Agapito Gherardi, his secretary
Ramiro da Lorqua, one of his Spanish captains
Michele da Corella, aka Michelotto, his strangler
Lorenz Behaim, his astrologer
Sebastian Pinzone, one of his spies

Oliverotto da Fermo, soldier of fortune and one of
   Cesare's captains
Paolo Orsini, soldier of fortune and one of Cesare's
   captains
Giuliano della Rovere, later Pope Julius II, enemy of the
   Borgia
Louis XII, King of France
Caterina Sforza, ruler of Imola and Forlì

If the present be compared with the remote past, it is easily seen that in all cities and in all peoples there are the same desires and the same passions as there always were.

NICCOLÒ MACHIAVELLI

I

Towards the Glorious Future
(1479–1498)

1

NICCOLÒ: I am late for the execution. This is annoying because I have been looking forward to this man's death for more than a year.

I have wasted time arguing with my mother, who says I cannot go out. 'Your father is worried about the plague, Niccolò. He is probably fretting over nothing, but he is your father. Right or wrong, you must obey him.'

'Please, mother. Please let me go. We don't have to tell Dad . . .'

'You're not suggesting we lie to your father?'

'You don't have to actually *lie*. Just don't tell him.'

My mother's face goes into odd contortions as she tries to get her head round this. How has she managed to live for more than thirty years without understanding anything about how the world works? I'm only ten and it's pretty clear to me.

I can see she is wavering, though, as much from weariness as from the logic of my arguments. Pressing home my advantage, I plead and plead, making my voice whiny and irritating. 'What he doesn't know can't hurt him,' I say. In the silence after I've finished speaking, we can both hear my father coughing up blood. My mother puts a hand to her forehead as though she is about to faint. Finally she sighs: 'Go, if you must. But be good. And come home soon.'

I am gone before she has a chance to change her mind. As the door bangs shut, I leave behind the stale warmth of the house and run down the street towards the happy roar and stink of the river. Out here, the air is cold. It is yellow-grey with dust and sunlight and smoke. Free at last, I let my legs carry me as fast as they can.

I am headed towards the Bargello, where all traitors are hanged. The name of this particular traitor is Bernardo di Bandino Baroncelli, and as everybody knows, he stabbed Giuliano de' Medici in the back of his head during high mass in April last year, crying out 'Take that, traitor!' as he did so. It was part of a conspiracy, organised by the pope and the Pazzi family: they wanted to take over our city. Lorenzo de' Medici was stabbed too – he got a blade in his throat – but he survived, and the conspiracy was crushed. That is why we call him Lorenzo the Magnificent. All the other assassins were hanged long ago, but this Baroncelli hid in the belltower and then, somehow, escaped Italy. But the Medici have eyes everywhere, so it is said, and they found him in Constantinople. And this morning he is to be hanged, and I . . . I am missing it.

I shove and wriggle my way through the crowds on the Ponte Vecchio, using my elbows as shields, and as I reach the end of the bridge, I see Biagio, the fool, waiting for me, hands on hips. I run straight past him. 'Come on, we're late!'

A moment later I feel his grip heavy on my arm and hear his cross voice, panting. 'I know we're late . . . whose fault is that? . . . too late to run now . . . already missed it . . .'

Biagio is fat. He does not like running.

'The executioner might be late as well,' I say, and pull my sleeve free of his grip. 'Come on, let's see!'

'The executioner is always on time!' Biagio shouts, as though I have personally insulted him by suggesting otherwise.

I ignore him, and keep running. I dodge the steaming piles of horseshit and leap over the stream of piss that runs down the middle of Via Por Santa Maria. I turn right and cut through the alley where my father's cousins live – sudden quiet; the backs of houses; washing hung on lines; a baby screaming and the smell of boiling cabbage – then emerge into the vast open space of the Piazza della Signoria. A game of *calcio* is taking place in the square, a large crowd gathered round it. I slow down, and look up at the palace: armed guards stand before the doors; soldiers on horseback patrol the square. *Power* is here. Still jogging, I bend my neck further back to see the high black tower: the clouds moving fast behind make it look like it's falling towards me.

I sprint forward: round the edges of the cheering, jeering crowd. As I pass, someone yells and several men topple over like dominoes in front of me. One of them stands up, blood pouring from his nose, and pulls a knife from his belt. I run in a wide circle around him, then up a sidestreet: darker, cooler, emptier. For a moment I believe I might not have missed it, but then I see the crowds spill – laughing, talking fast – from the street to my right, and I know they are leaving the Bargello.

Now I have no choice but to stop: the wave of adults is too strong to oppose. I stand in a doorway, getting my breath back, and keep a lookout for Biagio. He appears after a while, his face the colour of a beetroot, and slumps at my feet. Sweat drips from his head onto the cobbles. When he's recovered, he says, in a desolate voice: 'I told you the executioner is always on time.'

Outside the Bargello, only a small crowd remains. We stand beneath the body and look up at it: twisting, slowly, from left to right, and then from right to left. All spasms gone; the face dark.

Biagio whispers, 'Take that, traitor!' and I laugh.

Soon everyone has left except me and Biagio, and a man, further back, writing something in a notebook. The man is quite young, and finely dressed, but he doesn't look rich: more like a poor man who spends all his money on clothes. He has long hair, and his tunic and hose are pink. 'Are you a poet?' Biagio asks him. Biagio is always going up to strangers and asking them questions.

The man glances up from his notebook, and looks as though he's tasted something bad. 'Why ever would you think that?'

LEONARDO: I finish noting down the details of what the dead man is wearing, and then I look again at the sketch – at the man – at the sketch – at the man. The head, I see, is not quite right. Too skull-like. The man hanging above me looks alive still – only somewhat tired and sorrowful. Resigned to his fate. I sketch his face again in the bottom corner. The urchins move closer and stare at my open notebook.

The fat urchin says, 'Oh no, he's not a poet. Look – he's only an artist.'

Only an artist!

The thin urchin asks, 'Have you been commissioned to do a painting by the Medici?' He points to Botticelli's figures on the wall of the Bargello. 'Was it you who did those paintings of the other traitors?'

How can a small child know about such things? *Commissions* and *Medici* and *traitors* – these words like dust in his mouth. I look in his eyes and see no innocence, no joy. Only a small adult peers out from those eyes, above a thin, cruel Florentine smile. You grow up in this city and it stains you for life. I am thankful that I passed my early years among trees and hills and rivers.

from the hill near Vinci I could see my mother's house, the white smoke rising from the chimney

'No, I did not paint those other men. They would appear more real if I had painted them.'

The thin urchin looks unimpressed. 'Well, they say the artist got forty ducats for each one, whoever he was.'

I try to stop my eyes widening. But it is only money – there is no glory in such work. And it will not last. I close my notebook and replace it in my pocket. Leaving the dead man to the tender cares of the urchins, I walk down Via Ghibellina.

I go past the heavy black door of my father's office. I do not slow down. I do not knock. The last time I saw my father was the day before Christmas, and the conversation was the same as always –

When are you going to settle down and get married, Leonardo? What do you want to do with your life?

I wish to work miracles, father

Oh . . . sometimes I despair of you

I focus on the stones beneath my feet, the purple-shadowed walls and doorways that rise up either side of me. As I move towards the city walls, the voices around me grow quieter, the people fewer, the houses smaller and poorer. I turn right up a narrow sidestreet – so small it has no name – and left down another. And there, at the end, is my studio.

I walk inside – the familiar, mingled smells of turpentine, vinegar, walnut oil. The cat meows, the hens burble in the corner. I warm my hands over the brazier. Tommaso, my young assistant, glances up from his canvas and asks how I am.

'Fine,' I say, looking over his shoulder. I point to the mountains in the background of his picture. 'Remember the bases should be paler than the summits.'

7

Tommaso frowns, nods, concentrates on his work. The cat rubs himself round my calves. I can feel his warmth through the thin hose.

'Where's Ricardo?' I ask.

'He went to buy cinnabar. We're all out.'

'You gave him the money from the cashbox?'

'Yes . . . and some of my own.'

'Your own. Why?'

He hesitates. 'There wasn't enough in the cashbox.'

'It's empty?' I blush. 'I'm sorry, Tommaso. I'll take some money from the bank today, and pay you back.'

'Don't worry, master. There's no rush.'

But there is, and I know it. Time is a strong wind, pushing at my back. Nearly twenty-eight years old and what have I achieved? At my age, Masaccio had completed most of his life's work. If I died tomorrow, no one would even remember my name – my legacy would be a few small debts, some unfinished paintings. Several notebooks filled with questions . . . and barely a single answer.

I go back outside, walking faster now. The bells of Santa Croce start to ring. Further off, to my right, the bells of the Duomo echo them. I do not wish to pass my father's office again, so I turn randomly – right, then left, then right again. Down unfamiliar streets. The smell of dogshit, the sound of beggars coughing. I stare at motionless figures slumped in the shadows and wonder who among them carries the plague, who has already taken his last breath. In winter the infection is usually dormant, but during the last month it has claimed forty-two lives. These corpses are incinerated every morning in the plague pits the other side of the Arno – and if the wind is coming from the south, that sweet sickening stench is the first thing I breathe when I open the shutters of my room.

memento mori

My head is pounding and in my stomach there are jets of bile. I walk away – hurriedly, unseeingly, through stinking alleys and bustling markets, past hanging slabs of animal flesh and circles of men gambling with dice, no longer even aware of where I am going, only what I wish to escape . . . until I arrive, by chance, at the Piazza del Duomo. The pale sky vaulting high above. Thirstily I drink the cold air, and after a moment I start to feel better.

A sudden noise above me, as if the sky has been ripped like a sheet of thick paper – I look up and see a swarming dark cloud of wild geese flying over the city. Once more I puzzle over the way they navigate themselves. There does not seem to be a leader. The birdcloud is pulled in different directions by different groups, changing shape like drops of water on tilted glass, yet it never separates, never hesitates. There – *there* – is achievement! Perfection! Mystery! How do the geese find their way south? How do they fly, with such heavy bodies? Could a man fly thus? How does a man walk? How breathe, speak, hear, frown, smile, weep? These questions I have been asking myself since childhood. Asking other people too . . .

my uncle gently mocking me as we walked down to the vines from our house in Vinci – 'Tell me tell me tell me. Why? Why? Why?'

We are each of us living miracles. I look around – men and women buying, selling, gossiping, joking, thieving – and reflect that some of these people, of bad habits and little intelligence, do not deserve such a fine instrument, such an amazing variety of mechanisms.

Then, among the crowd, I notice a blind beggar, dressed in a monk's robes, his eyeballs coated white with cataracts, and I feel a swell of pity and gratitude. To be blind would be worse than death! He who loses his sight loses his view of

9

the universe, and is like one buried alive who can still move about and breathe in his grave. But I – *I* can see! I must never forget the wonder of this gift. I can see not only what other men see, but also, I believe, things they can't see. This sounds like boasting, and I wish to be humble, but . . . all my life I have been sneered at and doubted – because my father did not marry my mother, because my Latin is poor, because painting is only a 'mechanical art'. But the poets and scholars who make such remarks have no idea how much more Truth there is in a single painted shadow or flower than in all the useless words of Plato and his imitators. And to paint truly, one must *see* – the workings of the nerves and muscles beneath the skin, the wingbeats of a hummingbird, a drop of water on the petal of a rose, the movement of wind in a field of hay. And to see, one must understand. And to understand . . .

tell me tell me tell me why why why

For what is the inevitable precursor of all truth? A question. We must always ask – never cease asking. A verse from Lucretius returns to my mind –

> *I may at last gloriously uncloud*
> *For you the light beyond, wherewith to view*
> *The core of being at the centre hid*

– and then the cathedral bell tolls, breaking the threads of my thought. Again! Where has the time gone? I look up at the great dome – and at its peak the golden orb, which I helped fix there, eight years ago. I remember – standing on the roof of the world, looking down at the tiny people, the tiny houses, and imagining all the great works I would accomplish . . . soon. I was only nineteen then, my whole future ahead of me. And here I am still, lost in the crowd below, a nobody.

Soon a new year will begin. A new decade. Perhaps I should move to a new city, begin a new career? Away from the wagging tongues, the frowning eyebrows, the smirking lips, the stained minds. Away from the darkened past, towards the glorious future. What I need is a steady income – not too many strings attached. The freedom to pursue my experiments, to learn Latin, to read books, to paint or sculpt or discover or invent or build something that people will still talk about long after I am dead. *To uncloud the light beyond.* I should write to the pope perhaps, or the Duke of Milan . . . I must look into it.

But now the bell is ringing. The bank will be closing soon. I turn on my heel and walk briskly in the right direction.

When I reach Santa Maria Nuova and withdraw twenty ducats, the bank manager, Fra' Abbiata, warns me I have only eight left in my account. Eight! He rubs his fingers and thumb together. 'You need to earn more, Maestro Leonardo. Big paintings! Major commissions! And finish them, for once!'

'I know, I know, but . . .' I wave my hands to signal helplessness.

Never enough money. Never enough time.

2

NICCOLÒ: We kiss and finally I dare to put my hand up her dress. She does nothing to stop me. The insides of her thighs are as soft as dough and as hot as freshly baked bread. She keeps her eyes closed and moans softly as she breathes. Then, just as I am about to touch the Holy of Holies, she opens her eyes and calmly pushes my hand away.

'Not there.'

I sigh. 'Cecilia . . .' My eyelids are heavy, my breath thick with desire. I touch her bare arm, move my face closer. 'Please . . .'

'Oh Niccolò!' She looks away. 'You know I want to. But . . . my virtue is all I have. If you were to take it, what would become of me?'

'You've never . . .?'

'Of course not!'

We are in shade, surrounded by trees. There is no sound but the river and the buzzing of insects. I look at her: olive skin, black hair, green eyes, luscious lips; her chin a bit too long, perhaps, her teeth a bit too rabbit-like, the faintest hint of dark fur on her upper lip . . . but I don't care.

'Let's just kiss again,' I suggest.

But her eyes are wide open now. 'Can you hear bells?'

I listen: yes, the bells of the church in San Casciano are ringing softly in the distance. 'No,' I say.

'Liar! I've got to go.'

She stands up and I stand next to her. She is slightly taller than me.

'Tomorrow?' I ask.

'Maybe.' She smiles, biting her lip, and my soul melts. A final kiss, and then she is gone: running through the woods, out into sunlight.

Back at the house, I can smell burning. I go to the kitchen and see smoke pour from the iron plate hanging over the fire.

'Er, Dad?'

'Oh shit!' He comes running through from the garden, a volume of Cicero in his hand. 'The carp! I forgot all about it! I was so pleased when I caught it as well, thinking I'd be able to give you boys a proper meal for a change.'

The two of us stand there, looking sorrowfully at the burnt remains of the fish. 'You don't think we could save some?' I ask.

'No,' says Totto's voice behind us. His moonface expressionless, my brother proceeds to scrape the charred carp into the ditch while my father and I look on helplessly. Totto is thirteen going on thirty-five; dad is fifty-eight going on fifteen.

'Never mind,' I say, putting an arm round his shoulder. 'We can go to the tavern.'

'We've eaten at the tavern every day this week,' Totto moans.

'I'm sorry, Totto,' Dad says. 'Sorry, Niccolò. We're not such a family with your mother away and your sisters married . . .'

'Dad, it's fine!' I draw a finger across my throat while looking at Totto: a subtle reminder he should keep his fat mouth shut. The three of us cross the road to the tavern. 'Did you enjoy the fishing at least?' I ask.

'Oh, it was wonderful. Wasn't it, Totto?' My brother grunts. 'The sunlight on your face, the sound of the river, the smells of the countryside . . . you must come next time, Niccolò. Where did you go this morning, by the way?'

'Oh, just down to the woods,' I say, resting my arm on the bar.

Antonio serves us bread and tomatoes, cheese and dried figs, and a gallon of ale. We take a table in the corner, below the shuttered window. 'So what's her name?' my father asks.

In the deep shadow, he can't see me blush. 'Cecilia,' I mumble.

He laughs and smacks my shoulder. 'You're a boy after my own heart, Niccolò. Just mind you don't get her in trouble.'

We eat, and dad tells us a few priest jokes. The jokes are old, but they make us laugh; the bread is dry, but it fills us up; the ale is rough, but it cools us down. All in all, it's a good lunch.

'Oh, by the way,' my dad says, as I wipe my mouth on a cloth. 'I got word this morning that the Livy is ready at the printers. Would you go back to Florence and pick it up for me?'

I hesitate for a moment, thinking of Cecilia waiting for me in the woods tomorrow morning, but my father's happy, expectant face is too much to resist. 'Of course, dad. It'd be an honour.'

I ride our mule, all alone in this country of forests and hills, and my mind drifts. Oh Cecilia! At the sound of your name, my heart beats faster, my prick hardens, and my soul is tormented by a hollow, desperate yearning. In my head I compose a poem for her: tender, ardent, slightly rude. A bit like Ovid, but in Tuscan. I'm pretty sure Cecilia has no Latin.

By four o'clock, the poem is more or less finished and the heat of the day is at its peak. I stop at the inn in Tavarnuzze, where I see Filippo Casavecchia, the blacksmith: an old friend of dad's. He buys me a drink and I borrow a pencil and a scrap of paper from the barman, and scribble down the verses I composed on the journey.

Filippo sips his ale. 'Studying in your holidays, Nico?'

I look up, distracted from my search for a word to rhyme with ecstasy. 'No . . . it's a poem.'

He laughs. 'You screwed her yet? I guess not if you're bothering to write her a poem.'

'She's a virgin. I was . . . I was thinking of asking her to marry me.' This is the ale speaking: I had no intention of saying that to Filippo, even if the idea had crossed my mind during the long, hot journey.

'You were what? You're only seventeen!'

'But my Cecilia is virtuous. And I . . .' – I weigh the phrase on my tongue – 'I love her.'

'Cecilia . . .' He frowns. 'Not Cecilia Arrighi?'

'Yes. Why?'

'Cecilia Arrighi from San Casciano? Lives on the corner near the baker's? Dad's a cooper?'

I can feel my heart beat harder with foreboding. 'Yes.'

'Black hair, goofy, chin like a bayonet, nice pair of tits?'

'Yes, goddamnit! What about it?'

He laughs softly. 'She's having you on.'

'What do you mean?'

'She's about as virginal as the pope's mistress, that's what I mean. She's been ridden more times than your old mule out there.'

I stare at him with glassy eyes. 'I don't believe you,' I say. But I do. His tone is too sure. Already the hazy, perfect image of the girl I kissed this morning is fading, being replaced by this new, darker, unflatteringly detailed portrait.

I stare at the dirt floor, where the barman's dog is devouring a rat it's just caught. Filippo leans forward and prods me under the chin. 'You're too naïve, lad. You should wake up; be more sceptical. People don't tell you the truth just like that. Why should they? They tell you what they think you want to hear.' He gets up, squeezes my shoulder. 'Don't worry, Nico. There's no harm done. It's always better to know the worst. And maybe you've learned something too.'

I say nothing. Filippo says farewell and leaves the inn. I finish my ale and read through the poem I wrote.

Oh well.

Sod it.

I screw the paper into a ball and throw it on the fire.

The sky is turning red in the west when I reach the Piazza della Signoria. I am tired and depressed, but the sight of the city centre, buzzing with the impersonal joy of a warm summer's evening, lifts my spirits again. I do love Florence. As the proverb says: 'The countryside is for animals; the city for men.'

I ride to the printer's: hand over three bottles of wine and one bottle of vinegar to Signor Rossi. In return he gives me Livy's *History of Rome*. It is bound in vellum: a beautiful object. And, inside, all the wisdom of the ancients; all the virtues and heroics of the Roman Republic. My dad worked for months, indexing this volume, in order to pay for his copy; the wine and vinegar were just to pay for the binding. Holding the book proudly under my arm, I lead the mule through the city streets, across the Ponte Vecchio, and back to our house.

When I've stabled the mule, I sit in my dad's chair and open the Livy. Soon I am no longer in Florence, no longer in this timid and pygmy-like age; I inhabit a nobler time, a greater land. For hours on end I forget my petty woes, my amorous yearnings; I forget Cecilia and her lies (and even her thighs); I think only of power and glory. One day I will enter politics. Either that or be a famous poet; I haven't quite decided yet.

My reverie is broken by a knock at the door. I open up: there stands Biagio, stout and grinning. 'I heard you were back. Are you coming out for a drink? Everyone will be there.'

I laugh with pure happiness. 'Biagio! Boy am I glad to see you! Yes, I'll come out. Just let me get some money.'

I go upstairs and fill my pockets with coins. Enough for some wine, and perhaps a trip to the Frascato afterwards, to find a whore. It really is about time I cured myself of this damned innocence.

3

CESARE: Sun-glare and bloodstink. Sweat stings my eyes. Roaring then silence.

My horse is bleeding, trembling. I stroke her neck. Look round – thousands of eyes on me. Thousands of eyes on the bull.

The bull is bleeding. Three thin swords poke from its shoulders. The bull is weakening. Bloodpools everywhere. The bull is angry.

Head low, it charges. I hold the horse still. I can feel her heart beat under my thigh. I whisper in Spanish:

Calm. Wait. Soon.

The bull charges. The horse trembles. Time moves slowly. I slide another sword into the bull's neck.

Sweat foams on the horse's flanks. She tries to run – hooves slip on bloodslicked cobbles. The bull's horn touches the horse. The horse screams. She bleeds and runs.

The bull is swaying. I dismount, walk over. The bull stares up at me. The bull is angry but the bull is weak.

Roaring then silence. I wipe sweat from my eyes and raise the great sword.

The bull lifts its head. Strength for one last charge. But too late, too late.

My mouth is dry. My hands are soaked. Head empty, muscles loose. I've done this many times before.

I swing the great sword.

Silence then roaring. Bloodstink and sun-glare. The bull's head on the ground.

I wash my hands. I wash my face. The crowd chant – 'The bull is dead! Long live the Bull!'

The Borgia Bull, they mean. The Bull – our family's symbol.

I take off my shirt and wash my chest. The smell of blood lingers. Servants pass me clean clothes, gloves dipped in musk. Silk cool, leather warm on my skin.

Girls gasp: 'He's so brave! He might have been killed!' But I knew I wouldn't die. It is not my time yet.

I saw the stargazer last night. Lorenz Behaim. He cast my horoscope. It said I had two paths – two possible fates. If my father is pope, I'll win fame – and die young. If not, I'll live long – without fame.

'Like Achilles,' I said. Lorenz nodded. 'How young?' I asked. 'It's hard to say,' Lorenz said. 'How young?' I repeated. 'Like Alexander,' Lorenz said.

Alexander the Great died at thirty-two years old. Alexander the Great was King of the World.

I am nearly seventeen. More than half my life gone. Fucking hell – I have no time to lose.

I signal Fernando, my page. He comes running. 'Yes, my lord?'

'Still no message?'

'No, my lord. Rest assured you will be informed the moment . . .'

I wave my hand. He shuts the fuck up. I nod. He disappears.

Five days. That's how long it's been – the papal conclave. My father in Rome, in the Sistine Chapel – smiling, whispering. Promising, threatening. Bribing. Perhaps his last chance to be pope. A hundred and twenty hours. And each hour like a day.

Each evening – a message from my father. I know all that has passed. The shifting alignments of the two factions. The muleloads of gold sent to cardinals' palaces.

In his last message – the third scrutiny. Things going his way. The balance tilting. Hope – great hope. 'It is within my grasp at last.'

That was yesterday evening. Before then, waiting was a dull ache. Now it is burning – a raging fever. To lose it now would be –

Fuck. Don't go there. If only I knew . . .

A servant comes. He whispers. The arrangements for the *palio*. Bribes offered. A rival poisoned. Our tactics sharpened.

It is only a horse race. I have five hundred ducats riding on it. But what is five hundred ducats? O fate, O destiny, O Fortune . . . let me lose the race and win – the true prize.

Seconds drag by. Trumpets and drums, flags and chariots. The horses assemble. The crowd roars.

A servant comes, breathless. 'The messenger is here, my lord. But the guards have detained him . . .'

I stand up. Swords in my stomach. 'Take me to him. Run!'

I follow the sprinting servant. Fuck my dignity – my noble bearing. I must know. I must know NOW.

We push through crowds – to the edge of the square. Sienese troops have stopped the messenger. They are asking him questions.

I give them money. I tell them to disappear. They go.

I stare at the messenger. His clothes soaked with sweat. And the look in his eyes – tired . . . frightened? Does he bring bad news?

'Speak.'

A second passes . . .

'My lord, I have ridden all day to bring you the news . . .'

'Tell me!'

A second passes . . .

'Your father was elected the new pope this morning. He has taken the name Alexander. He sends you his . . .'

A second passes . . . and everything changes. Breathe in, one person. Breathe out, someone else.

I am the pope's son.

I walk a different path now. The path to glory. The path I left behind goes through lowlands. This one curves up high to peaks unseen. It's riskier – the falls are fatal. But all great things are dangerous.

Yes. Fucking YES.

I clench my fists. Turn my burning eyes from the messenger's face. Compose yourself. Straighten the mask. Give the messenger a purse of gold. There's plenty more where that came from. He kisses my feet – opens his mouth to pour out fine words.

I hold up my hand. 'Save it. Change your horse. Eat some food. Then ride back to Rome. Tell my father I am happy and proud at his deserved elevation blah blah blah. Use lots of fancy phrases. You can expect more gold at his end.'

'Yes, my lord.'

I call one of the servants. 'Get my carriage ready.'

'What about the horse race, your lordship?'

'Fuck the horse race. Get my carriage ready, I said.'

There is no time to lose.

4

LEONARDO: I turn my eyes from the stage to the faces of the audience, which appear and disappear with the flickering of the multicoloured flames. I watch as their faces show fear, wonder, amusement, shock. As we near the climax, I lift my eyes to the night sky. This part of the show is risky. It has never been done before – it might go wrong. I squint up at the blackness, and the first white flakes appear, seemingly from nowhere, drifting down lazily in beautiful spirals and eddies. I look at the audience – no one has noticed yet. Their eyes are still fixed on the darkening stage, waiting for the next miracle. And then, one by one, with gasps and exclamations, they feel the cold wetness on their faces – and look up . . .

'Snow!'

'But that's impossible. It's the middle of summer!'

Lucrezia Crivelli, the duke's mistress, smiles at me and says, 'Dear Leonardo, however did you manage it?'

I wish to work miracles

'He is a magician!' someone cries.

'Not at all,' I protest, as the fireworks begin, arcing and exploding through the sky. I lift my head to watch.

Soon the show is over. I bow as the members of the court cheer, and I kneel down to receive the thanks of his lordship the duke. He hands me a silk purse of coins. I kiss his gloved hand, then slip away.

I walk quickly through the courtyard, everywhere hung with red and blue satin. Furtively I weigh the bag of coins in my hand – it is not heavy. The duke has grown less generous lately – rumour has it his position is under threat. I pass the guards and cross the drawbridge. Seeing the vast crowd gathered a hundred feet from the Castello Sforzesco, I take the carnival mask from my pocket and put it on.

Elegantly anonymous now, I move past the mob. A few stare at me hungrily (do they wish to rob me? thank me?) but I walk onward, eyes to the ground. I leave the castle behind and go along Via Sanseverino until I reach Donnino Bramante's house. I knock at the door, remove my mask. The servant lets me in and tells me I may wait in the drawing room. Here I sit alone, eyes closed, remembering the most beautiful moments of the evening *Salai in his cloak of silver trimmed with green, the devilish smile on his face* until I hear the front door open and the clamour of familiar voices.

'Leonardo, there you are!'

'What are you doing here, all alone?'

'Everybody loved it, Leo!'

'But the snow! The snow! How did you *do* that?'

I stand up and kiss my friends as their voices wash over me. Il Sodoma, dressed in scarlet, wearing devil's horns on his head, leading his pet monkey in on a velvet leash . . . Giacomo Andrea, suave and handsome, who hugs me and tells me about a new church he has just been commissioned to design . . . Luca Pacioli, sober-faced, slightly embarrassed by the excesses of my other friends, talking to me about the divine proportions in the shapes of light made by the fireworks . . . Donnino himself, his hair such a mess you'd think he had just woken up, shining his genial smile at me and clapping his hands for wine . . . and

Tommaso, of course, my most trusted assistant – he has a beard now, but in his eyes is still the same zeal for learning, the same dry wit, that I liked so much when I took him on as a sixteen-year-old in Florence. I answer their questions – and then, in a whisper, ask Tommaso one of my own.

'Have you seen Salai?'

'Not since the start of the show.'

'I gave him some money. He said he wanted to buy something.'

'You astonish me.'

'I know you think I spoil him, Tommaso, but . . .'

'That is none of my business, master, but I'm sorry – I don't know where he is.'

his silver cloak disappearing, another shape waiting for him in the darkness

'Never mind – it doesn't matter.'

After that, the hours pass in a happy blur. We drink chilled wine. Some other guests arrive. Donnino plays the lute. Il Sodoma dances, lasciviously. Donnino sings rude songs. The monkey dances, lasciviously. At some point I ask Luca how to multiply square roots, and he shows me on a piece of paper. After that, my memories are vague, dark, flashing.

Eventually, exhausted, I ask Donnino if I may sleep on his bed for an hour, and he shows me to the room.

I take off my clothes and lie on the bed in the dark. It is hot in this room, even with the window open. My mouth is dry and the walls are spinning slightly. I close my eyes and, because it always brings peacefulness to my soul, remember the countryside around Vinci. The view from the hilltop near my mother's house – the cypress trees like dark candle flames and the lines of hills melting bluish grey behind them.

my mother smiling, her calm warm gaze – mamma I love you and I

Eventually I fall asleep . . . and dream that I am flying. Ahead I can see mountains, clouds, birds. Below me a large winged shadow moves silently over lakes and fields. This is a recurring dream – the most wonderful of all my dreams. I fly, and I am free.

And then I hear someone coughing and I open my eyes. I am lying in the harsh light of dawn in a bed with rumpled sheets, and around me on the floor are half a dozen strangers, their mouths slack, their odours fetid. One of them is snoring.

I dress myself, then tiptoe between the guests' sleeping bodies and go downstairs to the drawing room. The silent aftermath of the party – cushions on the floor, a broken clay jug, Donnino asleep on the couch. He was too kind to wake me, to send me home. I notice a sheet of paper on the table and pick it up – numbers, sums, explanations in Luca's tidy handwriting. And beneath, five words: 'Regular accounting preserves long friendships.' I smile wryly. So I must have been talking to Luca about Salai. I tear off a strip of paper and write a note to Donnino, thanking him for an enjoyable night and apologising for taking his bed. Then I put the rest of the paper in my pocket and leave by the front door.

Outside, Via Sanseverino is still in shadow but the air feels warm. I walk to the main road, and back towards the castle. Here the sun is low and bright. Squinting, I see stewards carrying pieces of wooden scaffolding and painted back-cloths through the gates. A quiet shock as I realise what they are – the props and scenery from last night's spectacle.

I love to create these illusions, but what if they are, as they pretend to be, life in microcosm – a glorious flaring, followed only by darkness, leaving not a trace of itself behind? What if all my work will, one day, be carted off so unceremoniously, dumped in a store room or burnt on a pyre?

I wished to carve my name in marble but . . . have I merely sketched a signature in dust?

But no, I am looking at the world through the queasy gloom of a hangover. I have already created something that will last.

I feel in my pocket for the key. Yes, I still have it. The duke must have forgotten. I finished the fresco nearly a year ago – or, rather, he told me it was finished, and forbade me to continue working on it. But odd nights, odd dawns, I let myself in and look at it, alone. Try to see it with fresh eyes. Each time, some imperfection sings out to me from the tableau – pleading for me to change it.

I walk to the monastery. From behind the stone walls I can hear the monks chanting, but it is too early for them to eat breakfast. Good – I will be alone. I unlock the door of the refectory, and walk to the middle of the room. Then I turn – and look. For the first time, I see it the way I dreamt it would be seen. Not as a painting on a wall, but a perfect illusion – the monks' dining room lengthened, another table added to the five at which they eat each day. And sitting at that table, Jesus and the twelve apostles.

And then I spot something on the floor, at the foot of the painting. Some spilt food, perhaps, or a dead insect. I walk over to the mark, intending to remove it, and close up I see tiny flakes of brilliant blue, tiny flakes of red. I crouch down, touch one of the flakes with my finger – it turns to powder.

In shock, I stand up and search the picture, my eyes darting from one part to another. I take a few steps back and look further up . . . to Jesus's blue cape, his red shirt. There are *holes* in the picture. Tiny holes, of course – I wouldn't even have seen them if I hadn't found the flakes, but . . .

holes

The paint is crumbling. I must have got something wrong in the mixing. And if after a year, half a dozen tiny flakes have fallen, how many will have fallen after ten years, fifty, a hundred? Five hundred years from now, my picture will not exist at all – it will be nothing, a blank wall, the image vanished like a ghost. I put my head in my hands and stare through the cage of my fingers at the floor.

merely sketched a signature in dust

I hear footsteps, voices – the monks coming for their breakfast. I let myself out and walk away, the sunlight hotter now, but the city looking even more desolate than before. A city of ashes, a city of dead hopes.

Someone calls my name. I look up and see one of the gentlemen from the court. He lifts his hands – 'The show last night, *bravissimo*! I won't forget that in a hurry.'

No, I think, but you will forget it – soon, nothing will remain of it.

I thank the gentleman politely and walk on, as my name is whispered by the people around me. They stare and point. Someone laughs. A thin, dirty child runs up to me and begs for a soldi. I throw him a coin and quicken my pace to escape the whispers and the stares. The cost of fame.

I enter Via Dante. More people on the streets now. Too many people – the city like a river in flood. I walk, the foul smells of pig's blood and rotting fruit assailing my nostrils, the loud noises of vendors' yells and hammered stone attacking my ears, the clinging bluish-black filth of smoke, dust and sewage smudging my clothes and shoes. If only they had let me build a new Milan to replace this dismal maze.

I drew them pictures of the city in my mind – explained to them the diseases they would prevent, the money they would save, the lives they would improve. I drew tall chimneys to disperse the smoke high above the city. I drew a system of locks and paddle wheels so the canals might be used to cleanse the streets. I divided the city into two levels – the lower level, with its tunnels and canals, for the warehouses and the traders' stalls, the movement of beasts and goods, and the upper level for houses, with loggias and courtyards and fountains, with wide avenues where people might walk freely amid flowering trees and breathe unpolluted air. Oh, I can see it all now, the dream city arching over the ruins of old Milan! But no . . . the duke preferred to spend his money on armies and parties and mistresses. My city was never built.

I walk past the clay Horse I sculpted, as mighty as ever – and as fragile. I was meant to cast it in bronze. But the duke used the bronze to make cannons instead. So my Horse will crack and crumble with the years, just as my Last Supper will flake and vanish. I have achieved so much since I came to Milan fifteen years ago – but what will it all count for, in the end?

a signature in dust

I walk through the Piazza del Duomo, past the beggars and sellers, the mules and the builders, until I reach the sanctuary of the Palazzo Vecchio. I climb the steps up to the roof.

Here, high above the city, there is a breeze and the air does not stink. I shield my eyes with my hand and look out over red rooftops, grey city walls, forests glinting silver in the heat haze . . . some swallows moving through the air like swimmers in a fast river, their shadows rippling over the dried earth . . . and, unreal as a painted backdrop, the distant mountains. Their peaks bluish with the perspective of loss.

I take the piece of paper from my pocket and memorise the sums that Luca wrote upon it, then I fold it carefully.

And I launch my paper bird through the air. It twists, flurries, loops, dives, soars, vanishes. It *flies*. Just as a man with wings large enough might learn to overcome the resistance of the air, and conquer and subjugate it, and raise himself upon it.

a winged shadow moving over lakes and fields

I stare up at the sky, where invisible Fortune watches me, and whisper, 'One day . . .'

5

CESARE: Treeshadow and insectbuzz. The scent of ripe melons and the sound of false laughter. Supper at our mother's vineyard – overlooking city and sunset.

A minor celebration – in my honour. My brother Juan gets the big celebrations.

Juan is the soldier. I am the churchman. I am the elder – it should be me with the sword. But Juan is our father's favourite.

The far end of the table – talk in Italian. Our end of the table – talk in Spanish. Me. Juan. Our cousin Fatty Lanzol – the Cardinal of Monreale.

I water my wine. Fatty sips his. Juan drinks like he's dying of thirst – as always. That thirst he can't quench. For other men's wives. For boasts and insults.

His sneering voice: 'Would you pass the salt please, *cardinal*?'

I look up. A second too late. The salt cellar near me. Our cousin reaching across.

'Still not used to being a man of the cloth, eh?' Juan taunts.

I stare. Zero expression. I say: 'Cardinals have power. And money. And the chance to be pope.'

'Yes, but captains have glory. And their own armies.'

'It's not your army. It's the army of the Church. And you haven't had much glory yet, *brother*.'

Blood rises to his cheeks. He slams the tabletop. Hisses: 'It was my first time. And I had bad luck. I'd like to see YOU do better.'

Oh – so would I, Juan. So would I.

Hoofclatter and torchlight. We ride through dark streets. Four of us – me, Fatty, Juan, a masked man. The last silent, nameless. An acquaintance of Juan's. Behind us – servants and grooms.

Past the Colosseum – ghostly in the gloom. I see the shades of Julius Caesar and Tiberius. Their names echoing into eternity.

Past corpses hanging from the walls of palace gardens. I see rats crawling round their shoulders. Men whose names are already forgotten.

The scent of roses. The stench of death.

Past our father's old palace. Past our mother's old house. Past the house where Juan and I grew up.

Memories stir – of fights and feasts. Ceremonies and kisses. And one pervasive feeling – that yearning for childhood's end.

So now it's over. Our father is pope. I am a cardinal. Power accumulating. The Borgia on the rise. But slowly. So slowly . . .

Still I look ahead and see my future – glorious and towering. But time is running out.

I must triumph before I die. I must conquer before death conquers me. I am twenty-two years old. Only ten years left. I clench my fists – no fucking time to lose.

At the Ponte Sant'Angelo, Juan says he must leave us.

Fatty says: 'At this hour? The streets are dangerous, cousin.'

Juan: 'I'll be fine.'

Fatty: 'Take a servant, at least. It is rash to go out alone in Rome . . .'

When everybody hates your guts. When everybody wishes you dead. But Fatty is too polite to say this.

Juan sighs – signals for his groom to follow. The groom on foot. Juan on his mule.

As he rides away, a dark shape moves behind him. The masked man – mounting the mule. His arms round Juan's torso. Silent.

We watch them go – vanish into night. The servants murmur.

Fatty frowns: 'Do you think we should have stopped him?'

I say: 'He's probably on the scent of cunt. He'd have killed you if you tried to stop him.'

Fatty: 'Yes. I daresay you're right. Who was that man though?'

I shrug. 'Juan has some strange companions.'

We ride across the bridge. The city silent as a morgue.

15 June, 1497

Another fine summer's day – alone in the Sala del Credo. I look out at the shaded courtyard. I walk across the room. Look out at the sunlit gardens.

I admire the frescoes in the lunettes. All these prophets, with their strangely familiar faces. Mine. Juan's.

Our long combed hair. Our neatly trimmed beards. Our handsome features. The paintings crude – you can hardly tell us apart.

From beyond the closed door – my father's voice. His footsteps hurried. Impatient knocking at the door.

'Come in, Father.'

His brows knitted. Eyes darting. 'Juan's servants tell me he didn't come back last night . . .'

'That's right.' I tell him of our parting – the groom, the masked man. 'Cardinal Lanzol was worried. But I presumed . . . a lady friend.'

'Yes, you're probably right.' He looks through the window – at the shadows on the grass. 'He should be back by now though.'

'Second helpings?'

My father laughs. His face relaxes. 'Or third, even, in Juan's case. Yes, yes – I'm sure you're right, Cesare. Are you coming to consistory?'

'Of course, Father.'

Time drags. The seconds like hours. The minutes like days. Consistory – Nones – Vespers. The shadows in the garden shorten, briefly vanish. They reappear, lengthen. Melt into darkness.

Muscles twitch in my father's face. A new one every hour. His hands writhe in his lap.

Juan's servants are called – every hour. My brother has still not been seen.

'There's something wrong. This isn't normal. He wouldn't . . .'

'He's done it before,' I point out. 'Juan forgets that people worry about him. He doesn't think.'

My father nods. 'I know, I know . . . you're right. But . . . Juan has enemies. What if he . . .'

'We could order the city searched.'

He stares at me, eyes wide. He has been waiting for me to say it. Waiting for someone else to voice his fear.

'You don't think . . . ?'

'No. But it's getting dark. Better safe than sorry.'

He nods – eyes on the ground. He orders the city searched.

We have supper in my father's study. He doesn't eat. He paces the room. He says: 'If he's dead . . .'

I eat. I say nothing. If my brother's dead . . . I'll take his place.

When my father's gone, I stand at the open window. Look out at the vast, invisible world. All the stars above. All the lands that lie beneath them. All of them waiting to be conquered.

I breathe the cool air. Shiver with desire.

Calm. Wait. Soon.

16 June, 1497

I walk beside the open bier. My brother – eyes closed. His face ghoulish in the flickering torchlight. People stare, murmur fearful – 'You'd think he was only sleeping.'

I look at his face – like looking in a mirror. The undertakers have done a good job. His beard trimmed. His hair combed. His slashed throat sewn up – the scar hidden.

They dragged the river – found his body. Fully dressed. His purse full of money. Bad luck for Juan. But we must all make sacrifices for the family.

My father spent the whole day weeping. Wailing and hammering the door of his room. Now he walks at the head of the procession.

My mother walks behind me. My sister Lucrezia behind her.

We walk by the Tiber. Mosquitoes whining. The river low and foul. Two hundred torches – reflected in the water. Dark. Flickering.

On the breeze I hear distant screams. Witnesses being examined. Suspects questioned. The city scoured for Juan's killers.

We enter the church. The nave crowded. The ceremony solemn – and dull, and long. It stirs memories of childhood.

The smell of incense. The stink of death.

My father sobs. My mother prays. Lucrezia trembles.

I watch Juan's face. I half-expect him to yawn at any moment.

22 June, 1497

We finish our meal. I dismiss the servants. My father stares at the table. I clear my throat. 'Father, I . . .'

He breaks me off. His voice abrupt. Emotionless. 'I've called off the investigation,' he says. 'I know who killed your brother.'

He stares at me. I stare back.

'Oh?'

He looks at the table. 'Yes. It was the Orsini. They've hated us ever since Virgilio died in our dungeons. They blame me for it. And, of course, your brother led the attack on their castles – even if he wasn't successful. This was their vendetta.'

'But you don't want to bring them to justice?'

'I want REVENGE! But it must wait. Now is not the time. When we are stronger, more secure – when they think I have forgotten – when they think the danger is past . . . *then* . . . then I will SMASH them!'

His fist bangs the table. His eyes flash white. I say nothing.

'Sorry, my son. I should not let my anger rule me so completely, but . . . *my Juan!*' Tears well in his eyes. His throat gurgles. 'I loved him so . . .'

'We all did, Father.'

A handkerchief pressed to his face. Seconds pass. His breathing slows. Voice low and broken-sounding now: 'I know, Cesare. You may not always have seen eye to eye with your brother, but . . . he was your blood. Blood matters. I know you know that. But now . . . now you are my only son.'

'There is Joffré too.'

He coughs. Or is it laughter? 'I am not entirely sure about Joffré's paternity. I am sure, however, that he is not worth a damn as a soldier. I suppose I could make him a cardinal.'

A crack of light. I see my chance. The words rush out. 'Father, I don't want to be a cardinal any more. I want to fight. I want to be your Captain General.'

A look of shock on the old man's face. But not surprise, somehow. 'No one has ever renounced the velvet, you know. No one.'

'Good. Then I'll go down in history.'

He's going to say yes. I can sense it. Can almost feel the swordhilt in my hand. Can see my future ahead of me – towering, glorious.

My father inspects his fingers. Sighs, long. 'The cardinalate is worth a lot of money. You'll be losing thirty-five thousand ducats a year. Not to mention the opportunity to become pope.'

'There are other ways of getting money. And of winning glory. There are other means of power.'

He nods. But his eyes are elsewhere. Seeing the ghost of Juan, I suppose. Sadness cloaks his face again. Voice cool and distant now: 'I'll see what I can do.'

6

NICCOLÒ: I follow in Biagio's trail as he shoves his way through the crowd, and Agostino comes behind me, apologising smoothly to all the people we disturb. There is a roar from up ahead, echoed behind and around us. Standing on tiptoes, I peer ahead: we are close to the gibbets now; easily within stone-throwing distance. I thump Biagio on the shoulder and say: 'This'll do.'

We put our crates on the ground and step upon them. The square is packed and there are people watching from the rooftops: eating picnics, drinking wine, enjoying the warm spring breeze. Outside the door of the Palazzo della Signoria, the three friars are being forced to take off their black mantles, their white habits. This is a smart move: remove their costume and you remove their mystique; in their undershirts, these three men might be ordinary criminals.

I look up at the black walls of the palace: silent faces fill the windows. In a week or two, I will be inside there, looking out. I will be a pen-pusher, a decision-maker. Barring a miracle, my election to the Second Chancery is already assured: I have spent the last four years carefully cultivating friendships with the men who count – Alamanno Salviati, Bartolomeo Scala – and writing learned papers for them on the future of the Florentine Republic. Before that, I composed poetry and wormed my way in with the Medici;

but they fell soon after the death of Lorenzo, and I had to start all over again. This is politics: you must back the winning horse and, if necessary, switch your bets in the middle of the race. Now it is time to collect my winnings. I have come here this morning to witness the final act in my own rise, and in the fall of Fra' Girolamo Savonarola.

Only a year ago, choirs of children sang while the friar burnt the city's mirrors and wigs and lutes and nude paintings. The bonfire of the vanities, he called it. Now the wind has changed and the city is burning the friar. In a couple of hours, we will all be free once again to admire ourselves in mirrors while wearing false hair, playing musical instruments and leering at naked women. Ah, liberty . . . how I've missed you! Four years of sobriety and virtue is enough for anyone.

All the way along the wooden walkway they shuffle: the three friars in their undershirts, their ankles held together by leg-irons. The hangman shaves their heads. The crowd goes silent. One by one, each friar climbs his ladder, and a noose is fastened around his neck. Someone coughs. In the distance a baby wails. 'Nice day out for the infant,' Agostino whispers.

I watch as the hangman hurls the first friar off the ladder. But his rope is too short, and the hangman was too gentle, so his neck is not broken. He takes an age to die, the poor fool, choking and repeating 'Jesu! Jesu!' as his feet kick desperately at the air.

The second friar is hurled off the ladder. This time, thankfully, the hangman does a better job: the second friar is dead within a minute.

The silence tightens, intensifies; twenty thousand people hold their breaths. We wait and listen: to hear what Fra' Savonarola will say. Will he confess his guilt? Will he prophesy disaster? Will he justify himself? But no. Bizarrely, he says nothing at all. His face betrays no emotion. He might as well be sitting on the toilet, thinking about the weather. Behind me, someone yells: 'Oh prophet, now is the time for you to work one of your miracles!' It's hard to tell if the man is joking or not.

The hangman hurls Savonarola from the ladder. I hear the crack as his neck breaks. The hangman jerks the rope to make the friar's feet dance.

As if a spell has been broken, the crowd roars and surges forward. I am knocked off my crate. The mass of flesh and bones crushes me and releases me, crushes and releases again, and I smell the acrid stench of a thousand sweating bodies in my nostrils; feel once more the terrible, unreasoning power of the mob. This is the same mob who chased the friar back to San Marco six weeks ago; who would have torn him limb from limb in their rage had he not been arrested and protected by guards. And yet, if you'd asked any of the people who were part of that mob, the next day, why they were so angry, they would just have shrugged their shoulders. They had waited all day in the rain for the trial by fire – the Dominicans versus the Franciscans – and nothing had happened: they were bored, frustrated, mildly pissed off. And then a few *arrabbiati* – the friar-haters – started yelling 'Let's kill Savonarola!' That's all it took. That's all it would take now. If someone shouted 'Let's kill Niccolò Machiavelli!', they probably would. Except that they don't know who I am. Anonymity has its benefits, I suppose. I begin to wonder if becoming second chancellor is such a great idea after all.

By the time the crowd has calmed itself and I have stood back on top of my crate, the fire has already been lit beneath the corpses. People are throwing bags of gunpowder onto the flames, making nice explosions. The bags were on sale in the square – only two soldi for three. People are singing now, laughing, telling rude jokes.

'Praise the Lord!' a loud, posh voice declares. 'Now we can all commit sodomy again!'

And then someone shouts 'A miracle! A miracle!' and we all go silent. I look at the hanging bodies: through the smoke, I see that Savonarola's right arm is lifting, the hand opening, displaying two fingers and a thumb. 'He is blessing us! It's a miracle!'

Women scream. Men sob. People fall to their knees and pray or run away in panic. I look sideways at Biagio. His face is white, stricken. He turns to stare at me. 'Do you think . . .?'

I say nothing. My muscles tense.

Agostino leans over and says: 'It's just the hot air, making his hand rise.'

'Oh.'

We look again and suddenly this seems obvious. The flesh is charred; black as rats. He is deader than a piece of wood. A gang of boys throws stones at the bodies, and a few seconds later the friar's arm has fallen to the ground, in flames.

My muscles relax; I breathe easy. I bask in the pleasant heat. He is not a prophet. He is not a saint. He was just a man, and now he's dead.

Agostino suggests we go and celebrate my election.

'He hasn't won yet!' Biagio objects.

'He'll win easily, Biagio. You know it as well as we do. With Salviati's support, he can't fail.'

'Yes,' I say, 'and don't worry, gentlemen – I won't forget my friends when I am in office.'

'Where shall we go?' Biagio asks. 'The Frascato?'

'Absolutely,' I say, and raise my hands like Cicero before the Senate. 'Today, it is our patriotic duty as good citizens to get drunk, gamble and fuck prostitutes.'

Everyone laughs.

You think me cruel? You think me cold and heartless? Yes . . . well, you're not the only one. But we must always move with the times. The friar was a good man, I do not deny it, but he paid the price for being an unarmed prophet. No one could have saved him today. As for my laughter . . . I can only quote one of my own poor poems:

> *I laugh, and my laughter does not touch my soul*
> *I burn and no one sees my passion.*

You see? I do have a soul. Even if it's unlikely now to be saved.

As we walk through the emptying square, we hear a roar of laughter behind us. We turn around. Someone throws a small black object in our direction. It lands on the cobbles, smoking gently. Some boys begin kicking it about. A man shouts: 'I always told you the friar was a heartless bastard!'

I smile thinly. We're all heartless bastards now.

Know Your Enemy
(1499–1502)

7

NICCOLÒ: I've been working in the Palazzo della Signoria for more than a year now, but the novelty has yet to wear off. I still feel a small thrill approaching the tall black tower, entering this vast cool lobby, climbing these stone stairs. Where I come from, stairs are steep, dark, narrow and noisy: the wood creaks; the air stinks; the close walls echo every sound. Power, I have come to realise, is a broad, shallow, light-filled staircase; power is the almost-silence in which I walk up these steps, the scentless air that I breathe.

All the same, I am beginning to feel more at home here. A year ago, I would have been too intimidated to come into the palace trailing dust and sweat. But this afternoon, I am in a rush; my presence is eagerly awaited. I have been away for several weeks: in Forlì, negotiating with the famous Caterina Sforza. An impressive woman, I must say: the heart and brain of a man, but with soft full lips and a heaving white bosom. She flirted with me, but only to get what she wanted from Florence; I did the same, to get what Florence wanted from her. In the end it was a stalemate, but an enjoyable game.

I climb three flights of stairs, then jog through a corridor; three more flights of stairs, and another corridor. A final two flights, my lungs wheezing, and I go through the Hall of the Lilies, where my boss Ser Antonio is spouting off pompously, as usual. My office is just through here: the narrow room with a small window.

'Hello Agostino. Hello Biagio.'

They lift their heads from their desks and their grey faces light up. 'Niccolò!' they yell, simultaneously. They stand up; we embrace. They tell me how much they've missed me; what a shit Ser Antonio has been in my absence. I give Biagio the portrait of Caterina Sforza he asked for, and he pins it proudly to the wall. 'Isn't she magnificent? What was she like in real life?'

'Magnificent,' I say. 'So what news of the war?'

'It's going well,' Biagio says, still staring at the poster. 'Things are starting to heat up, and I believe that Captain Paolo Vitelli will soon have captured Pisa and finally restored Florentine honour.'

'Never trust a mercenary,' I say, automatically.

'We all know your principles, Niccolò, but no one has any complaints about him at the moment. We've paid him and his brother Vitellozzo their twelve thousand gold ducats, and they've received reinforcements today. In another two weeks, the castle of Stampace should fall, and soon after that Pisa will be ours.'

'Well, I still have my doubts about the Vitelli, but that sounds like a good excuse to celebrate. Shall we go to The Three Kings? I'll tell you what Caterina Sforza wears under her skirts . . .'

Agostino laughs and Biagio's mouth falls open: his eyes are like saucers.

outside Pisa   *10 August, 1499*

VITELLOZZO: My artillery has done its job. The breach in the city wall is wide enough now to drive six horses through. Our footsoldiers are advancing easily with their swords and pikes.

This is not good news. A civilian may think I would want our troops to secure a quick and easy victory over the enemy but that's because civilians are naïve and understand nothing of military strategy. Put it this way: if we win today who is going to pay us tomorrow? And put it another way: the Pisans are paying us quite a bit *not* to beat them.

I take off my helmet and curse the hot weather then walk over to the tent where my brother Paolo is eating lunch.

'Sit down, Vitellozzo.' He offers me a chicken leg.

I shake my head. 'Paolo, I've just been watching the battle . . .'

'Is it going well?'

'It's going *too* well. We are losing control of our troops. Those young Florentine recruits – they're getting all these crazy notions of honour and pride and courage . . .'

Paolo spits out his food. 'Have they entered Pisa?'

'Not yet. But it will happen soon unless we do something.'

'Command the retreat.'

'I already have.'

'And they're disobeying your orders?'

'Come and see for yourself.'

He gets up and shouts for a page to help him with his armour. When it's on we go out to the top of the hill and look down at the small red and black figures below.

'Get our horses!' Paolo cries. 'Call our captains! We must drive them back ourselves.'

A few moments later we ride down the hill and enter the maelstrom of fighting. It is chaos as always. There are thick clouds of cannonsmoke and dust from the fallen walls. There are stray gunshots from the ground and flying arrows from the battlements. It's bloody dangerous, in short. I know what I'm talking about: my younger brothers

47

Gianni and Camillo both lost their lives in meaningless battles like this one. Sometimes I wonder whether it's really worth the money we're paid. But how else are we meant to make a living? If we tax the citizens of Città di Castello any more than we do now we'll have riots and insurrection on our hands. And that's even more dangerous than battles.

'Retreat you cocksucking Florentine swine! Go back you thick-headed peasant scum!' Paolo rides through the ranks of our more hot-headed troops. He smashes helmets with his broadsword and yells at them in his loud noble voice. I do the same.

One of our flag-bearers has the impudence to contradict me. 'But we're through! We've taken the church! The city is ours if we press home our advantage now! Why are you telling us to retreat?'

I ride slowly back to where his horse stands at the head of a column. The men behind him wear angry mutinous expressions.

'Take off your helmet, soldier. Show me your face.'

He does as I tell him. His face is beardless. I put my sword blade to his throat. He does not flinch. 'Never contradict or question an order from a superior officer.' I increase the pressure of the sword point on his neck. The skin hollows and his face pales. 'Do you understand me?'

'Yes, sir.' His voice low and resentful.

I press the sword harder: blood trickles down his neck. 'Louder!'

'Yes, sir. I understand. I'm sorry, sir.'

I remove the sword. 'Good. If this happens again I'll slice your goddamn head off. Now order your men to retreat!'

By nightfall we have all the men back in camp. We can see the Pisans repairing their fortifications. We can hear our troops muttering round their campfires. 'Word will get back to Florence,' I say. 'They'll probably accuse us of cowardice.'

'Those lily-livered pen-pushers!' Paolo shouts. 'What the hell do they understand about military strategy?'

'Nothing at all. But perhaps we should explain our decision to them. Write a letter to the Signoria . . .'

'Have you no pride, brother?'

I blush. 'Of course Paolo. But I . . .'

'God's death! There's no one in that palace of noble blood any more. They're all merchants and bureaucrats. Write them a letter? I *piss* on the Florentine Signoria!'

I hang my head. 'I'm sorry Paolo. You're right of course. I . . . I don't know what I was thinking.'

He comes close and hugs me tight. 'We're Vitelli. Don't ever forget that, brother. We're better than them.'

Florence   *26 September, 1499*

NICCOLÒ: It is gone midnight and I am the last person left in the palace. I have been here since dawn, and my body is exhausted; but my mind is awake with a grim excitement. Here at my desk, by the light of a single candle, there is one last letter I must write.

I have been writing and dictating letters every day for the last six weeks: encouraging, exhorting, warning; expressing our concern, our frustration, our impatience. But still nothing changes. The most recent excuse is an outbreak of malaria in the camp, which supposedly makes an assault impossible. The whole of the Signoria is tired of the Vitelli brothers now. The time has come to put an end to their excuses and their lies.

I dip the quill tip in ink and scratch it in my most elegant script across the paper. This particular letter will not be read out to Paolo and Vitellozzo Vitelli. If the commissioners do their job with all the prudence and subtlety which I demand of them, the Vitelli will not guess the contents of this letter until it is too late.

I sign the letter, dry the ink, fold the paper, and seal it in wax with the offical stamp of the Republic of Florence. Then I think about what I have done, and sigh with relief, satisfaction, and no little awe. I have written my name into the footnotes of history. I have proved that the pen can, in certain situations, be mightier than the sword.

The final sentence of my letter is a death sentence.

outside Pisa   *28 September, 1499*

VITELLOZZO: I lie awake with my eyes closed listening to the rain fall like stones on the tent. I feel weak and exhausted. Am I coming down with malaria? Hundreds have died of the fever already and many more are sickening. I wonder if we should have let the young Florentines finish off Pisa after all. We would have lost fewer men that way. And we would no longer have to deal with their sodding Signoria.

I hear voices outside the tent. I open my eyes and sit up as a guard rushes in. 'What is it?'

'My lord, I am sorry for intruding but . . .' – he swallows and breathes hard. 'Your brother Lord Paolo is captured and . . .'

Captured! 'But how? By whom?'

'The Florentine commissioners invited him to breakfast this morning . . .'

'I know. I was invited too. But I felt ill so I . . .'

'But when breakfast was finished they said to him that they wished to discuss more confidential matters. So he dismissed his attendants and . . .'

I close my eyes in despair. 'Those deceiving bastards!' If they execute him – I will find out the names of everyone responsible for the decision and I will kill them myself. One by one. Slowly. Painfully.

'Yes my lord, but they are coming now – for *you*. I ran all the way to warn you but you must hurry. They'll be here soon.'

Yes – I must save myself. If I am captured too then who will avenge Paolo? The Vitelli will be finished: none of us left but women and children. Our enemies will have the children slaughtered and they will take over Città di Castello. I must escape . . . but how?

'Please hurry my lord! They will be here any moment!'

I stare at the guard's pale panic-stricken face. Think Vitellozzo – think! Then it comes to me. It is a shameful thing to do but it is my only hope. I say: 'Take your clothes off and lie in this bed. Cover your face and disguise your voice for as long as you can. Tell them you are ill. When they finally see your face you must tell them who you are and that I forced you to agree to the deception. I have no doubt they will spare your life.'

The guard is undressing before I've even finished my speech. By the time I have put on his uniform he is groaning in bed. I leave the tent and hurry out into the rain.

Florence   *1 October, 1499*

NICCOLÒ: I stand on the rooftop of the palace. From the battlements I can see the square below, the people a dark mass in the evening halflight. I can hear them too: cheering and jeering, just like they did in May last year, when Savonarola was executed. Biagio taps me on the shoulder. 'It's time.'

51

I turn from the battlements and watch. The executioner leads the disgraced captain up the stairs from the tower dungeon and onto the rooftop. Paolo Vitelli is finely dressed; his face set in an expression of noble contempt. Behind him, the sky is bruise-coloured.

He was tortured yesterday, but he confessed to nothing. Some waverers wanted to postpone his execution, reconsider the evidence, but they were shouted down. I was proud of us: we are finally learning to act decisively. As I told the Signoria last night, this execution sends out a message: even the most famous captain in Italy cannot cheat the Republic of Florence and get away with it.

Vitelli is shaved and gagged, and his shirt collar is pulled down to his shoulders, baring the thick neck. He is forced to his knees. The priest grants him absolution, and Vitelli nods. Then he fixes all of us in a long, sweeping glare of accusation. I stare back: cold, righteous. He *is* a traitor, and he deserves what is about to happen to him.

Finally he is forced onto his chest, and strapped down. The executioner lifts the axe. The heavy blade falls. Blood spurts up, but the neck is not severed. One of the *priori* faints: his colleagues help him to the floor; they pour water on his face. The axe is lifted again. It comes down: this time the head rolls free. I exhale with relief. The executioner walks over to retrieve the head. A guard holds a pike ready, and the executioner impales the bloody neck on the sharp point. Then two more guards hold flaming torches close to it and the head is displayed in triumph to the crowd below. They roar their approval.

I turn to Biagio and Agostino. 'Thirsty?'

Afterwards in the tavern, strangers come up to me and slap me on the back. 'Good job!' they say. 'Beautifully done!' They are talking about the deception with which we captured Paolo: the invitation to breakfast, the quiet arrest. It was, I am told several times, a work of art.

I raise my glass and drink. 'I am glad the plan worked. Though it is a shame that the commissioners allowed his brother Vitellozzo to escape. We may come to regret that one day.'

8

LEONARDO: From the highest point in my garden, I can see them coming. When I arrived, just after sunrise this morning, they were no more than a faint blur on the horizon. Now they resemble a gigantic insect crawling through the hay fields, towards the city. By midday they will be here. The French army, with King Louis at its head.

I have done all I can to protect myself and those around me from the worst that might happen. I have emptied – but for a few coins – the cashbox in my studio, wrapped its contents in small paper parcels, and secreted them in various places. I have fitted locks to the doors of my little house here and to those of my studio and other rooms in the Palazzo Vecchio. I have also fitted a lock to the gate of this garden, though it would hardly be enough to stop soldiers intent on looting and spoiling. There is nothing I can do now but trust to Fortune.

and perhaps the king may offer me a

Finally I force myself to look away from the approaching army. I may as well try to enjoy my garden during these last hours, rather than waste the time worrying about what might happen to it. It was, ironically, a gift from the duke. He has not been the most reliable of patrons during my sixteen years in Milan, but for this I can forgive him almost everything. I painted him the Last Supper, and in return he gave me this piece of green earth – these three acres of Paradise.

Being here calms me, as always. I walk its length – down past the bridge, past the vines. The grapes were picked and pressed only last week – the juice is fermenting now in barrels behind the house. The leaves of the cherry trees are already the colour of flames. I can smell dead leaves burning somewhere in the distance – that sweet, sad, summer's-end scent.

Il Moro fled a month ago. After all his bravado about fighting to the death, the Duke of Milan just rode off one night in early September – leaving the castle empty, the city unguarded.

The bells of Santa Maria delle Grazie start to ring. I lock the door of the house. I do not know whether to feel hopeful or fearful. I am forty-seven years old, and I have been living in this city for most of my adult life. I did not ask for change, but change is what is coming. And perhaps after all, it need not be threatening. Perhaps this is my opportunity. *Perhaps the king* . . .

I walk through the crowded, noisy streets to the palace and climb up to the roof. Salai and Tommaso come with me. So do some of the servants. We sit and drink wine and eat wafers until the noise of the crowd rises. Standing up, I see that the gigantic insect has transformed itself into a butterfly – a flickering, translucent, many-coloured creature, glimmering in the autumn sunshine.

The king is a tall man, more handsome than his predecessor, simply dressed. Mona Marguerita, our housekeeper, points out the Venetians, riding behind him, and hurls abuse at them. But my own eye is drawn to the young man riding next to the king on a beautiful white horse.

'Who is that, on Louis's right?'

'The pope's son, isn't it?' Tommaso replies. 'Duke Valentino.'

Salai giggles. 'A man with the most evil reputation. If even half the rumours I've heard about him are true . . .'

smirking mouths whispering gossiping

'There is no reason why they should be,' I say sharply. 'In my experience, rumours are more often the result of envy in the teller than of vice in the talked-about.'

Valentino is taller than the king, his shoulders broader, his horse more prettily caparisoned. And the animal he rides upon is truly magnificent – a silver-white mare. I take the notebook which hangs from my belt and sketch the horse's mane and nose and forelegs.

Behind me, Salai tells Tommaso in a whisper –

'. . . they say he killed his own brother. And as for what he does to his sister . . .'

Tommaso touches my elbow.

'Oh, master . . .'

His voice is sorrowful.

I turn to face him. 'What is it?'

He points to the clay Horse, at the far end of the square. Some French archers are using it for target practice. Their arrows arc, descend, puncture the baked flesh. A thousand more, and it will crumble. Even a hundred more and the holes will let the rain in, cause the Horse to slowly disintegrate.

'We can protest,' Tommaso says. 'They have no right . . .'

'There's no point, Tommaso. All they are doing is hastening the inevitable.'

a signature in dust

I swallow, look away.

CESARE: I touch my swordhilt. Yes – I'm a soldier now. I've taken Juan's place. Captain General of the papal troops. Riding next to the King of France at the head of a conquering army. It beats being a cardinal any day.

We see Milan like tourists. Like tourists with swords. The vast gaudy Duomo – like a wedding cake. The ugly blood-red castle – unconquerable, so they said.

Funny to see the massive walls. The endless battlements. The cannons, the moats. Unconquerable – and conquered so easily.

Sforza fled, a month ago. Why? Because he knew he would lose. Why? Because the people stopped believing in him. Why? Because he stopped believing in himself.

A lesson – power lies not in weapons or fortresses. It lies in men's beliefs. A trick of the mind. Once you stop believing – so do your subjects. And your allies. And your enemies. And thus your power disintegrates – stones crumble to dust.

Conclusion – always believe. Never surrender.

VITELLOZZO: When it's dark I go to see Cesare Borgia at his room in the castle and prostrate myself at his feet. It makes me feel pretty sick but what can you do? I've met him before – when he was a kid. I thought even then he was an arrogant shit. And of course his blood's about as noble as sewer water. But the fact remains that he's the pope's son and the king's favourite . . . and I've heard on the grape-vine that he's got his eyes on Florence.

That's the clincher: if I can get a job with his army there's a good chance I'll be able to enter that city as part of an invading army. My artillery can smash down its walls and famous buildings. And I can go and do my private business.

To my surprise Borgia pulls me to my feet. I look in his face: he's taller than me but I am stronger. I'd have him in a fight. I bet he knows it too.

He embraces me. 'You are the greatest artillery commander in Italy and it would be a privilege to have you in my army.' Then he names the amount of money he'll pay me and the number of men he wants me to recruit. I'm gobsmacked. He's offering me double what I've ever been offered before. Must have more money than sense.

'Thank you my lord,' I say. 'I swear I will serve you faithfully.'

'I don't doubt it,' he says. 'I can tell just by looking in your eyes that you're a man of honour.'

CESARE: In his eyes – ambition and hatred. In his eyes – stupidity and betrayal.

But I let it go. Vitellozzo's a bad man, but he's a good soldier. I can use him.

I am building an army. The best army in Italy. Soon I will conquer my own cities. I will build my own empire. Imola, Forlì, Faenza, Cesena ... And then, one day, perhaps Florence.

I smile at Vitellozzo. I say to him: 'Show me what that is in the pocket of your cloak.' He blushes and stutters. He has no idea how I guessed his secret.

I say: 'You keep touching it so tenderly, it must be very precious to you.'

Pride flashes in his eyes. He takes out a folded sheet of paper. He gives it to me. I unfold it and read:

Rinuccio da Marciano
Pietro da Marciano
Piero Soderini
Francesco Soderini
Niccolò Machiavelli

'The names of the men you hold responsible for your brother's death?'

Vitellozzo nods.

'And the one who's been crossed out?'

'Was stabbed through the heart on my orders last month, my lord.'

I smile. I must keep a close eye on this Vitellozzo.

Next morning – the tour continues. We visit the Duke of Milan's stables. The most beautiful stables ever. Frescoes of the horses – lifesize, feeding, trotting. The gleam of light on their coats.

Next – the dining room of a monastery. Narrow, small, spartan. Less luxury than the horses' stables. Here to see the Last Supper by Leonardo da Vinci.

Everyone talks in whispers. The king starts to admire it – point out its wonders. Then is told he's looking the wrong way. Admiring the wrong fresco. He shrugs, turns round – begins again.

The king is a fool. I don't know much about art – but I know superiority when I see it. If these two frescoes fought a battle, it would be a massacre. The other artist's army dead and bleeding. His castle razed and smoking.

Leonardo is presented to the king. An older man – delicate, graceful. A hush of reverence round him. 'Genius,' they whisper.

The king says: 'We wish to take the fresco back to France.'

Everyone laughs. 'But it's painted on a wall of the monastery, your majesty.'

'We don't care. We will pay any expense. We must have it.'

'But, your majesty, it's impossible.'

'It's not impossible,' Leonardo says. His voice quiet, calm. 'It could be moved. But the fresco would be damaged.'

'I like it where it is,' I say. 'It fits this room perfectly. Anywhere else, the effect would not be the same.'

The artist looks at me. Curious. Grateful. Bows.

The king sighs. 'Very well. Then will you, Leonardo da Vinci, come back with us to France? The queen would like to meet you. You could work for us – perhaps paint our portraits. And portraits of our horses for the stables. And you could paint another Last Supper – in one of our dining rooms.'

The artist bows – goes down on one knee. He says he does not deserve such honours. But in any case he cannot leave Milan – he has too many projects here. He begs the king's pardon.

The king looks astonished. A painter has said no to him. I am intrigued.

I go through the reports in my head. Leonardo da Vinci. Forty-seven years old. Bastard son of a notary. One quashed sodomy charge in Florence. Painter, sculptor, musician. But also architect, scientist, inventor. If I could tempt him . . .

'I could recommend Andrea Solario, your highness, to go in my stead,' Leonardo suggests. 'One of my most able assistants. It was he who painted the duke's stables, which you so admired.'

'Oh really?' Childish delight on the king's face. 'Yes, that would please us.' Smile turns to pout. 'Still, the queen will be disappointed – it was you she wanted, not your assistant.'

'Perhaps you would allow me to paint something for your majesties here, and send it to you in France?'

'Yes.' The king frowns, nods. 'Yes – good idea. Ligny – arrange the details please.'

The Comte de Ligny takes the artist aside. The king turns his eyes to the fresco again. Pretends to admire it. Then claps his hands. 'It must be nearly lunchtime.'

LEONARDO: I slip the draft contract into my pocket and say farewell to the Comte de Ligny, who follows the royal crowd out of the door. Why did I say no to the king? There was just something too casual about the request – I had the feeling he would have forgotten all about me by the time I reached the French Court. And he is also notorious for being miserly. Still, it was quite a strange decision, given that I have no employer, no patron, no fixed abode. Sometimes I surprise myself.

I am about to leave the monastery, when I look up and see him – the young man who rode beside the king yesterday. The one who told the king my Last Supper should stay where it was. Cesare Borgia – the Duke Valentino. *A man with the most evil reputation* . . . Yet if it is true that men's faces show their natures, then Borgia's must be graceful and fair. His nose is like Salai's – no hollow at the top. His lips are thin, his cheekbones high, his skin milkpale and spoiled only slightly by the marks of the French disease. His tunic is black velvet, slashed with purple silk – the Spanish sombreness is not to my taste, but it suits him well. There are rubies the size of cherries in his black velvet cap. And his hands, I notice, are surprisingly long-fingered and delicate in their black kidskin gloves.

He presents himself, and when I bend to kiss his feet, he stops me and kisses my cheeks. The scent of musk is overpowering.

'You are too great a man to kiss my feet, maestro.'

He ushers me towards the Last Supper – 'It is remarkable. I have never encountered anything like it. One sees not a painting, but an actual table, with real people seated behind it.'

I look at it, but see only tiny holes, tiny flakes of paint on the floor beneath it. I am amazed that no one else has said anything – is it possible I am the only one who notices?

'Thank you, excellency. That indeed was my intention – to bring Christ and his apostles into this humble dining room.'

We walk still closer, and he examines the details. 'Extra-ordinary. I feel I could reach over and pick up that salt cellar.'

I smile. 'Thank you for interceding with the king – I fear that if he had moved the fresco to France, there would have been nothing left of it by the time it arrived.'

He looks at me, and I see in a flash that he understands. 'Yes – it is delicate. I saw your Horse too yesterday. A very great shame, what those archers have done to it.'

'It should have been cast in bronze. But the duke ran out of money, and he used the bronze to make cannons instead.'

Valentino laughs softly. 'For all the good it did him. I am afraid, however, that most rulers would favour weapons of defence over monuments if it came down to a straight choice.'

'Of course,' I say. 'I understood his reasoning. I just fear . . .'

'. . . that nothing you have achieved will last? Yes. That depends, of course, upon the nature of the work. I heard about a letter you wrote to Il Moro, offering your services as a military engineer.'

I open my mouth, but no sound comes out. How did he find out about that? That letter was written seventeen years ago, before I even moved to Milan. He seems to read my mind – leans closer to me. 'I have eyes everywhere, Maestro Leonardo. One must have – in order to gain and keep power.' His green eyes blaze. '*Aut Caesar aut nihil* – that is my motto.'

To be Caesar, or to be nothing. It is quite an ambition. 'You wish to work miracles,' I say.

'Exactly!' He grins. 'I wish to work miracles. Why would anyone settle for a lesser ambition?'

'My father would say that if you lower your expectations, you are more likely to achieve your aims.'

'Yes, my father would probably say the same thing.'

'But your father is the pope, my lord – mine is just a notary.'

'Which makes your rise to eminence all the more impressive.'

I look at him with a sudden dawning of shock. What a strange turn our conversation has taken. 'My rise to eminence?'

'You have just refused an invitation from His Most Christian Majesty. There are many lords and princes who would not dare do that.'

'You think I made a mistake, my lord?'

'No. I think you have a great future. Perhaps *we* have a great future . . .'

We?

In Latin, he quotes some ancient author – *'Alexander and Aristotle were the teachers of one another.'* I look up into his eyes. He takes my hands in his. 'It was a pleasure and a privilege to meet you, Maestro Leonardo.'

I begin to tell him what a pleasure and a privilege it was for me too, but he cuts me off. 'I must go – the king will be wondering where I am. I will be in touch. I don't know when exactly, but I will. When I am in a position to make you an offer you *can't* refuse.'

By the time I am outside, Valentino is astride his horse. That beautiful animal, its coat gleaming like ivory. He waves to me as the horse walks away.

I raise my voice. 'It is possible I may leave Milan, your excellency. If . . .'

'Don't worry,' he calls back. 'I will find you.' The horse breaks into a trot. 'I will send you a sign.'

9

CESARE: Through the visor – a grey blur. In my ears – the roar of rain on metal.

I take off the helmet. I look around. Behind me – ten thousand troops. Mercenaries – Gascon and Swiss. A thousand Italians led by Vitellozzo.

I ride through rainlashed streets. Crowds of people cheering. Their eyes grateful. I am delivering them from a cruel tyrant. They hate her – so they love me.

Her – Caterina Sforza. The amazing Amazon. The bloodthirsty big-titted bitch. I don't know her – but I know the stories.

Story one. Defending a castle – the besieging army threatened her children. Go ahead and kill them, she said. Lifted her skirts – showed her cunt. Look, she said – I have the mould to make more.

Story two. Her second husband butchered in front of her eyes. She took soldiers to the quarter where the murderers lived. Ordered them to kill everyone who lived there. Women. Children. Old people. Everyone. She stayed to make sure no one was left breathing.

There are more stories – but you get the idea.

The people have given me the town – but I must take the castle myself. The Amazon waits inside. She will not surrender.

Cheering turns to screaming. Grateful eyes turn fearful. I look round – what's wrong?

It's the fucking Swiss. Spitting and stealing. Burning and destroying. Raping and killing.

I shout at the French commanders. They shrug. 'We can't control the Swiss.' I shout at Vitellozzo. He shakes his head. 'Soldiers are soldiers. Let them have their fun.'

'No!' I yell. I tell them both – you control your troops. Or you answer for their crimes.

I shout for the Swiss commander. The order goes down the line. It comes back – the Swiss commander is with his troops. Spitting and stealing. Burning and destroying. Raping and killing.

I will never trust these mercenaries again. I stand up in my saddle and yell: 'If I live to remain your lord, I swear on my word – I will make it up to you for this.'

But no one is listening. They are running. They are screaming. They are weeping and bleeding and dying.

Then – a huge roar. Everyone freezes. I turn and stare – a house half-destroyed. The cannonball bouncing, smashing. Rolling down the high street. The Amazon is firing at us.

I put on my helmet. In my ears – the roar of rain on metal. Through my visor – the dark mass of the castle.

5 December, 1499

A week of bombardment – and barely a breach. The castle is strong. The Amazon is strong. At this rate, we'll be here till fucking Christmas. But I do not have time. I must conquer SOON.

I go to see Vitellozzo. He's eating breakfast in his tent.

'Is there any way to speed this up?'

'Not without reinforcements, my lord. More guns. Bigger guns.'

'They're coming, I told you. But in the meantime . . .'

He shrugs. 'You could try talking to her.'

'You think she'll listen?'

'I doubt it. But you never know. They might be starving inside there.'

'Yes. You're right. It's worth a go.'

Early afternoon – the message comes back. The Amazon will talk. 'You must come to the drawbridge,' the messenger says. 'Her excellency will meet you there. That way, you can confer in privacy.'

I wonder. I remember story three. My father sent the Amazon a letter. It said, you owe the Church money. Payment is overdue. My son will collect. She sent a reply, written on cloth. The cloth had been wrapped round a corpse. The corpse of a plague victim. The letter was intercepted – the messengers tortured. They confessed. My father survived. But the moral is clear – do not trust the Amazon.

My armour is removed. I am dressed in black velvet. But beneath I wear a chainmail vest. I secrete a dagger in my sleeve.

I walk to the drawbridge. Attendants follow. I wave my arm – they back off. The drawbridge lowers, creaking.

Beneath the portcullis – the Amazon waits. She wears a dress – red silk. Her eyes glisten. Bosom heaves. I want to touch her. I want to strangle her. I want to . . .

Drawbridge touches ground. I bow to the Amazon. She curtseys. She's alone – as far as I can see. She takes a step forward – onto the bridge. I mirror her. My foot touches wood. The wood moves. I hear the crank of metal. The grinding of gears. What the . . .?

Someone yells: 'It's a trap!' My right foot dragged up. I jump – land on my back in the muddy earth. Black velvet splashed brown. My cape drenched. The Amazon yells: 'You did it too soon, you fool!'

66

The drawbridge swings up – clatters shut. Another two steps and I would now be inside. At their mercy. A dead man.

I am surrounded by guards. They lift shields, fire arrows. I am ushered away.

I go to see Ramiro da Lorqua. My master of the household. Fat and bearded. Cruel mouth, evil glare. I've known him since I was a kid. He used to scare the shit out of me. Now he scares the shit out of other people FOR me.

In Spanish I tell him: 'Make a general declaration. A price on her head. Twenty thousand ducats if she's taken alive.'

Ramiro nods. Bloodthirsty smirk. 'And if she's dead?'

I want to touch her. I want to strangle her. I want to . . .

'Ten thousand.'

17 December, 1499

I lift the commander's baton – and bring it down. Silence then roaring. The mercenaries pour through the breach.

All is chaos. Smoke and blood. Yelling and swordclash. The air filled with arrows.

I put my helmet on. Spur my horse forward. Over the logs of wood that fill the moat. Over the corpses. Through the courtyard. Gunpowder and bloodstink. Through the orchard – the trees ablaze.

In the tower, I find the Amazon. Black silk, silver armour. Her bulging breastplates. Her proud pink face. A guard either side of her.

Ramiro whispers: 'We found her in the gunpowder stores, my lord. She was trying to set light to them. Luckily the fuse was damp.'

I do not show anger. I tell the guards to release their grip on her excellency. I give her a purse full of ducats. Utter fancy words. Ask her kindly to await my presence in the palace.

In her eyes – rage and hate. But on her lips only courtesies – sweet nothings.

I nod to Ramiro. He escorts her to my room. From the top of the tower I survey the conquered fortress. Blood and smoke. Flames and screaming. Piled corpses, smashed walls.

I lick my lips. The fun has just begun.

Her face in candleglow. Cool and powdered now. The servants take our plates away. I dismiss them for the night. Lock the door. Breathe in her silence, her fear. And then I go to work.

I pay her compliments. Talk smoothly. I have conquered her – now I must charm her.

The Amazon's eyes on me. Judging. Calculating. I stroke her hand. Tell her how soft the skin is.

I see the hate and rage and fear fade from her eyes. In their place I see desire. I see promise of pleasure.

I let my own desire show in my eyes. The desire is real. Only its nature is ambiguous. Like hers, I suppose.

I want to touch her. I want to strangle her. I want to . . .

She pays me compliments. Talks smoothly.

'If I could have chosen one man to be conquered by, my lord . . .'

'I fear you are trying to conquer me for a second time . . .'

'You are as skilled with words and glances as you are with artillery . . .'

The breach is opening. The big guns are primed.

We dance to silent music in the candled darkness. The mingled scents – my musk, her rosewater. Melting beeswax and sweet cypress smoke. Our lips close – breathing the same air.

I look in her eyes – see her calculations. She thinks if I fall for her, she'll stay free. She sees herself the Duchess Valentino – one day Queen of Italy. And then – a dagger in my back. My power at her feet. I can see it all – her visions, her greed. Her delusions. The Amazon does not know me.

We kiss. She breathes, 'Yes.'

I undress her, slowly. I touch her naked skin. She breathes, 'Wait.'

Lying on her front. Playing hard to get. She puts her hand on mine – to stop me. I take her wrist. Slide it up behind her back. Hold it there. She breathes, 'Oh.'

I stroke her back. I stroke her buttocks. I stroke the gorge between. Slowly. She breathes, 'No.'

She puts her hand on mine – to stop me. I slide it up behind her back. Hold it there, her two hands in my one. I can feel the pulse fizzing in her wrists.

I stroke her again. She groans with desire. She bends her knees, arches her back. She breathes, 'Please.'

The breach is open – the fortress surrendered.

I reach in the desk. Take out a silk scarf. I slide her hands down between her legs. Till they're touching her ankles. She breathes, 'Yes.'

I tie her ankles and wrists together. She breathes, 'Oh.'

She's trussed up like a turkey, her buttocks spread. I strip. I move closer. The cannon is loaded.

Then: 'Not *there!*'

I breathe, 'Yes.'

The tiny hole widens. The muscles contract. I conquer the bitch. I smash her defences. Blood on white silk. Screaming then silence.

I get dressed. She sobs. She begs: 'Untie me . . . please, Cesare.' Her voice tender. Calculating.

I lock the door behind me. Laugh softly. In the corridor, I hear her scream. 'You bastard! Come back! You BASTARD! Set me free!'

22 *December, 1499*

Candlesmoke and quillscratch. Night in my office. The faces of my servants, captains, secretaries, spies – glower and flicker before me.

To Ramiro, I say: 'When we leave, you stay behind. You are in command of Imola. I want you to enforce order, justice, discipline – by any means necessary. You understand?' He nods, smiles. 'Yes, my lord.' I dismiss him.

Next – Pinzone, my top spy. Squinting eyes under dark greasy hair. I say: 'You will be stationed with Ramiro da Lorqua. Serve him. Stay close to him. Watch him carefully. Listen to everything. Take notes. Report to me. Understood?' 'Yes, my lord.' I dismiss him.

Next – Agapito, my secretary. 'I want you to start a petition. Make it look like one of the people started it. Address it to . . .'

A sudden roar below. The banging of fists on wood. Agapito raises his eyebrows. I look out the window – the street filled with troops. Drunk and mutinous. The fucking Swiss.

We go downstairs. The door is opened. Their commander says they want more pay. If I refuse, they desert. Fucking mercenaries.

But I can do nothing now. Fifty guards inside the palace – five thousand out in the street. I promise them more food, I promise them more money. Finally they go.

In the distance – I hear screams, I see smoke. The night sky stained orange by flames. I will make them pay for this.

I call Michelotto. My most trusted henchman. Scarred face, broken nose. Hands the size of dinnerplates.

I write to the French general. I write to Vitellozzo. I roll up the papers – put them in Michelotto's huge hands. 'Tell them to come now. I want them ready in the square at dawn.' He nods, is gone.

I turn to Agapito. 'This should be interesting.'

23 December, 1499

Bleary winter light. Frost in the empty market square. I sit astride my horse. Below me – five thousand Swiss. Surrounding them – two thousand French. Surrounding them – a thousand Italian cavalry. Watching – the people of Imola. Frightened. Desperate.

The Swiss chant. They want more money. They want it now. If they don't get it – they'll burn the whole town to the ground.

I don't care about the money – but mutiny cannot be allowed. I must mount a show of strength. I must teach them a fucking lesson.

They chant. They stamp their pikes. They stare murderous.

I stare back, cool. I hold the baton of command. I bring it down. A thousand French archers aim arrows at the Swiss.

The Swiss shut the fuck up.

'Now listen to me,' I yell. I yell loud so everyone can hear – not only the Swiss. Not only the French. Not only the cavalry. But the people of Imola – hanging out of windows, hiding behind doors.

'You will be paid when we reach Cesena – and not before. IF I decide to retain you afterwards, you will be paid at the higher rate which I agreed last night with your commander. But I warn you – this is the last time you will defy me. If you do not agree to these conditions, I will order the archers to open fire on you. I will also ring the town bells. There are twenty thousand people in this town. I will let them have their revenge upon you for the crimes you committed against them. You think they are unarmed? You are fools. They have kitchen knives, they have axes. They have scythes and iron bars. They will tear you to pieces and spit on your remains. And they will do so with pride and without fear – because this is THEIR town.'

I stop – look up at the windows. Silence. And then roaring. The people screaming, cheering. Chanting my name. Chanting the town's name. Threatening vengeance on the Swiss. The same Swiss from whom they ran terrorstruck less than a month ago. The power of words!

I smile. My throat sore. My hands shaking.

I stare at the Swiss commander. Raise my eyebrows. He nods. Through gritted teeth: 'It will be as you have said.'

10

NICCOLÒ: Stray dogs howl from dark sidestreets as I walk across the Ponte Vecchio. It is midnight. Beneath me, the Arno hisses. My fingers are frozen inside leather gloves. My head spins with facts and figures. I smell of ink. I hurry past the sleeping bodies of the beggars and vagrants in Via Pitti. Perhaps the river will freeze tonight? Perhaps these men will all die? It would ease the administration of the city at least: fewer mouths to feed; more bread for the rest of us.

I reach the door of our house with relief. The warmth hits me as soon as I enter: the warmth and the smell of mulled wine. My dad must be feeling ill again. I go to his bedroom: yes, there he is, blankets up to his neck. 'Not the plague *again*, Dad?'

He laughs; coughs. 'You may mock, Niccolò, but in truth I do not feel well at all these days. I am afraid this year may be my last.'

'Oh, give over! You'll probably outlive me!'

'God forbid,' he says automatically. Then: 'Good day at work?'

I warm my hands by the fire. 'Madly busy, as usual. Valentino is expected to take Forlì in the next few days.'

'Ah, poor Caterina! She was a great woman in her way. I wonder what will happen to her?'

'She can look after herself, I'm sure. She's probably twisting the duke around her little finger at this very moment.'

'And you know whereof you speak!'

We both laugh.

'Shall I fix some dinner then? I take it Totto's not around?'

'I'm here,' says a small voice from the corner of the room.

I look: there he is, my younger brother; sitting in a chair, his legs crossed neatly at the ankles.

'We should employ you as a spy, Totto.'

He half-smiles. 'Fancy a game of chess later?'

'Absolutely! I've been thinking of a new strategy to defeat you.'

'I thought you were madly busy at work?'

'I was using chess as a means to resolve our political problems: Duke Valentino as your queen, inching ever closer to my king, which is Florence. How do I fend you off? How do I get the better of you?'

'Queens don't inch, Niccolò. They strike swiftly at will.'

'The Florentine Republic inches,' I groan. 'It wavers and prevaricates. It negotiates and temporises. It does everything in its power to avoid using its power to actually do anything.'

'Ah,' my dad says, 'so you're still frustrated by the slow workings of our Signoria?'

'I see *I* shall have to make dinner,' Totto says. 'Once you two get started on politics, you forget all about more earthly concerns.'

After Totto's dinner – plain and warm and filling, as usual – Dad has a nap and I lose to my brother at chess. Three times in a row. What is it about this game? I like the idea of it, but it always seems like there's some crucial ingredient missing. 'Why am I no good at chess, Totto? I feel I *ought* to be good at it.'

'Because of your brilliantly perceptive analyses of the ever-shifting political situation and your hard-earned experience of running a state government?'

'Something like that, yes.'

He smiles. 'Chess isn't life, Niccolò. It's just a board game. I play it more often than you do, so I'm better. I am a member of the chess club, you know.'

'Are you one of the best players, Totto?'

'No, I'm one of the worst. But I don't mind. Winning or losing is not important to me: it's just a pleasant way of passing the time. Life seems so long sometimes. I don't know what else to do with myself.' I stare at him: so calm; almost bovine. Does this person really share my blood? He replaces the pieces carefully. 'Another game?'

I stare at the black and white board; at the carved wooden figures. 'I've got it!' I say. 'I know what's missing from this game.'

'What?'

'Luck!'

He regards me dubiously.

'I'm serious, Totto. Fortune, so crucial in life, plays no part in chess whatsoever. If you wanted to make it realistic, one player should start with a much bigger army, and the other one should bring his friend's army in halfway through the game. Then the white pawns should all defect to the black side, and the black bishop should start secretly taking out his own side's pieces. And then, just when one side is close to achieving checkmate, a coin should be tossed. If it lands on tails, they have to swap positions. And you should play it outside, so the wind can blow the pieces around a bit. Yes, that sounds much more true to life! What do you think . . . shall we give it a go?'

LEONARDO: I cannot describe the strangeness of seeing my father again after a gap of two decades. He is seventy-four now, but he has changed less than I expected – a little more stooped perhaps, and he is bald, but he still has that iron vigour in his eyes, his bearing, his voice. His fourth wife, Lucrezia, fades into the background – she is fifty years his junior, but she looks worn out, prematurely old. Evidently, his shadow still withers.

We eat lunch and we talk. Everything is hurried – he must open up the office again at two o'clock. And it is all my fault for being late.

I don't know what I expected – a sense of triumph? a show of paternal pride? In any case, the reality is disappointing. I am probably the most famous artist in Italy, but still he manages to make me feel small, a failure – as if I am fourteen years old again. Always he sees the negatives, focuses upon them – turns the vice of his sarcasm and disapproval ever tighter. We talk of the Horse – 'another unfinished masterpiece' – and he lingers cruelly over its destruction, savouring it as if it were the moral to a story he is telling me.

it is said of the kite that when it sees its nestlings grow too fat, it pecks their sides out of envy

We talk of the Last Supper and the King of France, and he tells me I am a fool for refusing the king's offer. He asks me about commissions, and throws his hands up when I say I have none – or at least none I feel like doing.

'I am weary of the paintbrush, Father.'

'You should make the most of your current status. You are fashionable now. Fame doesn't last for ever, you know. Next year, it will be someone else, and the fees you command will be meagre again.'

I sigh. 'But if it means neglecting my experiments . . .'

76

'Your experiments!' he snorts. 'You have no business sense. You have no common sense.'

I wish to work miracles, Father

Sometimes I despair of you

I change the subject. We talk of Milan – the latest news is that the French have returned. Il Moro has been captured and put in prison. *He has lost his state, and his goods, and his freedom, and none of his works was completed . . .*

At five to two, the table cleared, my father tightens his cravat and says, 'That architect from Ferrara – wasn't he a friend of yours?'

'Giacomo Andrea? He still is.' I remember our parting – I was leaving Milan, while he had decided to stay. He thought the new government might give him work. 'A good friend. Why do you ask?'

'He was executed a few days ago by the French. Hanged, drawn and quartered.'

I stare at him. My mouth is open. I cannot speak.

'I must get back to work. The servants will see you out. Please do try not to be late the next time you come.'

11 May, 1500

NICCOLÒ: Well, you had the last laugh, didn't you Dad? You always insisted that what you had was serious, and in the end you were proved right. Never trust a doctor, you told me many times. I never will, now. Every time I start coughing or feel feverish, I will do as you did, and retire to my bed. And I will think of you, and talk to you, whenever I get the chance. Because you were more than just a father to me: you were my best friend.

I am drunk now, and the house is a mess: empty cups everywhere, breadcrumbs on the floor, melted candlewax on the tablecloth. I have laughed and cried so much that my eyes and jaw muscles are aching. Still, it was a good party: you'd have enjoyed it, Dad. Everyone came. We drank too much wine and ate too much cake and swapped stories of the things you'd said and done. I truly felt, at times, that you were here in the room with us: sitting in the shadows, laughing along.

I have spent so little time with you in the last few years; how deeply I regret that. I was always so busy, so exhilarated and exhausted by work. You were proud of me, I know, but I wish I'd put aside an hour each day to speak with you about it all. Now I feel like there's a great hole in the middle of my life. I remember every joke you told me, every piece of advice you gave me; I remember the gallons of wine we shared, the moments of silence on fishing trips or warm winter afternoons. How strange it will be, in this house, with only Totto for company.

I pick up some cups and take them to the kitchen. I should really go to bed: Totto keeps telling me he'll deal with the cleaning, and it's true that he's more efficient at such things than I am. It's also true that I must leave the house before dawn tomorrow in order to ride to Pisa, where I will meet with the war commissioners to discuss the current situation. The war is not going well: I tell the Ten that we should raise our own local troops, rather than relying on mercenaries all the time, but their response is always that it would be 'politically risky'. They're worried that someone in the Signoria will use the troops to engineer a military coup. Honestly Dad, I sometimes wonder if that would really be such a bad thing: at least it would put an end to the pointless discussions, the endless shilly-shallying, the spineless policy of neutrality . . .

Totto, like an old woman, is ordering me to bed. I say, 'All right, all right,' and pick up a half-drunk cup of wine and your beloved *History of Rome*. The copy I collected from the printer's myself all those years ago. You remember?

I light the lamp by my bed and sit up, fully dressed. For an hour or so, I read, and remember, and drink. And then, as I stare at the cobwebs on the ceiling, reflecting on the lessons of the Second Punic War, a new thought pops into my head. Perhaps I should get married? Before, I never wanted to be tied down, but now . . . I don't know, I feel older somehow, and I am suddenly comforted by the prospect of hearty meals, regular sex, a warm hearth. I'd get a dowry too: perhaps a thousand ducats. And with any luck, she'll be a better conversationalist than Totto. What do you think, Dad? It's a good idea, isn't it? Yes, I'll make some enquiries when I get back from Pisa.

Vinci   *14 May, 1500*

LEONARDO: I sit back in my chair. There's a silence – mellow, not strained. I have just eaten lunch with my uncle Francesco. Like my father, he hasn't really changed – he's just become more himself. His beard has grown longer and has turned the colour of ash, but he still smells of grass and earth. Spending such a long time on his own, surrounded only by nature, he's grown comfortable with saying nothing. He gets up to clear the table and I listen to the wind in the chimney, the flickering of the flames in the hearth.

'What will you do this afternoon, Leonardo?' he calls from the kitchen.

'I'm going to see my mother.'

I hear a plate smash.

'Francesco?' I get up, rush to the kitchen. He is standing there, white-faced, his hands empty. 'What is it? What's the matter?'

'Didn't you get my letter? I sent it to your address in Milan.'

A black whirlpool inside me. 'No. What did it say?'

'I'm so sorry . . . your mother's dead, Leonardo.'

calm warm gaze Caterina loving smile Mamma I miss you and I

'But you said . . . last November . . . you said she was getting better . . .'

'She was. She did. But she had a relapse. She died in February.'

I sit on a chair, feeling suddenly weak, and Francesco gives me a cup of wine. 'I had been gone for twenty years, Francesco – I didn't think a few more months would make any difference. I wanted to come unannounced, you see – surprise her . . .' I shake my head. My eyes are dry. I look out of the kitchen window. 'The rain's stopped, at least. I might go over there – she's buried at Campo Zeppi?'

'In the village churchyard, yes.'

'I'll go and pay my respects. Put some flowers on her grave.'

'Do you want some company?'

I manage a smile. Had anyone else asked me, I would have said no. 'Yes – thank you, Francesco. Some company would be nice.'

We walk the same path I walked a hundred times in my childhood. The path is muddy, and the landscape flatter and barer than I remembered. The sky is slate-coloured. For a long time, we say nothing, and I fall into a memory – of coming this way one spring morning, as a child. I must have been eight or nine. I was carrying a bottle of oil – a present for my mother from my grandparents. She had just given birth to one of my half-brothers. I was so happy at the thought of seeing her that I ran down through the olive grove – the same olive grove through which Francesco and

I are now walking. I must have slipped, or tripped, and the bottle . . . it fell from my hand.

the glass smashed, the oil soaking into the earth

I don't remember if I ever finished the journey to my mother's house that day. All that comes back to me is the terrible guilt I felt, and which I still feel now. I was always late for her – I never gave her what I should have done. A bad son. I am sorry, Mamma.

Her gravestone is small and round. Chiselled roughly into it are her name and the dates of her birth and her death. Nothing else – no epitaph, no loving tribute by children or husband. She was only a poor peasant girl, after all – impregnated by the local notary, then married off to a labourer, who beat her. I was the lovechild, her favourite. The light of her life, she told me once.

nobody else in my life has ever loved me like she did – and nobody else ever will

I put some wildflowers I've picked at the foot of the stone, and then for several minutes I stare at the earth beneath which she is buried. I try to remember her face. I see her eyes, and her mouth, and her hair, but somehow I can't put them together – I can only see them one feature at a time.

I feel the wind, soft and warm, on my skin. The grass below becomes stained with oil-like shadow – *my* shadow. Beyond the shadow's outline, the grass sings with sudden golden life. In the distance, waves of brightness move through the grove of olive trees – it is the wind, lifting the underside of the trees' leaves, which are always paler than their top sides. Closer to us, meadows of many-coloured flowers bend in the gentle movement of this wind, which turns back to look at them as it floats on. I breathe, almost laughing at the incredible beauty of it. And we take all this for granted! Sitting back on my heels, I look up at the sky. The greyish haze has cleared, and azure wounds shine through. In the east I see a cloud in the form of an immense mountain, full of rifts of glowing light. I shake my head – if I painted that cloud, who would believe it had ever been real, that this moment had truly existed? They would say it was allegory, the light of the Lord. But one need not worship the God in their scriptures in order to witness miracles. Nature provides them for us daily. All you need do, O wretched mortals, is open your eyes!

My mother is dead now – her lovely flesh is food for the worms. But the soul can never be corrupted with the corruption of the body. The soul is immortal, I believe that – but it is, in the body, like the air in the pipes of an organ. When a pipe bursts, the air ceases to make music. So, when the body dies, the soul ceases to sing. Its silence is eternal. And yet Lucretius says that nothing perishes ever to annihilation . . .

I open the notebook that I keep attached to my belt and sketch my mother's hair, her eyes, the lineaments of her smile. I look at what I have done – see it as if reflected in a mirror. It is not quite right, not yet, but the memory will come. I know it will.

I look up at Francesco.

'What is it?' he asks. 'You look like you've just seen an angel!'

'I'm going to paint her,' I say. 'I'm going to immortalise her. I'm going to bring my mother back to life.'

11

CESARE: Night in the palace. I dictate, Agapito writes. I sign, Agapito seals. Messengers on horseback carry my words into the night.

I send letters to my father. Demanding more money. He says I spend too much, but he can always make more. Sell blessings, sell cardinalates. Men pay to be cardinals – we get their cash. And we get more cardinals, loyal to the Borgia.

I say to Agapito: 'My castles must be made stronger. Who do we know that knows about castles?'

Agapito says: 'There's Leonardo da Vinci. The Florentine artist you met in Milan.'

Yes. I remember his eyes, his aura. I remember him saying no to Louis. Painter, sculptor, musician. But also architect, scientist, inventor, military engineer. If I could tempt him . . .

I tell Agapito: 'Send him a sign. Make him an offer he can't refuse.'

At three in the morning, I see the waiting envoys. The Venetian is first. Manenti, the pompous prick. He tells me his government's request –

A young noblewoman, Dorotea Caracciolo. Travelling to Venice tomorrow. Through my territory. I will kindly send an armed guard. To escort the lady. To ensure her safety.

Her name rings a bell.

'Of course. You may reassure your Signoria. It will be done.'

When the envoy's gone, I call for Diego. One of my gentlemen. A Spaniard – a trusted friend.

He comes – hair mussed, buttoning buttons. 'In the middle of something, Diego?'

He grins. He kneels. He kisses my hand. 'How can I help you, your magnificence?'

'Remind me of the name of that woman you fucked in Urbino. You said she was beautiful . . .'

'Dorotea? Oh yes, she's a jewel. Randy little bitch as well. Just been married off to some old fart in Venice, and she was angry about it. Did I tell you what she . . .'

I smile. 'Yes, you did. Dismissed.'

Face puzzled, he bows. He does not ask why. It's not his business. It's mine.

near Cesena   *13 February, 1501*

DOROTEA: It is dark through the windows of the carriage and its motion is lulling me to sleep when I hear the first cry outside. I sit up and listen. Across from me, Stefania is dozing with her mouth agape. Dead to the world.

I am glad she is going with me. That, at least, is some comfort. In fact, it is my only comfort. This marriage horrifies me. Officially, I am already his wife: Caracciolo, the middle-aged captain who supposedly fell in love with me on our first meeting in Urbino, but who left no impression at all on my memory. (I have been shown a portrait of him: he has grey hair, a stiff back; he wears a self-important expression on his pale, thin face. He looks cadaverously dull!) My father arranged the marriage: he says it will be good for me. And, doubtless, it will be prosperous and safe.

But I don't *want* to waste the finite hours of my life playing cards and breathing disappointment in beautifully furnished drawing-rooms, surrounded by people too stupid to manage even a decent conversation. I want to *live . . .*

What was that? Another cry. I listen closely again, my whole body tensed, and let out a little scream when I hear what sounds like the hiss and thud of a crossbow bolt. The carriage shudders, the horses speed up, and suddenly the air beyond the thin wooden walls is alive with voices: male, raised, angry, fearful.

Stefania is awake now: her face grey in moonlight, her eyes wide. 'What is it, my lady?'

'I don't know, Stefania.'

A few months ago, she called me Dorotea, and we giggled together. We were best friends; now she is my lady-in-waiting.

More noises – shouting and clanging metal – and then the horses are slowing down, the carriage shuddering to a halt.

Silence. We look at each other. My heart thuds beneath layers of quilted silk. Three knocks on the door – quiet, even, firm – and then it opens and a masked man leans into the carriage, holding up a lamp.

'Dorotea Caracciolo?' His voice is Spanish-accented, and his gloved hands are huge. There is a wide, livid scar running from his cheek down to his throat.

'Yes,' I say tightly. 'Who are you? What do you want?'

He leans close: his breath smells of garlic. 'Do not seek to know, my lady. You are in good hands and will be going to better ones, where you are awaited with high desire.'

The door closes again. The carriage moves forward. I look out of the window and see four horsemen, swords glinting at their belts. I look out of the other window, and see four more.

Some time later, the carriage halts again. The door opens and we are led out. Masked men surround us. I dare not ask what has happened to the men in our retinue. In silence, we are led to a farmhouse nearby. It is set on its own; I can see nothing else but flat fields for miles around. The windows of the house are dark and shuttered. One of the men shoulders open the front door. The next thing I know, the peasants who live in the house are awake, their faces dumb with fear, and they are being ordered about by one of the masked men. 'Light the fire! Make us some supper! Be quick about it and you won't be hurt!'

We are made to sit down at a rough wooden table. They give me a plate of food. I say I am not hungry. The scarfaced Spaniard says I must eat. 'My lord will not want you to faint with hunger. He wants you in top condition.'

My voice trembles. 'Your lord – who is it?'

'Enough, my lady. Do not seek to know more.'

Stefania and I are put to bed together, on a straw mattress next to the old peasant woman. Stefania whispers to me: 'You don't think it's . . . Duke Valentino . . . do you?'

Duke Valentino is the most infamous man alive. When I was at the court of Mantua, the marchioness was terrified of him, and never stopped sending spies to his court, each one laden with gifts and flattering, perfumed letters. In Urbino, Duchess Elisabetta spoke of him with distaste, but also a kind of dreadful respect. He is reputed to be the most handsome man in Italy, as well as the cruellest and the most cunning. Stefania dreamt about him all last summer. She would wake up in a sweat and say, 'I've had another nightmare.' Strange – I always had the feeling she secretly enjoyed those nightmares.

I remember the prayers I made last night: asking God to deliver me from my bond of marriage. This isn't quite what I had in mind.

A warning for the future: be careful what you wish for, Dorotea.

14 February, 1501

CESARE: Scarface and shadowloom. Michelotto clears his throat. I look up. 'Well?'

'She is here, my lord. Waiting for you in the green room.'

'What's she like?'

'I'll have her if you don't want her.'

I laugh. Give him a purse of gold ducats. Dismiss him.

Agapito looks sideways at me. 'I hope she's worth it.'

'It was only a few ducats.'

'You know what I mean. Why have you done this, my lord?'

'Because I felt like it, Agapito.'

'That's not a reason. You're jeopardising your alliance with Venice, possibly even your good relations with France, to satisfy a whim.'

'I don't need Venice any more. That's the point – I'm a power in my own right now. Fuck Venice.'

'And if the king comes out on their side? *He* needs Venice, even if you don't.'

'He needs me more. Anyway, I'm innocent. Dorotea Caracciolo? She was perfectly safe when she went through our territory. I can hardly be blamed for what happens to her in Venetian territory, can I?'

'You can and you will, my lord. But you know that already. Oh well . . .' He shrugs, relaxes. 'You may as well go and enjoy your prize. I'll finish up here.'

87

I walk to the green room. Guards bow as I pass. I tell the men by the door – you can go now. I enter the room.

She's standing by the window. I see her shiver. Her hair disarranged, her dress dirty and torn. Pretending to look out at the dark – but watching my reflection.

'Good evening, my lady.'

'How dare you do this to me?' She turns. Big dark eyes. Fist-sized white breasts. If only she were blonde – she'd be perfect.

'Because I am bold and fearless, of course.'

'I am the wife of a Venetian captain of infantry and I . . .'

I walk towards her. Lean back against the table. Slip off my gloves – first left, then right. 'Diego told me you were beautiful. He told me many things about you.'

White cheeks turn red. White fingers intertwine. She twists her wedding ring round and round.

'I resent your insinuation. What you have done is a criminal act, and I demand to see . . .'

'A representative of the Venetian government? One will be along in the morning, I'm sure. You will be free to go with him, of course. If that is what you wish . . .'

'Of course it's what I wish! What do you . . .?'

I slide off the table, move closer. Watch the tendons in her neck tense and twitch.

I know what you did. I know what you want.

'You may decide tomorrow morning, my lady. In the meantime . . . I will have some things brought to your room. To make your stay here more comfortable. If there is anything else you desire . . . do not hesitate to ask.'

I drop to my knees. She stares down at me. Frowns and swallows.

Women always look fearful when they look at me. Respectable women, I mean. I know why. They desire me – and know they shouldn't. They are charmed – and wish they weren't. They want to find me vile, repulsive – and can't. Poor them.

I take her hand. Skin like warm silk. Press it to my lips. A shiver runs through her. Disgust . . . or lust?

I stand. I bow. I exit. She stares out of the window again. Seeing not the darkness, but her own shocked reflection.

15 February, 1501

DOROTEA: Oh dear, what is happening to me? It is evening, I am tipsy, and my resistance is weakening. The last few hours have been so unexpected and overwhelming, I simply don't know what to think.

As soon as he left the room after our first interview, I began to tremble. I was annoyed with myself: not only did this arrogant man fill me with a desire so strong that I could barely stand, but he clearly knew it too. I did *try* to sound outraged and revolted, to treat him with the cold haughtiness he deserved; but then he mentioned Diego's name, and it was as if I were standing naked before him. I hated him for that: for being so crude and obvious. But then he left me alone, and started sending the gifts.

First came the boxes of candied quinces, the sweetmeats and Malvasia wine; then a servant entered and lit about a hundred candles, followed by four musicians, who stood in the corner and played beautifully. Maids came and brushed my hair, powdered my face, painted my nails; then another servant delivered a gold-framed mirror as tall as I am, and a lady-in-waiting brought a selection of dresses. She was charming, and the dresses were all gorgeous. I made her sit down with me and share some wine and quinces. Then I dismissed the musicians and we both tried on the dresses. I asked her about the duke.

Either she knew nothing about his evil side, or she was a good actress. I think she was in earnest, but evidently the duke had anticipated I would ask her questions and had chosen her accordingly.

By now, however, my outrage had been dampened by the wine, and I had to admit that the dresses were lovely. If he had come in then, I would have had a hard time being cruel to him. But this was only the beginning. Afterwards came servants bearing shoes and slippers, kidskin gloves, perfumes and silk scarves. Three ladies arrived, each holding a velvet case: in the first was a pearl necklace; in the second, a pair of ruby earrings; in the third, a diamond set in a golden ring.

So now I am alone, drunkenly admiring myself in the mirror: I look like a princess. I move closer and examine my face. On my cheeks, I notice, are two bright red spots. But I have not applied rouge, nor even pinched my own skin: these marks are entirely natural. Am I blushing with shame or exhilaration?

There is a knock at the door, and a fat, bearded man dressed in scarlet enters my room. He introduces himself as Ramiro da Lorqua. I recognise the name: the lady-in-waiting mentioned him as a cruel man; he had ruled in the duke's absence and upset many people with his violent excesses. I feel sick with apprehension as I think of this, but he seems perfectly courteous.

Bowing, he says: 'My lady, I am sent to ask whether you would prefer to dine alone in your room or in the company of the duke?'

'I would like to dine with Stefania.'

'I regret that this is impossible, my lady. But fear not, you will be reunited with your lady-in-waiting tomorrow morning.'

'Then I will dine alone.'

'As you wish, my lady,' Ramiro replies, bowing again, then walking to the door.

I watch until the last moment, fighting my curiosity, then blurt out: 'Oh, all right, I'll dine with his lordship.'

He turns to regard me, and bows again. His lack of surprise irritates me.

As soon as he has gone, I regret my decision. What if the duke's kindness is only a ruse to charm me into giving him access to my room? He might rape me; he might strangle me in the night and throw my corpse in the river. Oh Dorotea, what a fool you have been!

CESARE: Candlesmoke and rosewater. The flicker of fire and the pant of her breathing. 'My lady,' I murmur, 'I am sorry if my men frightened you . . .'

She opens her mouth to speak.

'But I think that what frightens you most is to waste your life in a marriage that feels like death.'

Across the table she blushes. Swallows and averts her eyes.

'I do not wish to possess you, my lady, but to set you free.'

She says nothing. I see her breasts tremble – heart pounding under the skin.

I glance at the feast laid out before us. 'I find I have no appetite,' I sigh. (This is not a lie – I ate breakfast an hour ago.)

I stare into her eyes. She wipes her lips on linen. The tremor of a smile. 'Strange. Nor do I.'

I order the table removed. Tell the servants to leave us. My gaze does not release her as I speak – nor in the long silence that follows.

She is beautiful in that dress – cool silk and warm flesh.

I kneel beside her, take her hand. Remove the kidskin glove. And I smile – she's wearing the ring I gave her, not her wedding ring.

Gently I brush my lips against the back of her hand . . . her knuckles . . . her fingers . . .

I suck her fingertip. The salty taste of her sweat. The gasp from her O-shaped mouth.

She pulls her hand away. Stands up. Walks to the window. Clearing her throat. Shaking like a leaf in the wind.

I breathe in the warm scented air, savour the moment. This is my favourite part. The seconds before surrender – when conquest is still in the future, not the past. When nothing yet is certain.

I move close behind her. My shadow moves over her dress, her bare skin. But I do not touch her. Do not speak. I only wait. Silently breathe.

I could take her now, but that would dim the glory. For she is not only a woman – she is Venice's possession. She is Helen of Troy. Forbidden fruit.

The abduction was audacious – the seduction will be sweet. And all the sweeter if I do nothing. Merely wait for the flower to open in the sun.

Her breathing speeds up. The catch of an 'Oh' in her throat. She turns around – face pale, eyes troubled.

I take a step forward. 'My lady, are you unwell?'

She blinks, pales, falls. Into my arms. The warm weight, the soft skin. Opens her eyes as I carry her to the bed.

'You have a fever?'

White neck bared, red lips parted. 'I . . .'

'I will call for a doctor.'

'No!' Her voice thick. 'There's no need.'

I frown. Touch the scarlet flush in her cheeks. The glow of sweat on her forehead.

She lifts her face closer to mine. I breathe the air warm from her mouth.

'I fear you sicken, my . . .'

And she stops my mouth with a kiss. Her lips to my lips, her tongue like a flame.

Her hands grip my neck and pull me down. I laugh as she writhes underneath me – sometimes it is almost too easy.

The branch of the tree hanging low with its load. The fruit so ripe it falls into your hand.

DOROTEA: Black, middle-of-the-night, insomniac thoughts, plaguing me, swarming over me like insects in the darkness: I have slept with a monster . . . I am intimate with a murderer. What was I thinking? What have I done? How could I, etc etc? And yet, it was easy; it was inevitable; it was – oh why not just admit it? – delicious.

The voice that routinely orders people's deaths told me how beautiful I was; the hands that have squeezed the life from countless throats gently caressed my body; and the *will* that is blazing a vast trail through our country conquered my own will without the slightest effort. The duke is so strong, it's frightening; but believe me, his true strength is not to be found in those muscles that tense and flex so prettily under his skin. It's entirely in his mind.

His side of the bed is still warm; he sneaked out, just now, when he thought I was asleep. Probably he has gone off to organise more murders, or to copulate with other women; yet I find that I do not care much either way. What is happening to me?

Oh, I wish now that I had played a little harder to get; yet I feared, genuinely, that he would have dined with me, left without incident, and handed me over graciously to the

Venetian envoy in the morning. And then where would I have been? Incarcerated in a dull marriage, forever regretting the opportunity I had let slip between my jewelled fingers: like someone woken rudely after a magnificent dream, vainly wishing they could fall asleep again.

Black, middle-of-the-night, insomniac questions: What was I thinking? How could I? What have I done? What is happening to me?

And the answers: I wasn't really thinking at all. Easily, and without any great qualms. I have saved myself from a fate worse than death. I am beginning to truly *live* . . .

CESARE: I rub my beard. I button my buttons. Lean against the balcony and yawn. 'Excuse me, secretary, for making you wait. But I was very tired. I spent the night in pleasures, you see.'

The Venetian envoy stares at the paper in his hands. He reads out the words written upon it. The paper trembles. His voice trembles.

'. . . this injury has been openly effected against the person and whole of our State, which you can imagine how it has penetrated to our very soul, seeing this to be the first fruit we gather for the love and our deserts towards your lordship.'

'Hmm. Who wrote that? Their grammar's a bit lacking.'

Silent at his desk, Agapito shakes his head. Manenti says nothing. His lips are blue.

I lean my face close to his. 'I hope your government is not implying that I had anything to do with this lady's . . . disappearance.'

'We have information. We know it was you.'

I laugh in his face. 'I do not exactly lack for women, you know. Why would I bother kidnapping a Venetian lady when those of Romagna are already so generous in their affections?'

'We have information. The captors were all Spaniards.'

'Am I the only Spaniard in Italy? Besides – it's an obvious trick. If someone wanted to discredit me. One of our enemies – to sow discord between us. What do they do? Hire some Spaniards. Kidnap a Venetian lady. Make it look like me.'

I wink at Agapito, then make my face innocent. I turn to Manenti – gesture with my hands. Implore his understanding.

He stares at the floor. 'We know it was you.'

I lower my voice. I hiss with menace. 'That is not something you should go around saying if you have no proof.'

'We will find the proof.'

'Would you like to search the palace? Come with me – I will show you my bed. The lady with whom I spent the night is still there now. Exhausted, poor thing. Her name, as it happens, is Dorotea. Come – you can tell me if she is the lady you seek . . .'

I drag the man towards the door. He pushes me off. Straightens his coat. 'Please do not insult my intelligence. Nor the good lady's honour. I know perfectly well she is not in your bed! I will report your words – and your actions – to the Signoria.'

And he goes – no bow, no farewell.

Agapito raises his eyebrows. 'So much for diplomacy.'

Florence 					*3 April, 1501*

LEONARDO: With my wrist straight, I make the cross-hatching which gives shade, depth, relief to the image. This is science, and it must be accurate, but there is no reason why it might not also be beautiful. I look at the half-skull on my desk – I can see the fine toothmarks on the bone's edge, where Tommaso sawed it in two for me – and back to the paper. With the ruler I mark out the lines of the grid. Where the line a–m is intersected by the line c–b . . . *there* will be the confluence of the senses. At least, so Aristotle seems to say. And if this common sense truly is located here – between the zones of impression and memory – then . . . *this* point must mark the residence of the soul.

The skull half-grins back at me – mocking, inscrutable. This is one secret it won't be letting slip.

I hear a commotion outside the door of my study. With a sigh, I get up and open the door to the studio. The usual chaos prevails – assistants, clients, cats and hens. From Tommaso's laboratory, I hear the hammering of metal. And then Salai's voice rises clearly above the hubbub ('Master, there is some-one to see you') and I notice a strange silhouette at the street end of the room. I walk closer. The evening sun illuminates a great white horse, standing at the entrance of my studio.

I will send you a sign

Outside, I stroke the horse's nose and look in its clear coalblack eyes. It is Borgia's mare. Standing by her side is a young boy – a child of fourteen or fifteen with golden ringlets and an angel's face. I am forcibly reminded of the angel I painted for the Annunciation, or indeed of Salai in the full bloom of his youth, before the world spoiled him. Suddenly I wonder if this boy has been chosen specifically for his looks – a strange and disturbing thought. *I have eyes everywhere, Maestro Leonardo.* But I do not say anything.

Silently, the boy hands me a letter, which I open. Inside are the words – 'A gift from Alexander to the great Aristotle.'

the pen must have the penknife for a companion, for one is not much good without the other

I look at the boy, who smiles radiantly. He says, 'My master begs the privilege of becoming your patron, Maestro Leonardo.'

Bologna   *29 April, 1501*

VITELLOZZO: I have left the artillery behind: they keep getting stuck on the muddy road and we are in a hurry. Paolo Orsini and I have been entrusted with bringing Bologna to terms. I ride beside him. We don't speak – we're not friends. Even his own troops call him Donna Paolo because he's such an effeminate little bastard.

I keep thinking about the red wound on my cock. I saw Borgia's physician yesterday and he told me it was the first symptom of the French disease. He promised it will heal itself in a few weeks and I will feel no pain. But afterwards I will get the second stage – and that hurts like hell. It wasn't the most reassuring interview.

Donna Paolo says something in that lisping voice of his. The sound of it makes me want to kill myself. Or kill him. No doubt he feels the same about me. My spies say he calls me a brute and a thickhead in front of his officers. Big deal. We don't have to like each other. And if he thinks I'm stupid – all the better. The fact is we are allies because our interests coincide. We both want Borgia to lead us into Florence. Donna Paolo wants his Medici relatives back in power and I . . . everyone knows what I want.

Vengeance. It is the one thing that drags me out of bed in the mornings. It is the one thing that powers me through the long weary days. It feeds my dreams at night and haunts my thoughts in daylight. I live for it and nothing else. The world is ashes to me now.

Giovanni Bentivoglio invites us into his office and sits across the table from Donna Paolo and myself. I look out the window at the courtyard as the old man reads through the contract we have brought from Borgia. I can smell the candied pears that Donna Paolo sucks all the time. I can hear Bentivoglio's noisy breathing. Bentivoglio puts the papers down and says, 'I agree to these terms. But I want you both to sign it too.'

Donna Paolo shrugs. 'Why?'

'Because I trust you more than I trust him. You are both of noble blood. You are both Italians. You are soldiers and I have known you for many years. This Borgia is a foreigner and a bastard. He is *marrano* scum.'

I say nothing. He is right of course but I can't say so. Donna Paolo might go back to Borgia and tell him what I've said.

Bentivoglio looks in my eyes and says, 'I know you're afraid of him Vitellozzo. We're all afraid of him because he's got the big boys on his side – the King of France and the pope.' I smile but say nothing. I'm not afraid of Borgia. Man to man I could take him – I know it. But the old man is right about the power of his allies. And Borgia is a clever bastard too. Sometimes I feel like he can read my mind. Or maybe his spies are reading my letters? 'I also know you think you can use him for your own ends but you want to be careful he doesn't use you. Can't you see where this is leading?'

He looks at us one after the other. In the corner of my vision I see the Adam's apple bob up and down in Donna Paolo's throat. Bentivoglio sits back and laughs. 'I'll tell you what we're like – we Italian princes. We're like condemned men sitting in a cell and watching their friends being hanged one by one but too cowardly to speak out . . . in case we are next in line. But the catch is – we are *all* next in line. Borgia will hang the lot of us if we don't do something to stop him.'

The image haunts me now. I can't get it out of my head. Bloody hell – what if he's right? I stare without a word. Smelling the candied pears and listening to the old man's breathing.

Pianoro   *6 May, 1501*

DOROTEA: I'm not in love. I'd just like to make that perfectly clear. I am under no illusions about his character, nor the way that he sees me. My value lies in the fact that I am stolen property. This is not the most romantic of notions, admittedly, yet it gives me a power that all his other women must envy. I am a secret. My whereabouts and movements are known only to a select few. I am, thus, part of Cesare's daily agenda. He must think of me at least once a day.

We are prisoners, effectively, Stefania and myself. Yet I feel more free, I am sure, than I would have done married to the Cadaver. It is not the easiest of lives: we pack and we

unpack; we wear veils and dress as servants; we ride in cur-
tained carriages and live in shuttered rooms. Perhaps, in
six months or a year, this kind of routine will drive me crazy
and I will yearn for normality. But for the moment, I am still
able to find the clandestine aspect oddly thrilling. For long
hours, we are bored; but there's also an anticipation, which
we share (Stefania has a lover here too). And then there
is the comic side of things. We often laugh out loud, and
pinch ourselves, as we eat from gold plate then disguise ourselves as peasants to make the next journey unrecognised.

We arrived in Pianoro yesterday evening and will leave
tomorrow morning. All I have seen of the town is a
twilit glimpse of rooftops and distant streets through the
gap between two shutters. However, I am less in dread
of growing bored with this life than I am of Cesare
growing bored with me. My unique status gives me some
protection, but ultimately it won't stop him jettisoning me.
He will not strangle me and throw my corpse in a river, as
I once feared; but if he were to hand me back to the
Venetians, then frankly I would prefer to be strangled. My
name would be dirt: no one would believe I was held for so
long against my will, that I did not finally succumb to him. No,
I have nowhere else to go: my bridges have all been burnt.

I suppose you could say I am a whore now, but no more
than those Handmaidens of Venus at the court of Mantua;
no more than all the housewives of Venice, for that
matter. And at least I am a whore who must use her brain,
not only her body. Were I to mouth inanities to Cesare, as
we were trained to do by the marchioness, he would soon
grow bored of me. You see, Cesare *talks* to me after sex. I
don't think he normally talks to his women. He was silent
with me the first time. But for some reason now, his tongue
runs loose; perhaps because he knows I cannot speak to

anyone outside his circle of confidantes. Well, no one except Stefania, but who could she tell?

So I am not in love, and I am a prisoner, yet much of the time I feel almost ecstatic. Why? Because I am living on my wits, my senses sharpened by danger. I am standing in a treetop, on the thinnest of branches, and the view that swims and gapes beneath me – that vision of waiting death – is what reminds me that I am truly alive.

Barberino *12 May, 1501*

CESARE: Another day, another palace. I sit in the throne. The Florentine ambassador kneels at my feet. We are in Florentine territory, so why does he kneel? Because I have an army – and Florence doesn't.

'What is it that you want, my lord?' the ambassador asks. His name is Piero Soderini. He's on Vitellozzo's list.

Vitellozzo sits beside me – glaring at him. Caressing his swordhilt. Paolo Orsini sits the other side – staring contemptuously. Planning Soderini's destruction.

'What is it that I want? I want a *condotta*. Florence is weak. I worry about your republic. Someone might attack you – and what will you do then?'

'We already pay a considerable sum of money to France for her protection, your excellency.'

'But France is far away. My army is here now. Pay me – let's see – forty thousand ducats a year. And I will leave five thousand troops here. To protect you.'

'To protect us . . . from whom?'

I smile. 'From people like me. From people like Vitellozzo and Paolo.'

He swallows. 'I will speak to the Signoria. I will convey your desires to them. You may expect an answer soon, my lord.'

'Soon? You Florentines don't know the meaning of the word. Tell your Signoria – my army is only three days' march from their walls. They meet my demands – or they meet their deaths.'

The ambassador sneaks away. I summon Agapito. I say: 'You think the Florentines will pay?'

Agapito laughs. 'You know they won't, my lord.'

Agapito is right. These Florentines are slippery as eels. They'll promise. They'll temporise. They'll make long speeches and wait for the French to save them.

But you can't survive forever on words. One day they will run out of lies. One day, Florence will be mine.

VITELLOZZO: I plead with Borgia to let me kill him. I even go down on my knees and weep. But that cold bastard just says no. 'It is impolitic to harm an ambassador,' he says.

God's blood he makes me mad! I yell that I will take my own soldiers to the city and bombard the walls till the people surrender that scumbag Piero Soderini and then I'll kill him myself.

'If you make any aggressive move towards Florence you will not live to regret it.'

'What the hell is that supposed to mean?' I shout.

He puts his face close to mine. 'It means that I will crush your army and order Michelotto to strangle you to death. Is that clear enough?'

I can feel the muscle in my neck twitching. I put my hand to my knife. I could kill that bastard here and now. But as soon as my hand moves I see a shadow loom behind me. In the corner of my eye I see Michelotto. The duke's Spanish assassin. That ugly scarfaced bastard. Touch my knife and I'm a dead man.

I calm down and apologise to Borgia for my insolence. I kiss his feet and I swear never to question his orders again. He nods and I leave. Afterwards I feel sick as a dog. My brother Paolo would never have done that – I know it and I am ashamed. But Paolo is dead and I must remain alive if I am to avenge his murder.

So for now I play it softly. I play it cleverly. I keep my anger locked inside a strongbox deep in my soul. And I watch my employer like a hawk.

In short I keep my mouth shut and my eyes wide open. It's the only way to survive in this world.

CESARE: Vitellozzo goes. Michelotto shakes his head. 'That man hates your guts, my lord. Sooner or later we'll have to kill him. If we don't, he'll kill you.'

'He has a strong neck,' I say.

Michelotto smiles. 'I have strong hands.'

13

NICCOLÒ: The wedding feast is held in my new house, a minute's walk from the Palazzo della Signoria. I am very happy with it, although Marietta, I can tell, dislikes the décor: she keeps looking at the wall-hangings as though they have been put there just to vex her. Still, never mind, I'll give her some money and she can amuse herself choosing new ones. She can refurbish the whole place as far as I care. I am indifferent to my surroundings, and at least it will give her something to do before the first child arrives.

The feast, as is usually the case with such events, is a fairly drunken affair. We have two roast geese, but that is not enough to feed thirty people, so we all end up nibbling salted walnuts and drinking too much wine. We laugh and sing and dance, and I wish my dad could be here to enjoy it all. Around midnight the guests go home and I lead my bride upstairs.

I have never slept with a virgin before. It is a strange experience. At least with whores, they know what to do; they know how to make you laugh and make you hard. With Marietta, in spite of the wine I kept pouring into her glass, all I get is nervous stiffness and an unblinking stare. She makes me blow the candle out, so I am not able to admire her young and voluptuous body, but I can feel it in my hands, once I've managed to get her clothes off. I kiss her and she suddenly hugs me tight, her whole body trembling, and says 'Oh Niccolò, I love you.' She sounds as though she is going to add a 'but', but she doesn't.

I put her hand, which is cold and plump and strong, on my cock, and as she begins to stroke it, I wonder – half with suspicion and half with relief – if she has done this before after all. But as soon as I touch her cunt, she closes her fist on my manhood so hard that I yelp with pain. 'Careful!' I say. 'You'll break it off if you yank it that hard.'

Bizarrely, she begins to sob. 'Marietta, what's the matter?'

'You shouted at me! And oh, I am so useless at this! I have never done it before, I don't know what to do, and it's our wedding night and now you are shouting at me, and . . .' She starts to grow hysterical, her words becoming less comprehensible as her voice rises in pitch and volume, so that finally I am forced to slap her face to bring her back to reality.

'I'm sorry,' I say, as she goes silent. It is probably a good job that I can't see her face in the darkness. 'But you need to calm down, Marietta. Now, where were we?'

Somehow I manage to get the job done. Marietta, it must be said, does not give me much help. She lies there like a slab of cold marble, silent and unmoving. When I kiss her face afterwards, I taste her tears on my tongue. I think she must still be angry with me for slapping her, and begin to apologise, but she hugs me tight again and, weeping, tells me how happy and relieved she is and how much she loves me and what a good wife she will be to me.

It takes several hours – and a long conversation about wall-hangings – before I am finally allowed to fall asleep. Marriage, I can tell already, is going to be a complicated business.

LEONARDO: I walk to the port and see the green shadows cast by the ropes, masts and yardarms against the white surface of the wall. I wonder why this is, then conclude that it must be because the wall is tinged not by the sunlight, but by the colour of the sea which laps beneath it. I write this in my small blue notebook and walk on to the end of the spit.

This, according to Borgia's agent, is the part of the town that most urgently needs fortifying. I look around me – he is right. This rise in the land provides a nearly perfect panoramic view of the surrounding lands and sea. In a few places, my view is obstructed by small hills. If I could remove these, flatten them, and build a citadel here, the cannons inside would command the whole area.

I walk to each of these hills in turn and, using the special eyeglass that I designed last year, measure their height. Afterwards I pace out their diameter and sketch their outline. I am so deep in my work that I forget how quickly time is passing. The cramping of the muscles in my stomach reminds me that the hour for lunch has passed, so I go to the market and buy bread and goat's cheese, an apple and some wine. I walk to a clifftop and eat my picnic sat on a boulder in the cold dazzle, seagulls cawing above, gusts of wind making the waves below rear up and crash down with an explosive weight, turning the water to spume. I think of Dante –

> *lying on a featherbed*
> *or under quilt, fame will not come,*
> *without which, your life consumed,*
> *you'll leave no more vestige of yourself on earth*
> *than smoke in air, or in the water spume*

– and my heart speeds up. I take huge breaths of sea air into my lungs. As I sit on the clifftop and sketch the citadel I plan to build, it grows in my mind into something greater – a new kind of fortress, with no more battlements or towers, no vulnerable angles or corners at which to aim cannon – nothing but curved rings, concentric circles, from which all bombardments will be deflected. *Perfection* . . .

If I had the time, I would map out this whole town. I could then, like God, rub out the parts that didn't suit me and sketch in other parts of my own invention. And, with the power of the duke at my fingertips, those sketches and erasures would be made be real. The land would change as I wished it, like clay on a potter's wheel. I would remake Nature in my image.

The sky is growing overcast and the wind colder, so I walk back through town to my lodgings. The high street is lined with vendors, all singing out their wares in the local dialect. I look hungrily at the trout on display in the fishmongers', but it is years since I have eaten anything that sees or feels. Tommaso taught me the principle, and I will not give it up now. I pass through the crowds gathered by the silk and damask stalls, and think of buying some pink stockings as a gift for Salai. Then I see a stallholder selling caged birds. Doves, pigeons, lovebirds. I buy one from him – a white dove – and, before his astonished eyes, open the door of the cage and set the bird free. It flies up to a windowledge. Then, after looking around at all the infinite possibilities suddenly open to it, the dove flies off, over the town, and disappears from sight.

The man tells me I am a fool – that this bird is tame and will soon be killed in the wild. 'Then at least it will die free,' I say, thinking, as the words come out of my mouth, how hollow they sound.

The man shakes his head, as if at a simpleton, and asks for the cage back – 'Now you won't be needing it.'

'You expect me to give you the birdcage?' I say. 'So you can imprison another bird within its bars?'

He stares at me ironically. 'Well, what else were you planning to do with it?'

I will keep it as a symbol, I decide. An empty cage, its door open – a symbol of my newfound liberty. I don't say this though. The stallholder would only make some sarcastic comment. Instead I walk off without a word, people staring at me as I go – the cage in one hand, my expression enigmatic.

14

CESARE: All winter and all spring – in this small dark room. All winter and all spring – working alone.

I rise at noon. I am dressed and groomed. I ask for news – they give me news. I ask for money – they give me money. I write letters, I make plans. I study maps, I recruit captains.

This is the year. The greatest year of my life. The year that will change everything. My Rubicon. My Issus.

It is written in the stars – the astrologer tells me. And anyway I can smell it – fame in the air. I can feel it – glory at my fingertips.

All winter and all spring – making plans. My secret plans. My shining plans. A trail of gunpowder – a long fuse. Soon I will light it. Soon . . . BANG!

It is evening now. I look out at the blueshadowed courtyard. I walk across the room. I look out at the twilit gardens. Silhouettes of trees against the violet sky.

I listen to my spies. I read their reports.

Report from Imola. Ramiro is a tyrant – the people of Romagna hate him. This is good. He crushes crime, he instils discipline. He does it by burning houses. He does it by killing children. I take the credit – he takes the blame.

Report from the cardinals. Della Rovere has escaped to Savona. He was plotting against us. Our most dangerous enemy. He wishes to be pope. He wishes to crush the

Borgia. We sent assassins – but too late. This is bad. He is free – for now. He is safe – for now.

Report from Tuscany. Vitellozzo's army lies outside Arezzo. In the town, his partisans spread revolt. In a day or two – the town will surrender. It will rebel against Florence. It will declare Vitellozzo its ruler. This is good. Florence gets the fear – Vitellozzo gets the blame.

A knock on the door. Michelotto enters. He tells me he has bad news – and good news.

'Give me the bad news,' I say.

He tells me Caterina Sforza is free. Released from the Castel Sant'Angelo – on the pope's orders. She will go to Florence – live quietly. She knows if she says a word about us, she's dead.

'Oh well,' I say. 'We should have killed her – it would have been safer. But too late now. And the good news?'

A slanderer has been caught. A madman, spreading lies about me. Michelotto cut his tongue out, stitched it to the man's ear – the symbol of false report. The man hangs from a wall of the Castel Sant'Angelo. He will die up there in the heat – slowly, silently.

I nod. Just as I wished. Word will spread. Fear will spread. Like blood – like fire.

It is better to be feared than loved. Sometimes I wish it were otherwise. Life in Romagna is more pleasant than life in Rome. To be loved is sweeter. But to be feared is surer.

And with Romans it is the only way. They laugh at kindness. They sneer at justice. Terror is the only language they understand.

Luckily for me, I speak it fluently.

near Arezzo   *7 June, 1502*

LEONARDO: I reach the remains of the camp in the late morning, as the main body of the army marches away from it. I am taken to the commander's tent, the largest of those still standing on the hillside, and I am presented to Vitellozzo Vitelli. He is a bear of a man – thick-necked, like the Judas in my Last Supper. The look in his eyes is at first cold, almost contemptuous. Then he is told my name and something different flickers in those blue irises – the sensitive boy he once was, perhaps, trapped beneath the hardened layers of soldier's skin. His voice comes out surprisingly smooth and quiet. 'Leonardo da Vinci – I am honoured to meet you.'

the strange magic of reputation

He bids me sit down and serves me sweet wine. 'It's a Malvasia from Venice – the very best.' I nod and smile uncomfortably. Around us are the sounds of an army on the move (the shouting of orders, the clanking of armour, the clatter of horses' hooves) but Vitellozzo, though half-dressed in armour himself, seems unperturbed by this clamour. He looks like a man settling down to a good book – calm, full of happy anticipation, as though he has all the time in the world to devote to our conversation.

I sip the wine, which is intoxicatingly strong, and we begin to talk (I don't know how it comes about) of the ancient generals, the ancient authors. Excited, Vitellozzo gets up and rummages about in his belongings. He comes back with a volume of Livy. 'I was reading this only the other night,' he says, and shows me the passage about the siege of Syracuse – how Archimedes, with his ship-shaking machines and his burning mirrors, defended the city walls from the might of the Roman army.

with his little finger, he could crush a battalion

I mention that I am seeking a Latin translation of Archimedes' mathematical works, of which a volume exists in the library at Borgo San Sepolcro. The general promises me eagerly that, upon entering that town, which will happen soon, he will send someone to secure the book for me.

I begin to thank him, but he interrupts me. 'I am told you are a genius on the same scale as Archimedes,' he says, and before I can protest, he continues – 'It would be worth much to a general to have such a man on his side.'

Something in his manner confuses me. Why does he say *would* rather than *will*? And why that hungry, nervous look? I reply that I hope to fulfil the Duke Valentino's expectations of me.

Instantly his eyes cloud over. 'Ah . . . Valentino.' His jaw tenses, his lips contort. He looks as though he would say more, then abruptly changes the subject.

As I leave the tent, he asks me whether I know 'any of the following men' – and recites a list of names. His eyes flash as he speaks. I recognise some Florentine family names, but none of the men are personal acquaintances of mine. I say this to Vitellozzo. The blaze in his eyes dies as suddenly as it had flared up, and I find myself looking, once again, at a hardbitten general, his eyes hooded, suspicious, weary.

'Who are they?' I ask, out of curiosity.

'Never mind,' he sighs. 'They will all be dead soon anyway.'

15

NICCOLÒ: The bishop groans that his buttocks are aching again, so we stop at the inn in the centre of town. We order a pitcher of ale and take it outside, where a patch of lush grass overlooks a stream and some fields. There is no one else in the garden except for an old priest, sheltering under a cherry tree.

'I'm sorry Niccolò,' the bishop sighs, easing himself to the soft ground. 'I know you're impatient to get there, but I am not as young as you, and my old body can't take the pace.'

'I'm not impatient at all, Francesco,' I lie. (I began our trip calling him 'your worship', but he is a friendly sort and begged me to use his first name.) 'I would happily stop at an inn in every town we pass. It's the Signoria who asked us to get to Urbino as quickly as possible. They are worried about Valentino. Not without reason, perhaps.'

'Yes, he seems a devil of a man all right. And if he did capture Urbino, it would put us in an awkward situation. But I honestly don't think there's any rush, Niccolò. I've seen these things many times before. You ride like the wind to reach a place, and then end up hanging around for weeks afterward, bored out of your mind. Valentino will probably still be setting up his artillery when we arrive. Urbino's a tough nut to crack, you know: a brave duke, loved by his people; a hilltop city. In fact, I rather think young Borgia may have bitten off more than he can chew this time.'

I smile – Francesco does love his clichés – and take a long draught of ale. When I put the mug down, I notice that the old priest is coming towards us. He is red-faced and looks oddly agitated.

'Good day, sirs,' the priest bows. 'Did I hear you two gentlemen discussing Urbino?'

'Yes, that's right.'

'Well then, you may be interested to learn that I have just come from there.'

'Oh really? And how did things stand when you left?'

And then, in the excited, indignant voice of one who is the bearer of bad news, the priest tells us that the town has already fallen. To gasps of incredulity from Francesco, he explains how Borgia tricked Guidobaldo out of his beloved duchy using only the words of a messenger. He asked to borrow Guidobaldo's troops, and reassured the poor fool by sending his message from a town a hundred miles south of Urbino. Then he led his men on one of the fastest night marches ever known, while other troops under his command closed in from the north, east and west. By dawn the entire papal army surrounded Urbino's borders, and there was nothing Guidobaldo could do but flee for his life.

I laugh at the sheer audacity of this plan. Francesco splutters with outrage. Speaking at the same time, he says 'What treachery!' and I say 'What idiocy!' He is talking about Borgia. I am talking about Guidobaldo. Both of us, naturally enough, are right.

Yet surely it is better, I say, for a prince to be treacherous than foolish? We debate this question along the remainder of our day's journey. I win the argument, over dinner that evening, by declaring: 'The traitor is – at the last count – Lord of Romagna, Duke of Valentinois, Lord of Piombino,

Duke of Urbino, and Gonfalonier and Captain General of the Holy Church. The fool is the earl of nowhere.'

Francesco shrugs and sighs. 'Yes. Unfortunately, that is the situation.' He is silent for a while, brooding over his wine. Finally he says that, in the afterworld, God will punish the treacherous more harshly than He punishes the foolish.

I concede the point. 'This may well be true – in the after-world. But here on earth it is not so, and never has been.'

'Then we are agreed,' Francesco smiles, as the serving girl brings us two steaming bowls. '*Buon appetito*, Niccolò!'

I eat some tripe and wonder what Cesare Borgia will be like. Will he speak with a forked tongue? Will he breathe fire?

Urbino   *24 June, 1502*

It is dark when we arrive at the city gates. Francesco dismounts with a moan, telling me how soundly he will sleep tonight after a good meal at our inn. 'Like a log, Niccolò,' he says several times. 'I will sleep like a log.'

We haven't even stabled our horses, however, before a soldier runs up to us and asks if we're the envoys from Florence. I say that we are. 'His lordship is expecting you now. Follow me please.'

'But we're still in our dirty clothes, my good man,' Francesco protests. 'Can't the duke wait half an hour, so we can get cleaned up and make ourselves presentable at least?'

'My orders are to take you up there now.'

'But what about our bags? And the inn where we are to stay?'

'Your bags will be taken care of. You are to spend the night in the palace. Now follow me please!'

Francesco and I exchange a look. 'Well,' I say, 'it's better than hanging around for weeks, getting bored out of our minds.'

Francesco says nothing. He looks bewildered.

We follow the soldier up the steep, wide road that leads to the Palazzo Ducale. Before we are even halfway, Francesco is complaining that his legs are killing him. The soldier turns around and growls rudely: 'His lordship will kill you if you don't hurry up.'

Francesco hurries up.

The palace has a ghostly, deserted feel as we cross the courtyard, the cream-coloured stone glowing in the moonlight. Most of the old duke's courtiers, it would seem, have already fled. We climb two flights and follow the guard through several dark rooms. Our footsteps echo. Finally we reach a closed doorway, guarded by four men with halberds, dressed in red and gold livery and standing to attention. The soldier tells them who we are and one of the guards knocks on the door.

'Yes?' says a deep male voice.

'The envoys from Florence, my lord.'

'Send them in.'

We walk through, and the guard follows us.

'Remain inside, soldier,' says the voice. 'And lock the door.'

Cesare Borgia is standing in front of a blazing fire, despite the warmth of the night, and has his back turned to us. He is a tall man, dressed head to foot in black. The sword hanging from his belt glints in the reflected firelight.

The room is large and contains no furniture except for two low chairs near the fire and a huge, unlit candelabra hanging from the high ceiling. The windows are shuttered.

I hear the bolt slam into place in the door behind me. At the other end of the room, an identical door is bolted by another guard, who stands in front of it. Are we envoys or prisoners?

The duke turns and I see his face for the first time: he is young, bearded, handsome; all of which I knew. But no one had told me about the look in his eyes. I have only seen eyes like those once before in my life: at the zoo in Florence. The eyes belonged to a leopard.

'Sit down, gentlemen,' he commands. He does not roar: his voice is low, smooth, unstrained. He speaks with the authority of a man who has never needed to shout in order to be heard.

We sit down in the two chairs. I choose the chair furthest from the fire. Even from here, I can feel its heat. Borgia paces around us in a restless circle, so we have to turn our heads repeatedly to keep him in view. All I hear is the sound of the duke's footsteps and Francesco's laboured breathing. Occasionally I shoot a glance at the guard by the door: he stares back at me, expressionless.

To break the awkward silence, Francesco begins to apologise for our lateness, explaining the delays that beset us on the journey. Borgia cuts him off. 'Enough. You are here now. To business.'

Another silence. Borgia stops pacing and stands in front of us. He towers over us: we have to bend our necks to see his face. His eye sockets, lit and shaded by the flickering firelight, look demonic. The emeralds in his velvet cap glow like cats' eyes in the dark. He leans closer: he is wearing musk and I am uncomfortably aware of the foul smell of sweat and filth emanating from our clothes. In a nervous voice, I congratulate him, on behalf of the Florentine Signoria, on his success in capturing Urbino.

'Oh yes,' he replies sarcastically. 'I am sure that Florence is delighted by my growing power.'

And then the attack begins. Our Signoria lied to him last year! Florence broke her promises! Nothing enrages him more than a broken promise. I look sideways at Francesco: he is gripping the arms of his chair like a man in a fierce wind.

Suddenly the duke's voice softens and he tells us that he wishes to be our friend. 'If you are my friend, you will have me always at your service.' A second later, he slams his gloved fist into his gloved palm and leans towards us: 'If not, I will have to assure myself of you *by any means necessary*. For I know your city does not like me.' He moves his face closer to mine: stares in my eyes. I swallow. He shifts his gaze to Francesco. 'You have tried to stir up trouble for me, both with the pope and the King of France.' I know perfectly well that he is talking about Florence, about the Signoria, and yet it is impossible not to feel personally accused of these crimes.

I do my best to defend the Signoria's actions during that fearful summer a year ago, when Borgia marched his army close to our city gates and we promised him forty thousand ducats to leave us alone. I do my best to block out the duke's looming presence and to argue coolly and lucidly the Florentine government's side of the dispute.

For a long time, the argument swings back and forth between Borgia and myself. Francesco sits silently in his chair, his forehead glowing with sweat. As I argue, the tiredness caused by the long journey fades and is replaced by a kind of exhilaration: to be so close to power, real power, and to converse as equals with this duke; to be – if only briefly – the focus of his attention . . . Several times I think I see Borgia smile in the darkness as I make my points deftly and eloquently. We are like a pair of swordsmen, testing out each other's defences. He knows I cannot pierce his, perhaps, but he is surprised by how well I defend myself.

And then I overstep the mark. I say that – in return for the good faith he demands from Florence – he himself ought to show his good faith by removing Vitellozzo Vitelli and his troops from Arezzo. The duke stops dead in front of me and leans down. In a voice rich with threat, he says: 'Do not expect me to do you any favours.' Then, moving two steps backward, he recites our names, savouring each syllable: '*Francesco Soderini. Niccolò Machiavelli.*' He raises an eyebrow. 'Your names are not unknown to me.'

We stare up at him, perplexed. This goes against all diplomatic protocol: as envoys, we are representatives of the Florentine government; our personal identities are of no consequence to anyone. The duke laughs quietly at our faces. 'Vitellozzo Vitelli carries a piece of paper around with him everywhere he goes. On this piece of paper are five names. They are the names of the men he holds responsible for the death of his brother Paolo. One of the names is crossed out: that man was killed on Vitellozzo's orders.' There is a pause, during which I fancy I can hear my heart beating. I wonder if Valentino can hear it too? 'Gentlemen, both of your names are on that piece of paper. I would suggest that it is in your interests to persuade the Signoria to agree a deal with me.'

He turns his back on us. The doors are unbolted and one of the guards leads us to a room in the palace. It is a large room with a fireplace, but the fire is not lit and there is no furniture except for a washstand, two mattresses stuffed with corn leaves, and a small table with two chairs. We find our baggage piled unceremoniously in a corner.

'He seems to have stripped the palace bare already,' Francesco observes in a whisper, when the guard has left us alone.

'Yes. It looks as if he doesn't intend to stay here long.'

'The French army probably won't *let* him stay long.'

There is silence for a while as Francesco washes his neck and face in a bowl of cold water, and I get undressed and go over the interview in my mind.

'An extraordinary man,' I say, thinking aloud.

Francesco turns to me. 'A dangerous man, certainly. One fears he is capable of anything.'

'Yes,' I agree, although our sentiments, I can tell, are not the same. Francesco seems to be trying to conceal his fear, while I am doing my best not to show my excitement.

I walk to the window and open the shutters. In the moonlight: a precipitous view of rooftops and plunging hillside. My head swims.

I close the shutters and take some paper, ink and a pen from my bag. Then, by the light of a single candle, I begin to make notes of the conversation that has just taken place.

Francesco gets in bed, grumbling about his aching muscles, and for a long time the only sounds I hear are his sighing and coughing and the scratching of my pen across the paper.

Suddenly he speaks: 'Niccolò, you're not going to mention . . .'

'The personal threats?'

'Yes.'

'No.'

'Good . . . good.'

(The Signoria would call our judgement into question if they knew Borgia had tried to frighten us.)

He falls asleep and I keep writing. When I have written down all I remember of what was said, I make my own personal assessment of the duke:

120

This lord is truly splendid and magnificent, and in war there is no enterprise so great that it does not appear small to him; in the pursuit of glory and lands he never rests nor recognises fatigue or danger. He arrives in one place before it is known that he has left another; he is loved by his soldiers and has collected the best men in Italy. These things make him victorious and formidable, particularly when added to his perpetual good fortune.

This is not what the stuffed shirts in the Signoria want to hear, of course. But it is the truth, and they are paying me to tell them the truth. Cesare Borgia is as dangerous to our republic as a lighted torch to a haybarn.

I get in bed and I close my eyes, but for hours and hours I do not fall asleep. In my mind I hear his voice repeat my name and see his leopard's eyes stare into mine.

16

DOROTEA: I don't know whether to feel happy or ashamed when I wake up in the duchess's bed. I can see slivers of daylight through the gaps in the bedcurtains, so I leave naked Cesare to his twitchy sleep, and dress myself before slipping out of the room.

How strange it is to be back in Urbino! I lived here for three years when I was a girl, and the duchess was always most kind to me; then, last summer, I came back for the midsummer festivities, which is when I met Diego, the Spanish captain, with whom I . . . well, you know the rest.

But it is so quiet and empty here now – like a palace in a fairytale, spellbound by some evil witch. Everywhere I go, I see, in my imagination, the tapestries and paintings that once covered these bare walls, the candelabras that once hung from these lightless ceilings, the chairs and couches on which we once lounged and flirted and drank and talked through the night . . . There is something brutal, almost shocking, about the way these rooms look now – like seeing a beautiful woman with her head shaved for execution.

I go to the kitchen – there are no servants and the stove is unlit – and take some stale biscuits for my breakfast. Being a fugitive, of course, I am not allowed to enter the dining-hall, where soldiers and envoys are now eating in the places once assigned to princes and poets, duchesses and cardinals. Oh Cesare, what you have done here is so sad! Why must everything turn to ashes when it is conquered? Why conquer it in the first place if you are not even going to feel any pleasure in its beauty? But I would never ask these questions of the duke. He would only sneer.

I sit on the marble windowseat in the ballroom, to finish my biscuits and watch through the window as the colour of the light changes in the square and the pigeons bathe in the fountain, and the stallholders assemble the daily market. I watch as porters bring barrels of wine and crates of grumbling chickens to the palace, and a small man on a horse shades his eyes and looks up at the palace, before turning to trot quickly down the hill. And, amid all this quotidian bustle, I see a face I recognise – a face I would not have dreamt to see here, now.

It is the famous artist whom I saw, the winter before last, in Mantua. He was there to paint a portrait of the marchioness. What was his name? Leonardo da Vinci. He has changed, aged – his long hair is greyer, his face more lined – but the wise, serene look is still in his eyes and his clothing and bearing are still uncommonly beautiful. He rides a tall chestnut mare, and behind him on mules are his two strange-looking servants. My heart lifts as I run to the other side of the ballroom and watch them enter the palace courtyard. Is this Leonardo working for Cesare? Here, I feel sure, is one Borgia conquest that will *not* turn to ashes in his hands.

NICCOLÒ: I rise early and give the letter to a messenger, who promises me it will reach the Signoria by tomorrow. I myself should be there the day after that. Which will leave me two days to persuade the Ten of War and the Council of Eighty and the five hundred deputies in the Grand Council that they must make an alliance with Duke Valentino.

I grab a quick breakfast in the dining hall and saddle my horse in the courtyard. Riding out into the square, I shade my eyes from the already warm sunlight and look up once again at the palace in which I first came face to face with power in its rawest, most concentrated form. I have spoken with the King of France, and he is more powerful, of course, in political terms, but nothing in his eyes or voice or body or manner would suggest so; Borgia *exhales* power.

The windows of the palace are mostly still shuttered, but in one open window I see the face of a young woman – blonde-haired, beautiful, melancholy. She looks like a princess in a fairytale, imprisoned at the top of a tower.

Not that there's much chance of *me* riding to her rescue. After all, I am but an envoy. I must content myself with my plain wife and the favours of certain Florentine prostitutes. And yet, there *was* something in the duke's words last night – something *under* the words, perhaps, or *between* them – that makes me wonder if I must remain a mere envoy all my life . . .

Anyway, enough dreaming. I should focus on the task in hand. I must make it to San Giustino by tonight if I'm to have any hope of being in Florence the day after tomorrow.

LEONARDO: We are met in the courtyard by a large, bearded, ferocious-looking Spaniard in a scarlet cloak who introduces himself as Ramiro da Lorqua, master of the duke's household. He shows us up to our suite of rooms on the second floor. There are two large and three smaller rooms. It is decided that I will occupy two of the smaller rooms (one for my studio, the other for my bed), and Salai and Tommaso the third. Tommaso will have one of the large rooms for his laboratory, and the largest of all will be our communal sitting room. Ramiro seems baffled that I should let my 'servant' have a bigger room than me.

'Tommaso and Salai are not servants,' I explain. 'They are my assistants. And I prefer small rooms because they do not distract my mind.'

The three of us spend the morning unpacking our belongings. I am still arranging my books in the cupboard when there is a knock at the door. I open it and a grey-haired, distinguished-looking gentleman in sober clothes looks back at me. His cheeks are ruddy, his nose bulbous, his eyes genial and complacent. He smiles and bows – 'Do I have the pleasure of addressing Maestro Leonardo da Vinci?'

I invite him in and he introduces himself as Francesco Soderini, Bishop of Volterra and envoy of the Florentine government. The name rings a bell, but I don't know how or why. Anyway, a cleric and a politician – what have I done to deserve such an estimable visitor?

I ask Salai to bring us wine, and the bishop seats himself in the room's most comfortable chair. 'Ah, I am still aching even now! The ride from Florence, you know – very long.'

I nod, smile, wait for him to begin.

'So . . . you are working for the Duke Valentino now, I hear?' The bishop's tone has become suddenly, unpleasantly familiar.

'That is correct.'

'May I ask in what position?'

'I am his lordship's military engineer.'

His mouth set in a grim line; head nodding as if to the music of a marching band. 'Indeed. So you see no conflict of interest in such a post?'

'Conflict of interest?'

'Maestro, if the duke attacked Florence, your home city, as he threatened to do only yesterday, in my presence . . . how would you feel about that?'

THE GROUND IS BURNING

I am silent for a moment.

questions I don't ask myself

'It would not be my choice.'

'No. I imagine your feelings would be rather complicated.' *Should I love Florence? Is it unnatural, this absence of
patriotism?* 'Still, I expect you are well compensated for any'
– he coughs – 'guilty feelings you may suffer.' *Why should I
love Florence? What is Florence to me?*

I am about to speak, but the bishop holds a hand up.

'I did not mean to insult you, maestro. Nor have I come
here to preach – but to offer you a way of serving your
beloved fatherland while also serving your new master.'

'What do you mean?'

He means that he wishes me to spy on the duke.
He wishes me to report my private conversations with
Valentino to the Florentine Signoria so that they may have
reliable information on the duke's hopes and intentions,
his thoughts and movements. I want to say no. I want to tell
the bishop to get out of my room.

a spy, sneaking in the dark – a spy, cheating and deceiving

I begin to speak, but Soderini is already out of his chair.
He is patting me on the shoulder. He seems to think a deal
has been done, that I have agreed to do what he wishes.

*Francesco Soderini . . . I remember, now, where I heard his name
before. He opens the door and bows, self-satisfied.*

'Vitellozzo Vitelli was asking after you, the other day,' I
say. 'He seemed eager to make your acquaintance.'

The bishop's ruddy cheeks turn the colour of old
snow.

In the evening, I am summoned by the duke. He has
changed, I think, since I last saw him – the daredevil boy
has vanished, and a harsher, tougher man stands in his

place. His face is thinner, his beard thicker. He still has that charm, that ease of grace, but it looks more polished now.

like a mask – like my own mask

'You have achieved greatness since we last met, my lord.'

'In Milan – yes, I remember it vividly. Greatness? Not yet, Leonardo. I am only beginning. Like you, I wish to work miracles.'

I smile involuntarily. I have been through that conversation so many times in my mind, but I did not dare hope that it made the same impression on the duke. His mind must be filled to the brim with plans, conquests, enemies, allies, numbers of men and ducats ... how is there still room in there for a precise memory of the words we spoke three years ago in a monks' refectory?

He asks me questions about my travels, my thoughts on the fortifications of Piombino and Arezzo, and so on. He listens respectfully to my answers, and tells me which other towns he would like me to inspect. The itinerary for my summer is already planned.

Afterwards he shows me the wonders of the palace, beginning with the old duke's famous library, where thousands of crimson leather volumes with silver clasps are lined up neatly on shelves. I read the names of many ancient authors – works on botany and mathematics and anatomy for which I have searched for years.

'I see you would stay here all night if you could,' the duke says. 'But don't worry, Leonardo, there will be time for you to study here in the coming days.'

'I heard rumours that you were selling the books, my lord.'

'Not all. You may choose which works you would like to keep.'

I bow my gratitude.

He shows me Federigo's studio, which is even more impressive than I imagined – the representations of armour hanging in half-open cupboards, done so perfectly as to fool the eye, and not in paint but in inlaid wood. By torch-light it is difficult to make it all out, but –

'Here too, I could pass several days, my lord.'

'This is where I work, Leonardo. But you may come here in the morning, when I am asleep. I will arrange it with Ramiro.'

After that, we take wine in the duke's sitting room and I show him the sketches of new weapons that I have been working on this spring – the scythed chariot and the armoured car, the exploding cannonball and the sword-cating shield. This is the most enjoyable part of our conversation – we are like two boys playing with new toys. And the duke becomes particularly excited when I tell him that Tommaso will be creating working models of the weapons in his laboratory.

There is a pause in our talk and then his lordship says, 'I have never said this to anyone before, Leonardo, because it is not something I have ever felt.' I look at him – he is staring at the floor, or into space. 'With most men I feel as though I am speaking to a lower life-form – as though I need use only one small part of my mind to deal with them. With you, however . . .' – his eyes meet mine – '. . . I do not feel that way at all. I feel as though your mind is as great, if not greater, than mine. It is, for me, a rare and exhilarating experience.'

'The feeling is mutual, my lord.'

He looks at me sharply. 'There is no need for flattery. I have more respect for men who are truly honest.'

'I promise you this is no mere flattery,' I say, with more sincerity in my voice, though in truth it is precisely that.

Can I honestly claim that this young warrior is the intellectual superior of Luca Pacioli or Donnino Bramante? No, but if I *had* been honest with him, I suspect Borgia would have enjoyed the experience less than he imagines. One does not slight a man like him without regretting it.

And yet there is certainly a vivid, questing intelligence beneath that handsome brow. Cesare Borgia is very far from being stupid or even mediocre. Ultimately, however, I know that I must, and will, always flatter him, never speak with him honestly, as true equals. Why? Because Cesare Borgia is not simply Cesare Borgia – he is an incarnation of power. And, because of this power, he is both more than, and less than, a man. What is more, I feel certain that he knows all this, just as he knows now that we can never speak of it. For a strange moment, I feel sorry for him – this ruthless brilliant conqueror sitting before me. I think how lonely he must be.

I stifle a yawn. It is late. I finish my wine, stand up, and bow my gratitude. The duke smiles, embraces me again, and then, as I am leaving, says, 'I believe you had a visitor today.'

I turn, surprised. 'Yes, my lord. Francesco Soderini.'

'He asked you to spy on me for the Florentine government?'

My heart pounds, in spite of my innocence. 'Yes. I tried to make it clear to him that I would never do such a thing, but . . .'

'He presumed otherwise.'

I nod. The duke goes to his desk and examines some papers laid out there. 'What would you say if I asked you to use his presumption – to act as a double agent against the Florentines?'

a spy, sneaking in the dark – a spy, cheating and deceiving

'My lord, I . . .'

Seeing the expression on my face, Valentino bursts out laughing. 'Don't worry, Leonardo. I would never make such a request. I just wanted to see your reaction. It is good. I know you are a man I can trust. And really – to ask a genius to act as a mere spy . . . why would anyone do that? You, I fear, would make a terrible spy. But I think you might have your uses in other spheres.'

He grins, and I blush. Relief rushes through me. Relief and admiration. I feel suddenly glad I am working for the pope's bastard son, and not those sly hypocrites in my 'fatherland'.

17

CESARE: Breathe the cool air. Feel the cool breeze. Glimmers in the darkness – above the eastern hills.

Not yet dawn. I've been up all night – in the palace at Urbino. Up all night – writing letters, making plans. Fighting fears. The palace a prison now. Bottled heat, endless waiting.

A relief to be out here. One hour's ride – another world. Here with my gentlemen. Here with my leopards – hunting in the hills.

The hours pass – fast. We chase, we kill. The bliss of unthinking, the bliss of cool air.

Afterwards, we slice up the buck. Build a fire. Cut and skewer, turn and burn the meat. Sit round the fire in the rising sun – laughing, talking, eating, drinking. The leopards asleep.

Happiness. For a brief moment. And then . . .

Anxieties crowd in. Worries swarm. Fears crawl over me – like dark insects. They buzz, they bite, they sting. I wave them away – leave me the fuck alone. But back they come. Circling, retreating, attacking. Anxieties, worries, fears.

I go through them, one by one. Isolate and analyse. Divide and conquer.

One – Lucrezia's ill. In Ferrara, eight months pregnant. Upset by the heat – and the coldness of those around her. She fears for the baby – I fear for her.

My beautiful sister. Ever since we were children, this closeness. No one knows me like she does. No one loves me like she does. And yes, I've heard the rumours – and no, they're not true. I would never do that to someone I loved.

But now she's sickening. Feverish, bleeding. If she were to die, I . . . the world goes black, everything collapses. Fuck. But nothing I can do. Only wait and hope. Powerless – the worst feeling ever.

Two – Louis's angry. This time I've gone too far. Taken too many liberties. I threaten Florence – I insult the king. He is coming back to Italy, and when he does – he'll put me in my place. So they all say. So Louis says in letters.

Three – the captains are angry. The captains are scared. So my spies tell me. They've realised the scale of my ambitions. They know I will swallow their little kingdoms. They can feel the chain tightening round their necks. Vitellozzo and Oliverotto. The Orsini and the Baglioni. Will they turn on me? Will my friends become my enemies? Yes – only a question of time now.

Four – Florence is bullshitting me. She's playing for time, lying through her teeth. She knows Louis is on her side. She knows his army is coming. She called my bluff – again. Soderini read me the letter yesterday. Empty words – the Signoria's speciality. I raged at him. It made me feel better – but it didn't help.

Florence is not my friend. The captains are not my friends. France is not my friend.

So . . . I have no friends. Only enemies. But it is always better to know your enemies. And things can change. Things WILL change.

What should I do? Sacrifice a pawn to Louis. Win him back to my side. Fuck the Florentines – it's the French who count. Fuck the captains – they'll turn on me anyway. May as well be now.

I'll tell Vitellozzo – get out of Arezzo. I'll make him angry. Make him show his hand. This will make Louis happy – make him my friend again. Two birds killed by a single stone.

Yes. A plan of action. My decision made, the fears cease swarming. Anxieties and worries fly away.

I chew the deerflesh – savour the blood. I stroke the leopards' warm flanks and stare at the eastern hills. The sun rises. The heat grows.

I ride back to Urbino. Back to the empty palace. Alone in the duke's dark bedroom, I fall asleep.

I dream of Lucrezia. In my dream, she is dying.

Cesena   *9 August, 1502*

LEONARDO: In the hours of daylight the air is like steam, and so bright it hurts my eyes. I have experimented with hats of different brim widths, but they do not help with the glare that reflects from the brightly coloured house walls or the pale cobblestones or the surface of the river I am mapping. There must be some way of solving this problem. Perhaps I could make some special spectacles – diffuse the light with stained glass, as they do in the windows of cathedrals?

why do I feel

So the days are harsh and humid here, but the nights . . .

why do I feel so

Standing on the balcony of my room, I breathe air that feels like velvet and look up into a sky illuminated by a thousand stars – each one, I believe, a globe, like our earth, or like the moon, all reflecting the light of the sun, which is

the centre of the universe, although very few people understand this. I am naked but no one can see me – the people
of this town are all asleep. Behind me, in my bed, I hear the
sound of his dream-haunted boyish muttering.

why do I feel so happy?

Yes, the drought has ended. Salai crawled into bed with
me last night for the first time in nearly five years and kissed
me on the mouth. I was three-quarters alseep, and for a long
time as we kissed and stroked each other, I thought I was
dreaming. It is not an uncommon dream for me. But no, he
was there (*is* there) – flesh and skeleton, strong muscles and
warm blood, sweet-smelling curls and sweat-sticky skin.

I sigh, wondering what I have let myself in for. I had
thought all that was finished. I am anxious, I suppose, in
case our physical love brings back the storms it used to
spark so often in Milan. But in spite of my worries, I am
happy. An animal happiness, a bodily exhilaration, that is
all the more glorious for my having almost forgotten how
it felt.

remove the mask for a moment – no one can see you now

I know I will not fall asleep for hours yet, but for once
I don't feel like doing anything useful – no algebra exer-
cises, no geometrical doodling. I only wish to savour the
moment. So I put some clothes on, walk downstairs through
the silent palace and out into the starlit square.

Even the insects are quiet now. The sole sound to be
heard is the falling of water in the old fountain. But what
sounds it seems to make, now that all else is silence! I
listen, spellbound, to the various notes created by water
falling from different heights into a bowl of varying
depths. It is music. I could make harmonies from such an
instrument.

My mind drifts . . . Why did Salai choose to come to my

bed tonight? The answer is probably not too flattering. He has been bored and miserable ever since we left Urbino – inspecting fortresses is not his idea of fun. He moans about the people of Romagna. He mocks their dull clothes, their provincial accents, their narrow minds. He feels alone, trapped. And he is a young man, with a young man's needs and desires. I cannot blame him – it's perfectly natural. I only hope he will not be awkward or embarrassed with me tomorrow.

But never mind tomorrow. Never mind why. These things are unimportant. Never mind the fear of becoming dust, being forgotten – *now* is bliss. If only I could stop time – suspend my life here, in this moment, as in a painting . . .

I don't know how long I stand here, by the fountain, listening to its music, breathing the velvet air . . . but I do know that I am happy.

How many times in my life have I felt true happiness? Such moments rear like mountain peaks through the mist of my past. The problem is that most of the time I am on the other side of the mist, the underside, and I cannot see them. All I can see is the dark valley through which I walk, the path before my feet, the abyss plunging down beside me.

I must remember those mountain peaks. I must remember not to forget them

Afterwards, the moment over, I go inside – to lie next to Salai, under the mosquito net. I close my eyes and let the sound of his slack-jawed breathing slowly lull me to sleep.

When I wake up the next morning, he is gone. His side of the bed is cold.

Florence   *11 August, 1502*

NICCOLÒ: Agostino and I are whispering urgently when I

feel a strong hand pinch my arm. 'Ouch. What's the . . .?' I look up: Biagio is staring gravely at two men who are passing along the other side of the lobby. I recognise our loathsome boss, Ser Antonio, straight away, due to his ridiculous walk, but I have to squint to make out the identity of his companion. When I realise who it is, my mouth hangs open. Alamanno Salviati, who is widely tipped to become the most powerful man in Florence (a Gonfalonier for Life will be elected next month), has his arm round our boss and is talking most warmly to him. As we watch, Ser Antonio looks suddenly in our direction, scowls, and says something to Salviati. The latter glares at me, then nods at something Ser Antonio has said. Then the two of them disappear upstairs.

We exit the palace in silence, and – as soon as we are outside – Biagio yells: 'That rheumy prick! I wish him bloody shit in his asshole! Sucking up to Salviati like that, just so he can get us fired.'

'You don't *know* that's what he was doing,' Agostino says.

Biagio stops dead and stares at him. 'Are you joking or what? Did you see the look he gave Niccolò? And we all know that Salviati was behind the plot to have Niccolò removed from his post last year.'

'That was only a rumour,' Agostino objects. 'Nothing was ever proved. Anyway, let's not forget it was Salviati's influence that helped Niccolò get his job in the first place.'

'That's true,' I say. 'But I must admit he does seem colder towards me these days.'

'Colder?' Biagio laughs. 'He's had it in for you ever since you said we should ally ourselves with that bastard Valentino. What the hell were you thinking of, by the way? And God only knows what poison Ser Antonio's been whispering in his earhole. I tell you, if Salviati wins the election, all three of us are . . .'

'Doomed?' I say. 'Yes . . . you may be right, Biagio. In which case, it might be wise to support the other main candidate.'

'Piero Soderini?' Agostino nods. 'Good idea. Shall we go to The Three Kings and discuss it?'

Cesena   *12 August, 1502*

LEONARDO: Romagna is the chief realm of all idiocy. On that, if on nothing else, Salai and I are agreed. I have wasted the entire morning talking to leather-brained castle guards and jobsworth officials whose only satisfaction in life seems to be to prevent me from seeing what I need to see in order to improve this sorry town's fortifications. Four hours waiting outside locked doors, signing useless documents, listening to endless repetitive petty arguments . . . an exercise in futility.

Finally the heat and dazzle of the sun grow so strong that we can stand it no more, and the three of us retire to a tavern, The Angel, where my little devil sits in the corner, scowling and sulking like a fourteen-year-old (though he was so much prettier and sweeter at that age), and Tommaso and I struggle with the waiter, who refuses to admit that it is possible to provide a cooked meal without the flesh of dead animals. 'You can have flatbread then,' he says, folding his thick arms and staring down at us.

Flatbread is Romagna's only culinary speciality. It is bread, which is flat.

'Vegetables! Fruit!' Tommaso cries. 'You must have *something*.'

'We do not serve peasant food, sir,' the waiter declares proudly.

Quietly I say, 'We should go somewhere else.'

But Tommaso is already laughing violently, that stubborn, satiric expression on his face, demanding to see the pantry, to talk with the cook, to choose the food himself. Eventually he wears the waiter down, as a river erodes rock, and the two of them go off to inspect the vegetables. Salai, who has ordered steak, eats it silently, staring at the ugly patterned tiles on the floor. He has been like this ever since the night we spent together – as if he is angry with me.

I ignore him, and begin drafting a letter to Valentino. I explain that his minions are making my task impossible and wasting not only my time but his money. I write what I feel, and then tone it down afterwards, adding *your lordship*s and *respectfully*s and *while I understand, of course, that your excellency's mind is much occupied*s. When I look up, Salai is killing flies with his hand. I force myself not to say anything.

'Well, that's sorted!' Tommaso shouts, returning triumphantly from the kitchen. 'I've talked to the cook, and she's perfectly happy to prepare us a dish of salad leaves, tomatoes, avocado and soft goat's cheese. She's really nice. It's only her husband who's an obstinate fool.'

'Cesena seems to be full of obstinate fools,' I observe.

'Cheer up, master – at least we'll eat well. Oh, and she's sending her son to get some cool water from a spring for us to drink. She says the well water they normally serve is dark yellow at the moment, on account of the drought.'

I sign the recopied letter and roll it into a cylinder. 'Have you got any string?'

'Well done Tommaso – thank you so much!' he mocks. 'What ever would I do without you?'

'I *am* grateful, Tommaso. Sorry. But do you. . .'

'String. Yes.' Sighing, he reaches a hand into his knapsack and pulls out a tightly wound ball of hemp and a penknife.

And then, looking from Salai's blankly miserable face to my cross, preoccupied face, Tommaso offers to deliver the letter to Borgia himself.

'But he's in Milan,' I say.

'That's all right. I fancy a long ride.'

Ferrara   *17 August, 1502*

CESARE: In her room – the smell of death. The air close and sad. Flickering candleshadows on the walls. Above the sheets, her face hovers ghostlike.

The doctor did as I told him to. He saved Lucrezia. He let the baby die. This is good.

But my sister's in mourning. Her heart is broken – she doesn't want to live. I must heal her heart. I must bring her back to life.

The doctor wants to bleed her. He says it is necessary. But she won't let him. She is frightened of the blade. I must persuade her to take the pain.

I sit down on the bed. Lucrezia looks at me – smiles sadly. 'You came.' The palest reflection of joy.

'Of course I came.'

'I lost my baby, Cesare.'

My hand on her hand. 'You must not think about that. It's over now. You must think of yourself.'

'He was so tiny. So sweet. His little face was perfect. But he never breathed. Not once.'

'You will have other babies.'

'But what if they . . .?'

'You must regain your strength, Lucrezia.' I touch her hair, I touch her face. 'You must get well – then your babies will be well.'

'And you, Cesare? Is everything well with you?'

'It's fine. Everything's under control. You mustn't worry about me.'

'I know. You are so strong.'

'So are you, little sister. You always have been.'

She smiles. Looks sad.

'You must be strong now. The doctor wants to bleed you.'

I tickle her feet – she laughs. The doctor comes into the room – the prearranged signal.

I tickle – she laughs. Like when we were children. I hold her foot – gently, firmly. She smiles, waiting. Tears in her eyes.

The doctor slices her flesh. Lucrezia bites her lip. I hear the blood pour in the bottle.

'Well done,' I say. 'Brave girl.'

Lucrezia goes pale. She utters the ghost of a laugh. I squeeze her hand. There's a long silence.

The doctor closes the wound. He opens the windows – the candle flames gutter in the breeze. The doctor leaves the room, and takes the silence with him.

'Your husband – is he treating you well?'

'Yes. Truly he is, Cesare. Ever since . . .'

I nod.

'. . . he's been very good to me. Very kind.'

'Good,' I say. Good – I won't have to kill him.

'How long are you staying, Cesare? Will you leave tonight?'

'No – I'll stay until you are better.'

'But what about your affairs? I heard about your captains . . .'

'I told you. It's under control.'

'But what if they . . .?'

'Lucrezia, if you don't stop talking about my affairs, I will be forced to do something drastic.'

An eyebrow raised. 'Like what?'

'I will send in Michelotto. He will caress your throat until you stop talking rubbish.'

She squeals. She laughs. 'Oh, don't – that's not even funny!'

'How do you dare stay alone with that big bad murderous villain Cesare Borgia?'

'How do *you* dare stay alone with that evil wanton seductress Lucrezia Borgia?'

I laugh. 'They're probably listening at the door now. Waiting for us to start fucking.'

'Or plotting someone's death.'

'Imbeciles. I'd get rid of them all if I could.'

She frowns dozily. 'Who?'

'*Them.* All of them. Everyone in the world but me and you.'

She sighs. Her hand touches mine. She leans back on her pillow and closes her eyes. Oh, Lucrezia – will I ever see you again?

Cesena   *20 August, 1502*

LEONARDO: Bang! Bang! Bang! It is past midnight, and a thunderstorm is booming and crackling somewhere over to the east – but that was not the sound of thunder. Salai and I have been arguing again; there are tears on his cheeks. The two of us freeze, as though we've been caught committing some crime. I listen, breath held, to make sure I am not mishearing, and there it comes again – a furious banging at the door. I say, 'Enter.'

The messenger is soaking wet – from rain, not sweat. I hear the hissing drops hit the ground as the door opens. He enters – a young man, eager eyes – and kneels down before me. He recites a message from the Duke Valentino: how sorry his lordship is that my important work has been disturbed and delayed through no fault of my own; how much his lordship loves and respects me; how his lordship has published a passport which will give me sweeping powers over all his dominions. And then the messenger carefully removes the document from his inside pocket and, in a grandiloquent voice, reads it out.

'Caesar Borgia of France, by the grace of God Duke of Romagna and Valence, Prince of the Adriatic, Lord of Piombino etc, also Gonfalonier and Captain General of the Holy Roman Church: to all our lieutenants, castellans, captains, condottieri, officials, soldiers and subjects to whom this notice is presented. We order and command that the bearer hereof, our most excellent and well-beloved architect and general engineer, Leonardo Vinci, who by our commission is to survey the places and fortresses of our states, should be provided with all such assistance as the occasion demands and his judgement deems fit. He should have the freedom to travel within my dominions, with all expenses paid for him . . .'

I glance at Salai, who has turned back towards me and is listening, wide-eyed, to the messenger. He feels my eyes on his face, and looks at me. A quiet smile, a suppressed laugh.

'. . . should be received with friendship and permitted to view, measure, and carefully survey whatsoever he wants. Other engineers are hereby constrained to confer with him and conform with his opinion. Let no man presume to act otherwise unless he wishes to incur our wrath . . .'

When he has finished reading, the messenger bows, hands me the passport, politely refuses the money I offer him, and leaves. I cast my eyes over the paper – the ornate handwriting, the red wax seal, the imperious CAESAR at its head – and Salai stands next to me, his chest touching my arm, to look at it over my shoulder.

'So if you show this to me,' he whispers, 'does that mean I have to let you view, measure and survey whichever parts of me you wish?'

I feel his hand stroke my thigh, and I turn. 'Oh Salai. Why must we always fight?'

He lowers his eyes. 'I don't know. I'm sorry.'

the high peaks of mountains rising above the mist

I kiss him on the cheek and gently set the passport down on the table. It is a precious document. If its magic works even on Salai, it will surely work on everyone else.

Arezzo   *21 August, 1502*

VITELLOZZO: My servant wakes me: a messenger has arrived. 'From the Duke Valentino.'

I am dressed and go through to the reception room. There sits Michelotto. The bastard's Spanish assassin. He looks up at me insolently – his yellow-toothed grin like an obscene graveyard in that scar-covered face.

I tense. I touch my swordhilt. I look round at my guards – signal them to search the Spaniard for secreted weapons. He's clean. I have the room searched – no one behind the curtains and no one under the table. Michelotto laughs silently as he watches me.

'Give me the message,' I say.

The message: get out of Arezzo now. Take your troops. Your presence here is offensive to the duke and to the King of France. You have twenty-four hours: if you're not gone by this time tomorrow the duke will march upon Città di Castello. He will take your home town – and it will be easy because all the nobles in that place have already begged him to be their lord.

The assassin spits the words out – as though he's talking to a servant or a dog. My blood rises. I yell in rage: 'How dare you show such contempt to me?' I unsheath my sword. 'I challenge you!'

A cool smirk. 'We will fight no duels. You must know that the contempt is not mine but my master's. I am merely treating you as he commanded me to.'

'And that's supposed to make it better?'

He shrugs. It's not his problem.

'Get out,' I hiss.

'Any message for my master?'

'Yes. Tell him to go to hell.'

The assassin raises his eyebrows. 'Is that all?'

I stare at the wall. I think of my palace in Città di Castello. I think of the gardens that surround it. I think of my horses and my dogs. I think of my wife and children. I think of my enemies laughing at my downfall. Through gritted teeth I say: 'Tell his lordship I will do as he commands.'

I watch the Spaniard go. As soon as he's out of sight I call for messengers. I send word to Oliverotto and Bentivoglio and the Baglioni and the Orsini. I tell them: it is time we met. We have much to discuss.

II

The Castle of Crossed Destinies
(Autumn 1502)

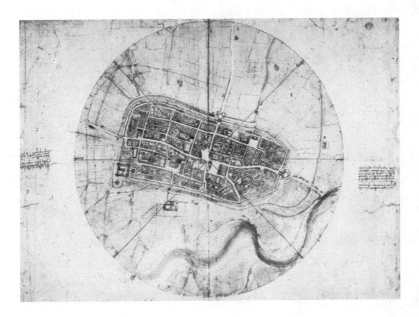

18

NICCOLÒ: I knock on the carved double-doors and am told to enter. I have never been to this part of the Palazzo della Signoria before: it used to belong to the first chancellor; now it is the headquarters of the Gonfalonier for Life. I open the door and walk into a vast, light-filled room, the walls decorated with scenes of glorious Florentine triumphs through the ages. 'Nice office,' I say, looking around.

'It's not too shabby, is it?' Piero Soderini smiles.

Yes, you will be pleased to learn that our candidate won. This is particularly good news for me, as Soderini's brother Francesco – the bishop, with whom I went to Urbino – has already told him that I am 'the most able man in Florence'. The only downside to his election is that Alamanno Salviati now hates me even more than he did before.

I sit in a wooden chair facing the desk. My chair is several inches smaller than the gonfalonier's.

'All ready for your journey, Niccolò?'

'Yes, your excellency. The horses are waiting outside.'

'Good. I realise you have already been given your commission, but I wanted to talk to you personally before you left. I am sending you, as you know, because you have already met the Duke Valentino, and according to my brother, you dealt with and understood him extremely well.'

I incline my head.

'No need to be modest, Niccolò. Francesco also told me that he felt the duke *liked* you: that he showed you affection and took you into his confidence.'

'The duke is capable of great charm,' I say. 'It would be naïve to confuse that with affection.'

'Perhaps,' Soderini replies. 'But my brother says he was not like that *at all* with him; that he was brusque and mistrustful. Anyway, my point is that you should use any favour he shows you for the benefit of our republic. We wish to be on friendly terms with the pope and his son, and we also wish to know exactly what his plans are. So it is your task both to gather useful information on Borgia – to help us know him thoroughly – and to keep our republic in his good books.'

'I understand, your excellency.'

'I also have some important news for the duke, which you may deliver to him. We have information that some of his captains have become alienated from the duke, and that they are currently in a secret meeting at Magione, concluding an alliance against him.'

I sit up. 'Any other details? Who's involved?'

The gonfalonier consults some papers on his desk. 'Vitellozzo Vitelli, Oliverotto da Fermo, Gianpaolo Baglioni and Paolo Orsini. They're the important ones, though there are also representatives from Urbino and Bologna at the meeting. You may tell the duke that our republic has been invited to send a deputy there, with a view to coming to some understanding with them. We have refused to do so, not only because Vitelli and the Orsini are enemies of this republic, but because we are resolved to remain on good terms with the duke, with His Holiness, and with His Most Christian Majesty.'

'Very good, your excellency. I will give that message to the duke as soon as I arrive.'

The gonfalonier stands, and so do I. He embraces me stiffly. 'I have great faith in your abilities, Niccolò. May Fortune be with you.'

I leave his office and run down the stone stairs, flight after flight. When I get outside, the sun is shining brightly and the air smells of burning leaves. I feel excited and full of hope. If I can reach Imola in time, perhaps I can be the first to give the duke the news about his captains. Perhaps I might even help save his state. What rewards might there be for such an action?

As I mount my horse and ride to the city gates, I settle into a long and pleasant daydream about my future.

Imola   *5 October, 1502*

DOROTEA: There is a Stefania-shaped hole in my life now. She left this morning, to join her lover in Rome. Without her here, my days will be so empty.

Still, I have more freedom than I used to. I am allowed to wander about town now, with a bodyguard following at a discreet distance. I look different these days, too, so my identity is less likely to be discovered. My hair is the palest of blondes (I have been dyeing it in the sun every day since the spring, at Cesare's request) and I am thinner. Sometimes, in the mirror, I think I look older too: I am not sure that even my mother and father would recognise in me the nineteen-year-old girl who was abducted a year and a half ago.

Cesare has been in Imola for a month now, and he has already been to see me five times. That's not too bad, considering the vast choice of women on offer to him. Clearly, despite my old hag's face and bony body, I still hold *some* appeal. In spite of this, I can't help worrying that one day soon he will simply grow tired of me, and I will be left behind in one of these castles or palaces along with all the other bits of junk abandoned in an army's wake: battered breastplates, empty barrels, pregnant virgins.

No, it will not do, this constant anxiety. I must think of something. Something to fill my empty hours, and to keep Cesare's interest. I spend all day and all evening wondering about this, as I drink my pennyroyal tea and cover up the agelines on my face with strawberry paste, but I can think of nothing.

Around midnight, Cesare comes to my room and we make love. 'I've got to go,' he says afterwards. 'I'm seeing one of my spies.' And the idea pops into my head, just like that. It pops into my head and jumps out of my mouth before I even have time to think it through. I'm not sure if this is a good thing or not.

'Cesare, why don't you use *me* as a spy? I'd like to be useful to you.'

He is silent. I can't see his expression in the darkness, and have no idea what he's thinking. Most men would probably have laughed in my face, but Cesare is not like that: he doesn't care if you're a woman or a commoner or whatever; what he cares about is intelligence, and loyalty. The longer the silence lasts, the more sure I am that he will say yes. Eventually he does. 'But first, you must prove yourself to me.'

'All right. As long as it doesn't involve killing anyone.'

'No, that would not be your forte. And I have many others who are good at it. Of course, I also have many others who are good at spying. But perhaps your ... *charms* ... would give you access to ... certain information ... that is closed to them.' He sounds like he is thinking aloud. 'Yes ... I think it might work.'

'You have someone in mind you want me to spy on?' This is exciting. 'Who is it?'

'I'll tell you later. The next time I see you.'

He gets out of bed, dresses himself in the darkness.

'When will that be?'

He kisses me on the lips. 'The next time I see you.'

San Leo   *7 October, 1502*

LEONARDO: I throw a piece of flatbread to the cat which yowls and purrs around my feet. He swallows it and yowls for more. I look to my right – Salai sleeps on the grass in the warm autumn sunshine, looking like a gigantic cat himself. He is tired out, poor thing, by the rigours of army life. I look to my left – the hillside plunges down into a sea of treetops, among which I identify firs, pines and laurels, all blackish green, some walnuts and pears, their leaves yellow shading into orange, chestnuts and holm-oak, which are a darker yellow, and the dark red foliage of cherry trees. I sketch the shapes of several of these trees, eat the rest of the flatbread and lie back on the grass next to Salai, my eyes closed against the fierce blue glare of the sky. I am rather tired myself. All this riding and walking and fresh air . . . I smile as the illuminated veins in my eyelids transform themselves into the shapes of flying birds.

so this is how it feels to be free . . .

I am woken by angry yells and the thunder of hooves. I sit up, look around – knights on horseback, perhaps a hundred of them, are riding towards the castle. They do not look friendly. Hurriedly I wake Salai and the two of us run into the woods to hide.

'Who are they?' he asks.

'I don't know. But they're not the duke's men.'

'They must be rebels then.'

'Whoever they are, I think we should stay out of their way.'

The knights speed past us towards the fortress, which I have spent yesterday and this morning inspecting, giving orders for its reinforcement. As Salai and I crossed the drawbridge an hour ago and came out here to eat our lunch, the carpenters were already going in, carrying beams and tools.

With all these castles, my brief is the same – to make them impregnable. And in a few days' time, San Leo would have been precisely that. However, the rebels have been clever. They must have told the carpenters to leave some beams on the drawbridge so that it couldn't be closed. Now they enter the castle by the easiest route possible, smashing the guards out of their way with broadswords.

It all feels oddly remote, as though we are watching an exhibition of arms, until one of the duke's men rides towards us. He shouts as he rides, trying to rouse Don Michelotto's troops, who are camped at the foot of the hillside. As he comes closer, I see his face – he is a Romagnan boy, younger even than Salai. He sees us and shouts – 'Insurrection! They have taken the castle!'

We stare back in silence. What does he expect us to do?

Closer and closer he comes, still yelling the same words and staring now into the dark shadows of the sloping forest. I drag Salai out of the way and we watch as, only a few horselengths from where we stand, the boy's redcheeked face freezes, his mouth open but suddenly silent, and he falls, in a slow, dreamy arc, from the saddle and onto the grass. I hear the crunch of metal on earth and the horse's panicked breathing as it gallops on, into the trees, down the hill, out of sight.

so this is how fear feels . . .

I watch the horse until it has vanished, and then I look down at the ground. The boy lies before us, his young body encased in polished armour, his gold and scarlet uniform torn and muddied. His arms are spread out to the sides, like Christ's. His helmet is lying in some long grass a few feet from his body. His eyes are open but unseeing. His soul has left the broken body – it will sing no more. Through his neck, spearing the Adam's apple, an arrowhead points to the sky. Its tip glistens red.

I hold tight to the trunk of the tree, which seems to tremble in my hands. Behind me, I hear Salai quietly sob.

Magione

VITELLOZZO: 'Let's all just cool down and look at this rationally.' Donna Paolo is lecturing us. Again. 'Borgia still has the support of France. If we do something rash now we may not live to regret it . . .'

That coward! That turncoat! Does he really think we haven't seen him whispering in corners with his kinsman Roberto? That we don't know who sent this Roberto to Magione? Is he really stupid enough to believe that we take his protestations at face value?

Sod it. I call my servants and tell them to take me to the dining room. I can't stand any more of this bullshit. And I want some supper. But as the door is opened to let me out a messenger rides across the courtyard. We listen as he delivers his news but none of us can quite believe what we're hearing: the fortress of San Leo has fallen to rebels and Urbino is back in the hands of the Montefeltros. The first great crack has appeared in the Borgia empire.

Gianpaolo whispers, 'Yes.' Donna Paolo goes white with shock.

The game has begun. The first move has been made. It's too late to back out now – like it or not. We are at war.

Imola

NICCOLÒ: It is evening as I reach Imola. The town is small, but it seems prosperous and well ordered. I pass several brightly lit taverns; I smell the pleasant odour of frying sausage. I pause in the market square, where a crowd has gathered in the warm twilight, chattering cheerfully in their strange dialect. There are, encouragingly, lots of young women. (Since my daughter Primerana was born in the summer, nights with Marietta have been about as romantic as a report on slum sanitation.) As I reach the end of the main street, I see before me the square redbrick castle, with its round towers at each corner: an ugly thing, but solid-looking. I might be grateful for that solidity if the rebellion against the duke gathers strength.

Eager to deliver my news while it is still fresh, I leave my horse with a servant and report to the duke's quarters still dressed in my riding clothes. This time there are no guards on the door, and the room is smallish; the air cool despite the blazing fire. The walls are bare stone but for a red and gold flag with, at its centre, the menacing shape of a black bull: symbol of the Borgia family. Either side of the flag is hung an executioner's axe. The candelabra has not yet been lit, so the room is sunk in crepuscular gloom. His lordship smiles when he sees me. I bow, and kiss his gloved hand. The glove is soft leather and smells of ambergris. I present my credentials: we sit down on cushions in the stone windowseat, eyeball to eyeball, separated by only a few feet of air. The duke rings a bell and a servant brings us wine in heavy, ornate golden cups.

I give him the news about his captains. I watch his face as I speak, but no emotion shows in its expression. I tell him that Florence has been invited to join the league, but has refused, and he smiles slightly. Finally, when I have passed on in full the message of friendship from the gonfalonier, the duke replies politely, thanking the gonfalonier for his kind words and explaining how he has always wished for our city's friendship, and how any aggression towards her in the past was due entirely to the malice of Vitellozzo and the Orsini. He says all of this in a neutral, almost bored tone of voice, but his eyes, while he looks at me, are crinkled in a kind of ironic smile, as if he is secretly saying: 'We are both intelligent men and we know that these words are meaningless, but still, we have to say them, for form's sake.'

I take a sip of the wine: delicious. I begin to relax. And then the duke leans forward and touches my arm. 'Niccolò, you must be relieved that Vitellozzo Vitelli is now my enemy.'

'I . . . what do you mean, my lord?'

'Come now, you know what I mean. Your name is on his list, remember. As, by the way, is the name of your new gonfalonier.'

I tense: I was not expecting him to bring this subject up again. Indeed, I was rather hoping he might have forgotten about it.

'I met Piero Soderini last year – he was sent to me as an ambassador. He struck me as a rather nervous man: easily frightened. Easily *manipulated*.' He stares into my eyes. 'I gather you are his personal favourite?'

I blush. This is all highly irregular. 'My lord, if you . . .'

'Relax, Niccolò. You see, *my* name too is now on Vitellozzo's famous list. He hates me and has vowed to kill me. So we are allies, you and I – and your gonfalonier too.'

I remember Soderini's words to me: 'You should use any favour he shows you for the benefit of our republic.' But what would the gonfalonier say now, were he listening to this conversation? Am I supposed to go along with Valentino; to pretend that I will help him control my own boss? Am I clever enough to play a double game with this duke, so practised himself in the arts of deceit?

He leans back in his seat and sighs. 'Tell the gonfalonier that, if Florence wishes to be my friend, *now* is the time to make an alliance with me. Before, it was difficult because I was also friends with your enemies. But now your enemies are my enemies. This opportunity will not last for ever. Tell your gonfalonier it is now or never. Persuade him, Niccolò. Use that silver tongue of yours.'

DOROTEA: It is after midnight when Cesare enters my room. I open the bedcurtains and pull the sheets down, thinking he has come for the usual reason. But he shakes his head. 'I am here for business, not pleasure. I have the name of the man that I want you to . . .'

'To spy on?' I can't keep the excitement out of my voice.

In the light of the lamp he carries, I see Cesare frown. 'Not exactly. I want you to get to know him better.'

'What do you mean, "get to know him better"?'

'I mean what I say. I want you to be able to tell me the contents of his soul. His hopes and fears, his ambitions and weaknesses, how much power he has, what he thinks about me. How you get that information is entirely up to you.'

'I'm not going to sleep with him if that's what you mean.'

'I leave the details in your hands. All I care about is the results.'

'So what is this man's name?'

'Niccolò Machiavelli. He's the envoy from Florence.'

I feel a little disappointed: I was hoping for a more romantic quarry than a mere envoy. In my mind I see a grey-haired, pompous official – resembling the portrait of the Cadaver, my supposed husband.

'And how will I meet him?'

'I'll throw a party. In a few days' time.'

Magione   *9 October, 1502*

VITELLOZZO: We sit round the long table in the windowless cellar room of the Orsini castle. The air is damp and cold and smells of earth: it feels like a dungeon. In silence they pass me the treaty. I sign it, then shove it along the table and watch as the others follow suit. No one looks at their own signature. When all ten names are down the paper is laid out in the middle of the table and goblets of wine are brought round by the servants. Gianpaolo makes a toast: 'To the league against Borgia!'

I am in terrible pain from the French disease, so I drink until the pain's a blur. Around midnight most of the others go to bed, but I stay up and play cards with Gianpaolo and Oliverotto. When I've lost all my money I call my servants to carry me to bed, but Gianpaolo whispers: 'A word with you both first.' I tell the servants to leave the room and Gianpaolo swears us to silence. 'If news of it gets out, I will have you both killed.'

I nod. 'What is it? Good news or bad news?'

He leans back and smiles. 'Very good news. One of Borgia's most trusted commanders has come over to our side.'

'Who is it?'

Gianpaolo whispers the name in our ears, one after another.

'God's blood!' I say.

'How do you know you can trust him?' Oliverotto asks. 'It could be one of Borgia's tricks.'

'You'll see,' Gianpaolo says. 'He's not going to come out openly against Borgia. He's going to act for us as an inform-ant: a spy on the inside. It will be easy enough to judge if his information is good or not.'

19

LEONARDO: I hear my name called, and look up to see one of the young Spanish captains. 'The general wishes to speak with you, maestro.' I follow him to the front of the column, passing ranks of footsoldiers who are, I notice now, standing still. When we reach Don Michelotto, he is staring, arms folded, at the river which blocks our path, talking to Ramiro da Lorqua. I greet both men and dismount.

Salai says that Ramiro looks like a sleazy tavern-keeper and Don Michelotto like a common thug, and I must confess I am minded to agree. The scar on Don Michelotto's face is particularly troubling – like a vertical smirk. Yet he treats me with the greatest courtesy and respect, unlike Ramiro, who seems cold and suspicious. It is Don Michelotto who speaks to me now –

'Maestro Leonardo, we are in need of your expertise. According to the map I was given, there should be a bridge here, but as you can see, no bridge exists. I do not wish to go miles out of our way to find another one, but the water is too deep for us to risk crossing with horses. Can you think of a way to construct a bridge?'

'What materials do we have, general?'

'There is this pile of timber, which our scouts found in a local landowner's barn, but unfortunately the lengths are all too short to span the river.'

I look where he points. They are planks of oak, green and unseasoned, all cut to the same thickness and length. But the planks can be no more than sixteen feet long, and the river – perhaps twenty-five feet wide. 'Do you have any rope, or nails?'

'Nothing, I'm afraid.'

'Is it impossible?' Ramiro asks.

'No, it's not impossible. Just a moment, please.'

And opening the small notebook that I keep attached to my belt, I begin making calculations. I see the bridge form in my mind – the numbers determining its shape, its strength. A few minutes pass. The sun re-emerges from between two clouds. I can feel the soldiers' eyes on me as I work. The problem is similar to some of the mathematical puzzles that Luca used to set me in Milan. The only difference now is that men's lives might depend on the outcome.

The operation works itself out. I check it again, to make sure. Then I order the men to move the lengths of wood to the side of the river. I supervise their movements. I use Tommaso's string to make measurements. Tommaso himself is back in Imola, working on my design for an automatic crossbow.

and his neck his neck the arrowhead pointing to the sky and

When the bridge is ready, a young soldier is ordered to cross it on horseback in order to test its strength. I tell Don Michelotto that I will go instead. 'I will stand or fall by my own calculations, general.'

He stares at me, hesitates, nods.

I mount my horse – the white mare that Borgia gave me, whom I have named Caterina after my mother. She steps onto the bridge and I feel it sway slightly beneath us. The water rushes below, its surface reflecting the white sky. Caterina walks across slowly, nervous. But my calculations are correct. The bridge is strong – it holds. We cross to the other side and I look back. Don Michelotto is grinning. Ramiro da Lorqua is frowning. The footsoldiers are cheering. I beckon them to follow me.

Imola

NICCOLÒ: My head is spinning, the way it does when I've had too much wine. Yet I have had nothing to drink since dinner. Why, then, do I feel so strange? It might be the lateness of the hour – midnight struck some time ago – combined with my own exhaustion after a day spent inspecting the duke's troops and artillery. Or it might be the lack of light in here: the duke's chamber is lit by a single candle which, when I look into its flame, blinds my eyes, but conceals the duke's face in its shadows. Or it might simply be *him*: his presence, his scent, the unsettling power of his words . . .

On the face of it, the duke is in a perilous position. The rebels have retaken the duchy of Urbino, and are moving towards Romagna. They have more than ten thousand men, while he has fewer than five thousand. He is in danger of losing not only the little empire he has worked so hard to create, but quite possibly his life. And yet he looks like a man who has just eaten a good meal – or fucked a beautiful woman.

He is telling me now about the measures he is taking to build up his army. I listen, and nod, and watch his white teeth glimmer in the candlelight. But still I am mystified by his absolute self-assurance. Finally, I ask him straight out: 'Why are you so certain that you cannot lose? Is there something I don't know about?'

'Because my enemies are frightened . . . they are frightened of *me*.'

'But if they attacked you now, you would . . .'

'Yes. But they won't. They are afraid that I am only feign-ing my weakness. They are afraid of walking into a trap.'

'But you aren't pretending. It isn't a trap. Is it?'

There's a silence. 'I will tell you, Niccolò, because I see you are a man who understands power. But this is for your ears only. It is not to be mentioned in your letters to the Signoria. Understood?'

The duke is taking me into his confidence: this is good. He is asking me to withold information from the gonfalonier: this is bad. Still, I do not really have a choice. Our conversation is already so intimate, and his will is too strong to oppose. And it is such a *small* sin he is asking me to commit . . . hardly a sin at all, in fact.

'Yes, your excellency.'

'No, it is not a trap. If they attacked me now, all would be lost. But their fear, as I have said, will hold them back. They know me as a man of subtlety and deceit: thus my reputa-tion protects me. And of course, each hour they delay, their chances of success slip away – and mine increase. Because I have the King of France on my side; I have the people of Romagna; my father is pope and can procure me whatever money I ask for. What do this congress of failures have on their side? Nothing but their hatred. Believe me, Niccolò, the ground is burning under their feet and they do not have enough water to put it out.'

There's silence again. I feel ever more light-headed, as though I am floating up, out of my own body, and looking down on the two of us from the ceiling. A few moments later, I realise that I am holding my breath. *The ground is burning under their feet and they do not have enough water to put it out.*

I breathe out, and then in again.

'Goodnight, Niccolò,' the duke murmurs. 'You know I will set fire to the ground beneath *your* feet if you ever breathe a word of this to anyone?'

I will not breathe a word, of course. I am as frightened of the duke as his enemies are. And I know, now, that my letters to the Signoria are being intercepted and read. But why did he entrust his secret to *me*? What has he gained by admitting his weakness? I feel as though I am being tested; tried out for something. Though what that something might be, I have only the faintest of ideas.

The duke rings a bell and the door opens. A blaze of light from the guard's torch enters the room. I stand up and walk carefully towards it. As I reach the doorway, the duke says: 'Until tomorrow night, Niccolò.'

'Tomorrow night?'

'Yes. I am hosting a party. Your invitation will be delivered in the morning.'

Fossombrone

LEONARDO: We are met by one of Valentino's scouts, who tells us that the people of Fossombrone have just rebelled and driven the duke's guards out of town. I watch Don Michelotto's face as he receives this news and the expression is so terrible that I have to look away. 'It is an insult too far,' he says, in a frighteningly quiet voice. 'We must pay them back for their temerity.'

A messenger is sent to Imola with this news. We keep on, at a faster pace, to Fossombrone. It is a pretty town. I was here in the summer, with Salai and Tommaso – I inspected the town walls and the fortress.

Arrows whistle through the air as we approach, all of them falling short. Don Michelotto orders the artillery to be set up on a nearby hill. I think of the lives that will be lost to those arrows, those cannonballs.

at night in dreams I see the boy's face his neck

'Perhaps there is an easier way for us to enter the castle,' I say.

Don Michelotto turns and stares at me. Since the episode of the bridge yesterday, his attitude towards me has changed – from respectful to awed. I keep telling him that it was simply the logical consequence of mathematical knowledge, but he seems to regard me now as some kind of magus. 'You know a way, maestro?'

'I think so. When I inspected this fortress before, I noticed a flaw in its layout. I recommended it be changed, but it looks to me as though nothing has been done.'

He asks me what the flaw is, and I explain that a secret escape tunnel leads from the innermost refuge to the underside of a bridge further down the River Metauro. 'This exit will be guarded, of course, but . . .' Don Michelotto nods excitedly. He leaves the main body of the army in the command of Ramiro da Lorqua and selects a band of footsoldiers – perhaps thirty or forty – to accompany us.

I point out the bridge from a distance, and the men run towards it. The general walks beside me, thanking me for the gift of my great knowledge. Being esteemed by Don Michelotto is a little like being loved by a huge and vicious dog – flattering but also rather worrying. By the time we reach the tunnel, the two guards are dead. Their bodies have been dragged to the side of the exit. I see one of their throats half-severed, the blood still flowing from the wound. I look away.

his face mouth open eyes unseeing and his neck his neck

One of the soldiers lights a torch while another unlocks the door with the keys from the dead guard's belt. We enter the tunnel.

Imola

NICCOLÒ: At the washstand in my rented room, I scrub my neck and behind my ears. I shave my face and comb my hair. I have no perfume, so I buy a lemon from the market and squeeze some of the juice onto my skin: it stings like mad. When I look at my dim, distorted reflection in the rusted tin kettle, I see that my cheeks have turned the colour of a smacked arse. I am thirty-three years old, but look about twenty-two. Biagio once said I looked so young I resembled a foetus, and with those pink cheeks of mine I can see what he meant.

Oh well. I'll always have my wit.

I put on my trusty old cloak, straighten my collar, adjust my codpiece, cough up a bit of mucus, and then I'm off. As I walk up the street towards the castle, it's just beginning to get dark.

DOROTEA: I rub pumice on my teeth and perfumed oils on my breasts. One maid cleanses my face with beautifying water, then adds powder and rouge, while another brushes and braids my hair. A third files and paints my fingernails. Two more maids bring the crimson dress. They help me to put it on, then stand back and cover their mouths. 'Oh my lady,' one of them says, 'you look . . . ravishing!' I smile, and scrutinise myself in the mirror. The poor envoy won't know what's hit him.

I tell the maids they may leave, and give them each a ducat. They thank me and go off twittering.

I think through everything Cesare has told me about the envoy. His name: Niccolò Machiavelli. His age, height, appearance, background, marital status, official position. And, above all, his character. 'Don't underestimate him,' the duke told me last night. 'He has a sharp mind. And don't be too forward – let him make the moves. He'd be suspicious otherwise.'

I look in the mirror again and consider my new identity. I am not Dorotea Caracciolo, of course; that lady has long since disappeared. My name is Stefania Tozzoni, and I am an illegitimate daughter of one of this town's noble families. This is all Cesare gave me; the rest I must invent myself.

I spend an hour or so walking around the room, looking at Stefania Tozzoni in the mirror and imagining all the details of her life. She is bored of life in Imola, I realise: who wouldn't be? She is mischievous and witty, and possibly not a virgin. There is a secret unnamed tragedy in her past. She is naturally reserved and not easily impressed. What she likes in a man is someone who can make her laugh. She is, in other words, all Niccolò Machiavelli's wildest dreams come true.

I send for a servant to bring me wine, and drink two cups quickly – for courage. At eight o'clock, the master of the household comes to my door to escort me to the ballroom.

Fossombrone

LEONARDO: We walk through the tunnel, bent forward in a crouch. The air here smells noxious and the floor is treacherous with slime – a couple of times I slip and have to put my hands out to the curved walls, which are also slimy, and ice-cold. In the torchlight I see the shadows of rats scurry past. Everything is loud in my ears – our footsteps, the soldiers' voices. When we draw close to the tunnel's end, I tell Don Michelotto that we must be quiet or the guards inside the castle will hear us. He stops and orders silence. At the door, the soldier with the key unlocks it and enters, sword held out in front of him. I can hear the other soldiers' breathing now – fast and harsh in the darkness. The soldier at the door signals that the way is clear and we go through. I am near the front, just behind the general.

We are in a small, dimly lit room – empty but for two benches and a wooden chest. A single other doorway leads from the room. We climb a narrow stone staircase. It ascends in a spiral, lit only by the torches we carry. Round and round, up and up we go, until we reach a door. It is half-open and through the gap we can hear laughter. Don Michelotto draws his sword and signals the other soldiers to do the same. I hear the hissing echo down the staircase.

The general tells me to wait behind the door. I nod, and stare at the dark grain of the wood as the soldiers file past. On the other side of the door there are noises. Yelling, laughing. Begging, screaming. The clash of metal on wood and stone.

or flesh and bone

I watch my hands – they are writhing, white, like maggots. I am afraid. I remind myself that fear protects life, just as courage imperils it. Fear is a good instinct, not a source of shame.

I hear another sound now – a kind of gentle roaring. Then I hear my name called and walk through the doorway. The air is smoky and there is too much to see in one glance, but several images embed themselves in my memory – a flower of yellow flames cascading upwards from a dining table . . . a man with his elbows on the table, his headless neck and shoulders slumped over a plate of beans . . . an old woman sobbing by the fireplace, with a dead child lying like a rag doll in her arms . . .

My name is called again – more violently now – and I hurry through to the next door, coughing and weeping in the smoke. The air is hot on my skin. My foot slips and I look down – a pool of nearly black blood and, at its centre, like an island, a man's head. The old woman cries out to God – 'Why hast thou abandoned us?'

I see Don Michelotto at the door, beckoning me.

'Hurry, maestro. This place is going to burn.'

'But the old woman . . .'

The general says nothing – only draws his index finger across his wide, muscular throat.

why hast thou abandoned us?

We clatter down another spiral staircase, and emerge outside on the castle battlements. I have to tread carefully to avoid the freshly severed body parts on the steps. Below I see the duke's soldiers running after guards, peasants, women, children – they laugh as they run, like boys chasing hens. Above me I see black smoke pouring from a window of the tower.

Imola

NICCOLÒ: Entering the ballroom is like entering a different land: most of the palace is elegant but plain, the walls bare and pale, but here there are tapestries on the wall and dried rose petals on the floor; velvet curtains hang over the windows, while opposite them a huge fire burns in the hearth. Two silver candelabra illuminate the dancefloor, but for the moment it is empty: the few other guests stand in a small circle by the curtains, drinking wine and looking smugly at the liveried musicians who are playing in the far corner of the room.

I walk towards the group of men and see two faces that, in spite of their carnival masks, I recognise: the Mantuan envoy, Capello, and the duke's secretary, Agapito. The

envoy seems pleased to see me, but personally I am disappointed by his presence: not only do I find him super-
cilious and annoying, but I had hoped that tonight's
guestlist would be more exclusive.

Capello introduces me to the other two guests: a pair
of poets called Sperulo and Justolo. I have never heard of
either before, and can tell at once that they are worthless
parasites: they are dressed in slashed, particoloured velvet
tunics and wear their hair long. Sperulo is short and fat and
Justolo tall and thin, but otherwise they are identical. I tell
them I used to be a poet myself. They look at me dubiously,
and Sperulo asks me how, 'in that case', did I end up as
an envoy? 'I wanted to do something useful with my life,'
I reply.

They scowl and turn away, but Agapito laughs and takes
me aside. 'His lordship is very pleased with you, Niccolò.'

'He is?'

'Yes. He believes you are a man with whom we can do
business.'

I frown and nod, unsure whether this is a compliment.
I can't help noticing the fine materials and beautiful cut
of Agapito's clothing – and feeling rather shabby in com-
parison. Still, at least he is friendly, and after a few drinks I
am feeling less self-conscious. As the ballroom starts to fill
with guests, Agapito takes me by the arm and makes intro-
ductions. I meet three of Cesare's Spanish gentlemen, two
more poets, an elderly German astrologer, an artist from
Urbino, and several local noblemen. There are also, I am
glad to report, quite a number of youngish, good-looking
women. After five goblets of wine, I am so high-spirited that
I begin rating them in my head, as Agostino and I used to
do in Florence in our bachelor days:

Yes.

Yes.

No.

Only in a dark room.

After a few more drinks, perhaps.

Not bad . . . oops, fat arse.

Too skinny.

Too old.

Too young.

High risk of the French disease.

God. In. Heaven.

I stand and stare, too drunk to dissemble my desire. This lady reminds me of someone I've seen before, though I can't think when or where. Whoever she is, her face is exquisite, her body voluptuous; and she wears a dress the colour of blood, cut so low on the shoulders and bust that, were she to stand behind a low wall, one might easily imagine her naked. She is talking to another woman when I see her, and she must feel my eyes on her because for no apparent reason she suddenly looks up at me and . . . *smiles.*

DOROTEA: Oh, I think I have his attention now! The envoy – tonight's prey – gives me the same look that men have been giving me all evening. It is an odd expression: they look, these men, almost *terrified* by the desire my appearance provokes in them. This must, I think, be a question of power: tonight – masked, glamorous, unknown – I have the whip hand. I am the man, and they are all mere women. As I think all of this, I smile – and that smile produces its own response in Niccolò Machiavelli. He looks suddenly hopeful, emboldened: a dog who notices the stick in his master's hand. He moves towards me . . . and asks for the pleasure of the next dance.

Everything about the envoy is small and bony: his face, his neck, his shoulders, wrists, legs and fingers. Next to

Cesare, he hardly seems a man at all – more like a little boy. When we dance, he steps on my feet and stares frankly, disbelievingly at my breasts. His skin smells oddly acidic. And yet he is not wholly unattractive: something about the smallness, perfectly proportional, makes me want to play with him like a doll. And he is funny.

'Sorry – I'm not the greatest dancer in Italy.'

I smile.

'In fact, I may even be the worst in Imola.'

'Now you go too far.'

'You have danced with someone more maladroit than me?'

'Many.'

'My poor lady, Fortune does not favour you.'

I laugh. 'You're not *that* bad!'

'Ah, I see. We are playing a game in which only lies may be spoken.'

'Not at all.'

'You have confirmed my suspicions. May I ask your name?'

'Stefania Tozzoni.'

'Stefania Tozzoni? A likely story. Hmm, I wonder what your real identity might be.'

His eyes, behind the mask, seem to penetrate my own and I am half-afraid that he is onto me. But we keep talking and it soon becomes clear that our conversation is just an extended joke; an opportunity for Niccolò to flirt without doing so overtly.

The song ends and I ask if he would accompany me to one of the windows as I wish to breathe some fresh air.

'Indeed. Let us go and enjoy the warm summer breeze – it's freezing in here.'

'Really? Then why is the sweat pouring down your face?'

He looks at me with faux seriousness. 'My lady, that is not sweat. I am weeping with laughter at how ugly and clumsy you are.'

For a moment my jaw drops – and then I get the joke. I smack his arm playfully and lead him to the cool, private space behind the heavy curtains.

'Are you from Imola, Donna Stefania?'

'Yes. I have lived here all my life.'

'Ah – a foreigner! Myself, I am Romagnan to the bone.'

I ask him about his job, what he thinks of Imola, and – pretending to be coy – his marital status. Without blinking, he tells me he is married with nine children – thus implying, of course, that he is single and childless. A double bluff. He is an accomplished liar, this Niccolò. I must watch out for him.

We talk some more, and he gently holds my gloved hand in his. He clearly has only one thing in mind, and yet I can't help liking him. It is like being chatted up by a clever child: flattering, amusing, harmless.

We go out to dance again and I spot Cesare entering the ballroom. Instantly the music stops and the fawners surround him, thanking him for the magnificent feast and proclaiming him a new Alexander. 'How dignified they all are,' Niccolò mutters. 'Those poets in particular strike me as men of the greatest talent and sincerity.'

I laugh. Oh Niccolò, you are so droll! I am almost sorry for what I am going to do to you.

Fossombrone

LEONARDO: I do not look at the corpses any more. To begin with, I told myself it was necessary – experience is the mother of learning, and here, in these sliced-open human bodies, is anatomy. After all, when I was a younger man in Milan I went to the dungeons to observe the contortions of criminals under torture. I went to the hospitals to see deformed bodies and amputated limbs. I went to the madhouse to sketch the grotesque faces of the inmates. But here, my curiosity has been sated. In a human slaughteryard like this one, the dissections are too crude to reveal anything of value.

I also tried looking at the scene as a picture. A few years ago, in preparation for a fresco I never completed, I wrote pages on how to represent a battlefield in paint – the quality of the dustclouds near the horses' hooves, the pale faces and pained expressions of the conquered, the muddy ground trampled with gore. But that was before I had seen real killing. Now I find these are not details one notices. The sight of congealed blood in sunlight does not make me wonder what combination of vermilion, black, lead-white and lead-tin yellow would be needed to reproduce it on canvas – it just makes me feel sick.

And so I look away. I admire the gyre of a hawk in the white sky above. I sketch an interesting gargoyle on the castle wall. Above all, I try not to touch anything. All is filthy, corrupted by murder. I walk as if on a narrow bridge that sways beneath me.

the abyss plunging down beside me

And then I chance upon a sight from which I cannot possibly look away. A little girl, perhaps four or five years old, wanders alone from a smoking barn, holding a rag doll to her mouth and crying quietly. I move towards her and she recoils with fear. Her face is smeared with lines and clouds of dirt. I show her that I carry no weapon, that I am here not to hurt her but to help her, and with the desperate wariness of a wounded animal, she stands still while I edge towards her.

When I finally persuade her into my arms, she falls asleep almost instantly. I am shocked by the lightness of my burden. I stroke her half-burnt hair and carry her in the direction of the town. At the drawbridge, a drunken guard laughs at me and asks where I think I'm going.

how fear feels

'Please let me through. I need to find someone who can look after this little girl.'

'Bit young for you, mate, isn't she?' the soldier sneers. 'You dirty old bugger!' And, intending I think to frighten rather than wound, he slashes at me with his sword. I am so astounded by this sudden violence that I do not even notice the burning pain in my forearm until much later.

Rigid with terror and anger, I back away and take the passport from my cloak. I hold it out in front of the guard and say: 'When I tell Don Michelotto what you have done, you will regret your actions.'

The ugly grin fades from the man's face as he stares at the passport, and I think I see terror in his eyes. He cannot read the words, but it is an impressive-looking document. Evidently he is very afraid of the general, and it occurs to me in that moment that he is much younger than I first imagined – not much more than a boy. Without a word, he runs off into the gathering darkness, and I cross the drawbridge and enter the town.

Away from the castle, the terrible noise fades to an almost-silence of exhaustion, relief, mourning. In the centre of town, in the softness of veiled moonlight, I find a convent hospital. An elderly nun takes the little girl from my hands and promises me they will look after her. 'There will be many orphans tomorrow, I fear,' she says.

Then she looks at my arm and asks me if I would like her to wash and bandage it. Surprised, I look down and see a wound, six inches long, in the flesh of my forearm. It is superficial, but it has bled profusely and the blood has dried and caked my skin so that it appears much worse.

She washes the wound in warm water and alcohol. It stings and I gasp. It looks like a tiny mouth, the viscera pink beneath the skin. A tiny mouth crying out silently at all these offences against the human body.

As the nun bandages my arm, she tells me I'm a lucky man – I won't even have a scar.

Imola

CESARE: In the blackness of her room, she tells me everything. How he asked her to dance. How she led him behind the curtains.

She tells me of his game – every word a lie. How she made him stop lying. I like your wit, she said. But I don't like your lies. Tell me the truth. Only the truth.

How he opened up his soul. Confessed the wife, confessed the child. Confessed his fears and hopes.

'So what is your verdict?' I ask.

'He loves his wife,' she says. 'But in a guilty way. He's not in love with her.'

'Fuck his wife,' I say. 'Tell me about his work. Tell me about power. Loyalty. Temptation.'

'He loves his city,' she says. 'But in a guilty way. He despises its government. He loves the idea of the republic, but hates the reality.'

'He has some power – the ear of the gonfalonier. But also many enemies. He fears they're conspiring against him. He feels undervalued.'

'The Florentines hate you,' she tells me. 'The Florentines fear you. Niccolò thinks it will be hard to persuade
them to be your friend.'

'He's been sent here to talk. He's been sent to watch. But
to promise nothing. To agree nothing. He wishes it were
otherwise.'

'He admires you,' she says. 'You're a kind of hero to him.
But in a peculiar way. It's not your charm – it's your actions.'

'He looks at power like an anatomist looks at the human
body. He dissects it, examines it. He thinks you're a new
breed. A superman.'

'In the depths of his heart, he dreams of your triumph.
He loves Florence – but he also loves Italy. He dreams you
will conquer us. He dreams you will unite us.'

I see my future – towering, glorious. Florence mine,
Machiavelli its governor.

'What does he want?' I ask. 'For himself. In return. What
does he desire?'

'He needs money,' she says. 'But that's not what he
dreams of. He dreams of power. Not over you – under you.
He dreams of his ideas becoming real.'

I think through what she's said. I think about Niccolò
Machiavelli. How can I use him to get what I want? What
method shall I employ?

'I like him,' she says. 'He's funny and he's clever. I want
him to like me. Not for the dress, not for my breasts – but
for me.'

I stop listening. She's drunk, she's rambling. But I
know what she means. The envoy is smart – I enjoy his
approval.

I'm surrounded by flatterers. They crawl after me, beg
at my feet. Arselickers, wannabes, yesmen. They bore me
to death.

I thirst for intelligence, for honesty. Like with Leonardo. Men who see clearly. Men who think for themselves. Who are brave enough to tell me the truth.

I say: 'How did it end?'

'He tried to kiss me. I pushed him away – gently. He said: "Will I see you again?"'

'What did you reply?'

'I said, "You never know."'

'Good.'

'Are you pleased? Did I pass the test?'

'Yes you did.'

She kisses me. 'What next?'

'You'll see him again. But not yet. Let him sweat – let him dream. Let him grow thirsty for you.'

'What about Leonardo, the artist?'

'What about him?'

'Could I "get to know" him?'

'Leonardo's on our side. I don't need information on him.'

'That's not like you,' she says. 'To be so unsuspicious.'

'I'm growing suspicious of *you*,' I say.

'Why?'

'Why are you so interested in Leonardo?'

'Because he's brilliant. And famous. Because I'm bored.'

'I don't need you to spy on him.'

'Could he paint my portrait then?'

I laugh. So this is all vanity? But yes – her portrait. She is mine – my courtesan, my spy, my stolen prize. But one day, I might have to dispose of her. If I had her portrait – a souvenir . . .

'All right – he can paint your portrait. I'll hang it on my bedroom wall.'

20

VITELLOZZO: Early morning: I am wearing full armour and the doctor has given me pills which will keep the agonies of the French disease at bay for the rest of the day. Afterwards I will suffer doubly he says – but I don't care. The joy of victory will soothe my pain.

I exit my tent and look out at the hillside stretching below me. It's blue in the twilight and there are small campfires everywhere like stars. The men are eating their porridge and dressing quickly in the cold air. I breathe in the familiar scent of smoke and sweat: for the first time in ages the eve of battle gives me that physical thrill.

I see Gianpaolo emerge from his tent and the two of us walk to the far end of the hilltop. From here we can see the enemy. How small and vulnerable they look from this distance – like I could smash them with one of my hands! Their campfires are low and red: only embers.

'Apparently our informer rode off with a small group of men last night,' Gianpaolo says. 'So we can kill everyone without compunction. Are you still worried that this might be a trap, Vitellozzo?'

I shrug. The pills make me indifferent to danger. 'We'll find out soon enough.'

Two scouts approach us. They report that most of the enemy are still sleeping and that their scouts have been killed on sight. The alarm has not yet been raised.

Gianpaolo says: 'It's time.' I nod agreement.

We go back to the camp and begin ordering our troops into battle positions. I think of Michelotto skewered on the end of my sword and laugh like a madman. These pills are good stuff.

Imola

NICCOLÒ: I drag myself out of bed at half past eight. Usually I wake earlier than this, but I have been sleeping badly ever since the night of the duke's party. I can't get her out of my head. Stefania Tozzoni. I do not remember everything I said to her, but I know we spent most of the night talking, just the two of us. And she likes me – I can tell. Enough to go to bed with me? I'm not sure. But even the smallest possibility of that happening seems to infect me with a haunted nervousness; a frantic lust that gnaws at me, day and night.

Especially night.

Yes – in those long dark hours I imagine it all in my mind, so vividly that afterwards I can hardly tell if it were dreamed or actual. I see the two of us kissing, caressing, undressing, and – in long, insatiable repetitions that keep waking me up with a hard-on all through the night – making love. I see her on top of me, her head thrown back, her blonde hair cascading down her back, and . . .

Oh, but it's more than mere lust. This fever *consumes* me. It is with me all the time, everywhere I go. I walk to the castle and talk to Borgia's secretaries, his treasurer, the other envoys, the French captains, hunting for gossip, and still It follows me. I eat lunch at a cheap tavern near my lodgings and read the letters from Florence – Agostino warning me about my enemies in the Signoria; Biagio telling me that Marietta is angry with me for staying away from home so long – and in every word I see only It. I eat dinner and I go to the palace and I wait with the other envoys and I am shown in to see Borgia (always first, and always for longer than the other envoys – why is that? – I don't know, but it's making them jealous) and I sit in his dark, menacing, charming presence and we talk about power and war and conspiracies and alliances – the very stuff that used to occupy my mind all the time – and still . . . all I can think about is It. Oh Christ, will I ever snap out of this? Distractedly, I read through Agostino's letter again:

> I am sure, by God, that you are held in great honour there, you whom the duke himself and all the courtiers favour, so that they heap praise on you as a prudent man, surround and flatter you. That is a pleasure, since I love you dearly. Nevertheless, I would not wish you to neglect what may soon keep you from completing your work. My Niccolò, even if those things now creep and slink about, they must soon come out into the open. You know the nature of men, their deceptions and secrecy, their rivalries and hatreds, you know what they are like, upon whom a man depends entirely at this time. Therefore, since you are prudent, you must look out for yourself and for us, plan for our common advantage.

I frown, wishing I were better able to concentrate on my work. I wonder what he means by 'those things that creep and slink about'? It sounds rather sinister.

Calmazzo

VITELLOZZO: I urge my horse down the hillside. All around me in the halflight are the dark rushing shapes of cavalry.

Hooves thunder the earth! Metal bangs on metal! I yell and my voice catches in my throat. The early-morning darkness and my visor and my watering eyes make it impossible to see anything clearly.

We enter their camp and I swing my sword at anything that moves. Their soldiers are dazed and half-dressed and half-awake. Some fight back but most just run. In confusion and darkness they crash into tents. They stumble through campfires and trip over each other's feet. Dogs howl and growl. Horses bolt and kick. Some men scream for mercy and some play dead: you see them prone and ride on, then look back and they're running the other way.

But there is nowhere for them to go – nowhere to hide. Our cavalry is like a whirlwind crushing and cutting and from three sides our infantry closes in at walking pace – ready to kill all who try to flee. The only escape route is behind the camp. But here there is a deep river and only a single narrow bridge over which the men can run. Some risk swimming the river but it is wide and the current strong and for every one who makes the opposite shore at least two are swept away to their deaths. Already there is a bottleneck at the bridge: thousands of men just queuing up to be slaughtered. The rising sun turns the grass from blue to green and the river from black to silver . . . but all is going red. Blood in the water and blood on the grass: a scarlet dew.

I leave the enemy footsoldiers to their fate and ride off in search of Michelotto. The officers' tents have been abandoned. I order them torched and look around. Where is that bloody Spaniard? And then I see him: down by the river but far from the bridge. On horseback he barks orders at a group of infantrymen who are crowded over something on the ground.

I yell at my men to follow me and charge the enemy guards. The clash of sword on shield. My arm is heavy now but still I feel no pain. 'Michelotto, you ugly bastard!' I shout. 'I'll teach you to be insolent to a nobleman! Show some guts – come and fight . . .'

I see his face through a gap in the circle that protects him. He stares at me and says something then turns his horse and . . . crosses the river. There was no bridge there before but now there is a bridge. How did they construct it so quickly? And with what? I stare as my prey rides over the water and away. How the hell did he . . .

My thoughts are interrupted by an axe blow to my shoulder. The force is enough to knock me off my horse. For a moment I lie flat on my back. I'm helpless as an overturned beetle and I'm thinking what a shit way to die but then my pages arrive and help me to my feet. My horse has fled so they usher me from the danger zone.

And now . . . now I feel it. Pain in my shoulder and pain in my arm. The pills are wearing off. I lift my visor and vomit on the bloody grass.

Imola   *18 October, 1502*

NICCOLÒ: I dress and shave in my room, then go downstairs and eat breakfast. I walk to the castle – it is a clear, cool, sunny morning – and talk to Agapito. I mutter in corners with other envoys, and talk French to one of the captains, with whom I have become friends. But there is no new gossip: only more details about the slaughter in Fossombrone, and further rumours that Paolo Orsini is in secret negotiations with Borgia. At midday I walk back down the main street and eat lasagne in The Bell. The pasta is as dry as sunbaked mud and the wine tastes like vinegar, as usual. When

I've finished, I go to my lodgings. I say hello to my land-lady, who is knitting by the fire, moaning about the French soldiers, and climb the stairs to my room. I open the door, and then I see it: on the floor. I bend down and pick it up. A sealed letter: expensive paper, perfumed. My name written in elegant script. My heart is hammering now. I open the letter and read the message:

> Will you see me again?
> Yes.
> Meet me in three days' time at dusk on the south-facing battlements of the castle.
> Stefania

I lower myself carefully to the bed and stare in wonder at the stains on the ceiling. I am so happy, I can hardly believe it. But three days! So much for my chances of getting a good night's sleep this week . . .

21

LEONARDO: It is evening when we return to the castle. I decline all offers of food and drink and go straight up to our suite in the palace. Tommaso, excited, greets me with the words, 'The automatic crossbow is ready, master. Will you come and see it?' Then he notices the look on my face and the bandage on my arm and asks if I am all right.

his mouth open eyes unseeing the red tip glistening and

'I am very tired,' I say. 'Don't worry about this, Tommaso, it's only a scratch. I will see the crossbow tomorrow, if you don't mind. Now I must sleep.'

In my room I undress and get in bed. I close the bed-curtains and I close my eyes, but I cannot shut out the images in my mind's eye. I am truly, desperately tired, yet sleep is impossible. I am condemned to lie in darkness and relive the horror, moment by moment.

the flames on the table and the head on the floor and the old woman sobbing and the little boy dead and the black smoke pouring from the window and the little girl waking up alone in the dark her mother and father gone for ever and

Eventually I fall asleep. But in my dreams I am at Calmazzo again, and to the horror and pity and guilt I felt before is added the urgency of fear. It is *me* they are hunting, *me* they are trying to kill. In my dream I wake up before dawn as usual, while all the others are still sleeping, and walk through the camp. I sketch the shape of the field, with the pine forest at one end and the hillside rising above, and the smouldering fires dotted over the bluish landscape . . . and then I see it.

the black wave coming down the hillside

And I dream I am a little boy in the fields near Vinci, running towards my mother's house. Thinking of her face – the kindness of her eyes, the warmth of her arms, the curve of her lips. But as I get closer to her house, I see black smoke pouring from its window and

I wake up. My breathing is ragged. My neck and chest are soaked in cold sweat. *Oh, Caterina – I swore I would bring you back to life, but . . .*

19 October, 1502

When I wake again my muscles and joints are stiff, perhaps from all those nights sleeping on straw, but inside I feel calmer. I open the bedcurtains and walk to the window. Outside it is still dark. This seems strange – have I really slept only a few hours? I creep to Tommaso's room, and to my surprise I find him awake, reading a book.

'Isn't it the middle of the night, Tommaso?'

'The middle of the night? No, the sun only set two hours ago.'

'What? Then I have hardly slept at all . . .'

He laughs. 'Master, you have slept all night and all day.'

I sit down, shocked by this thought. I have not slept so long since I was a child. 'All that time wasted,' I whisper to myself.

'Not wasted,' Tommaso says. 'It has done you good. The fever seems to have left you.'

'Yes,' I say. 'Although what I saw will never leave me.'

He asks me what I mean and I tell him of the outrages I witnessed in San Leo, in Fossombrone, in Calmazzo.

Terrible, how these innocent names of villages and towns, unknown to me until the past week, are now a shorthand for horror and infamy. I tell Tommaso that I wish him to stop work on the automatic crossbow – I say we must not create weapons whose only purpose is to destroy life.

he who does not value life does not deserve it

'But the model is finished, master, as I told you, and his lordship has seen it. He was . . .'

'The duke has seen it?'

'Yes – he is very pleased. He sent word, just now, that he would like to see you. He wants to thank you personally.'

The duke treats me like an invalid. 'My dear Leonardo,' he says, putting a hand on my shoulder and leading me towards the fire. 'Come, sit down with me. It is a cold night – would you like some hot wine?'

Before this, I had thought I was doing a good job of covering my emotions. But Valentino can see through masks, it seems. I drink the wine, which is sweet and heavily spiced, and listen as his lordship tells me how impressed he is by the model of the automatic crossbow. 'To enable one man to shoot four times as quickly as before – this is the future of warfare! You are a true visionary – bravissimo.'

the arrowhead spearing his Adam's apple

'I must also thank you for saving the life of Don Michelotto. He told me about the bridges you made, and how the bridge at Calmazzo was the only thing that prevented him and his men being slaughtered by Vitellozzo. Don Michelotto is the most trusted and important of all my generals, and the man who saves his life deserves the richest of rewards.'

The duke stands and walks to a dark corner of the room. When he returns, he is holding a beautiful sable fur cape.

186

'This was given to me by the King of France. I think the style will suit you. Please don't offend me by refusing my gift, Leonardo. Try it on – how is it for size? If it's too large, I will ask my tailor to fit it for you.'

I place the cape over my shoulders – it is warm and heavy and smells of musk.

The duke takes a step back and examines me. 'It suits you very well,' he says. 'Better than it does me, in fact.'

I thank his lordship for his generosity, but he waves me silent and bids me sit down on a bench before the fire. The flames give out a tremendous heat, so I remove the cape and fold it across my lap. The duke sits next to me and, in a gentle voice, says, 'I never intended you to experience the horrors of battle so closely, Leonardo. I understand that you must have been shocked by what you saw . . .'

'My lord, I knew perfectly well what warfare was – what it must be. It is only that I . . .'

'Hush.' He touches my bandaged forearm, like a mother quieting a sobbing child. 'You are a great artist and a great scientist – you are not a soldier. There is no shame in feeling fear or revulsion in such a situation. Perhaps later, you must experience this again – it might prove unavoidable – but for now I can find you some safer and more agreeable duties.'

I bow my head. 'I will do whatever you ask of me, my lord.'

'You told me once that you knew the art of mapmaking?' I nod. 'I require a detailed map of this town, with the towns surrounding it marked for their direction and distance. Would you be able to provide such a map in, let us say, two weeks?'

'I think so. I will do my best.'

'Good. You may work on the map in the daytime. I was also wondering whether you might not paint a portrait for me in the evenings?'

'Of yourself?'

'No. A friend of mine. Her name is Stefania. She has a room here in the palace.'

Internally I sigh – I am weary of the paintbrush. But to the duke I say, 'It would be an honour.'

He laughs. 'You don't have to do it if you don't want to! But meet the lady first, and then decide. I will have you taken to her room tomorrow evening. About seven?'

'Very well, your excellency.'

I finish the wine, which is tepid now, and stand up. The duke stands too. He gives me a silk purse of gold ducats, then arranges the cape around my shoulders and ties it close to my neck. He presses his hands down hard on my shoulders and kisses me on both cheeks. Even after he releases me I can still feel the pressure of those strong hands.

Walking back through the corridors of the palace, I am struck by the strange thought that the cape is not a gift, but a burden. The knot is uncomfortably close to my throat. Its scent is foreign and overpowering. Rather than me possessing the cape, I feel it is the cape that possesses me.

20 October, 1502

DOROTEA: I have dismissed the servants and now I flit around the room, tidying this and rearranging that. One moment I am looking in the mirror at my modest dress and shawl, the next I am poking the coals in the fire. Finally I hear the knock at the door and say 'Enter' in an unnaturally high voice.

I smile and curtsey – I am truly happy to see the great Leonardo da Vinci in my room – but his face looks more careworn than I remember it. Back in Mantua, and even

188

in Urbino, I had the impression that those green-grey eyes saw and knew and understood all; they were not weary, but serene. Today, however, the artist's face seems more deeply lined and his eyes flash an emotion that I cannot quite name. It's not desire – I've seen that in other eyes lately, and it is a much simpler expression – but some kind of troubled recognition. Does he remember me? If so, the memory is not an entirely happy one.

I begin to talk – to chatter, as Cesare would say – in order to disguise this awkwardness, and Leonardo too, after a few tense moments, recovers his habitual grace and calm. He moves my chair closer to the window and we discuss the weather, the kind of light that one sees at this hour, how I should sit, and so on. And yet, beneath this smooth civility, the early strangeness of our meeting does not really fade. It lingers in the room, like an unidentifiable scent.

I send for apples and wine, and Leonardo orders a lute-player. He arranges the Spanish veil that Cesare asked me to wear so that it covers my hair but not my face, and as the daylight fades he sits across the room and begins to sketch me, with chalk on paper, explaining how he will first pre-pare a full-size cartoon, which will be pricked onto canvas, and afterwards he will paint my portrait. 'There will be no need for your presence at that stage, my lady.'

I smile and ask questions, and for an hour or so we talk in this way, until gradually the silences grow longer, Leonardo becomes absorbed in his work, and my mind starts to drift. I think of my rendezvous tomorrow night with Niccolò. Cesare wants me to coax more detailed confessions from him, to name his enemies' names, but I am nervous at the thought of this. Or perhaps guilty is the right word. Still, it was my idea to become a spy, and I must prove myself adept at it if I am to have any future with the duke. The last time we slept together, I could tell it was my information that excited him more than my body.

Something snaps me out of my reverie – perhaps the silence? The lutist, I notice, has stopped playing, and I cannot even hear the soft scrape of chalk on paper. I look at Leonardo and see tears in his eyes, delicate streams running down his face. He is staring into midair, apparently transfixed.

I signal for the musician to leave and hear the door close behind him. Then, very slowly, I stand up and walk over to the weeping artist. He looks up at me wonderingly as I move close to him, and then seems to wake from his dream. He turns away from me and with a handkerchief wipes his eyes and cheeks. Staring at the floor, he apologises and begs me not to report this to the duke. 'Of course not,' I say. Instinctively I press Leonardo's face to my chest and stroke his long hair. I feel his body heave with sobs. Tears come to my own eyes as I watch my hands caress the beautiful brown and silver hair.

Slowly his body relaxes into mine. When he has calmed down, I ask him what the matter was.

LEONARDO: I leave her room feeling embarrassed, but also elated. It has been a long time since anyone held me like that. *Perhaps not since I was a boy, and my mother . . .* It has been a long time since I wept, as well. Both acts have done me some good, I feel, though how and why I cannot say.

I return to my room and sit at my desk, and idly I sketch geometric shapes on a fresh sheet of my notebook – dividing and subdividing the small charcoal squares, taking comfort in their regularity, their finite variation. But after an hour or so I feel suddenly weary. Candlelight blears and doubles. I look up at all my other notebooks, these records of past investigations, ideas, experiments, idle thoughts, arranged on the shelves of the bookcase – and their bare spines stare back at me, reproachfully, like the faces of abandoned children. I still haven't finished them. I still haven't put them in order. One day soon, I must get round to it. But not tonight . . .

I decide to go outside – to cool my fever, to set my thoughts free. So I put on my cloak and overshoes and walk out of the palace, through the gardens, up onto the battlements. It is dark, the moon waning, and an icy wind blows my hair. I can feel the chill traces of tears on my face. I walk all around the castle walls, the guards muttering salutations as I pass. In each direction I look out at the dimlit landscape – fields and distant hills to the south and east, the sleeping houses of Imola to the north and west.

Tomorrow morning I will begin to map this place. I am excited about this. While in Cesena this summer I developed a new technique, using my special eyeglass. I am sure that if I apply it to the whole town, I will be able to create something unique, something never seen before. It will be a modern map – drawn to scale, viewed from above. Not from one particular point, but from *every* point. The humble town of Imola as seen, before this, only by God.

I contemplate these ideas for a while, and then I feel the rustle of paper in the pocket of my cloak – the sketch of Donna Stefania! I retrieve it, and discover that the paper has been creased. Cursing my own carelessness, I smooth it out on the flat stone of the battlement. In the moonlight I study the image I have made of her. It is ghostly, almost not there. And yet it *is* her face that looks back at me. Nearly her face. The more closely I study it, the more I feel that the smile is wrong. I close my eyes and try to recall the shape made by her lips when I looked up at her after my weeping fit, after her embrace, and she . . .

calm warm gaze I miss you Mamma and I

But now I am confusing myself. What does this Stefania have to do with my late mother? Why do memories of poor dead Caterina, so vague and faraway that I cannot even trust their veracity, keep merging with the present reality of this young noblewoman?

I promised I would bring you back to life but

I sigh, and walk back to the palace. These thoughts are going nowhere – they spiral inwards like a vortex. So I cast them from my mind and think only of tomorrow morning. The clean, accurate lines of the map. The exact measurements.

21 October, 1502

NICCOLÒ: I uncrumple the note and read it again: . . . *at dusk on the south-facing battlements of the castle.* Well, here I am. And there, a red stain on the horizon to my right, is the setting sun. But where are you, Stefania?

The last three days have been the longest of my life. I thought I would never get through them. There hasn't even been any event of note to take my mind off her: aside from Michelotto's defeat in the skirmish at Calmazzo, and persistent but unconfirmed rumours that Paolo Orsini is in communication with Borgia, nothing seems to be happening at all. Just an eerie waiting. It seems like the duke was right about his foes: they are too afraid of him to strike.

Still, this delay – however tortuous – has at least given me time to order from Florence five ducats' worth of good wine and the velvet mantle which I wear now. It is sewn up in front, a style I am unsure about, and is slightly too large for me, because the tailor cut it to fit Biagio, but on the whole I am happy with it: it is more elegant than the coat I brought with me, and it will keep me warm now the nights are growing colder.

The sun has disappeared completely now. I walk up and down the battlements and rub my arms. I am on the point of giving up and going home when I see her walking towards me. Stefania. Something about her is different: she wears a red silk scarf around her neck and her hair has been cut or brushed in a new style, but I don't think it's either of these things. And then I realise what it is: she is not wearing a mask. She does not look as merry or sensuous as the other night, but in an odd way, with her face uncovered, she seems even more mysterious to me. My heart aches; my mouth is dry as dust. We embrace and I hold her gloved hands. I had a joke prepared for her arrival, but something in her look tells me this would not be appropriate, so I simply ask how she is.

'Fine,' she replies. 'And you, Niccolò?'

'The three days since I received your note seem to have lasted about three years. But apart from that . . . yes, I'm fine.'

I smile, and her lips mirror mine, albeit briefly.

'Well . . . shall we go somewhere warmer, Donna Stefania?'

'Yes. Do you have a room?'

'Of course.'

'Is it private?'

'Yes.'

'Good. Let's go.'

Her briskness takes me aback, but we walk together out of the castle and into town and I take pleasure in the looks we receive. Even dressed modestly as she is tonight, men's eyes follow her everywhere.

I feel a clench of shame as I open the door of my land-lady's small, ugly house and lead Stefania inside. She looks unfazed, however, and follows me upstairs without a word. Inside the room, she asks me to close the shutter and lock the door. I light a few candles and open one of the bottles of wine sent from Florence. I pour two cups, then kindle a fire in the hearth.

'Don't you have a servant?' she asks.

'At home, yes. But I'm afraid the Signoria is rather ungenerous with expenses for its envoys. They seem to think I should be able to survive on air.'

Stefania smiles but says nothing, and an awkward silence takes hold as I use the bellows to get the fire going. When this is done, I turn around and smile at her. She is sitting on the room's only chair, staring into the flames.

'Are you hungry?' I ask. 'I'm afraid I don't have much to eat. Just some salami and some dried figs . . .'

She shakes her head. 'I'm fine, thank you.' She looks like she is waiting. What else is there to do? I put a hand on her knee. She gently removes it and asks how my work is going. To cover my embarrassment, I tell her. I sit on the bed, stare at the floor, and the words come flooding out of my mouth. I fear if I stop speaking she will get up and leave. Or ask me what I thought I was doing with my hand on her knee. And so everything comes out; I am hardly even aware of what I am saying. I have a vague memory of drunkenly telling her, the night of the party, about Marietta and Primerana, about Salviati and my other enemies. She seemed to like my honesty more than my wit, so I blurted out everything.

It's the same now. She asks questions. She nods and smiles. She seems so interested – so pleased, at last, to be here – that I do not dare break the spell by changing the subject; I just keep answering, like a prisoner threatened with torture. After an hour or so, I open a second bottle of wine. We are both sitting on the bed now, and I am making her laugh. The time seems right to make another pass. I lean across and kiss her on the neck.

DOROTEA: I push him away and go to sit down on the chair. I thought he'd got the hint the first time, but . . . oh well, I can't blame Niccolò really. It must look like a seduction scene, with the shutters closed and the door locked. How is he to know that my ulterior motives are not the same as his ulterior motives?

He kneels on the floor at my feet. 'Donna Stefania, I'm so sorry. I know you are a lady of the purest virtue, and . . .' I try to interrupt, to stop him making a fool of himself, but he takes my hands in his, looks into my eyes and says, 'Please. Let me finish.' He clears his throat and stares tragically at our hands. 'I'm falling in love with you.'

The worst part is that I think he means it. Niccolò is a professional dissembler, but this, I feel sure, is not just a line. I wish it were. I wish he were still roguishly, playfully trying to get me into his bed. Listening to Niccolò speak without irony, without wit, is like seeing his face for the first time without a mask: odd, incongruous, faintly disappointing. Oh, why are men suckers for mysteriousness? How can such a brilliant judge of men be such a terrible judge of women?

Well, I have all the information I need from him now. I had hoped that we could be friends, but I like and respect Niccolò too much to lead him on any further. I don't want to hurt him, so I resolve to be clear. I must leave no room for doubt or ambiguity, however callous it may sound. 'Niccolò, I'm sorry. But I'm not in love with you. Not at all. You must not let yourself fall in love with me. It is hopeless.'

Silence. I risk a glance at his face. He looks like a man who has just lost everything. 'But you . . .' Still the awful hope in his voice.

I wasn't going to do this, but I know I must extinguish that last spark of hope. And perhaps I owe him some honesty at last. 'Niccolò, I came here on the duke's orders. He is my employer . . . and my lover. He asked me to discover certain information about you, and that's what I've done.'

He stares at me. 'Then you are not Stefania Tozzoni?'

'No. It was only a role I was playing.'

'So . . . who are you?'

A flash of fear: I shouldn't have confessed the truth.

'My identity is irrelevant.'

'*Irrelevant?*' The first flaring of anger in his voice.

'Niccolò . . . I am sorry,' I repeat. Then I get up to leave.

22

CESARE: A cup of wine – halfdrunk. A chicken – halfeaten. A candle – halfburnt.

Agapito brings news – Paolo Orsini is here. *Yes!* I knew he'd crack. I targeted Paolo at the start. The thread always breaks where it's weakest.

I call for wine and candied pears. I order more wood for the fire, I order the doors guarded.

Paolo slinks in – frightened, hopeful. He falls to his knees – kisses my feet. He swears he is sorry – that it wasn't his idea.

'I know, Paolo. I know it was Vitellozzo. I know it was Oliverotto. I know you urged caution – told them not to fuck with me. But they wouldn't listen, would they?'

He nods like a puppet. Repeats what I've said. He damns Vitellozzo. He damns Oliverotto. He begs my forgiveness.

I tell him: 'Sit down by the fire. Have some candy, have some wine.' Relief and triumph in his eyes. He thinks he is safe now.

We discuss a treaty – to make the peace. I tell him: 'If you can persuade the others to sign it, I will make you lord of Imola. I will raise you above the other captains.'

He asks for concessions – I give him concessions. He asks for security – I give him security. I tell Agapito to draw up the contract. Paolo drinks his wine. He sighs with satisfaction.

I invite him to play chess. I tell him I'm good. I let him beat me. Now he thinks himself a master of strategy.

Chess is for fools. I play chess for real. I play it with knights and castles – with bishops and pawns. Real ones – not wooden ones.

Paolo belches. He crosses his legs and licks his lips. He purrs and flirts and smirks.

I think about having him killed. Seeing the leather straps tighten round his throat. Seeing his eyes bulge out of their sockets – that smirk wiped off his face.

All I'd have to do is ring the bell or clap my hands . . .

But no – not now. First I must gather them all. First I must be patient.

Calm. Wait. Soon.

A cup of wine – empty. A chicken – bones and grease. A candle – smoke and waxmelt. Nearly dawn – I go to her room.

She's asleep. The candlelight wakes her up. She tries to kiss me – breath foul, skin warm. I tell her no – business first. What happened with the envoy?

She reaches across – hands me a sheet of paper. I read her words. Everything I wanted to know. The contents of Machiavelli's soul. The details of Machiavelli's life.

I say: 'Good.'

'You're welcome. Now can we make love?'

'How did you leave it?'

'With Niccolò?' Her voice gone strange. Something to hide. She's afraid – ashamed.

'Yes, with Niccolò. What's happened? What went wrong?'

'Nothing,' she lies.

I squeeze her throat – my thumb in her windpipe. She pushes and scratches. 'Life is short,' I whisper. 'I will make yours even shorter if you don't tell me what happened.'

I let her go. She coughs. 'I told him the truth.' Fear in her voice – shame in her voice.

'The truth?'

'That you sent me to spy on him. That I was your lover . . .'

'What! Why?'

Silence. I slap her face. 'WHY?'

'I got all the information you asked for. There was nothing else to learn.'

I put the candle near her eyes – stare into her soul. She squints, looks away. 'You felt sorry for him,' I say. 'You felt guilty.'

'Yes. Cesare, I like him. I didn't want to . . .'

'You're weak. I should have known. You're not cut out for this.'

I'll send her to Venice. No . . . wait. She knows too much. She can't leave here alive. Only one solution.

She sits up – she grips my arm. 'Cesare, I'm sorry. You're right – I was weak. But I'll grow stronger. I won't let you down again.'

'No,' I say. 'You won't.'

'Please,' she says. Panic in her voice. Can she read my thoughts? 'Please, Cesare.' Calmer now. 'Give me one more chance. I did get the information you wanted.'

That's true. She has talent. But can I trust her? Perhaps I can use her – in a different way. Now Machiavelli knows what she is, I can use her to squeeze him. I can use her to oil him.

'How does he feel about you now?'

'He's in love with me.'

'After what you told him? He's not a fool.'

'He's human.'

I laugh. 'Unlike me, you mean?'

'Yes. Unlike you.'

'I want you to see him again,' I say. 'Arrange a meeting.'

'But he knows that I'm . . .'

'You will be my mouthpiece. You will tempt him with great rewards. You will cow him with great punishments. You will do EXACTLY what I tell you. Understood?'

'Yes,' she says. 'I am at your command.' Her voice says – *Please don't kill me.*

I will put a tail on her. A spy to spy on my spy. An ear to the wall – an eye to the keyhole. I will not kill her. Not yet. Give her enough rope – see if she hangs herself.

She whispers my name. Breath foul, skin warm. 'Please can we . . .' I stroke her throat. I stroke her breasts. I stroke her cunt.

I flip her over – and fuck her in the arse. I fuck her till she screams. I fuck her till she bleeds.

Afterwards she weeps. I whisper in her ear: 'Don't fuck with me again. Or I will fuck you up.'

Città di Castello   *24 October, 1502*

VITELLOZZO: I knew that I would suffer for my exertions at Calmazzo, but I had no idea the suffering would be so great or last so long. It is ten days since our glorious victory, but still the fever rages as I lie here in bed and my dreams are all of slaughter and desolation. I see men rushing from behind closed curtains – their swords drawn. I see my children skinned and bloody – piled high like carcasses in a butcher's shop. I see my wife raped by Borgia. I feel Michelotto's ligature tighten round my neck.

I wake up screaming again, then slowly my breathing returns to normal. I open the bedcurtains: grey daylight through the windows. I am soaked with sweat but the pain has gone – for now. I tell the servants to send for my secretary.

'My lord,' he says, 'I am relieved to see you looking so much better. Do you feel well enough to receive visitors now?'

'Depends who it is.'

'Don Paolo Orsini arrived this morning. He wishes to speak with you urgently.'

My face creases with disgust. But he may bring important news. I say: 'Send him in.'

Donna Paolo enters and pretends to be concerned about my health. He looks sickeningly well himself. And smug. I wonder what tricks he's been up to? 'Get on with it,' I say. 'Why have you come?'

His hatred shows briefly in his eyes. Then he smiles. 'I have something to show you.' He takes some folded sheets from his pocket and hands them to me. I read the first few lines and realise what it is.

'You traitor!' I yell and make a lunge for him. But the slick little bastard dodges my grip and I begin coughing. Shards of broken glass in my chest. I groan.

'You should read the whole treaty,' the traitor lisps. 'He is offering me very generous terms. He may offer you something similar – if you make your peace now.'

'If you'd just show a bit of backbone we could still defeat him.'

'The Orsini have long held an alliance with the King of France,' Donna Paolo says pompously. 'As long as the duke has the support of Louis we cannot go against him.'

'Bullshit! That's not why. You're the duke's bumboy – that's the *real* reason! You bloody fancy him.'

His eyes narrow. His back stiffens. 'You are delirious. You are talking nonsense. I will leave you to read the treaty and to consider your position more carefully when you have regained your wits.'

'I'll talk to you when you've regained your *balls*! If you ever had any . . .'

He ignores this and moves to leave. 'Don't delay too long though, Vitellozzo. If you are the last one to make terms it's a fair bet you will be the first to pay the consequences.'

I scrunch the treaty into a ball and throw it at his departing shadow.

Imola   *27 October, 1502*

NICCOLÒ: I shit liquid fire as the cold wind howls below me. For the sixth morning in a row, I feel as though someone has been smashing my head against a rock all night. I wipe my arse and shut the privy lid, remembering the whore I went with last night (older than me, and uglier too) and wondering if she's given me the French disease. I get dressed and count the money in my purse. I feel sick. I count it again. *Oh God.* I do not even want to think about how much cash I've wasted in the last week on booze and prostitutes. And that special wine from Florence! And that velvet mantle! And all of it for nothing . . .

For a couple of days after my rejection, I was at least revitalised by the desire to find out the lady's true identity. I went everywhere, asked everyone. Then Agapito summoned me to his office and ordered me to end my investigation. 'The identity of your lady friend is a secret and will remain so,' he said. 'If you persist in causing trouble, you will soon feel the duke's wrath.' I left his office trembling like a naughty child, and wondering how everything had gone so wrong so quickly. Only a few days before, he had told me how pleased the duke was with me. Now, it seems, I am *persona non grata* in this court.

I am not angry with the duke: I should have expected no less from him. I am not even angry with *her* – not really.

It is with myself I am angry. How could I have been such a fool? I shiver with self-disgust and write another letter to the Signoria, analysing the situation here and begging them to send me home:

> I entreat your lordships again to accord me my recall
> ... My own affairs at home are falling into the greatest
> disorder, and moreover I cannot remain any longer
> without money, which it is necessary to spend here.

All of this is true – my position in the office is apparently under threat, Marietta is upset with me for being gone so long, and I am horribly poor – and yet I doubt I would feel so eager to return had Stefania (or whatever her real name is) given me a different answer the other night. I also doubt whether the gonfalonier will grant my request, but I have to try. At the very least, they might send me some ducats to keep my head above the water.

I go to the castle to find a messenger who can deliver my letter to Florence, and bump into one who's looking for me. He hands me a note from Francesco Soderini. It is mostly pleasant nonsense, as the bishop's letters tend to be, though he urges me to send friendly greetings on his behalf to the duke, as he's eager to be made a cardinal. He also suggests I should look up a Florentine artist while I'm in Imola: one Leonardo da Vinci, who is currently working as the duke's military engineer, but who has agreed to pass on information about his employer to the Signoria.

I learn where this Leonardo is living – he has a plush suite of rooms in the palace itself – and go there to see him. But he is out all day, according to his odd-looking assistant. I ask when he might be back and am told that such things cannot be guessed. I get the distinct impression that the assistant is trying to get rid of me, so I write a quick note to the artist, explaining who I am and where I am staying, and ask that the message be passed on. The assistant smiles at me as if I have the word 'PRICK' drawn on my forehead and says, yes, he will certainly pass my message on.

I go to the tavern to get drunk.

29 October, 1502

LEONARDO: I rise before the sun does, wash and rebandage my wounded arm, scent and dress myself, then go to Salai's room so I can wake him. He scowls at and curses me, as always (Salai does not like mornings), but there is nothing to be done about this. It is both agreeable and necessary for me to be in town before the crowds, and with Tommaso working on the model of the siege tower for the duke, Salai is the only assistant I have here. I could borrow one of the duke's servants, I suppose, but I prefer to work with someone I know – no matter how grumpy they are.

We breakfast in silence, then walk out of the castle, over the moat, and into town. Salai carries the hodometer and the ball of string, I hold the compass and the eyeglass. At the centre of the market square, I check the disc I have planted there. It has not been harmed. I tie the string to it and measure the morning's first path with the compass. We will do the eight lines between Scirrocho and Mezzodi today – that will complete the basic measurements for the whole wind-rose, and I can spend the next few days transcribing these, with the aid of the old map I found in the town library, into drawings, rather than a series of numbers. From mathematics to a single image – a miracle of a kind.

As usual at this time of day, I am filled with energy and optimism – pacing the blueshadowed streets, breathing the cold smoky air, knowing that I am awake and working while everyone around me sleeps. I unreel the string and walk the line dictated by the compass and the eyeglass. Salai follows me with the hodometer. He is meant to be counting the clicks himself, but I instinctively do this, knowing that his concentration tends to waver. As we go, I jot down details of street intersections and the lengths and widths of buildings. We reach the outer wall, then walk back to the disc in the market square.

By the time we've got there, the sun is up, the stall-holders are arriving, and I can hear cocks crowing, smell the sweet warmth of baking pastries. I buy one for Salai and we share some hot spiced wine. He shivers, so I lend him the cape that the duke gave me. My assistant manages his first smile of the day. While he eats the pastry, I sketch a couple of men arguing in a doorway – just stick figures, representing the movement of their hands, the postures of their bodies. I hear an old peasant woman say to her companion, 'He who possesses most must be most afraid of loss,' and note this down, next to a list of other wise-seeming sayings I have heard from the mouths of the people of Imola –

A small truth is better than a great lie.

He who takes the snake by the tail will presently be bitten by it.

To speak well of a base man is the same as speaking ill of a good man.

Perhaps it is only my imagination, but often these sayings seem to speak of Valentino, and of my relationship with him. Is he the snake whom I hold by its tail? Is he the base man?

We have finished the final eighth of the map by half past one so Salai and I go back to the palace, where Tommaso has prepared lunch. We eat together at the long table and

Tommaso describes the progress he has made on the siege tower. My face must reveal an emotion I was not aware of feeling, for Tommaso says, 'Siege towers don't actually kill anyone, Leonardo.'

I try not to think about what I saw in Calmazzo and the other places. Sometimes the images come back to me in dreams, but on the whole I am doing a good job of forgetting my horror. The pictures in my mind are only pictures, after all. Their reality is in the past now. The suffering is over, and so is the fear. Even the thin white scar on my forearm has almost vanished now.

In the afternoon I retire to my room to begin the drawing of the map. It is painstaking work, but satisfying, both in its precision and its miraculous beauty. *To see the town as only God can see it . . . to fly, if only in my imagination . . . to be omniscient.* I finish up at six and read some Archimedes. At seven, I go to Stefania's room.

I knock on the door and enter, and am rewarded with that smile. I have attempted to sketch it a dozen times already, but somehow its essence eludes me. I can reproduce the curve of the lips, the lines in the skin around the mouth caused by tensed muscles, the shadows and highlights cast by the evening light, but not the feeling that pervades it, emanates from it. Her smile comforts and haunts me – it reassures and tantalises. I could watch it all day.

'Will I see you tomorrow evening?' she asks as I pack away my chalks.

'Yes, my lady. The usual time?'

'Yes. And Leonardo, could you stay a little longer afterwards? I will arrange some food to be served. There's someone I'd like you to meet.'

'Of course,' I bow. 'May I ask who it is?'

'A countryman of yours. His name is Niccolò Machiavelli.'

23

Imola   30 *October, 1502*

NICCOLÒ: I walk down the main street as dusk falls. It is packed with promenading families, guards on horseback, scavenging dogs; a rich man's carriage ploughs through the middle of this crowd, the driver calling out for people to clear the way. Two young women giggle as I pass: one of them is quite cute, if rather young-looking, so I turn around to check out her figure from behind, and see her staring at me. She blushes and her friend howls. You see, Niccolò? You haven't lost it completely. When I turn back to face the way I walk, I notice I have stepped in a mound of fresh horseshit.

Yes, my pride is still wounded from the rejection. But perhaps tonight will be the occasion of its healing? The note from 'Stefania' was delivered this morning, though I'm still not sure what to make of it. A week ago I thought we would never see each other again, and now she is inviting me to dinner with Leonardo da Vinci: it's all very odd. Still, I do want to meet him, and I wasn't getting anywhere through the usual channels . . . And I'll get to see *her* again.

Not that I particularly want to. But I will if I must. I'll pretend that I feel nothing: that it was all a drunken jest. I no longer hold out any hope that she's secretly in love with me. I realised the absurdity of that last night, as I thought about her in bed with the duke. I mean, how could I ever compete with *him*? Rumour has it that he had his way with Caterina

Sforza too, before he took her prisoner: Jesus Christ, I envy him that! But let's face it, he's more god than man. And that's without even mentioning his vast wealth and power.

In fact, it occurred to me last night that I've been thinking about this whole thing in the wrong way. I need to be more objective about it, more detached. If I remove my own feelings from the equation, it is easy to see that love is essentially the same as war or politics: a conflict of power; a constant flux of alliances and concessions, conquests and surrenders. And, as with politics, one must always be pragmatic, realistic. That girl I passed on the street, for example, represents a feasible medium-term objective. The whore I took the other night was an easy, short-term satisfaction. My marriage to Marietta is a complicated, long-term negotiation. And 'Stefania'? Pfft . . . that would be like Florence planning an invasion of England.

As I cross the drawbridge into the castle and walk towards the door of the palace, I ask myself how I'm feeling.

Calm, myself replies. *Cool, detached, objective.*

Liar, I say.

Myself shrugs, and keeps walking.

DOROTEA: Niccolò smiles as he enters, then kisses me lightly on both cheeks and, looking casually out of the window, apologises for his behaviour the other night. 'Very ungallant of me – getting drunk and pretending I loved you, just to try and get you into bed.'

He looks at me hopefully, as if to see whether I will go along with this version of events. I smile: 'Don't worry, Niccolò: we all say things we don't mean when we've had too much wine. Let's just forget it, shall we? I think you'll enjoy meeting Leonardo. He's a great man, and he has the confidence of the duke. As do you, of course . . .'

He looks sceptical. 'Do I?'

'Naturally. His lordship was saying to me only last night
. . .' – Niccolò blushes; I go on, as if I hadn't noticed –
'. . . that he was glad it was you who'd been sent by the
Signoria.'

'I wrote to the Signoria two days ago, asking them to
recall me,' he says sullenly. 'The duke would make more
progress if they sent an ambassador instead.'

'Perhaps,' I say, 'but his lordship would take less pleasure
from the conversations. And the duke believes that, with
your influence over the gonfalonier and your . . . *persuasive-
ness* . . . you might well be able to convince the Signoria to
give you the power to negotiate an alliance yourself.'

Seeking to hide his pleasure at this compliment, Niccolò
changes the subject. 'People in Florence are worried about
the accord the duke has signed with the Orsini. Do you
know anything about that, my lady?' There is a slight con-
descension to his tone; clearly he is expecting a negative
answer.

'I have read the treaty myself,' I say.

'Really?' And his eyes light up like candles in a black
room. What a change comes over his face at the scent of
news! All the sadness and self-pity that have clouded his
expression this evening are suddenly gone, and the razor-
minded questioner returns. 'What were its terms?'

Reciting the precise phrase that Cesare made me learn,
I reply: 'The terms were so meaningless that a child would
laugh at them.'

'What are you implying? That the duke does not intend
to honour the treaty?'

'Do you really believe a man like the duke would make
peace with people who had betrayed him? Who would have
killed him given the chance?'

'No, I never believed it,' he says eagerly. 'Are you saying then that this whole peace negotiation is a ruse? If so, I will reassure my Signoria that they have nothing to fear from an alliance of the duke and his enemies. For, if they did unite again, Florence would surely be the most obvious target of their combined armies.'

I lean closer to him, without fear now of being misinterpreted. He has only one thing on his mind, and it is not my body. 'You did not hear this from me, Niccolò, but your city has no reason at all to fear such an alliance. His lordship is not interested in making friends with his enemies, but in wiping them from the face of the earth.' He nods. 'You may write that down if you like.'

'I don't think I'll need to, my lady. It's quite a memorable phrase.' That strange little smile of his slides across his face. Niccolò is himself again.

'But enough of politics,' I say. 'For tonight, at least. In a few moments you will meet one of your most esteemed countrymen.'

He bows. 'I have heard of your friend Leonardo, of course, although I must admit I have no great knowledge of art.'

'Leonardo is not only an artist – you will see.'

'Tell me: why did . . .'

But his question remains unasked: he is interrupted by a soft knock on the door.

LEONARDO: Niccolò Machiavelli – I have heard his name before. Not only in the message that Tommaso gave me the other day, but somewhere else, from someone else . . . I frown and puzzle over this for hours before it comes to me. Yes, I'm almost sure – his was one of the names on Vitellozzo's list of the soon-to-be-dead.

He looks well considering. An interesting face – foxlike, boyish. Thin rounded nose, thin mouth, small ears and eyes, but the latter flash with a rare intelligence, and that mouth, when it smiles, is curious too. Ambiguous, complicit . . . a very Florentine smile. The envoy's odour and clothing are not to my taste, but on the whole, and to my surprise, my first impression of Niccolò Machiavelli is a good one. I suppose I was expecting another pompous politician in the mould of Francesco Soderini. I offer my hand, and he clasps it in both of his – 'It is a great honour to meet you, maestro.'

I tell him that my great-grandfather was an envoy for Florence.

'Really? I don't think any of my family have ever been artists. Or military engineers, for that matter. Mostly it's just an unrelenting line of notaries and lawyers.'

'Yes, my father's family is the same,' I say. 'Why didn't you follow your father in the notarial business, if you don't mind me asking?'

you have no business sense, you have no common sense

'He went bankrupt when he was younger, so our name is on the blacklist.' A defiant smile at the misfortune of this stigma. 'I was lucky to get this job.'

'Lucky?'

He concedes the point. 'I made the right connections. You know how it is in Florence.'

'Yes – I was never very good at that. I'm sorry to hear about your father's bankruptcy.' Niccolò shrugs, as if it's nothing, but I feel bound to make my own confession in exchange. 'I was never in line to take over my father's notarial office because my mother was not his wife.' I watch the envoy's face as I say this, but see no distaste or disapproval – evidently he is not a snob. 'So we are both, in a sense, outcasts.'

I utter this last line lightly, mockingly – Niccolò understands my meaning.

'Yes, if only I could stop running through these corridors of power and settle down in a quiet dusty office somewhere. And you, I suppose, would much rather sign forms all day than be the most celebrated artist in Italy. How much happier we both might have been, were it not for the intervention of cruel Fortune . . .'

He laughs, I smile, and Stefania places a hand on each of our arms. She says she is glad that we have so much in common, as now she does not feel guilty about leaving us for a few moments while she goes to supervise the preparation of dinner.

As soon as she is gone, the atmosphere in the room seems to change. It grows cooler, the room smaller. Niccolò looks at me with different eyes. Or perhaps he simply removes the mask he was wearing?

'So,' he asks, as though this were the question to which all other questions have been secretly leading, 'What do you think of your new employer?'

I say nothing for a moment. Then, in a voice loud enough to be overheard from the other side of the door – 'I fear there has been a misunderstanding, Niccolò. Your colleague Francesco Soderini approached me in Urbino and asked if I would provide information on the duke to the Signoria. He seemed to believe that I had assented to this, but . . .'

'He was mistaken?'

'Yes. I am not a spy, Niccolò. Nor do I wish to become one.'

He nods. 'I see.'

'I am sorry if this upsets your plans,' I say, voice lower.

'Not at all – I quite understand. People like Francesco take others' views for granted sometimes. They imagine that everyone sees the world the same way they see it.' He takes a swig of wine and leans back in his chair. 'And actually, it gives me the evening off work. Now that I know there is no information to be gleaned, I can simply relax – and enjoy your company.'

After that, we fall to talking about places in Florence, and of certain people. We talk of the Medici, and from there the conversation turns to Lorenzo the Magnificent and his patronage of art, his poetry. Niccolò, it turns out, was a poet in his youth. Inevitably, we begin to debate the rival virtues of poetry and painting.

the poet can write an exact description of skies, rivers, faces – but the painter can so depict them that they will appear alive

Stefania returns and seems amused to find us engaged in a theoretical discussion. It is a dispute I have had many times during my life. In my younger days I would grow angry and inarticulate, but I know all of the opposing arguments by heart now, and am able to put them out, one by one, like a servant extinguishing candle flames.

now tell me which is nearer to the actual man – the name or the image? the name of man differs in other countries, but his form is changed only by death

'My advice,' I conclude, 'is not to trouble yourself with words unless you are speaking to the blind.'

Niccolò, like most advocates of the written word, begins to bluster in the face of this logic and, intuiting perhaps that my command of Latin is rudimentary, he uses examples from Plato, Cicero and others to support his ideas.

'Anyone who brings the ancient authors into a discussion is using not his intelligence,' I say, 'but merely his memory. He who can drink from the fountain does not go to the well.'

213

To my surprise, Niccolò laughs. 'Actually, I agree with you there. Any fool can quote the ancients and make themselves look learned. Doesn't mean they have any idea what they're talking about.'

'Ah, I am glad you have a found a point you can agree on at last,' Stefania says, 'because it is now time for us to eat. And it is unwise to argue too violently while swallowing food. One might easily choke on one's words.'

DOROTEA: I lead them to the table and we sit: Leonardo to my right and Niccolò to my left. It is a pleasure to see them together like this, and to be the cause of their meeting. Just in case you're wondering, the duke did not order this; my motives in arranging it were entirely innocent and personal. My life here is an uncomfortable mixture of boredom and fear, and the company of Niccolò and Leonardo is a welcome distraction from both.

Throughout dinner, I struggle to get a word in: a fact which amuses rather than irritates me. Listening to these two Florentines is a masterclass in the art of argument. They are always right, even when they are wrong. Niccolò argues like a man hammering nails, one by one, into the lid of a coffin, inside which you are entombed alive. Leonardo speaks like an expert swordsman, slicing you up in beautiful shapes, and so quickly that you feel nothing and hardly even see the blade flash.

We eat, and I listen to them talk of science and mathematics, of nature and religion, before Niccolò starts telling jokes against priests. I look up at Leonardo while this happens, wondering if he might be offended, but he laughs in a way I have never seen him laugh before – like a young boy, forgetful of all but the joke being told.

Niccolò too seems happily forgetful. He barely even looks at me – not because he is avoiding my eye, but because he is so interested in Leonardo that my presence becomes ghostly to him; peripheral. Only when the conversation touches on the duke does he remember me and look narrowly in my direction, weighing his words with the thought that they will be reported afterwards to Cesare. I want to tell him he may speak freely; that the duke is no longer interested in what he thinks or says, but only in what he does; but I know Niccolò would not believe me even if I did say this. So I keep quiet until the meal is over, then embrace them and watch as they walk down the corridor together, still intently talking; free now to say whatever it is they truly wish to say.

NICCOLÒ: As we walk towards his suite of rooms, Leonardo whispers to me: 'There's something I wanted to warn you about. When I was with Vitellozzo Vitelli in Arezzo, he showed me a list . . .'

'My name was on it.'

'Yes. You knew already?'

'The duke told me. Until recently, I was quite concerned about it. Now Vitellozzo is his lordship's enemy, however, I feel suddenly much safer.' As long, I think, as the duke is not also *my* enemy.

'Yes – he's a strange man, Vitellozzo. I met him in the summer and he struck me as slightly . . . unhinged.'

'The duke will unhinge him,' I say, 'with a battering ram.' I laugh, pleased with this metaphor. Then I hear footsteps behind me. I stop and turn, peer into the darkness: in the corridor in which we walk, only one torch hangs from the wall, so both ends – before us and behind us – are submerged in dense shadow.

'What is it?' Leonardo asks.

I shrug. 'Probably nothing.' And follow him to the door of his suite. His two assistants are in the large common room, playing cards at a table. They look up as we enter, but say nothing, and Leonardo ushers me into his studio. He lights candles as I examine it. It is surprisingly small: no bigger than my own cramped lodgings. There are a couple of paintings on the wall, a neat stack of papers on the desk, a brazier filled with bright orange coals, and a small window overlooking the palace garden; but the room's most interesting feature is the wall opposite this, where a wooden case is filled with a multitude of books. 'Quite a library,' I say.

Leonardo nods. 'I have been collecting for many years. Feel free to look through them.'

I pick up one of the candles and scan the titles. I see several which I have read – Livy, Lucretius, Pliny the Elder – and many more I wish to read. Among these is Plutarch's *Lives*, which I have read before, of course, but which I have been longing to consult again ever since arriving in Imola. I flick through Leonardo's copy, and a phrase flashes up at me from the page: *His many successes, so far from encouraging him to rest and enjoy the fruits of his labours, only served to kindle in him fresh confidence for the future* . . . Now who does that remind me of?

'Would you like to borrow it?' Leonardo asks.

'I would like that very much,' I reply. 'I have ordered it through friends in Florence, but apparently there are no copies to be found in the whole city.'

'Please take it. You may return it to me when you have finished. Your desire to read it seems quite urgent, Niccolò.'

'Yes . . . I keep seeing parallels between the duke's methods and those of Alexander, Julius Caesar and others. I am haunted by the feeling that all the events and conflicts through which we are living now have already occurred, somewhere in the past, and that if we could only learn the lessons of the past, we might better understand the present . . . and light our way, dimly, into the future. That sounds extravagant, I suppose?'

'Not at all.' Leonardo looks at me intently, as though there is something on my face (or in my eyes) that he has only just noticed. Slightly embarrassed by the intensity of his gaze, I move towards the desk and glance idly at the papers there, covered in sketches and a peculiar hand-writing. Then I look more closely, struck suddenly by the realisation that I can't read a word of what is written. I squint, lean closer. 'Is this some sort of code?' I ask.

'The simplest kind of code.' Leonardo picks up a small, flat mirror and places it at the side of one of these pages. 'Look into the glass.'

I do, and see a line of perfectly legible Italian. 'What . . . ?'

'Mirror-writing, Niccolò.'

'But how? Why?'

He shrugs. 'I am left-handed. It comes naturally to me.'

Shaking my head in wonder, I walk to the wall: near the door is a map that resembles maps I have seen of Tuscany, but there is something different about this particular map. Something odd. I put my finger to a mass of orange sur-rounded by pale green. 'This is Florence, isn't it?'

Guardedly, Leonardo agrees that it is.

'But I don't understand. The Arno doesn't flow that way.'

On the map before my eyes, the river leaves our city and flows directly to the sea; in reality, as we know to our cost over many years, it flows through Pisa, which thus controls all sea trade.

'Not yet, no,' he says.

'Not *yet*?'

'This is a projection, Niccolò: a plan for diverting the river so that Florence would have a port and Pisa would be cut off. It would be a way of finally winning the war against the Pisans – without any loss of life.'

'What a magnificent idea! But surely it's not possible?'

'Oh, it's possible. It would be expensive, of course, but no more so than the current war – and it would pay for itself within a few years due to the vast increase in trade.'

I look at Leonardo again. What a strange and mysterious man this is! I have never met anyone like him.

'Leonardo, may I mention this to the gonfalonier?'

'Yes. But do so discreetly, Niccolo. I am not sure how pleased the duke would be if he discovered I was working for Florence.'

I remember, now, the blunder I made earlier – expecting him to work as a government informer – and cringe at my own crassness. I begin to apologise, but Leonardo waves away my words. 'You are forgiven,' he says lightly. 'But let me ask you what you asked me then, Niccolò: what do *you* think of my new employer?'

'I presume your reluctance to work as a spy extends to both sides?'

'You have my word on it. If I am honest, I have very little interest in politics – it seems to me like the clash of large beasts: one watches it primarily to avoid getting crushed beneath their hooves. However, I can tell you are a true authority on the subject, so I would value your opinion as to the qualities and prospects of the man I serve.'

So I tell him: of the duke's power base (French and papal support), of his cunning and ruthlessness, his boldness and self-belief, and of the astounding good fortune he enjoys, which is a result, I say, of his impetuous nature. 'Fortune is a woman. If you wish to master her, you must beat her. She is more easily conquered by the rash and the violent than by those who act more slowly and coldly.'

'I feel sorry for your wife, Niccolò.'

'I speak metaphorically.'

'I understand. But can the duke rely on Fortune continuing to favour him? After all, to extend your metaphor, women are notoriously capricious.'

'The duke's great weakness is the age of his father,' I say. 'Pope Alexander is apparently in rude health, but all the same he is more than seventy years old. Were he to die soon, the duke would need to influence the papal election. If he could arrange it so that the next pope is one of his own men, or at least someone he can bribe to do his will, then . . .' – Leonardo raises his eyebrows – '. . . then I think there is no limit to what he might achieve. He is an extraordinary man.'

He nods, as though I have said what he was thinking. 'Something drives him. Something I have seen in few other men. The duke seems to me like the fuse of a cannon, smouldering towards some great explosion.'

'Yes,' I say. 'That's exactly it. Do you know what he said to me the other day? He was talking about his enemies – Vitellozzo and the other rebels – and he said: "The ground is burning under their feet and they do not have enough water to put it out."' I laugh. 'I liked that. But you are right, Leonardo. He acts rather as if the ground were burning under *his* feet.'

There is silence in the corners of the room. The coals in the brazier glow red; they crackle and darken. Leonardo says: 'The ground is burning under *all* our feet. I can feel it, Niccolò. Can't you?'

24

LEONARDO: For the past two weeks, ever since that first conversation with Niccolò, I have been in a terror of dying – of dying without having left something of myself on earth. Something that will endure. Something great, something imperishable . . . but *what?* I am fifty years old and still I have not found what I am looking for.

that my course should not be sped in vain

Niccolò came to see me again a few days later and I showed him my notebooks – told him all they contained. If only I could organise and edit them, I would be able to publish books on anatomy, architecture, astronomy, geology, music, painting, shadows, water, zoology, each going further into these disciplines than any of the ancients ever went. 'Then you must,' he said. 'What if there were a fire in the castle? All of this would be ashes.' I felt the cold fingers of panic as he spoke – tightening around my heart.

to leave some memory of myself in the minds of mortals

I wake up before dark every morning and measure the land beyond the city walls. Salai follows me – muttering, cursing, the hodometer clicking over rocks and through mudflats – as we traverse army camps, climb hills, cross rivers. It rains and we get soaked. Beggars follow us. Salai complains, but I tell him to be quiet. I am ruthless now in the pursuit of my objectives. I've been too lax in the past. Time is running out, the end of my life approaching – I must not waste an instant.

for what is sleep? sleep is the cousin of death

After lunch I draw the map. I use watercolours to make it clearer and more beautiful – red for the houses, green for the fields, blue for the moat and the river. I complete the map because I must. Because the duke needs it. But what will become of it in time? Ashes. Dust.

why then do you not create works that after your death will make you seem alive?

I work with Tommaso on designs for new weapons – he regards me ironically as I talk of the need to fire arrows more quickly, or to destroy the enemy with a single blow. He thinks I have forgotten the horror I felt after Fossombrone and Calmazzo – and perhaps he is right . . . I look at my forearm, where the drunken soldier's swordblade opened my flesh, and there is not even the ghost of a scar there now – the skin has healed perfectly, the tiny mouth vanished. If my body can reconstitute itself so miraculously, then why not my mind?

for those who sleep through life are like the sad dead

In the evenings I draw Donna Stefania – I am happy with her hands, her hair, her eyes . . . but still the smile eludes me. Am I wasting my hours puzzling over this? Sometimes I think so, but other times I feel it is at the heart of all I strive for. That if only I could understand the mystery of that smile – discover the mathematical formula for it, the scientific forces behind it – all else might somehow fit into place, the overarching truth be revealed.

time devours all with the relentless teeth of years

And now, after dinner, in the darkness of my room, sitting at this desk by the light of a single candle, I go through my notebooks, copying out passages on different sheets, trying to separate the intertwining strands of my thought.

Yet what catch my eyes, what lodge in my mind, are not my calculations and conclusions, but these fragments of old frustrations – these reminders to myself to work, not to sleep, to seek fame, immortality, to create that Something which will endure a thousand years.

the ground burning beneath my feet

But it is too much. The task is beyond me. I find myself befuddled by the labyrinthine paths of my own thought. I become lost in a maze, of which no map is possible, in which I can discern no path that will lead me where I wish to go, no pattern which will spell out the answer I seek.

I stare at the flame of the candle and consider its beauty. I blink my eyes and look at it again. What I see now was not there before, and what was there before is not there now. *Who is it who rekindles this flame which is always dying?*

I write this down. For this is what I seek, isn't it? Not only immortal fame, not just glory for myself . . . but *to uncloud the light beyond.* To uncover the face of God. To look Him in the eyes, if only for a single moment.

I attempt to sketch the candle flame, all the while knowing that it is impossible – that it will never once be still, but will keep being made and remade until the wax has all melted and the flame sputters and turns to sweet smoke, ultimate darkness.

And then, as I hear the rain shushing outside, weariness overcomes me. I fall asleep at my desk, my head on a pillow of papers.

CESARE: I pace the floor of my small dark room. Listening to the rain, falling all night. I pace and I brood. I read and I brood.

I read a spy's report. Hours of conversation – dozens of pages. I flick through. Then that phrase snares my gaze, and I read more slowly.

THE GROUND IS BURNING.

I said it about my enemies. But Machiavelli is right – it is true for me too. I brood over time running out. I brood over my weakness.

How did Vitellozzo know where to find my army? How was he able to surprise them? The evidence all points one way – a traitor in our midst. But WHO?

I read more reports. I analyse past conversations. I suspect everyone – eliminate them one by one. I must find the traitor. Sniff out the rat. I brood on this for hours.

My father always says – you brood too much. Ever since I was young – these dark moods, these hours of circling thoughts.

But what if he dies? What would happen if the pope died NOW? Everything collapses . . . the world goes black? No. I must be ready.

I have the Spanish cardinals – eleven men in my pocket. I have Cardinal Amboise – an ally, but ambitious.

And then there's our old enemy – Cardinal Della Rovere. A dangerous man. A serpent to be crushed.

I have an emergency plan. The day the pope dies, I seal off Rome. I have Della Rovere killed. I bribe Amboise – not to be pope.

And then . . . the new pope in my pocket. A puppet pope – my hand up his arse.

But how do I seal off Rome? If my troops are there, it's easy. But what if I'm here? What if I'm fighting?

I need troops in Rome – men I can trust. I need the Orsini. That's why Paolo is still breathing – why I signed his stupid treaty.

There is another solution. If I could take Florence, I wouldn't need the pope. If Tuscany AND Romagna were mine, I'd be a power on my own. As great as Venice. Greater.

But Florence is protected by France – always the same problem. If I invade, Louis crushes me.

I must make Florence mine – not by force, but by cleverness. A binding treaty. The thin end of the wedge.

So I squeeze her envoy. I oil her envoy. I use my secret weapon – the spy he loves. She whispers threats in one ear, promises in the other.

I read Machiavelli's letters – he's on my side. He fears me, admires me. He tells the Signoria – you should sign an alliance. He says – the duke's a dangerous enemy. He'd be a powerful friend.

Machiavelli recommends. Machiavelli advises. Machiavelli persuades. But is it enough?

My spies in Florence say that Machiavelli is the gonfalonier's pet. Soderini would give him more power – if he dared. But Machiavelli has enemies. Soderini has enemies. They must tread carefully.

I sit and I brood – in my small dark room. Staring at the human chessboard.

Thinking – what if?

Thinking – but how?

Thinking – and then . . .

Calculating odds. Adding up costs. And all the time . . . the ground burning under my feet.

I am twenty-seven now. Only five years left.

I clench my fists. I grind my teeth.

The rain falls hard – I hear it all night. The rain pours down. But it can't put out THESE flames.

LEONARDO: Asleep, I dream of flying. In the dream I stand on the roof of the Palazzo Vecchio in Milan, looking out over red rooftops and grey city walls, to the forests glinting golden in the dawn light and the distant bluish mountains, and where once I let go of paper birds and watched them soar and dive through the air, now I myself am the bird. Or rather, I am a man, inside a winged machine like those I sketched years ago, and it is I who jump from the palace rooftop, who soar and dive and fly . . . The world beneath me recedes until it is nothing more than colours and shapes – like a vast painting, a breathing map.

In the distance, I see a castle. An army is besieging it – vainly bombarding its walls with cannonballs, vainly shooting arrows of fire at its battlements. Vainly – because the castle is so designed that it deflects everything. It is the castle I sketched in Piombino – the perfect, rounded castle of the future.

And then . . . I fly high over the battlements. The soldiers turn their faces up to watch me. Their mouths are open in wonder. Like a giant hawk, I swoop down on them. Exploding cannonballs fall from my wings. Flames engulf the trees in the orchard. Blood flows like a river through the gutters. The soldiers' mouths widen in horror – they scream silently, as only the dead can.

In the dream, I am happy. I am triumphant, ecstatic. Death is all around me – and immortal glory is mine.

I stare up at the sky – to look God in the eyes. And see my own face looking back.

25

DOROTEA: I stand in front of the window, watching the rain turn the garden dark and sad, and remind myself who I am going to be for the next hour. I am playing so many parts these days that it is easy to get mixed up.

I am meeting Niccolò, so that means I am 'Stefania Tozzoni' – not the naïve, sincere Stefania Tozzoni I was when he first met me, but 'Stefania Tozzoni' the mysterious whore and spy. I brief the Florentine envoy on the duke's secret wishes, and drop hints that if he succeeds in his task, he will gain entry not only to the duke's powerful inner circle but to a paradise of flesh beyond his dreams.

With the duke, I am Dorotea Caracciolo, but I am not myself. I fake my desire, and conceal my fear and revulsion. This is new. For a long time, I admit, I was thrilled by Cesare's presence in my bed. I found the danger of sleeping with a monster exciting – and besides, I did not truly believe that he *was* a monster; I thought the monster was a mask he wore to scare people. Then came that night, two weeks ago, when he took off his Charming Cesare mask and I saw that underneath was the *real* monster. It was not only the pain and humiliation of what he did to me that night: it was the knowledge, the total destruction of all doubt to the contrary, that – if he ever deemed it convenient – he would have me killed without a second's thought. It crossed his mind that night: I saw it in his eyes.

My sole objective now is to kiss the duke goodbye without kissing goodbye to life. And so my mask must never slip; my voice must never waver.

With Leonardo, I am Stefania Tozzoni, yet I am also myself. But even this is not as simple as it sounds. When so much of your time is spent pretending, it isn't easy to stop. It is like breathing or walking when you are thinking about breathing or walking: what was natural becomes awkward and laborious. I also have to be circumspect in what I say and how loudly I say it: the monster has spies everywhere.

Still, the hours that I spend with Leonardo are the only ones to which I look forward with pleasure. With Niccolò, what I feel is power – and guilt. With the duke, it's powerlessness – and fear. But with Leonardo, I feel . . . wonder and comfort . . . sweetness and awe . . . divinity and humility . . . sadness and euphoria. I feel (why be afraid of the word?) *love.*

I have never met anyone remotely like him before. Indeed, I do not believe that anyone like him has ever lived. He is charming and handsome, but that is not what makes me feel as I do: it is only the silk wrapping on a gift of inestimable value. How to articulate this? The more time I spend with Leonardo, the more I listen to him speak, the more it seems to me that his words, his facial expressions, the lovely elegant gestures he makes with his hands, are no more than odd waves, mere splashes of foam on the surface of a vast ocean – an ocean of thought and feeling that extends deep deep down into dark, unplumbed, never-seen beauty and strangeness. Yes, I realise how fanciful this sounds, but I am more convinced with each day that passes that I will never *know* Leonardo, the way I know Cesare or Niccolò. And yet, oh! how I yearn to explore those quiet depths . . .

Of course, there is no shortage of rational objections and dissenting arguments to my daydreams of Leonardo. I essay them myself all the time. He is older than my father. He prefers boys to girls. He probably regards me as nothing more than another tyrant's mistress whom he's been commanded to paint. And Leonardo wears a mask, like everyone else. A well-mannered, inscrutable mask. But I have seen him without it, for that one strange moment. I have held him in my arms while he wept, like a little boy, and confessed to me his most secret fears and wishes. And that moment, though never mentioned, is with us always in the room, a tender ghost.

But ... oh, I hear the bells ringing! Is it five o'clock already? Niccolò will be here any minute! I must get into character. I am 'Stefania Tozzoni' and tonight is when I tighten the screw. The monster made that clear to me last night, with his hand around my throat. It is time to get results, he said. If not . . . I dread to think.

NICCOLÒ: I meet with 'my friend' (as I always refer to her in reports to the Signoria) in her room in the palace. This is a regular occurrence now. She closes the shutters, lights candles, locks the door, and we sit side by side on her couch in the dimness. The air is thick, as always, with the sweet, rich scent she wears. I turn towards her and she turns towards me. Eye contact is maintained throughout, so I cannot look down at her thighs, but I can hear her skirt rustle and hiss as she crosses and recrosses them. And I can feel the silk brushing the cotton of my hose and – occasionally, never for more than a second or two – the pressure of her flesh against mine.

Yes – the pressure.

I know what she's up to, of course. Caterina Sforza used similar tactics: the oblique promise of sexual surrender if only I succeed in persuading the Signoria to meet her demands. This is politics. This is power. It has nothing to do with love.

And yet a little voice inside me argues the contrary. *Will you really let your heart rule your head, Niccolò?* it demands. *Will you let the welfare of the Florentine state be determined by the adolescent yearnings of its envoy?*

Not at all, I tell myself. In fact, there is no need for all this heavy flirting. Because, as it happens, I think the duke is right. It *is* in Florence's interests to make an alliance with him.

Yes, myself agrees: *let the duke be paid for 'protecting' Florence. Give him control of the troops that guard her walls. And when the time is right, have the useless gonfalonier killed and rig the election so that you are voted his successor. And there you have it: Niccolò Machiavelli, Gonfalonier for Life; trusted adviser to the great Cesare Borgia, future King of Italy.*

That never even crossed my mind! I love my country more than I love my soul. I would never betray its interests . . .

But that wouldn't betray them, would it? You'd be a good gonfalonier: firm, decisive, judicious. What does it matter if you're not from a noble family? The ideal republic is a meritocracy, and you – as the gonfalonier himself has said before – are the most able man in Florence.

Perhaps, but the ideal republic is not controlled by a foreign tyrant.

The duke is Italian, Niccolò. And besides, when republics are in danger, they must have recourse to a dictatorship – otherwise they will always be ruined when misfortune befalls them.

That is true.

And, as you well know, the manner in which men live is so different from the way they ought to live, that he who unerringly follows the path of goodness will find that it leads him to disaster rather than safety.

Yes, that is also true, but . . .

But what?

Will the Signoria agree to the duke's proposals? God knows they are suspicious of his motives after what happened last summer.

'You must *persuade* them to agree, Niccolò. You must turn the screw. You must increase the pressure.' Her thigh against mine. The warmth of blood, the rustle of silk. 'If you succeed, his lordship will be so grateful that the rewards will be beyond your imagining.'

I'm not so sure about that, 'Stefania'. I have a pretty strong imagination.

'And *I* will be eternally grateful too.' Her naked hand touches mine. Her lashes lowered, lips parted. 'Convince them, Niccolò. Use your pen like a sword. I know you can do it. I believe in you.' ,

17 November, 1502

Late morning, four days later. The letter from the gonfalonier is delivered into my hands. I pay the messenger and walk to a deserted corner of the castle courtyard to read it. The sky is blue; the sun shines down; the air smells of horse manure and burning leaves. In the centre of the courtyard, a pig is being slaughtered, and a crowd is gathered round to watch it die.

I open the seal and unfold the letter. It shakes slightly in my hands. It begins 'My very dear Niccolò' and then waffles pointlessly for half a page. I skim through this, until I get to the good bit:

After long and vigorous consultation within the Signoria, it has been decided to accede to your suggestion. Niccolò, I am sending you the official stamp which will allow you to negotiate and ratify a treaty with his excellency the duke. It is a great responsibility, and you are still a young man, as has been pointed out to me by certain of my opponents, but I have faith in you and I am sure you will not let us down. The fate of Florence is now in your hands . . .

My heart races as I read and reread these lines. What I have wished for so long is finally mine: *power*. I fold the letter and put it back in my pocket. The crowd in the courtyard roars and the pig squeals in terror and pain, then is silent. When the clamour has died down, I can hear the gurgling of blood into a tin bucket.

Power!

I laugh, and look up at the sky. Fortune smiles down at me; she beckons me towards fame and glory.

I walk to my lady friend's room to give her the good news.

26

DOROTEA: My heart sails as I climb the stairs of the palace. In many ways I hate Imola: this castle and this palace have become receptacles of fear for me ever since I found out the truth about Cesare; but Leonardo's presence – the promise of it and the memory of it – give even such grim places a kind of secondhand glory, like the grace that appears on the faces of ordinary people in those still, silver seconds when the rain stops falling and the sun comes out.

I go to my room and prepare for his visit. I have sent the maids and servants away for the night, so I perfume and dress myself; I arrange the fire and stare out of the window at the bittersweet beauty of the sky darkening over the castle walls. The trees in the garden look melancholy now, their branches almost leafless, but I smile as I gaze at them. Before, autumn was always a sad season for me; the beginning of the end. Now, it will forever be the season in which I first found love; the beginning of true life.

I hardly recognise myself these days. Or rather, I hardly recognise the woman I was before. I think of the way 'I' used to feel and to see the world, and it is as though I am looking through a thick mist or cloud of smoke which shrouds everything in its deathly greyness. Only now am I alive; only now do I see. Oh, I am *consumed* by life! Leonardo told me one of his riddles the other day. How did it go? 'One shall be born from small beginnings which will rapidly become vast. It will respect no created thing, but will, by its power, transform almost everything from its own nature into another.' I guessed that he was talking about falling in love. He said the correct answer was fire, but that my response was more beautiful. He looked away from me as he said this – to hide his feelings? I do not know, but the hope has been kindled in my heart that he feels for me as I do for him.

The shadows in my room lengthen slowly as I wait for him. Finally he arrives and he sketches me on paper while I chatter away, as meaninglessly and joyfully as a bird singing to greet the dawn. For those brief hours, everything is as it always is between us, and – I tell myself – as it always will be. And then, as he puts on his cape and moves towards the door, he tells me that my presence is no longer required in order for him to finish the picture.

'What do you mean?' I ask.

'As I told you before, my lady, I have everything I need now. The colours are all in my memory, and . . .'

'I won't see you again?'

I cannot believe it: just as I have finally fulfilled my odious duty and persuaded Niccolò to do the duke's will; just as the duke's threatening grip has been released from my throat and I am able to breathe freely again . . . just as all this happens, the one *good* thing in my life is to be taken away from me! It is too much to bear.

A look of concern passes over Leonardo's face, and suddenly I am no longer in control of my actions or emotions. I begin to sob and I cannot stop. Leonardo leads me gently to the couch – the same couch where I so coldly and politically flirted with Niccolò – and holds me as I soak his fur cape in tears.

The cape smells of Cesare's musk, and that, in the end, is what brings an end to my crying fit. I imagine a spy listening behind the door and my breathing grows faster, shallower. Leonardo's body is tense, but his eyes are patient. 'What is the matter, my lady? Please tell me. You listened to me, once, as I unburdened my soul. The least I can do is to return the favour.'

I look into those calm grey eyes of his – their wisdom and strength. I put my lips close to his ear and whisper: 'I will tell you, Leonardo. But not here. The walls have ears. Could we go for a walk, or . . . ?'

'Come to my room,' he murmurs. 'The door adjoins not the corridor, but our common room, and I can ask Tommaso to play music so that our words cannot possibly be overheard.'

I nod, and follow him through the corridor. Tommaso, his wild-looking assistant, regards me curiously as Leonardo whispers into his ear. But when the explanation is over, he nods and picks up a lute. Then he starts to play and to sing as we enter the small bedroom. Leonardo locks the door behind us.

'I am afraid there is not much space,' he says, sitting on the only chair and signalling that I should sit on the bed. But I take his hand and pull him next to me as the tears come to my eyes again. I rest my head sideways on his chest and hold him tightly, and I feel his hand stroke my hair. 'Stefania . . .' he sighs.

'My name is not Stefania. That is the first thing I must tell you.' And, my throat welling, my voice breaking, I narrate the short and sordid story of my life: my years as a Handmaiden of Venus in Mantua; my betrothal to a man I didn't know; my abduction by Spanish soldiers; and how I became a whore and a spy for a man who, until yesterday, was thinking of having me put to death.

LEONARDO: I am sorry for her, of course. She is a sweet girl – and I have not forgotten her kindness to me, before. But it is an uncomfortable situation, all the same. I can hear Salai's voice now, outside the door, interrupting Tommaso's tired-sounding music. I cannot make out the words of their conversation, but it is easy enough to imagine –

S: Where is the master?

T: In his bedroom.

S: Oh, I'll go and see him then.

T: You can't. The door's locked.

S: Why, is he asleep?

T: No. He's . . . with a woman.

S (laughing): A woman! The master?

But it is not only their reaction which bothers me. I also have to consider the duke. He is a dangerous, unpredictable man. Will he become suspicious of me when he is told I took his mistress/spy to my bedroom? Would he be more angry at the idea that I was talking privately with her, or the idea that I was making love to her?

fear and desire

I have been close to so few women in my life that I do not even know if my reaction is just a physical reflex, like that which jerks your knee if someone taps a hammer against it, or whether it means something. Because the nerves sometimes act of themselves without the soul's command, as when sick people shiver, or when the tail of a lizard, cut from its body, continues to flicker. Either way, if this lady, holding me tightly around the torso, moves her arm any lower, she will come into contact with something that may give her the wrong idea altogether.

I am just about to make my excuses when she kisses me – her lips to my lips. They are soft, they smell like strawberries. She opens them slightly and I feel her tongue in my mouth. Soft, sweet. She is not so different to Salai when he was younger. I have not lain with him since the summer, in Cesena. I close my eyes and imagine him there beside me. She kisses me harder and then she says my name and I open my eyes – *her* eyes look like they wish to swallow me whole.

'I love you so much, Leonardo.'

The sincerity tightening, nooselike.

Her hand on my erection.

I swallow, and glance down at the strange curves of her body, the lines graceful, the skin flawless, the flesh warm, and beneath this the tendons and bones and pulsing organs, the labyrinth of veins and arteries and, further down, the vagina in hiding, like a hungry mouth like a dark cave *compared to the size of the womb, woman has larger genital organs than any other species of animal* and I hear Salai's laughter through the locked door, feel the chill draught of air from the unshuttered window, and I detumesce.

Politely, apologetically, I disentangle myself. I whisper to her that I was forgetting myself, that this is perhaps not a good idea, that we will be the cause of vicious gossip – perhaps life-threatening gossip – and that in any case I have much work to do, and . . .

To my astonishment, she smiles – sweetly, humbly, mysteriously.

'I understand,' she says. 'I will leave you now. But . . . could I see you tomorrow? Leonardo, I don't want you to disappear from my life. Not so suddenly.'

'Of course,' I say, without really thinking. 'But I am working outside the town walls tomorrow – mapping the land, you know.'

'I could help you.' She blushes. 'If you wanted me to.'

I consider this. It is not a good idea. It would slow down my progress, distract me from my objective. But the hope in her face is so delicate – I do not wish to be the cause of its breaking. So I say, 'Yes, if you like. But I leave early in the morning. Before dawn.'

'Come to my room,' she says. 'I'll be waiting.'

18 November, 1502

DOROTEA: We walk through the dark grey mizzle of dawn, our breath steaming. Both of us wear overcoats, boots, fur hats and scarves. The town is deserted, the air nearly silent. *Click click click*: Leonardo pushes some special wooden measuring machine (he did tell me its name, but I forgot) along the ground as we walk, and every so often he stops to write something down in a small blue notebook.

We pass the guards at the gate – Leonardo shows his passport and they bow respectfully – and walk through the slum town of ramshackle daub houses that has been built up against the town walls. The air smells of sweat and excrement, and involuntarily I pull a face when I breathe in this stench. Leonardo takes a handkerchief from a pocket in his coat and passes it to me. It is embroidered silk, the colour of ivory.

'Hold it to your nose,' he whispers. 'It's been soaked in lavender water.'

As he speaks, a small boy runs up to us and silently holds out his hand.

'Are you hungry?' Leonardo asks. The boy nods. Like a conjurer, Leonardo takes an apple from the same pocket and passes it to the boy, who bites into it greedily and then follows us like a stray dog, eating it as he walks.

Away from the town wall, the houses are replaced by cloth tents. The path that winds between them is muddy, with channels and puddles of strange-coloured liquid.

I hold the handkerchief more tightly to my nostrils. The walls of the tents shiver in the wind.

'The people inside must be so cold,' I say.

Leonardo nods. Then he turns round to face the boy, who has already devoured the apple. He kneels down so their faces are at the same level. 'Do you live in a tent like this?' he asks gently.

The boy nods.

Leonardo takes the long woollen scarf from around his neck and winds it around the boy's. 'That will keep you warm at night,' he says.

Still the boy does not speak or smile. He only stares; first at the scarf, then at the man who has given it to him. Then, as if it is the only gesture he knows, he holds out his hand again.

Leonardo laughs: 'I will make you smile, child, if it's the last thing I do.' He stands up and tears a sheet of paper from the notebook that hangs from his belt and begins to fold it in an elaborate pattern. The boy watches, expressionless. After a few seconds, Leonardo holds up the sheet of paper, which is now shaped like a bird, and throws it over the boy's head. Astonishingly, the paper bird flies in a swift graceful arc before suddenly lifting its beak and diving down into the mud.

At this point a miracle occurs. The lips of the tiny, solemn child lengthen in a smile of slow delight, revealing a mouthful of yellow teeth – and then they open wide as hoarse, shaking laughter pours from his throat. Leonardo smiles and bows farewell as the boy runs across to pick up the strange new toy.

We exit the slum town and walk out into the countryside. I want to touch Leonardo's hand, to tell him how kind and gentle he is, but I know he would only be embarrassed. He would make a good father though: that much is certain.

Through clouds of smoke, I see little red lights in the distance. I point, and ask what they are. 'That is the army camp,' Leonardo replies. 'It grows bigger every day. Strange, isn't it? All the talk is of peace, yet the duke continues to make preparations for war.'

We draw closer and I survey the camp: it stretches out, seemingly, for miles. A cloud of smoke hangs above the soldiers' tents and their voices come to us as no more than a vast murmur, like a hive of bees.

By the time we have left the camp behind, the sky is light; or as light as it will get on this bleak wintry day. 'You would think we were at the ends of the earth,' Leonardo says, looking around. 'Dorotea . . . do you ever think about the future?'

My heart betrays me by swelling when he asks this. Is he talking about *us*? My mind compounds the betrayal by imagining, as fast as a leaping flame, Leonardo and me married, living in the same house, having children, being happy, growing old together, dying in a tender embrace. 'Of course,' I say. 'I often think of what will be when we . . .'

'I mean a future beyond our brief lives. The future of the world – a hundred, five hundred years from now. Do you ever think of that?'

Blood rises to my cheeks. How foolish I was to think that he meant . . .

'I think of it often,' he continues. 'Of how the world may be. For the last thousand years or more, progress has been slow – when Rome fell, we went backwards, into darkness, and only now are we emerging once more into the light. The light of knowledge, I mean. But from this point on, I think the pace of progress will increase. When my friend Luca talks to me of mathematics, I can see it – all these possibilities . . .'

He is staring at the horizon, or perhaps beyond it. And then his expression darkens. 'When I was a young man, I used to wish that I could live long enough to see this glorious future. I imagined a world like the ideal cities drawn by philosophers and artists. A place where everything worked perfectly, where human beings lived in harmony. Where science had defeated disease. Where people could travel great distances, more quickly than we can even imagine today . . . where people could *fly*, like that paper bird . . . as high as the moon, perhaps. Wouldn't that be wonderful? To stand on the moon and see the earth below you – to see the waters on its surface, and to be illuminated by it the way our earth is illuminated by the moon at night?'

I touch his hand. 'Yes,' I say. 'That would be wonderful.'

LEONARDO: But, I say, that is not how I see the future any more. She asks me why. What do I mean?

exploding cannonballs fall from my wings

'I am an old man, Dorotea. I have lived fifty years on this earth, and only now have I come to realise the terrible truth about the future. You see, all of the ideas I've had to make the world a better place . . . they would have worked.'

'I'm sure they would, Leonardo. I mean, they will.'

flames engulf the trees in the orchard

'No, you don't understand. For ideas to become reality, one must have power. But when I showed my ideas to powerful men, to dukes and kings and generals, they weren't interested. What interested them were my *other* inventions, my *other* visions of the future. What they wanted – what they *all* want – is new ways to kill, to conquer, enslave, exploit. This world will not be perfected in the future, Dorotea – it will be slowly destroyed. Not by the wrath of God, but the folly of mankind. With our strong hands and brilliant minds, we will devastate vast forests. With our monstrous weapons and ingenious tools, we will stab not only one another but the flesh of Mother Earth herself. The blood of her waters will pour from these wounds, and one day nothing will remain on the earth or under the earth or in the water which will not be crushed, gutted, utterly sucked dry.'

I fall silent, my prophecy ended. Dorotea looks at me as if I, rather than humankind, am the one suffering from this death-seeking madness. I smile to reassure her that I have not lost my mind.

'Dorotea, if I make a flying machine, the duke will use it to drop cannonballs on people. Does that mean I shouldn't make a flying machine?'

'I . . . I don't know.'

'No – neither do I.'

We walk along the path for some time, in silence except for the clicking of the hodometer, and then some peasants pass us, coming from some nearby olive groves. We hear them before we see them. Their laughing voices come to us on the breeze. Three young men – not much more than boys. They are carrying heavy sacks, clowning around. When they see us, they go silent, and nod respectfully. Then, as soon as we are behind them, laughter breaks out again. Dorotea smiles, and I remember the old man, several years ago in Milan, whose body I dissected. I talked to him before he died – he was more than a hundred years old, and had not a single ailment of which he could complain. He told me of his farm, just outside the city, and the wife whom he met as a young man and who bore him ten children before she died. He was an ordinary man – a happy man. A man without ambitions, without desire for fame, a man whose life was quickly forgotten, whose name was never known outside his own village . . . but did *he* care? Would those peasant boys care? I think of the farmlands and vineyards of Vinci, of my uncle Francesco, of a life that might easily have been mine . . .

'Why do we chase the phantasm of immortal glory,' I ask, 'when happiness is here, all around us, in the fields and the river and the smoke-scented air?'

Dorotea looks at me shrewdly. 'Good question, Leonardo. What's the answer?'

tell me tell me tell me why why why

I shake my head. 'I don't know. Perhaps it is nothing more than curiosity.'

We keep walking – *click click click*. A flight of swallows swoops screaming across the sky, heading south for the winter. I watch them somersault and soar, then fade to invisibility, wishing I could do the same. The landscape around us is dark bluish, the leaves all falling or fallen. These are the death throes of autumn.

We come to the river and I stare into its turbid rushing bends for some time, watching the movement of the water, thinking of the apocalyptic future and the unhappy present. Then I turn to Dorotea, to ask her to count the hodometer's clicks for me, and see that smile shining back *calm warm gaze I miss you no one ever loved me like* and it is like a reminder, human or divine, that all will be well again, that spring will conquer winter . . . that, in spite of all this chaos, this darkness, this destruction, this fear, there is goodness in the world, and love – an absolute, invincible, unconditional love, like that which a mother feels for her child.

that will look whitest which is against the darkest background

We take all the necessary measurements and then walk back towards the town gates. In the army camp, the soldiers are standing in line, being inspected by Spanish officers. They look so young, so ordinary – no different from those peasant boys except that they carry swords instead of sacks of olives and wear uniforms instead of rags – and I ask myself if I really saw what I thought I saw at Fossombrone, at Calmazzo. Would young men such as these really kill and burn and rape? And if so, why? Simply because they are ordered to? But then I turn the question on myself – why am I, who so fear and detest violence, designing machines that will help these men kill other men more easily? Why? I do not even have the excuse of being compelled to do it. I could argue, I suppose, that my weapons on their own cannot kill anyone, but it is a sophism, fit only for one of my riddles –

> *One who by himself is mild enough and void of all offence will become terrible and fierce by being in bad company, and will most cruelly take the lives of many men . . . Of what do I speak?*
>   *Of swords and spears.*

I think of Niccolò. He enjoyed my riddles, but he would see through the false logic of that one straight away. I have a sudden urge to speak with him – he is always so clear, and so sure about everything.

NICCOLÒ: For the second night running, I cannot sleep. I am a bag of nerves. All my life, I have wished for, dreamed of, crawled towards *power*. But now that it is here, in my hands, I am paralysed; afraid to wield it. Warm saliva fills my mouth as I stare at the fearsome object on my dressing table: the official stamp of the Florentine Republic.

I feel like an inexperienced surgeon, holding a scalpel above the scarless white flesh of a patient whom he believes to be in need of surgery. Certainly, I know that, if the operation can be performed as it ought to be, the wound I am about to inflict will heal, and the body strapped to the table below me will be restored to perfect health; indeed, in future years, the patient will heartily thank me for my intervention, knowing full well that I have cut out the tumour that might otherwise have killed him. And yet, at this very moment, all I can think of is the pain my poor patient must suffer; the skin sliced open, the blood pouring out; and the possibility, however remote, that I will fumble the scalpel and accidentally sever a vein or a nerve essential to the vitality of the body politic.

All night, I argue with myself.

Myself assures me that my fears are baseless. He chides me for my cowardice, my indecisiveness. He whispers seductive promises of power; of a glorious future in which Niccolò Machiavelli is the most venerated man in Florence; of ages to come when my name will be mentioned in history books, statues erected in my honour . . .

I cover my eyes with my hands and try to ignore these gross and selfish temptations. I just wish there were someone I could talk to about this. I wish my father were alive, or that Agostino were here. Oh, there must be someone in this town with whom I can talk! Someone whose mind is not under the sway of the duke's. Someone who can look at the situation objectively. But who?

27

Imola   *19 November, 1502*

CESARE: A touch on my shoulder. I open my eyes – see daylight through the shutters. Agapito leaning above me. 'What is it?' I demand. Agapito wouldn't wake me before sunset for nothing.

'A disturbance in the square, my lord. Three French soldiers were seen urinating on a shrine to the local saint. Word spread. Now the townspeople want their blood. But the French captain won't surrender his men to the mob. He's threatening to open fire on them.'

As he speaks, I jump out of bed. My servants dress me. My pages arm me. My bodyguard surrounds us – me, Agapito, Michelotto. We march downstairs, we march outside.

Coldgrey and windmist. I mount my horse and ride through town. The streets deserted. Hear the buzz and yelling ahead.

We reach the town square – two armies stare and scream at one another. Five hundred French aiming arquebuses and crossbows, holding swords and shields. A thousand townsmen wielding axes, stones, knives. Spitting hatred. Ten yards between them. The gap closing.

Memories stir. This is where I made that speech to the mutinous Swiss. Where I made the people of Imola love and trust me. I look up at the balconies and windows, filled with faces. I must not lose them now. But I can't lose my army either.

I tell the bodyguards – stand back. I ride into the gap, alone. The screaming fades. Faces raised in hope. Both sides thinking – our saviour is come.

But the hum of tension remains. The threat of violence. If I say the wrong word, there'll be carnage. I'll be crushed in the collision.

My horse can feel it – she edges backwards, nervous. I dismount. Stroke her mane. Tell her to be calm.

I summon the French general. I summon the mayor of Imola. Each gives me their side of the story. They curse one another. Spit and grapple. The buzz of anger in the crowds. I shout: 'Enough!'

Silence.

I summon the three French soldiers. The townspeople bay for their blood. They walk to me proud and fearful. They tell me they were drunk – they didn't know it was a shrine. 'Those fucking superstitious country folk,' they murmur. I tell them to shut up.

I summon the man who saw them piss on the shrine. A pious fucking busybody. He thinks he's won a prize. Some of the people cheer him – many don't. He's not the kind of man people love.

I turn to the people. Shout: 'Listen to me!'

Silence.

I say: 'No one will be killed.' Murmur of dissent. I raise my hands. 'But the guilty will be punished.'

Silence.

'These three men desecrated your shrine. But they did so not with their hearts or minds or mouths. They did so with their cocks.'

Laughter. The busybody grins. The soldiers tremble. They can guess what's coming.

'If your cock causes you to sin, cut it off and throw it away. For it is better that you lose your cock than that your whole body be thrown into Hell.'

Roaring. Laughter. The French general hisses: 'No! If you do this, you will lose my men. They will mutiny.'

I tell him to shut the fuck up. To the crowd I shout: 'Listen to me! You might all have been killed today. Your wives might have been raped, your children murdered. But not only because of these soldiers' cocks. Because of THIS man's eyes.'

I point to the busybody. His grin fades. Can he guess what's coming?

The French general looks at me. The French general nods. He understands. A compromise – three cocks for two eyes. We must all make sacrifices for the public good.

NICCOLÒ: I watch in disbelief as the three French soldiers are stripped naked and held still by their own comrades. The French general himself performs the amputations. The soldiers' screams are drowned out by the acclamations of the mob. It's a horrific spectacle, but you have to hand it to the duke: he controls the emotions of the people like a master lutist bringing forth sweet music from some strings and wood. What happened today might easily have led to disaster, but he's turned it to his own advantage.

What I don't understand is how he convinced the soldiers to accept their punishment. Normally this sort of thing would lead to mutiny. I push my way closer to the front of the crowd, and then there is a surge behind me and I am carried, as on the crest of a wave in the sea, to the first row. And now, suddenly, I do understand.

I am only about ten yards from the duke himself, held back by one of his bodyguards. Behind me, the roar of vengeance dies down and is replaced by an eerie silence. There are mutters, whispers, murmurs, but the duke's voice rings out above them and for the first time I hear his words clearly: 'If your eyes cause you to sin, pluck them out and throw them away.'

Oh my God – he is going to punish the man who witnessed the desecration! It is cruel, horrific, unjust, and yet it is, I see at once, a masterstroke. The man, shaking and feebly screaming, is held from behind by the giant figure of Don Michelotto, and the duke signals that the mayor should perform the deed. The mayor turns bonewhite; he shakes his head helplessly. The duke smiles; he stands in front of the condemned man and announces: 'If your mayor will not take responsibility, I will do it myself. And, people of Imola, think before you howl. Let this be a warning to all of you. Soldiers, you must show respect to the citizens of this town, or you will suffer the consequences. But citizens, *you* must not seek out trouble; sometimes it is better to turn a blind eye.'

There is frantic muttering all around me, and then silence as the crowd swells two or three feet forward again, and the bodyguards strain to keep us at bay. I am so close to the duke when the moment comes that I could have a conversation with him without even raising my voice. I watch, heart pounding, as he puts his gloved hands either side of the man's face and squeezes. He looks as though he's going to give him a big wet smacker on the lips.

CESARE: I hold his face still – crush his cheekbones between my palms. Veins pop blue in his neck. I stare in his eyes – fear and disbelief, my own reflection looming.

Slowly, firmly, my thumbs dig in. The eyeballs like marbles. The man shakes, the man screams, the man vomits.

I push harder. Gouge and squelch. My thumbs deep in warmth. And then . . . the eyeballs pop like corks! Blood and jelly explode!

The man collapses. Michelotto holds him upright. His sockets black and empty now, blood all over his face. The ghost of a scream pouring from his mouth.

His eyeballs stare up at me from the cobbles. Outraged, reproachful. I laugh and crush them under my boots.

The sound of a thousand people biting their tongues. Swallowing their own vomit. Men gasping, women wailing. A boy laughing.

The stink of puke. The stench of piss.

I peel off my soiled gloves. Throw them into the crowd. The busybody is led away, sobbing crimson tears.

I look at the faces of the people. No love in their eyes now. But trust, respect, fear. They know not to fuck with me. They know not to fuck with the Borgia.

Fear spreads – like blood, like fire. Like falling in love. Transforming everything from its own nature into another.

I signal that the show is over. The crowd melts away. The French retreat.

I turn to Agapito – yawn and grin, stretch my arms. 'Well, that went well. I think I'll go back to bed now.'

NICCOLÒ: Half an hour later, walking back to my lodgings and agonising once more about my dilemma, I pass Leonardo in the street. I ask if he saw the show.

'Show?'

I describe the events in the market square, expecting him to recoil with horror, but he only blinks and nods. 'It is shocking. And yet I am not surprised.'

'Leonardo,' I say. 'Could I see you tonight? I wish to ask your advice about something.'

He smiles. 'I was about to ask you the very same question, Niccolò. Come to my room at eight. I will tell Tommaso to prepare some food for us.'

At the appointed hour, I knock at his door and Leonardo invites me into his study. There we drink wine and warm our hands by the brazier. It's only then that I notice the unusual agitation on my friend's face: beneath his smiling, wise-eyed mask, he seems almost as nervous as me.

'So, Niccolò, have you been reading the Plutarch since I last saw you?'

'Every day,' I say. 'Well, except for the last two days. Just recently, my mind has been . . . otherwise occupied.'

'And what conclusions have you reached – from your readings?'

'Conclusions?' I force myself to think about Plutarch's accounts of the lives of Pyrrhus and Marius, of Lysander and Sulla, of Alexander and Caesar. 'This, I suppose: that in times and places of great virtue, the most virtuous man will be the greatest; but in times and places of great evil, the virtuous man will be easily destroyed; and to be great, one must sometimes commit evils.'

Leonardo stares at the floor as he slowly nods. 'And the times we live in now?'

'Are evil, without a doubt.'

'You are saying, then, that virtue is useless in an age such as ours?'

'I am saying, Leonardo, that attempting to achieve virtuous ends through virtuous means is practically impossible now. Take what happened in the square today. The duke committed two atrocities: we are agreed on that. But if he hadn't done so – if he'd taken Christ's advice, for example, and turned the other cheek – what do you think the consequences would have been? The mob would have murdered those three French soldiers – they'd have torn them limb from limb. And then the rest of the French would have opened fire on the people. Hundreds of innocent civilians would have been killed. You may call Borgia's solution brutal if you like, but it's a lot less brutal than the alternative – which is what Christ's charity would have got you. In evil times, you see, the path of goodness often leads us to the house of evil. Yet we may sometimes reach the house of goodness by taking the path of evil. And you must surely agree that our destination is more important than the journey we take to reach it? The ends, therefore, justify the means.'

The words sound so inevitable, carved in stone, once I have spoken them. Leonardo looks at me as though he is looking into a mirror and is disturbed by the reflection that he sees within. I, on the other hand, feel strangely calmed by this discussion. Suddenly my path seems clear. The ends justify the means: I must risk the liberty of Florence today to ensure her strength and security tomorrow.

Leonardo puts his face in his hands, and groans. 'Oh *philosophy* . . . If only the world of mankind were as clear and shadowless as the world of numbers! In mathematics one does not argue if two times three makes more or less than six, or that the angles of a triangle are less than the sum of two right angles: all argument is reduced to eternal silence, and those who are devoted to mathematics can enjoy them with a peace which the lying sciences of the mind can never attain.'

Mathematics, I think: perhaps here is an answer? To examine men's minds and morals with the cold, analytical objectivity of a mathematician . . . to reduce our emotions and decisions not to ethics but to percentages, probabilities. Remove shame. Remove nobility. Remove all the lies and hypocrisies, and what is left? *The ends justify the means.* Yes, there is something here . . . I must think more on it.

But Leonardo has refilled our goblets now and recovered his habitual calm, so we sit and talk for a while of greatness and fame. We talk of Archimedes; of Aristotle and Alexander; of how, if a man, in the early days of Rome, had known how to build a cannon, he might have won everlasting glory. 'Think', Leonardo says, 'how quickly the Romans would have conquered every country and vanquished every army, had they possessed such a weapon! What reward could have been great enough for such a service? How famous would the inventor be now?'

'True,' I say, 'although if you really want immortal glory, the surest way is to found a religion – to be a prophet or a saint. You might not be rich or famous in your lifetime; you might even be executed as a criminal . . .' – I flash on the memory of Savonarola's hand rising, in the hot air – '. . . but after you're dead, the world is yours. I mean, Christ lived one and a half thousand years ago, yet we still talk about him constantly; his image is everywhere; his words are repeated and debated. Will even the *names* of anyone alive today be remembered a thousand years from now? Even five hundred years?'

LEONARDO: His question echoes within me. *To leave some memory of myself in the minds of mortals* . . . I think of Christ's words – 'I shall always be among you' – and wish I could say the same. Then I speak: 'But neither of us, I think, will found a religion, Niccolò. What other means would you say are open to us if we wish our names and feats to be remembered?'

He smiles. 'You are asking the right man. I wrote a dissertation on this very subject when I was twenty-one.'

I nod, and lean forward. 'So?'

'Well, the second best way is to found a republic or a kingdom. I suppose the duke has some hope of being remembered a thousand years from now. If he were to create a Borgia empire that united Italy and perhaps later conquered other parts of Europe . . . he could be another Romulus, another Alexander. Third in the list . . .' – he counts on his fingers – '. . . would be army commanders who have added to the extent of their country's dominions – a Caesar, for example, or . . .'

Impatiently, I interrupt him. 'Is there no room on this list of yours for men of learning: inventors, philosophers, artists?'

'Actually, I was about to say that men of letters of many different kinds – poets, philosophers, and so on – are of equal rank to the great generals. And, below them, I would place men who excel in some art . . .'

Excel in some art! I try not to let Niccolò see the anger that flares inside me, but evidently my mask is not in place, for he raises his hands in self-defence.

'I am not talking about my own views, Leonardo, but of the world's habits of attributing fame. Personally, I would say that Dante is worthier of a splendid grave than all twelve apostles put together.'

There is a silence, during which I sip my wine and stare at the coals in the brazier, thinking of the everlasting darkness into which that poor man was plunged today at Borgia's hands.

like one buried alive who can still move about and breathe in his grave

253

When I speak again, my emotions are under control, my voice calm. 'You are perfectly right, Niccolò: it is with the world, not with you, that I have my quarrel.'

He grins with relief. 'Of course, we shouldn't forget that, in the *Divine Comedy*, the lost souls in Hell beg Dante to keep alive for them their fame on earth, while those in Purgatory only entreat his prayers for their deliverance. Perhaps our desire for immortal glory is a sin, Leonardo?'

He says this jokingly, but I think of my dream from the other night, of the dark future I glimpsed this morning on my walk with Dorotea, and a heavy sigh escapes my lips.

'Certainly, it can lead us into sin. I don't know, Niccolò . . . I suppose you are right about the ends justifying the means. But what if . . . what if the ends are *always* evil? Wouldn't it be better, in that case, to use virtuous means?'

Puzzlement on his face. 'Always evil?'

'Yes. I mean, what if all the different paths open to us lead, ultimately, to the same bad place? What if the future is not an infinite array of glorious possibilities, but a single, inevitable darkness?'

Niccolò frowns. 'In that case, it makes no difference which path we take. But why . . .'

'It makes no difference?'

'Well, no. If you're saying they all lead to the same place . . .'

'But surely, in that case, the only difference we can *ever* make is by choosing the right path – the path of virtue?'

He looks at me suspiciously. 'Are you *sure* you're not thinking of founding your own religion?'

I laugh – it feels good, to laugh.

I was going to ask Niccolò the question I asked earlier of Dorotea, but I see now what his answer would be. And that the answer I seek cannot be found in the mouth of any other person. It is something I must seek in my own heart.

I stand up, straighten my mask. In a light voice I say, 'Yes, I'm sorry Niccolò. I am just in a strange mood, I think. Perhaps we should have dinner now, and open another bottle of wine?'

'Now *that*', he says happily, 'sounds like the path to take.'

DOROTEA: I listen at the door of my room until I hear their voices – Leonardo's warm and low, Niccolò's slightly drunken and high-spirited – and then Niccolò's footsteps on the corridor outside. As he passes my room, I open the door and whisper to him. He comes in and regards me ironically. 'Surely I'm not going to receive my reward before the treaty's even signed?'

I take the insult without a murmur: I have earned it, after all. 'Niccolò, about the treaty . . . are you sure you're doing the right thing?'

He laughs theatrically. 'Is the thought of going to bed with me really that repulsive, Donna Stefania?'

'Not at all, Niccolò.' I touch his arm. 'And I know very well that I have spent the last week persuading you that an alliance between Florence and the duke was in your city's interests, but . . .'

There is a noise outside in the corridor. I hold my breath and listen. Niccolò watches me, with a sly, amused expression. 'Perhaps I should not tell you this, my lady, but I did not actually need to be persuaded. I was always in favour of an alliance with the duke. However, I am very happy to accept my reward from you anyway.' He moves towards me, puts his hands on my hips. I smell wine on his breath. 'And don't try and wriggle out of your promise just because . . .'

Three knocks on the door: quiet, evenly spaced, frighteningly familiar. Niccolò sighs and removes his hands. I open
the door to Michelotto's leering, scarred face. He looks at
Niccolò, smiles, and a chill runs through me. I have been
afraid of him ever since he poked his head in at the window
of my carriage that fateful February night. And I have been
even more afraid of him since I realised Cesare was thinking of having me killed. Michelotto and I both know that, if
the order were given, it would be *his* hands that tightened
the ligature round my neck.

'Yes, Michelotto?' I manage to ask.

'Excuse me for intruding, my lady, but his lordship has
urgent business with Signor Machiavelli. Would you kindly
release him?'

'Of course.'

I curtsey. Michelotto bows. Niccolò winks at me, whispers
'Until later, my lady', and follows the strangler out of my
room and down the corridor.

CESARE: The envoy enters. I order the doors bolted. I order
the fire fed. I order wine and roast squabs. I haven't eaten
breakfast yet.

Machiavelli puts up a hand. 'No food for me, your lordship, I beg you. I have just had dinner.'

Yes, with Leonardo – I know. I wonder what they talked
about? My spy caught only a few words.

'May I congratulate you, my lord, on the justice you dis-
pensed today? It was a brilliant solution.'

I look in Machiavelli's eyes – ambition and alcohol. But also
sincerity. He's not licking my arse – he means what he says.

'I expected you sooner, Niccolò. The official stamp
arrived yesterday, did it not?'

'You know everything, my lord.'

'Was the burden of power too heavy for you?'

He blushes, smiles. 'Perhaps. But I see now that there is nothing to fear. My decision is made – we only have to discuss certain details.'

'I have taken the liberty of having a draft treaty drawn up.' I hand him the paper. 'Of course, if there is anything which seems to you unjust . . .'

He sits up. His eyes sharpen. He studies the contract – quickly, efficiently. As he reads, his eyes widen. My terms are generous.

'No, my lord. Everything seems in order. I believe this treaty will mark the beginning of an important and enduring alliance.'

I smile. I utter fancy lies. How I always felt the warmest affection for Florence. How our misunderstandings were the fault of Vitelli and the Orsini.

'Of course, Niccolò, you may take the treaty home with you to study it more carefully, if you wish.'

'There is no need, my lord. I am ready to sign it now.'

I invite him to use my desk. 'I am impressed by your decisiveness, Niccolò. And I am glad that the Signoria has finally given you the power that your abilities merit.'

If only HE were gonfalonier, my power would be secure now. A puppet gonfalonier – my hand up his arse. Yes, this is only the beginning for Niccolò Machiavelli.

'Thank you, my lord.' He signs both copies. Hands them to me.

'And the stamp?'

Machiavelli smacks his forehead. 'It is in my lodgings. I did not think to bring it with me.'

'That is not your fault, Niccolò. You were not to know that I would summon you tonight. Don't worry – I will send a servant to fetch it.'

In his eyes – fear and calculation. 'No, my lord. The stamp is hidden, and it will take longer to describe its whereabouts than to go there myself.'

'Very well. You may ride one of my horses – and I will send a guard to accompany you.'

He bows, retreats. 'Thank you, my lord. I will return presently.'

NICCOLÒ: The cold air sobers me as I ride back through town, but it does not change my mind. I have made the right decision: I have no further doubts on that score. My worries were a virgin's nerves – nothing more. Still, I did not think it was a good idea to have one of the duke's spies rifling through my belongings, so I lied about the where-abouts of the stamp: it is, in fact, still on the bedside table, where I left it.

We reach the house, and I ask the guard to wait for me outside. I run upstairs, as quickly and quietly as I can (my landlady will be sleeping now), and unlock the door of my room. I walk past the bed to the bedside table and pick up the stamp. How light and small it feels in my hand! And then I notice something that wasn't there before: a letter with my name on it. The handwriting is Biagio's, but the seal is not official. It must have been delivered while I was out. I turn it over: on the back, Biagio has scrawled the words 'URGENT AND SECRET'.

I open up the letter and read. It is written entirely in code, so it takes me a few minutes to make sense of what Biagio is saying. When I have done so, however, I inspect the stamp, then call out of the window to the guard that something unforeseen has happened, and that he should go back to the castle without me. 'Please tell the duke I will see him tomorrow,' I say. The guard stares at me suspiciously: he probably has orders not to allow this, but I don't care. Heart pounding, I close the shutters, lock the door, and read the letter again. It is dated the 18th – yesterday – and Biagio wrote it at home, not in the office. This is what it says:

Niccolò, do NOT sign that treaty! You are walking into a trap. The whole business of sending you the stamp has been orchestrated by your enemies, foremost among them Alamanno Salviati. As I warned you before, your constant calls for an alliance with the duke have raised suspicions against you. The duke is feared and hated in Florence, and you were a fool to think you could change that. Your enemies accuse you of corruption and treachery. The gonfalonier defended you, but was forced to accept this test of your loyalty. The stamp they sent you is not the official one – take a close look at it if you don't believe me.

I told the messenger this was a matter of life and death, and paid him extra to get it to you today – but if it's too late, you must know this: the treaty is not worth the paper it is written on, as the stamp is false. And as soon as confirmation is received here that you have ratified it, you will be arrested as a traitor. No one knows better than you what that means. I pray that you have not done anything you will regret. Your friend, BB.

28

VITELLOZZO: Ramiro da Lorqua watches me silently as I order my secretary into the room. We have just eaten dinner together. He is the informer: the traitor in Borgia's ranks. Ramiro eats like a pig – a fat bearded Spanish pig. Why must I always keep the company of men whose presence makes me feel physically ill? A picture of Donna Paolo flashes in my mind and the usual revulsion is mixed now with feelings of regret and anger. So much wasted time! So many lost opportunities! We could have crushed Borgia . . .

But not now. It's too late. The league has fragmented: the rats have all fled. There is only one course of action left open to me. I should probably have done this before but pride blinded me – and the fever clouded my brain. Now that I have finally crawled out of my sickbed I can see the situation more clearly.

I dictate the letter to my secretary and he writes it down. He must know it by heart now. I have dictated this same letter to him half a dozen times before but each time I have ended by throwing it on the fire. No doubt my secretary thinks the same thing will happen again. But it won't.

This time I abase myself and kiss the duke's feet and arse and apologise for the whole 'misunderstanding' – not futilely but to some purpose. I buy myself time and I make Borgia believe he's already won. I give him a false sense of security.

When the letter is finished I sign it and tell my secretary to have it delivered this very night.

He hesitates. 'Are you sure my lord?'

'Yes. Send it now.'

He bows and leaves the room.

There's a long silence and then Ramiro says: 'You're really giving up then?'

'To his face I give up. But I'll still defeat him. I'm going to use the same treachery on him as he's used on everyone else.'

'How?'

'A sniper with a crossbow.' I formulated the plan during those long dark days in my sickbed. In my mind the deed is already done.

With a lurch of panic I look at Ramiro. He is wiping his beard with a napkin. Never trust a traitor!

'You are the only other person who knows about this,' I say. 'If Borgia finds out I'll have an arrow put through *your* neck too.'

Ramiro laughs. 'Why would I tell Borgia that? I want him dead as much as you do.'

Imola   *21 November, 1502*

CESARE: Wind howls in the chimney. Shutters rattle. Flames gutter. Outside a hailstorm rages – inside I am calm.

Machiavelli is pale. Machiavelli is sweating. He's had a scare – the arrow whistled past his ear. Now he fears the monster's going to devour him.

'I am angry with your enemies, Niccolò – not with you.'

He's told me about the plot against him. The false stamp. He's not lying – my spies have confirmed his story.

'My opinion of you hasn't changed. You are a man of great intelligence and integrity. Fear not – we will defeat our enemies, you and I.'

'Thank you, my lord. But I think perhaps I . . .' – cough, cough – '. . . ought to distance myself from, uh . . .'

'From me?' I laugh. 'Of course you must. Your letters about me must be cool and measured. Objective. Insulting, even. But don't worry, Niccolò – you'll be proved right. This is my year, you see.'

'Your year?'

'Yes. It's written in the stars.'

Machiavelli frowns – he doesn't believe in astrology.

'You want proof?' I tell him about my army – huge, drilled, ready. I show him the reports from Urbino – my troops took control today. I show him letters from Orsini, Baglioni, Vitellozzo – grovelling letters. Please-don't-kill-me letters.

'The rebellion is over, Niccolò. My enemies are my friends – or so they think. Things are speeding up now. Soon the iron will be hot. Soon . . .' I hold my hand over the desk – then suddenly smash it down. The papers jump.

Machiavelli looks at me as if I'm mad.

'You'll see,' I smile. 'And so will your enemies. Before 1502 is out, your Signoria will be BEGGING me for an alliance.'

At two in the morning, the hail turns to snow. At three in the morning, Pinzone arrives.

He's ridden from Rimini. He gives me the report on Ramiro – pages and pages. I heft the paper – look up at him.

'Tell me,' I say.

'He betrayed you, my lord.'

'How?'

'He was in league with the rebels.'

'You're sure?'

'Yes. It's all in there.' He nods to the papers. 'Secret meetings with Vitellozzo, with Baglioni, with Oliverotto. He gave away our position at Calmazzo – then left the field the evening before the attack.'

I nod. So I have sniffed out the rat. I am disappointed – but not surprised. Ramiro was useful to me. Now his usefulness is at an end. Unless perhaps . . .

'Shall I arrest him, my lord?'

'No – not yet. Give him no sign that he's under suspicion. Keep watching, keep listening. I will read your reports. When the time is right, I will send word.'

'Very good, my lord.'

Pinzone bows. I give him a bag of gold ducats. He thanks me. He goes.

I open the shutter. Look out the window. Snow falling – white everywhere. The colour of innocence. But only a mask – the same filth lies underneath.

I think about Ramiro. Yes, he can still be useful to me. One last time. He will be my messenger to the world. The message – DON'T FUCK WITH ME.

LEONARDO: It is the middle of the night and my head is spinning with exhaustion. I have worked at my desk for nearly twenty hours today. Outside, the town sleeps under silent snow, while here on my desk are sketches, measurements, ideas to change the world. I look through what I've done, and I *know* it would work. The world's first flying machine.

to conquer the air – to write my name across the sky

But I also know the uses to which such a machine might be put. If all paths lead to the same end, then I must take the path of virtue. It aches, my decision. Not to fly – to erase my name from the sky. And yes, I know that someone else will, in the end, make the same calculations, the same measurements. Someone else will take the glory. Someone else will feel the air beneath their wings. Only I will know the truth – the bitter truth. But at least I will not dream of killing any more.

cannonballs fall from my wings

I pick up the papers and carry them to the open window. The air is cold. All is white. Snow everywhere, like a benediction. I hold the candle and feed the papers, one by one, to its flame. My dreams are blackened, consumed – they turn to smoke. I watch them fly up as sparks, bright against the black sky, and then fall to earth as ashes.

the flames engulf

The snow continues to fall. Soon the dark stain on the whiteness below will vanish. It will be as if it never was.

The Peak of the Mountain
(Winter 1502/03)

29

LEONARDO: By evening the map is complete. I go to see his lordship – to present it and to ask about money. I haven't been paid since October, the day he gave me the fur cape. I am shown in ahead of the waiting envoys and the duke greets me cordially. Yet I can detect a new shadow in his eyes. Perhaps he is merely preoccupied with mighty matters of state. Or perhaps it is something else.

the walls have ears

I show him the map and he admires it, but with less enthusiasm than I had expected. 'Is this not what you required, my lord?'

'It is precisely what I required. But I required it a month ago, as I told you.'

For the last three weeks I have been working secretly and zealously on the project to divert the River Arno. No one knows about this as yet, except for Niccolò, myself and the gonfalonier of Florence. And no one else must know. As for the map, I had actually forgotten about it until I opened the cashbox this morning – and found it empty. But I can't tell the duke that.

'My lord, I am sorry – I wanted the map to be a work of art as well as a practical guide. And you did ask me to make the portrait of Donna Dorotea as well, and . . .'

He waves his hand in a brusque silencing gesture. I stop speaking. This encounter is uncomfortably similar to several that I had with the Duke of Milan – patience and charm evaporated, the ruthlessness all too visible. I wait for the duke to speak as he paces the room.

'The portrait of *Donna Dorotea* . . .' (he pronounces her name sarcastically, and I realise this is information I am not meant to know) '. . . is it finished?'

'The cartoon is finished, my lord. Now I must prick the outline onto canvas and . . .'

'I know how it works. Do you have the cartoon with you?' I nod. 'Show me.'

I take the chalk sketch from the sheaf of papers I have brought and hold it up for the duke to see. He stares in silence for half a minute. Then, slowly, he nods. 'Yes. It is beautifully done.'

'Thank you, my lord.'

'Only . . . Donna Dorotea is a sexy lady. She is my mistress, as I'm sure you know. The woman in this picture is not sexy. She is beautiful, but you don't want to fuck her.'

I blush. Why is he speaking to me like this? Words stutter out of my mouth. He waves me silent again.

'Perhaps you should paint her naked?' His eyes on mine – green and cold. 'Or would that be too much temptation?'

I say nothing. This is not a conversation – it is a torture session. The duke is punishing me, though for what precisely, I cannot be sure. For growing too close to his mistress? What does he know? What does he suspect? 'My lord, if you are angry with me, I wish you would tell me why. Have I done something to offend you?'

The duke looks astonished. 'Angry? Why, whatever do you mean, my dear Leonardo? What could you possibly have done that would offend me? You have drawn me a beautiful map and a magnificent portrait of my mistress. I am deeply grateful.' He bows to his knees. 'I do wonder, however, what happened to all those weapons you dreamed up. The sword-eating shield and the exploding cannon-balls. Where are they? Have the map and the portrait really taken *all* of your time, maestro?'

Does he know about the Arno project? No, it's impossible. Isn't it?

eyes everywhere

'My lord, I . . .'

To my relief, there is a knock at the door. The duke's secretary enters. They converse, the duke issuing orders (for the movement of troops, I think) in a harsh whisper, while the secretary's eyes flick frowningly towards me. 'Relax, Agapito,' his lordship says. 'Leonardo is not a spy. If he has a fault, it is that he says too little, rather than too much.'

I stare at the floor, like a chastened child. 'My lord, may I . . .'

'Yes,' the duke says. 'Go. I will send for you when I need you.'

Relieved, yet deeply troubled, I exit. Only later do I realise that I never asked about the money he owes me.

10 December, 1502

NICCOLÒ: I eat breakfast watched by my landlady, who launches into her daily moan about the French troops – 'Those beasts! Scavenging animals!' – so I drift into my own thoughts for a while, nodding and saying 'Mmm' to make her think I'm still listening, and it's only as I'm dipping the last chunk of stale bread in my wine that I notice how cheerful she seems.

'Well anyway, good riddance to bad rubbish I say, and I pray that those foreign savages never come back.'

'What?' I look up at her. 'Come back from where?'

269

'Why, that's what I was just telling you – no one knows yet. They left early this morning down the Via Emilia so . . .'

'The army has left? All of it?'

'Are you deaf or something? What have I just been saying?'

'And the duke?'

'Why, he's leading them of course. I'll be sorry to see *him* go, I must say. I know he's got a bad reputation, but . . .'

'But I was with him last night. He never said anything about them leaving today!'

She laughs. 'Ah, he's the devil in disguise, that one. I'm glad he's on our side, and not against us.'

I finish my wine, wrap my mantle round my shoulders, put on a pair of overshoes and rush out of the house. It's snowing heavily and the street is empty, but I can hear a crowd cheering down by the town gates so I run there as fast as I can on the icy cobbles and push my way through the mass of bodies until I reach the road. There I see the departing tail of the army marching south: mules dragging heavy artillery, pursued by a few laughing boys.

I turn to the man next to me and ask if he has heard where they are headed. 'They're going to meet up with the king's men on their way to Naples,' he announces confidently. Another man says this is nonsense and the duke is just going south to put people off his scent: he is actually planning to turn suddenly north and attack Venice. I smile: if the duke *was* going to do such a thing (and it's not beyond the realm of possibility), even Agapito wouldn't know about it, never mind some random old man. Still, it is strange that they should leave so suddenly – and in such bad weather. Puzzled, I walk back to my lodgings to pack my bags.

Cesena   *12 December, 1502*

DOROTEA: I sit before the fire and try to get warm: after three days of travelling through snowstorms, the chill is deep inside me. When the duke came to my room on that last night in Imola, I thought I knew what he wanted; but he just told me to have my belongings packed quickly because we were leaving at dawn. His manner was cold, as it has been for weeks now. I spent much of the journey fearful that my carriage would halt in the middle of nowhere and I would be dragged out, strangled and thrown in a river. But it never happened, and now I am here: in a room of the palace in Cesena, overlooking the market square and the fountain. The room is large and high-ceilinged: a handsome place, but cheerless. I shiver with self-pity. I don't know where Leonardo or Niccolò are. I have not seen anyone apart from soldiers and servants since I got here.

After dinner, I go out to explore the town. It is a clear night, the moon nearly full. I walk through the snow, which is more than a foot deep in places, and follow the main street from the market square to the principal gate. I do not see Leonardo or Niccolò, but I do see a lot of minor horrors: French and Spanish soldiers stealing openly from people's houses, shoving old men around, urinating against the walls of the church. I say nothing until I see two drunk French officers laughing as they rip open a young woman's dress. She is standing at the front door of her house, barring the way, and a small child is clinging to one of her thighs, crying its eyes out. One of the soldiers takes his sword and pokes it close to the child's face. He says something in French: I don't catch all the words, but it is clearly a threat.

The woman catches my eye as she bends to protect her son. Knowing perfectly well what a reckless act I am about to commit, I shout at the soldiers in their own language: 'Stop that now! You should be ashamed of yourselves. The duke has given orders that the townspeople are not to be molested, and . . .'

The one with the sword turns slowly towards me. 'And who the fuck are you, *madame*, if you don't mind me asking?'

I open my mouth, hesitating over what form of words I can use to describe myself. I am the duke's spy? I am his lordship's personal courtesan?

'This lady is my friend,' says a low voice from above and behind me, in perfect French. 'The question is, officer, who are you, and what are you doing?'

I do not need to look behind to know that it's Cesare. I recognise his voice, of course, but more than that I recognise the fear in the eyes of the soldier with the sword. He stutters his own name and company and begins making some weak excuse.

'*Ça suffit*,' the duke says, before the man has finished. In a deliberately loud voice he continues: 'You have broken my commandments and you will pay the price.' I look around: Cesare is on horseback; either side of him are half a dozen of his personal bodyguards. In Italian, he says: 'Guards, seize these men and execute them. Display their bodies in the market square so that the people of Cesena and the rest of the troops may know what happens to soldiers who disobey my orders.'

The Frenchmen try to run, but they are caught and beaten by the guards, then dragged screaming and pleading down the street. Cesare watches them go, expressionlessly, then finally looks down at me.

'Thank you, my lord,' I say.

He laughs derisively and lifts me onto the saddle in front of him: 'Angel of mercy now, are we?' he whispers.

He steers his horse back along the main street. 'No, I was . . . I was looking for my friends,' I say. 'For Leonardo and Niccolò.'

'Oh, Niccolò Machiavelli is your *friend* now, is he? Does he trust you?'

'Probably not. I can't blame him for that, given how I've treated him.'

'The envoy doesn't trust you . . .' He lets a silence fall. 'Then you're not much use to me, are you?'

I say nothing. I know too well what is coming next. We ride into the market square, past the crowds watching the two soldiers being taken to the gibbets.

'What about Leonardo then? Does *he* trust you? I bet he does.'

'Yes – and I would never betray his trust.'

'Never say never, Donna Dorotea,' the duke says in that horrifyingly quiet, gentle voice of his, as we dismount in front of the palace. 'Never say never.'

Then, before a gaggle of watching servants and soldiers, he puts one of his gloved hands down the front of my dress and the other up the back of my skirt and, with his mouth wide open, kisses me savagely on the throat. I close my eyes and keep perfectly still. I am reminded of a story that Leonardo told me – about how, one day at the zoo in Florence, he had seen a lion lick a lamb. 'With a few licks,' he said, 'that lion took off most of the lamb's fleece. Then he ate it.'

When I am finally released, I walk trembling through the doors of the palace. In a loud, insolent voice the duke says: 'Tell your maidservants to wash and scent you tonight. I may feel like paying you a visit.'

As the soldiers laugh and cheer at this, I force myself to turn, smile, curtsey, and it occurs to me what a neat reversal my relations with the duke have undergone. When I first met him, I shivered with desire and feigned disgust. Now, I do the exact opposite.

30

LEONARDO: I study my plans for moving the Arno and pretend not to watch as Salai packs his trunk. He is travelling back to Florence today. Ostensibly he is going to supervise the running of my studio – but in reality, as we both know, he is leaving because he can't stand my company any more.

please no more war Salai I surrender

I had hoped that our return to Cesena would rekindle the happiness the two of us shared in the summer, but it was not to be. Salai is bored of me. He hates Romagna and he misses his friends. He wants to go to bed with people who are not old enough to be his father – people who are not his lifelong employer. I am saddened . . . but I understand. And I will find it easier to concentrate on my work, perhaps, now that we are not constantly fighting all the time. But I will miss him all the same.

Still, I am not alone. I have Tommaso – and my new friends Dorotea and Niccolò. And friends, despite Salai's insinuations, is all they are. Dorotea was infatuated with me before, I suppose, but she accepts now that the love we share must remain platonic.

in kissing, said Plato, the soul comes to the lips so that it may

I see her every day. Her smile is a balm for my anxieties. In the late afternoons, before the fall of darkness, we meet and go for walks through the town. I like Cesena – perhaps only because of the ghosts of summer happiness with Salai it contains, but still . . . I feel more at ease here than I did in Imola. It helps that the palace is not located inside the castle walls, but in the centre of town, overlooking the fountain that makes such exquisite harmonies.

The duke is friendlier with me now. He did not apologise for his behaviour towards me a week ago, of course (I doubt if he has ever said sorry in his life), but the next time I saw him, a few days ago, he was back to his usual charming self. I know it is an act, a mask he wears, but that is all right. *For if I pull away his mask I will see the* Sometimes falseness is preferable to truth.

horror beneath

He has asked me to prepare designs for the scenery and spectacles of the Christmas party. This is a pleasant task – the same frivolous, unremembered work which so frustrated me, towards the end, in Milan. But now I am grateful for the distraction.

For the most part, what I do during the days here is supervise Tommaso and his metalworkers, the stonemasons and painters, the plumbers and carpenters, the musicians and poets who gather each day in the great ballroom. But lately I have been setting more and more time aside to contemplate the Arno project.

When I first mentioned the idea to Niccolò, I did so without expectation. I wanted to find an invention that might create peace, rather than war – a way to bring immortal glory upon myself without the stain of blame. I did not believe that anything would come of it, but the more we talk, the more convinced he seems that he can persuade the gonfalonier to approve the scheme. Our visions of the matter are not identical, of course. Niccolò thinks only of defeating the Pisans, while I see my fingerprints erasing God's – the glorious works of Nature being perfected under my direction.

When Dorotea and I walk into town, we often call at Niccolò's lodgings – and then the three of us go either to a tavern or back to the palace for dinner. I daresay we make strange companions. Salai calls Niccolò 'the straight' (I prefer not to repeat what he calls Dorotea), and he has a point, I suppose. I never thought I could be friends with a man who works for the Florentine government, who has no appreciation of painting, who wears dark blue hose like it's going out of fashion (was it ever *in*, Niccolò?), and whose idea of a subtle scent is to mix lemon juice with cheap musk. But what can I say? He is not what he seems.

Niccolò is clever – and not only in the usual sharp, shallow manner of Florentines. He has an original mind. He is not a hypocrite. And he makes me laugh, which is not a quality to be underestimated. As the man himself said last night, 'Entertainment is more than ever necessary in these turbulent times.'

Salai finishes packing and stands before my desk. 'Well, goodbye,' he says coolly. I can see he is eager to go – like a dog being let out for a run. Risking his irritation, however, I stand up and walk around the desk to embrace him. His body is tense in my arms – tense with the memory of recent disputes, of too many harsh words.

I kiss his smooth cheek. 'Salai, forgive your old master for his temper.' He says nothing, but drops his forehead to my shoulder, as he used to do when he was young. It is all the forgiveness I need.

'Be careful on your journey,' I say. 'The roads are dangerous.'

'You be careful too, master. Try to stay out of the way of arrows and cannonballs.'

I smile. He goes. I return to my desk and stare emptily at the pale blue lines of ink that meander across the paper.

NICCOLÒ: It is an odd feeling – not to mention a huge relief – to be able to kiss the lips and inhale the scent and admire the eyes and mouth and gleaming white cleavage of Donna Dorotea . . . and not feel even the slightest twinge of desire.

Don't get me wrong: she hasn't grown ugly. If anything, she is even more attractive now than she was a couple of months ago. She's added some flesh to her bones; she wears less powder; her cheeks glow, her eyes shine. And if her mysteriousness has evaporated since she told me the true story of her life (including her real name), then it has been replaced by a tender compassion. The poor girl has suffered so much, it is easy enough for me to forgive her for the torture she put me through in Imola. And, of course, I tease her with the reminder that, the day Florence signs an alliance with Valentino, she will be mine.

The reason for my sudden indifference lies not with her, but with me. Or, to be more precise, with my new landlady, who is – how can I put this delicately? – shagging the life out of me.

To begin with, I thought Fortune was smiling on me for once. Not only did I find cheap lodgings quite near to the centre of town, but the landlady was a young, attractive widow. I didn't get to sleep at all that first night, and not only because of the fleas that bit me all over my body. We were at it till dawn, and my God it felt good! Seven nights and about five hours' sleep later, however, I am so tired, and so sore, that even the *thought* of sex makes me want to curl up in a ball, protecting my privates, and sleep. I am like a man who has eaten a nine-course meal and drunk two gallons of wine, then gone to bed and been woken at six the next morning and told he must eat the same feast again for breakfast.

So I kiss Dorotea and smile at her desirelessly. She looks puzzled, as though she knows something is wrong but can't quite put her finger on it. 'Are you all right, Niccolò?'

'Fine,' I say. 'Just a little tired.'

Then I embrace Leonardo and we sit down to eat our evening meal together. This ritual is good for two things: it saves me money (as Leonardo buys all the food, and Dorotea all the drink), which I am in desperate need of saving; and it gives me something resembling my old social life in Florence. Leonardo and Dorotea's company is not quite as relaxing and amusing as that of Agostino and Biagio in The Three Kings, but it's the closest thing I'm likely to find in this godforsaken little town.

So we eat and play cards, and Leonardo gives us a few of his riddles, and I tell them stories of Caterina Sforza, and Dorotea is just about to sing to the accompaniment of Leonardo's lute when I hear a loud noise in the corridor outside. I open the door and see a group of French captains talking loudly in their own language, gesticulating wildly, as they walk away from the duke's quarters. I watch them pass until I see a face I recognise – that of Baron de Bierra, whom I got to know in Imola. I go up to him and ask, in my best French, what's happened. He speaks very quickly, but the gist of it, I think, is that the duke has dismissed all his French soldiers. They've been told to return to Milan, and must leave within the next three days.

I walk back to Leonardo's room and, excusing myself, go to his desk and write a letter to the Signoria, informing them of this astonishing news. Then I say goodnight to my companions, and go off to find a messenger who can deliver the letter to Florence.

When this is done, I walk to my lodgings, going through all the possible reasons for the duke's decision. Can he really have run out of money to pay his troops, as the rumours have it? Or might the indiscipline of the French have outweighed their reputation as soldiers in the duke's mind? Or perhaps the French commander never forgave the duke for castrating the three soldiers who urinated on the shrine in Imola?

I think about this until my thoughts are soup and I am suddenly, horribly aware of the weariness in my body. Whatever happens, I must not give in to my landlady's demands tonight.

When I reach the house, I turn the key softly in the lock and ascend the stairs like a cat. In my room, I undress in the dark and slip into bed. *Finally* I can get some sleep. Then I hear the door squeak open and her voice whisper: 'Niccolò . . . is that you?'

Città di Castello   *21 December, 1502*

VITELLOZZO: In a rare show of emotion my father once told me: 'We become what we despise.' I had no idea what he was on about at the time – I was always the thick one in the family. But now I think about those words and wonder if they're true.

Until three days ago I was turning into Cesare Borgia.

It started with the insomnia. I would lie awake in bed all night worrying about his spies feeding him details of my plan. Worrying about his assassins getting to me before mine got to him.

Then I thought sod it – why stay in bed? If you're going to be awake all night you may as well put your nervous energy to some use. So I began working in my office from dusk to dawn.

I slept little but when I did my nightmares haunted me: I dreamt that armed men were hiding behind the curtains in my room. I became suspicious of the people around me. I suspected my secretary and my servants and my cousins – even my own wife. I had everybody searched and interrogated. To my shame I ordered the torture of some old friends. Eventually I sent them all away – banished them from Città di Castello. But this purge didn't do any good, as I immediately started suspecting their replacements.

Finally I got a letter from my wife. She said she understood why I was so suspicious and fearful of everyone and she forgave me for sending her away, but if she would not be allowed to see our children any more then she would rather be dead: 'Please send an assassin to finish me off Vitellozzo because my life is no longer worth living.' I became very emotional when I read that letter. I realised what a monster I was becoming and I vowed not to let the evil take me over completely.

I decided to trust people again. Yes, they might betray me. But it is better to die like a man than to live like a reptile – constantly hiding under stones. Your skin as thick as chainmail. Your blood as cold as ice.

I sent a messenger to bring my wife back to the palace and I watched with tears streaming from my eyes as she was reunited with our children. In that moment I felt myself become a man again. A true Vitelli. That was three nights ago.

I didn't make love to her because I am afraid of giving her the French disease, but we held each other and miraculously my insomnia was cured: for the first time in many weeks I slept peacefully. And I swear that in my dreams that night I saw my brother Paolo looking down on me from heaven – and his face was *proud*. And he said to me: 'Even if you are defeated you will still be victorious.'

But you mustn't think that I'm giving up in my battle with Borgia. No bloody way. My wife was adamant on that point. So against him I use all the tricks he has used against others. I write letters to him proclaiming my love and loyalty while behind his back I organise the sharpest welcoming party that bastard's ever had.

Cesena   *23 December, 1502*

CESARE: Dead of night. Ramiro's shown in – grinning, bowing. Fat and bearded. He kisses my hand. He thanks me for the gifts I sent him. We embrace.

'My old friend,' I say. 'I have known you since I was a boy – haven't I? I have always trusted you. Never doubted you.'

He tenses in my arms. 'You said you had good news, my lord?'

I hold him tight. I whisper in his ear: 'Yes, good news. We have caught a traitor. That's good news, isn't it?'

He tries to pull away – but can't. He laughs – ha ha. 'Yes, good news.'

My arm tight round his neck. 'My old friend. My trusted lieutenant. My right-hand man.'

'May I ask . . .'

'Who the traitor is?'

I feel him nod. I feel his heart pound. I feel his heart stop. He's fucking terrified. He's fucking GUILTY.

'I think you know the answer to that already, Ramiro.'

I let him go. I stare in his eyes. Guilt, terror. He says: 'My lord – surely you do not suspect . . .'

'I suspect nothing,' I say. 'I know it was you.'

He trembles. He falls to his knees. Tears in his eyes. 'My lord, it's not true. Who has accused me of this? Tell me and I'll . . .'

I yawn. I ring the bell. The guards appear. I say: 'Arrest this man. Take him to the dungeons.'

Ramiro weeps. Ramiro shakes. Ramiro pleads. Ramiro prays.

'I'll see you soon, Ramiro. I have another gift for you. A surprise.'

Terror in his eyes. Ramiro is an old friend – he knows me well.

31

DOROTEA: A hundred times a day, I ask myself the same question: why won't Leonardo go to bed with me? I think he loves me, even if he never says so. He wouldn't spend so much time with me if he didn't enjoy my company, and . . . well, you can just tell, can't you? Likewise his sexual preferences. Yes, I know his reputation, but when we kissed, his reaction was that of a normal man. So why hasn't it happened again?

Am I dressing too modestly these days? I changed my style because of something Leonardo himself said – that he thought unadorned peasant girls were often more beautiful than court ladies who *encrusted themselves* (those were his very words!) with jewels and powder. But perhaps he has grown too used to this plainness? Certainly, the other men in my life seem to have lost interest in me: Cesare, despite his threat, never visited my chamber that night, and I have barely seen him since then; while Niccolò, whom I see every day, looks at me as though I'm a man, or his sister, or an item of furniture. Under normal circumstances, I might have greeted this development with relief, but in my current situation I have to confess that I find it disconcerting.

Whatever the cause, it will not do. As happy as I am to talk and sing and laugh with Leonardo, I want more. And if the only way to get him into my bed is to use some of the tricks I learned as a whore, then so be it. Once the act has happened, I feel sure, everything will take care of itself. He will love me fully.

And tonight is when that will happen. What better time than the eve of Christmas? What better occasion than a magnificent party, designed by Leonardo himself, to which the whole of Cesena's aristocracy is invited? I call the maids to my room and say to them: I wish to look like a million ducats; can you help me? They giggle conspiratorially.

CESARE: Castlegloom and shitstink. Chainrattle and wallslime. We descend the narrow steps – me and Michelotto. Down to the dungeons.

The jailer opens the door. We go in. He locks it. He gives me the keys. I wave my hand – he fucks off.

Ramiro stands up. Ramiro's eyes widen. Ramiro swallows. He opens his fat mouth.

He's had all night – to make his excuses. To perfect his pleas. To think up a really good lie.

But panic dulls the brain. He stutters and sweats. He bullshits and weeps.

I stand, arms folded. I stare and smile. I listen to Ramiro. I listen to every lying stammered word he has to say.

Michelotto gets his tools out – he spreads them on the floor. The razor and the poker. The pliers and the saw. The hammer and the nails. Nothing fancy for Michelotto – he doesn't mind getting his hands dirty.

Ramiro keeps talking. But his words are drying up. His eyes keep flicking to Michelotto's tools. His concentration wavers.

Finally there's silence. I say: 'Have you finished?'

Ramiro stares at the floor. 'I am sorry,' he says. His voice quiet.

Sorry?

'Ramiro,' I say, 'I've known you since I was a boy. You were with me in Perugia. In France and in Rome. I gave you my trust. I gave you wealth and power. And how did you pay me back?'

Silence. Floorstare. Tears – but of fear, not remorse. He's not fucking sorry. He's just fucking terrified.

'When I was young,' I say, 'you used to scare me. You had that big reputation. You had those cruel eyes. But without power . . . you're nothing.'

I look at him now. Fat belly, greasy moustache. Like a fucking whoremonger.

Michelotto sharpens his razor. Ramiro watches, swallows. Michelotto oils his poker. Ramiro twitches, mumbles.

I think of his crimes. The murders committed, the cruelties inflicted. The conspiracy with Vitellozzo. The insult to Lucrezia that my spies heard him make.

I don't need to think of all this – I could torture him without it. But I wouldn't enjoy it as much.

Michelotto stands up. He nods. We're ready to begin.

NICCOLÒ: The market square is lit by hundreds of torches and packed with most of the town's citizens, there to watch the night races. I stay in the crowd to see the prostitutes run barefoot around the icy square. Apparently the duke had fifty of them brought up from Rome especially for tonight's festivities: rather an expensive treat for someone who supposedly can't afford to pay his troops. They slip and slide, shove and squeal their way around the course, their elegant nightgowns getting soaked and muddied and ripped, revealing the prize white flesh beneath. I bet I'm the only man here without an erection. The spectators cheer and jeer and grab hold of the whores' body parts as they run around – for four laps – until one of them, finally, is declared the winner, and gamblers start arguing over who owes whom.

I show my invitation at the door of the palace and am led upstairs by one of the duke's gold-costumed servants. Leonardo has been dropping hints all week about the party he was preparing, so I knew the theme was Ancient Rome, but even so I am amazed. The walls are painted to look like the walls of a ruined Roman bath: uneven piles of old pale stone and, beyond these, an ancient cityscape, seen as if from a hilltop, and a blue summer sky with thin white clouds floating through it. It is all so real-looking that I laugh out loud, and move forward into the buzzing crowd.

That's when I notice the stone dais in the centre of the room, inside which is a vast bath of steaming water. I have no idea how this is heated – probably one of Leonardo's miraculous contraptions – but it is evident that the water is genuinely warm because bobbing calmly in the green liquid are several naked women. These, I surmise, are some of the prostitutes brought from Rome; my theory is confirmed a little later when they are joined in the bath by a growing number of red-faced beauties who run, giggling and unclothed, between the startled party guests and jump into the water. By this point I have had two goblets of wine and my cock is beginning, like a treebranch suddenly budding one warm day in March, to spring back to life again.

Servants in togas walk around offering trays filled with morsels of fish and meat and dried fruit. Musicians play and sing, and dwarves dance with whores (now dried and dressed, their faces charmingly pink from the race and the steaming bath). Then the music stops and we are told that the wild boar races are about to begin. Everyone rushes to the windows, which are opened onto balconies overlooking the square, and from here we are able to see the creatures being ridden around the oval circuit, crashing into spectators, throwing their jockeys, escaping into side-alleys and generally causing mayhem. It is all very entertaining, and only when it is over do I recognise the tall, smiling man beside me. 'Leonardo!' I say. 'I must congratulate you on a dazzling illusion.'

'Thank you Niccolò. You're enjoying the party so far?'

'Having a marvellous time. But my cup is empty – and you don't even appear to have one – so let us go and get some wine!'

We stand together in a corner and make several toasts: to moving the Arno; to everlasting fame; to friendship; and to staying alive throughout our adventure with the duke. I get the impression that Leonardo would quite like his adventure to end soon, although he doesn't actually say this.

He points out a few curiosities to me, including a handsome young man chatting to a prostitute; the man's name, he says, is Piero Torrigiani. 'He has won a small measure of fame for being both a soldier and a sculptor.'

'An unlikely combination,' I say. 'Is he any good at either?'

'I don't doubt that he is a much better soldier than you or me, but as for his sculpture . . .' He pulls a face and shakes his head.

I laugh. 'Not a genius then?'

'I'm afraid not, although I have rather warmed to him since he told me that he once broke Michelangelo's nose with a well-aimed punch.'

'Michelangelo?' The name rings a bell. 'Oh, the young sculptor that everyone says is . . .'

'A greater genius than me?'

I begin to protest: that is not what I was going to say. But Leonardo is smiling.

'Yes, that's the one.'

'And what do *you* think? Is he as great as they say?'

'I think he is a very gifted artist and an arrogant, aggressive and generally unpleasant young man.'

'Ah.' Best not to say anything else, I decide, and people-watch for a while. 'Where's Dorotea, by the way?'

'I don't know,' Leonardo says. 'I was just wondering that myself.'

And then I see her, walking slowly through the crowd, which parts to let her pass, all eyes converging on her body, sheathed in pale blue silk and silver thread, and – yes – what seemed impossible only a couple of hours ago, suddenly happens: effortlessly and naturally, pleasurably and cripplingly. '*Mamma mia,*' I say.

Leonardo frowns.

CESARE: On the floor – a pool of piss. On the floor – spatters of blood. On the floor – two fingers and an ear.

Chained to the wall – Ramiro da Lorqua. Naked and fat. White and hairy. Screaming and bleeding and praying.

'I never knew you were religious, Ramiro. Michelotto, did you know Ramiro was religious?'

Michelotto shakes his head. 'I knew he was a pussy though.'

I laugh. 'He is – isn't he? A giant fucking pussy! Just two fingers and an ear – and you've confessed to almost everything.'

'Everything!' he screams. 'I've confessed to EVERYTHING! What else do you want from me?'

'No need to raise your voice,' I say. 'Unlike you, I still have both my ears.' I smile – then stop smiling. 'I just have the feeling that you're holding something back.'

'I'm NOT!' Ramiro screams. He sees my face. 'I'm not,' he says – his voice quiet, shaking. 'I swear to you, my lord. I have told you everything.'

'Hmm . . . let's go through it again, shall we? So you admit you were in league with Vitellozzo and Oliverotto? That you conspired with them against me?'

'Yes. Yes, I did. And I am sorry.'

'I forgive you, Ramiro.'

He stares at me – mouth open, eyes wide. 'You . . . forgive me?'

I open my hands. 'Yes – why not? I'm a merciful man. It's Christmas time. You've said you're sorry. So I'll let you off.'

I look in his eyes – hope battling disbelief. Hope winning.

'Let him down, Michelotto.'

Michelotto moves towards him.

'Oh thank you, thank you, my lord!'

'But wait,' I say. Michelotto stops. Ramiro freezes.

'I just remembered something,' I say. 'Something unpleasant. When you escorted Donna Lucrezia to Ferrara. Last January – you remember?'

'M-m-my lord?'

'DO YOU REMEMBER?'

Ramiro swallows. His lips tremble. 'Y-y-yes, my lord.'

'Good,' I say. Gently, kindly. 'Good. Then perhaps you also remember something you said to Donna Lucrezia. One evening during that journey. Something that . . . impugned her honour.'

'My lord, I don't know w-w-what you . . .'

I punch Ramiro in his big fat belly – feel the flesh, muscles, organs give way like dough. He gasps. His head smashes back against the wall. He moans with pain. His eyes roll back in their sockets.

I inspect my glove. White kidskin. Smeared with sweat and blood. I peel it from my fingers – drop it on the floor.

'I know what you said, Ramiro. There were many witnesses. But I want YOU to tell me. Tell me the exact words you used to insult my sister.'

He shakes his fat head. 'I can't . . . can't remember . . .'

To Michelotto, I say: 'Slice off his cock. It's so small, he'll hardly miss it.'

Ramiro squeals. 'NO! NO, PLEASE!'

'Tell me what you said to my sister, fuckface.'

'I said . . . I said . . . uh . . .'

I nod to Michelotto. He pulls Ramiro's cock – slices through it with the razor. Blood spurts everywhere. I wipe it off my shirt. The cock lies on the floor – a white slug, oozing red slime.

Ramiro screams, bangs his head against the wall. Blood pours from his mouth. The idiot's bitten his tongue.

'Don't fuck up your tongue, Ramiro. It's the only part of you I'm interested in.'

Ramiro jabbers. Ramiro screams. Ramiro weeps. Ramiro prays.

Seconds pass. Minutes.

'Enough,' I say. Ramiro closes his mouth. Ramiro sobs. Blood and snot shoot out of his nose.

'I said ENOUGH! I have a party to get to. You're wasting my time. Now tell me what you said to Donna Lucrezia before Michelotto pulls all your teeth out to stop you biting your fucking tongue off.'

Ramiro tells me.

'Good,' I say. Then I nod to Michelotto. He picks up the pliers and moves towards Ramiro.

DOROTEA: Damn! My cunning plan to turn the heads of every man in the room has been foiled by Cesare's half-naked Roman courtesans. But still . . . it's not going too badly. I saw the old desire flash in Niccolò's eyes when we met, and there is a long queue of men waiting to dance with me. The expression on Leonardo's face is more difficult to read. He looks . . . troubled.

I drink wine between dances, but not too much. I flirt with Niccolò in a light, ironic way, and smile, touch, talk to Leonardo. But each time I am interrupted by a male voice begging me to grant them the honour of the next dance, and to Leonardo I shrug as if to say 'What can one do?', and am swept away once more across the dancefloor. Still Leonardo doesn't ask me to dance. He just stands in the corner talking to Niccolò. Is he too shy? Should I ask him? Perhaps he needs to drink more wine?

When the next dance ends, I move towards my friends once more. Niccolò, who I can tell is already blotto, grabs three goblets from a passing servant. I propose a toast – to parties – and we all drink our wine to the bottom in one go. Three more cups, and Niccolò makes a toast: to the fairer sex. We drink the wine down again. Now it's Leonardo's turn. He proposes a toast to me. Niccolò shouts his agreement. I blush slightly; we all drink. Leonardo's eyes are on mine; they are *in* mine. The next song starts up and I take his hands. 'Aren't you going to ask me to dance?' I say.

CESARE: On the floor – two ruined gloves. On the floor – a cock and three molars. On the floor – shit and piss and snot and puke. And blood – blood everywhere.

Ramiro no longer screams. Just emits a low wail – like wind in a chimney. His eyes are white. He's all alone in a land of pain.

'Maybe we should just dump him in the square now?' I say to Michelotto. 'Let the citizens of Cesena take care of him . . .'

Ramiro snaps back to life. 'No . . .' A bloody, parched whisper. 'No . . . please.'

'But they love you so much here, Ramiro. Surely you don't think they would do you any harm?'

'Please . . . no.'

'Oh, you think maybe they remember watching you burn that child alive? Your foot on his head to stop him moving. You remember that? Remember how you forced the child's mother to watch?'

Ramiro closes his eyes. Ramiro shakes his head. 'On your . . . orders.'

'I don't think so, Ramiro. Did I ever tell you to burn children?'

'You told me . . . any means . . . necessary.'

'Yes . . . that's true. You had your uses. I recognise that. But these days you're only useful to me dead. Shall I kill you now, Ramiro? Put you out of your misery?'

Silence. Then sobbing. 'Yes.' The word pronounced with sudden precision.

'All right. We'll spare you more pain. All you have to do is tell us that one last thing. The thing you're holding back.'

Silence. Bloody breathing. The low windlike moan.

'Fuck it – Michelotto, cut him loose. Dump him in the square.'

'NO! Please . . . I'll . . . tell you.'

'I'm listening.'

And he tells me – of Vitellozzo's plan. The sniper with the crossbow. The show of friendship – the surprise assassination.

'Good,' I say. 'Michelotto, you have till dawn. See if you can get anything else out of him. I'll be back before daylight.'

DOROTEA: We dance to three fast songs, and then we take a breather and talk. Leonardo is smiling and laughing now; afterwards I will not remember what we talked about. What I will remember is his hands moving, gesticulating as he speaks, and me moving closer to hear what he says, and his fingers, his forearms, brushing my breasts, as if by accident.

At one point I notice Niccolò dancing with a prostitute: the two of them drunk and stepping on each other's feet. Leonardo and I share a glance, and laugh. A little later, I notice Cesare's entrance. Or rather, what I notice is Leonardo growing suddenly tense in my arms. I whisper in his ear: 'Relax – the duke doesn't care about me any more.'

Later still, I see Cesare kissing a young Cesenan noblewoman, and her husband watching mutely from a distance. I point the scene out to Leonardo, who nods. His face seems oddly slack, his breathing heavy. But then there is a slow song and we dance more closely together. And I know how the night will end.

LEONARDO: The air in her room smells sweet and warm – a cedar log burning in the hearth. I hear the door locked behind me and close my eyes. I have drunk too much wine tonight. She is dear to me and I was jealous when I saw her dance with all those other men, but I did not mean to lead her on. Now I feel as if I am walking fast downhill – I want to stop, go back to my room, but it is too late. *And nothing can be loved or hated unless it is first known.* But she puts her arms around me, kisses my neck, then undoes the buttons of my shirt and kisses my chest, breathes hot and rubs her teeth over my stomach. *And they will be inflamed to seek those things which are most beautiful* . . . She slides off her dress and pushes me through the curtains onto the bed. In here it is dark, the air close. I feel like a cat in a bag. She kneels astride my hips and leans over me until her breasts touch my chest and her tongue is in my mouth. . . . *in order to possess them and utilise their vilest parts.* I close my eyes, I think of Salai – Salai when he was young. And she lowers herself on to me. Tighter, hotter, softer than I imagined. For a moment all is good – the warm ecstatic colours in my eyes, like sunlight through cathedral windows. And then darkness falls, and I feel her breath, her heat, her weight, and I say I'm sorry and she says, 'No – don't be sorry, don't be sorry, my Leonardo, I love you, don't you know? Oh, I love you Leonardo, so much . . .' She stares at me, her eyes light in the darkness, her gaze hungering to penetrate my mask, to my soul, to hold me have me – *in order to possess* – and I think of the empty birdcage in my room, the door left open. Where is that bird now?

Hours pass before she finally falls asleep and I see the ashen light of dawn creep in through the gap between the bedcurtains. I free myself from her embrace and slip silently out of bed. I look out of the window – there is a small crowd gathered in the market square. They are all standing in a circle, staring at something.

I dress quickly, let myself out of the room and descend the stairs of the palace. I walk into the market square. I can hear the people's voices now – they are stallholders, but they are not setting out their wares. I see an egg on the ground – the shell smashed, the yolk broken. I hear laughter. I hear someone say, 'A Christmas gift from the duke.'

I reach the circle of bodies and say 'Excuse me.' Shoulders move aside. Faces turn towards me. I reach the front and see what they are staring at. In the centre of the square, on the bloodstained cobblestones, lies the body of a man, dressed in a scarlet cloak – his hands gloved, his head missing.

His neck rests upon a wooden block, and next to this lies an axe, the blade crimson. To the right of this a lance has been hammered into a crack in the ground. On top of the lance is the man's head. I force myself to look. Ramiro da Lorqua's double-chinned, thickly bearded face stares back at me, his lips bruised, his eyes wide open. He looks furious.

32

Cesena   *26 December, 1502*

CESARE: Oliverotto da Fermo stands by the window. His back rigid, his drink untouched. He turns quickly when I enter the room. Nervous, ratface?

He kisses my feet, he bows and scrapes. It's the first time I've seen him since the rebellion started.

I look at him – orange hair, rodent mouth. In his eyes – fear and hate. I knew him as a kid. He hated me then, he hates me now. But he's too shitscared to show it.

Oliverotto must have drawn the short straw. Vitellozzo and Paolo sent him here – into the lion's den. To see if he'd be devoured. To see if my forgiveness was real.

I smile, embrace him. Stand next to him at the window – and the two of us look out. Ramiro's body and head below us in the square. Dried blood shines in winter sunlight.

Here's another reason why he's nervous. Oliverotto was in league with Ramiro. He's afraid I've uncovered their plot – that he'll be next to lose his head.

I say: 'You heard what he did?'

'No, my lord.'

'He insulted my sister.'

He breathes out. 'Is that all?'

'What do you mean – is that all? No one insults my sister and lives.'

'Sorry, my lord. I didn't mean that. I . . .'

I clap him on the back. 'Relax, Oliverotto. I know you would never disrespect Donna Lucrezia. So tell me . . . how do things stand in Urbino?'

He gives me his report – he's a good commander. Then he gives me his message – from Vitellozzo and the Orsini.

They say: 'If you wish to invade Tuscany, give the word – we are ready to join you. If not, we will besiege Senigallia – in your name.'

I say: 'I do not wish to invade Tuscany – Florence is my friend. But Senigallia . . . yes. It would please me greatly if you captured that town.'

Senigallia is an enemy state. Ruled by the Della Rovere family. I was planning to take it anyway – but this is better. This is perfect.

Oliverotto makes bold promises. Oliverotto swears undying loyalty. Oliverotto kisses my feet. Oliverotto goes.

I call Agapito. I call Michelotto. I tell them where to send my troops. I tell them we leave today.

Sogliano al Rubicone   *27 December, 1502*

NICCOLÒ: My landlady cried when I told her I had to leave. She cried, and then she hugged me, and then she dragged me back to her bedroom for a valedictory shag. It was hours before I could get out of there, and I had to ride full pelt to catch up with the army, who'd left yesterday evening. Not that there *is* much of an army now: the duke appears to be travelling with only his personal guard, which is strange. I wonder where the rest of his troops are?

When I finally reach them, it is midday and they are near the village of Sogliano. Leonardo is supervising the installation of the portable bridge he invented in Imola. I ride up and say hello to him. He seems a little distant. I ask if

298

he's seen Donna Dorotea and he shakes his head. Then the duke rides over to me. Smiling, he asks if I know the name of the river we are about to cross.

'No, my lord.'

'This is the Rubicon, Niccolò. I am going to cross the Rubicon.'

I could point out to him that this is not actually the same river which Caesar crossed fifteen hundred years ago, and that – even if it were – the duke's action would carry none of the same meaning, as it no longer marks the border of any significant territory. But he probably knows all this and doesn't care. And if he doesn't know . . . well, *I* don't want to be the one who has to tell him.

Pesaro   *28 December, 1502*

DOROTEA: I am the happiest and the saddest person alive. What happened with Leonardo on Christmas night fulfilled all my hopes and desires, and it will stay with me for ever. But by the time I woke the next day, he was gone . . . and I haven't seen him since. Is it possible the duke has had him arrested?

The guards came to my room on Christmas morning, just after I'd woken. They told me to dress and pack quickly. Then I was taken to a cell in a tower of the castle, where I watched the colour of the sky change from white to black through the high, narrow window. I expected to hear the key turn in the lock that night: the signal that I was to be taken to my execution or (my greatest fear) the torture chamber. But there was no sound until the next morning, when I was escorted instead to a waiting carriage with blacked-out windows.

During the journey that followed, I had many thoughts: of my life and death, of my childhood and parents, of lost friends and lovers, and odd, forgotten incidents from the past . . . but mostly I thought of Leonardo. I remembered all our moments together; I daydreamed of a future which may never exist; of Leonardo's seed in my womb; of our child. That brought me hope, quickly followed by despair: if I *am* pregnant by Leonardo, his son or daughter will be killed with me. In the end, it was the memory of his face, his voice, his presence that soothed me in those uncertain hours. At least I have known love, I told myself; no matter what happens now, at least I've *lived.*

These thoughts soothe me still, as I sit on the bed in another anonymous room – this time in a palace in Pesaro, or so I am told by the serving girl who brings me food. I asked her how many nights I was supposed to stay here, but she only shrugged. Afterwards I realised what a pointless question it was: I live by the hour now, not by the day.

Fano   *29 December, 1502*

LEONARDO: Another night, another palace. Well, you always wanted to travel, Leonardo – and now you're doing it. But . . . this isn't what I had in mind. During daylight hours we ride through the barren winter landscape of Romagna. Each evening, I wait to be assigned a room in another hastily evacuated mansion while Tommaso scours the town for something to eat. We see nothing of interest, we speak to no one but each other. Travel broadens the mind, they say, but I feel it is dulling mine – turning it blank and fuzzy.

Outside it is dark and snowflakes float gently through the air. I sit on the bed and try to read Archimedes, but I can't take anything in. I put the book aside and lie back on the bed, wondering what has happened to Dorotea – did I somehow wish her out of existence? There is relief in her absence, but I miss her as a friend. I miss Niccolò too – I have seen so little of him lately.

There is a loud knock at the door. 'Come in,' I say, feeling too tired to sit up.

Don Michelotto fills the doorway. His scar smirks at me. 'His lordship wishes to see you now, maestro.'

'Of course,' I say, not without a slight surge of fear.

his head on the lance, lips bruised, eyes wide open

I follow Don Michelotto downstairs, outside, and through the silent town to another, larger building.

The duke smiles when he sees me – not his usual smile of charm to put you at your ease, but a simple reflection of the pleasure he feels at getting something he wanted. I am that something. He invites me to sit down, offers me wine, asks me how I am, but before I have had a chance to respond, he says, 'Senigallia. You went there in the summer, didn't you?'

This sounds like an accusation. 'Yes, my lord. You asked me to inspect the fortress. Is there something wrong?'

'Nothing wrong at all, Leonardo. Did you happen to make a map of the town?'

'I didn't have time to make a map, my lord . . .'

His expression darkens.

'. . . but I did make a few sketches. I have them with me – in this notebook.'

'Show me.'

I open the little blue notebook that has spent the last six months hanging from my belt and find the pages I filled in Senigallia. 'They're only rough sketches, I'm afraid, but I could copy them out for you.'

'Yes please.'

'Er . . . now?'

'Yes, now. Why, is there a problem?'

'Well, it's just that I haven't eaten yet. Could I . . .'

'My dear Leonardo!' He beams suddenly. 'You shall eat with me this evening. I will instruct the cook to do something without meat. Now, if you will kindly copy those sketches for me . . . I need to know how many gates the town has, and where each is located. I need to know the layout of the main street, and the location of the Borgo in relation to the castle. Do you think you can manage that?'

I look at my sketches – only a few simple strokes of charcoal. So I close my eyes and remember the town. It was a pretty place – a hot day. Salai and I had spent the night together in a guesthouse overlooking the beach. I see the castle, the moat, the houses and shops near the southern gate. I see Salai laughing, hear bees in someone's garden, smell the salt air carried on the breeze. I remember being happy.

'Yes, my lord,' I say. 'I'm sure I can.'

I do not ask what it is for. It is better not to know.

Senigallia   *30 December, 1502*

VITELLOZZO: The messenger reads out Borgia's letter. It takes me an effort of will not to punch the air. Yes – he is coming tomorrow morning. And yes – my spy has confirmed that he is marching not with an army but only a small personal guard. The fool! He is walking into the trap that I have set. Soon I will tighten my fist around him and . . .

But I can't let my triumph show now: not in front of Borgia's messenger. Not in front of Donna Paolo and his cousin. So I just listen while the detailed orders are given: all troops with the exception of Oliverotto's to be withdrawn from the town; all gates to be locked except for the northern gate; my troops to be moved down the coast and into the hills in preparation for the march south to take Ancona.

An expression of unease crosses Oliverotto's face while these conditions are announced, but I tell the messenger I accept – and Donna Paolo does the same. Oliverotto can hardly refuse after that. As soon as the messenger has gone he takes me aside and whispers: 'What the hell was all that about? We're leaving ourselves undefended.'

'What else would you do, Oliverotto? If we'd shown any suspicion he'd have started suspecting *us*. And anyway, for one thing he only has a small number of soldiers with him. And for another thing he'll be dead as soon as he sets foot in Senigallia so it won't make any bloody difference where our troops are. You think Borgia's men will continue to fight for him after he's dead?'

He snarls at me: 'I *think* that plans can go wrong.'

'This one won't go wrong.'

'What if your sniper misses?' he shouts. 'Have you thought about that?'

I grab his throat. His face turns red. 'Keep your bloody voice down!' I yell. He pushes me. For a second there's the crackle of violence in the air . . . and then it's gone. I laugh.

'What's funny?'

I say: 'Look at us. We're so bloody nervous: like a pair of virgins at their first ball. Let's have a few drinks and relax. It's going to be fine.'

'A pair of virgins my arse!' Oliverotto hisses. 'The difference is, Vitellozzo, that I don't *want* to get fucked.'

near Fano

CESARE: The sun's a silver disc in the west. The sea's a silver gleam in the east. Hoofclatter and breathsteam – the messenger arrives.

He gives me good news. I give him gold ducats. I send six more messengers – to the captains of my armies, hidden in the hills. I tell them – meet me at dawn, by the River Metauro.

I call Michelotto. I give him a message – to take to Vitellozzo. The message says nothing – it's just fancy words. But it gets Michelotto inside the town. There, he has duties – things he must do.

I call my commanders. I tell them the plan. I say – you are the only ones who know. No one else. If the plan succeeds – a thousand ducats each. If the plan fails – you all die.

The sun sets behind the mountains. The sea fades to black. The torches are lit.

I can't sleep. I can't sit still. I walk through the camp, envisaging my triumph. Tasting the glory in my mouth.

I see Machiavelli – shivering by a campfire. I tell him: 'I have crossed the Rubicon, but that was nothing. Now for an act worthy of a true Roman.'

He frowns – he has no idea what I'm talking about. I laugh. 'You'll see tomorrow, Niccolò. The whole world will see tomorrow.'

I said it all along – this is my year. And the year is not yet over.

33

near Senigallia   *31 December, 1502*

CESARE: To our right – the stilldark mountains. To our left
– the silver sea. Before us – Senigallia. Behind us – fifteen
thousand men. They met us at the river two hours ago.

I wear chainmail and a breastplate. I wear a helmet, I carry
a sword. I am surrounded by my bodyguard. Crimson silk and
cloth of gold – CAESAR emblazoned on their shoulders.

We move along the Via Emilia – my army magnificent in
the dawnlight. Black bulls on banners. Red and gold shine
against fields of white frost.

We march to the beat of drummers. We march in perfect
symmetry. Ahead of us, my captains wait.

They must be shitscared.

VITELLOZZO: I hold my cloak tight against my body but it
does not stop me shivering. A vast army marches behind
the duke. What the hell happened to his small personal
guard? Is this some cruel deception? But I say nothing: I
do not let my fear show. This is the decisive moment. I ride
a mule and I am unarmed. Now I must take the greatest
risk of my life: to greet my enemy as a friend. To make him
believe that he is so mighty and I so humble. To lead him
smiling through the gates of the town . . . to his death.

Beside me Donna Paolo laughs with his page, but I bet
he's just as nervous as I am beneath his bravado. Unless
he's cut some deal with . . .

Bugger it! It's too late for such thoughts now. Borgia is here before me. I ride towards him then dismount. I remove my cap and hold it in my hand. My other hand I hold out in friendship.

Borgia is armed. Even his neck is covered with chainmail. Christ's blood – what if he . . . ?

But no – he's dismounting now. He takes off his helmet and passes it to his page. He walks towards me. He removes his gauntlet and puts his hand on mine. He says my name. We embrace. I tense because I'm half-expecting a dagger in my back but nothing happens. The duke tells me how glad he is to see me again – how glad that we are friends and that the great misunderstanding is finally behind us. I echo his words and watch as he greets Donna Paolo in the same way. And I exhale with relief.

CESARE: I embrace them and I frisk them. I feel a dagger under Vitellozzo's cloak. Paolo is unarmed. Vitellozzo looks worried, Paolo smug. I scan the horizon – no snipers here.

I ask them where Oliverotto is. They say he's in the Borgo – the slumtown outside the walls. Him and a thousand men. I tell Michelotto to bring him here.

We wait and we talk. We talk and we laugh. We are all friends together. I wipe away a tear of joy.

When Oliverotto arrives, I embrace him. His face is gaunt, his body wooden. Nervous, ratface?

We mount our horses and ride towards town. I ride beside Vitellozzo. Me on my horse, him on his mule. He has to crane his thick neck up to look at me.

I stare in his eyes and see treachery. I see a sniper aiming a crossbow at my throat. I see hope battling fear – hope winning.

But not for long, Vitellozzo. Not for long.

VITELLOZZO: Afterwards, I will remember hardly anything we talked about as we rode towards Senigallia. Did the duke ask me about the French disease? He's suffered from it himself. Did I ask about our plans after Camerino? I've got no idea.

The truth is I am talking automatically now: not even thinking about what I'm saying. My thoughts are elsewhere: they are flying ahead to when we reach Senigallia. Over the bridge and into the Borgo. Round to the left and through the town gate. Up the main street and there – from the first-floor window of a corner house I've rented – will come the ultimate surprise welcome. A crossbow bolt between the eyes. Borgia will fall and all hell will break loose. I'll dismount and go over to him – the loyal captain heartbroken by the death of his commander. And I'll make sure the bastard's truly dead – with a dagger in the ear if necessary. After that it'll be a question of staying alive and getting inside the castle. Borgia's personal guard will be there but so will Oliverotto's men. Let them fight it out between them: I'll take Borgia's horse and ride to safety. It won't be easy – I know that. I'm taking a huge bloody risk. But the rewards . . .

I smile up at the duke who rides high beside me. I can tell from the complacent look in his eyes that he doesn't have a clue. The fool hasn't even put his helmet back on. He looks like a man on his way to a ball. And so he is. But this time he will dance with Death.

LEONARDO: To my relief, the Borgo and the town are as I remembered them – and as I drew them for the duke. The streets are thick with frozen mud which cracks under the horses' hooves, splashing up their forelegs. Poor Caterina – I must buy wine and oil to wash her coat and soak her hooves tonight.

We cross the bridge into the Borgo (I am in the train behind the duke and his captains) watched by rows of cheering commoners, to whom the duke's servants throw silver coins. There is a flourish of drums and trumpets, and ahead of us the cavalry execute a difficult manoeuvre in which they split into two columns and wheel round to face each other. A funereal drumbeat begins, and the crowd goes silent. They sense that something is going to happen.

We pass between the two rows of soldiers and I look from side to side at the gleaming armour, the drawn swords, the soldiers' breath steaming in the winter sunlight. I do not know the precise purpose of this move, or of the maps of the town that I made for Valentino, but I do know that I'm starting to get an ominous feeling about what will happen next. Perhaps all is not as friendly between the duke and his captains as it appears from their manner and their conversation.

lips bruised, eyes open

I glance behind me at Tommaso, but his gaze is fixed on the ground. Idly I wish I had accepted the duke's offer to borrow some armour.

VITELLOZZO: The drumbeat's slow and steady but my heartbeat's getting faster. My hands are sweating inside their gloves. If the cavalry forms another guard of honour inside the gate my sniper won't be able to get a clear shot. Why the hell didn't I think about this?

But we go through the gate and . . . it's all right. The street here's too narrow for a guard of honour. We go along the main street. The windows are all filled with faces: cheering and frightened and curious. I look up at the first-floor window on the corner house: it's open but I can't see anything inside. No face. No silhouette. No movement.

Come on – where the hell are you?

Borgia says something.

'I beg your pardon my lord. What did you say?'

'I just asked if you were searching for someone in particular?'

A cold fist round my heart. HE KNOWS.

I turn my face upwards to see him smiling down at me
and then I look back up to the window. Please let the sniper
be there. Please release the bolt. Put it through this bastard's grinning face!

But the window is empty.

Borgia says: 'You look like you could do with a drink
Vitellozzo.' He raises his voice: 'Come with me all of you
– I know a good place. We can celebrate our renewed alli-
ance.'

I glance round at Oliverotto. His eyes scream at me –
silent and fearful. Donna Paolo says something about having business to attend to and I begin to make my excuses
too but the duke cuts us both off: 'I insist. You would
offend me if you refused my offer. And besides I have some
urgent business of my own about which I must confer
with you.'

Donna Paolo bows his head. 'Then of course, my lord.'

I look for an escape route. That scarfaced bastard
Michelotto blocks my path. He grins sardonically at me.
How I wish I'd killed him at Calmazzo . . .

The others are dismounting now. I have no choice. One
false move and I'm a dead man. And perhaps after all the
sniper simply lost his nerve? Perhaps the duke really does
just want a drink? My hands shake as I let myself down from
the mule.

I follow Borgia through an arched gateway into the
courtyard of a palace. What is this place? How does the

duke even know of it? He hasn't been to Senigallia before – as far as I know.

I have a knife hidden under my cloak. I could stab the duke in the back with it now. But he is wearing full armour. And Michelotto walks just behind me – I can hear him breathing. I let my hands hang by my sides and keep walking.

CESARE: We go through the courtyard. We climb the stairs. Michelotto has done a good job – the sniper is dead and this place is perfect.

We enter the salon. The long curtains closed. The fire lit. The table set for four.

We sit down in our places – Vitellozzo and Oliverotto one side, Paolo the other. I take the far end. Michelotto guards the door.

I order wine, I order food. I eat and I drink. The others stare at their plates.

'Gentlemen,' I say. 'Aren't you hungry? Surely you don't think I would try to poison you?'

Ha ha ha. Their laughter forced, tense. They can't wait to get out of here.

Nervous, ratface? Nervous, Paolo? Nervous, Vitellozzo? Good – you fucking should be.

I look at their faces, one by one. Lying eyes, mean mouths. Their fingers white on the bloodred tablecloth.

They betrayed me. They would have killed me, stolen my empire.

I stand up, make a speech: 'I am grateful that you have taken this town in my name. I am also relieved that we have made the peace between us. You are all great soldiers – and I sleep more soundly knowing that you are my friends, not my enemies.'

I make a toast. 'To the future – may it be glorious.'

They echo my words: 'The glorious future.' None of them believe what they're saying.

I smile at them, one by one. I do not even glance at the curtains.

I look at Michelotto. He nods.

'Gentlemen,' I say, 'Nature calls, so I must leave you for a moment. But I will be back soon.'

I stand up – walk to the door. Michelotto lets me through. The door closes behind me. I descend the stone stairway.

I hear the quick thunder of footsteps. I hear swords drawn, voices raised. I do not break my stride.

VITELLOZZO: So I wasn't going mad. All that time I was *right* to be afraid. Just as in all my dreams and nightmares there are men behind the curtains. I watch them slide the dark velvet back and I see their blades flash in the gloom. Donna Paolo cries out like a woman: 'But you *promised* Cesare! You gave me your word!' Oliverotto swears. I stand up and grab the knife from my cloak. I stab the first of the guards who moves towards me: the sound of wounded flesh and the grimace of pain. I start to yell that I will kill them all, but before the words are even out of my mouth my arms are pinned behind my back and my knife clatters and spins on the floor. I smell Michelotto's garlic breath and hear his Spaniard's voice sneering in my ear: 'Vitellozzo Vitelli – your treachery is foiled. You are the duke's prisoner now. I promise you death will come as a relief.'

NICCOLÒ: I had a lie-in this morning: partly because I was tired, but mainly because I didn't want to enter Senigallia at the same time as the duke's troops. It is always chaos when fifteen thousand soldiers descend on a small town, and I was hoping that, leaving a few hours later, things might have settled down by the time I got there. Even before I reach the town, however, it is obvious I miscalculated.

Hundreds of people are leaving Senigallia as I ride towards it: an old man in tears, pushing a wheelbarrow filled with blankets and cutlery; children clinging to their parents' legs; a dog with its tail cut off, limping and leaking blood along the Via Emilia. Everyone says: it's hell in there. Everyone says: the soldiers are devils. Then they look fearful as they suddenly wonder who it is they're talking to.

Even these dire warnings do not fully prepare me. I have heard and read descriptions of towns being sacked before, but I have never seen it with my own eyes. What happened in Cesena and Imola was a tea-party compared to this. I'm not going to write a list of all the horrors I witness. As soon as you put them on paper, they just sound commonplace: exactly the kind of thing you always read and hear about. Yes, I saw a man get a swordblade in the face. Yes, I saw a woman being raped. Yes, I saw a child on fire. Yes, I saw all of this, but I didn't hang around to observe lots of interesting details – I just kept riding, half-suffocating in the pall of smoke and trying not to meet the eyes of anyone carrying a weapon.

It's inevitable, I suppose, this slaughter. These men, whose occupation is terror and violence and death, who have been drilled to do maximum harm to the enemy, have reached this victory without spilling a single drop of blood. It has been too easy, too dull, too unprofitable. This is their reward for all those months of waiting. It sickens me, watching it happen, but I can understand the logic of it. It's a tactical atrocity.

In the midst of the carnage and mayhem, I hear my name called. Stiff with dread, I slowly turn around – and see the duke on horseback. Grinning, he tells me that Vitellozzo, Oliverotto and the Orsini are his prisoners. 'I thought you in particular, Niccolò, would be pleased to know that Vitellozzo will soon have breathed his last.' I nod and thank him, as graciously as I can with all the screaming and burning and killing that's going on around us.

'I wanted to tell you this yesterday morning,' the duke adds, 'but I couldn't give the secret away.' I remember now, his strange hint: *an act worthy of a true Roman.* So this was what he meant?

The duke orders one of his bodyguards to escort me into the walled town, where the streets are safer. 'I will call for you tonight, Niccolò,' he says, 'and tell you the whole story. It is a tale worth hearing, believe me.' I don't think I have ever seen his lordship in such a happy, benevolent mood.

I follow the soldier through the northern gate and then ride through the town alone until I find somebody willing to put me up for the night. In a cramped and dusty storeroom, I dump my bags and write a short letter to the Signoria:

> It is now an hour before sunset, and the greatest turmoil prevails. I am extremely worried. I don't even know if I'll be able to find a messenger to take you this letter. I shall write more fully in my next message, but in my opinion the prisoners will not be alive tomorrow.

LEONARDO: I leave the town and walk to the beach. It is a bright afternoon, quite warm in the sun, although the breeze has an icy edge to it. I take off my shoes and hose and feel the fine sand between my toes. I cannot hear the noises of the town from here. Staring out at the calm blue-grey sea and sky, the horizon between them almost invisible, I think of the countless centuries through which the waves have been breaking, gently, on this coastline, slowly turning great rocks into this soft pale dust. Next to all of that, what am I? What are any of us? Each a mere grain of sand in a beach far wider and longer than we can ever imagine – all of us destined, one day, to be reclaimed by the sea that made us.

To pass the time and to satisfy my curiosity, I count the intervals between waves, noting down the numbers of seconds. When I look through the list afterwards, I do not find any pattern at all. This is, almost certainly, because I did not conduct the experiment for long enough. Or because I was distracted, and miscounted the seconds. There is no reason to think that nature would descend into chaos simply because humanity is doing so.

the horror beneath

The wind blows cold and I shiver. I do not feel well.

I walk a weaving line, just out of reach of the slowly encroaching waves. Beneath my feet are thousands of shells. Some I crush, unthinking. Others I pick up, examine, sketch, caress, and then discard. Only one do I keep. I choose it on a whim – for no particular reason at all.

There are some fishing boats in the water – silhouettes in the distance. Perhaps the men on board those boats do not know what is happening inside the city walls? Or perhaps, like me, they know only too well.

where is Dorotea? I dare not ask

I go back into town as the light begins to fade. The smoke has cleared, and all is quiet. By chance, I see Tommaso walking through the muddy, deserted Borgo. He tells me he has found us a room for the night, and shows me the food he has procured for our supper – bread, cabbage, eggs, wine. I ask him how much he paid – I will give him the money. He says, 'I didn't pay anything. The shop-keepers weren't around.'

His face is grim.

'Everything seems calm now,' I observe.

Tommaso says, 'The dead don't scream.'

DOROTEA: It is night-time now. Earlier today, I closed the shutters in a vain attempt to silence the noises that came from below. Now I open them so I can listen to the sea. I feel both relieved and bereft: my monthly blood came this morning. I stand at the window for a minute or so, breath-ing the salty air and staring out over the black rooftops, but then the cold grows unbearable so I close the shutters again and lie on the bed, under the blankets, trying to get warm.

An hour later, the servant asks if I would like to attend midnight mass. The master of the house is very godly and thinks it wrong that anyone, even a prisoner, should be denied the chance of communing with the Lord. I have not been to church since I was a girl but I say yes straight away, grateful for even the slightest hint of freedom.

I walk to the church behind the family and in front of the servants, accompanied by two of Cesare's guards. The town is silent, except for the groaning of the wounded in the hospital that we pass and the snoring of drunken sol-diers slumped in doorways and on benches.

The last time I went to church was in Urbino, and there the nave was always filled with prostitutes and gossips and moneylenders. Here, however, there is no one: only a cou-ple of confession boxes, through the doors of which I can hear the ghostly, wordless murmur of sins. I think of all I could confess and have a sudden urge to do just that, but no . . . I'd be here all night. So I follow the family into a row of pews near the back of the church and am amazed to see that nearly every row before us is full. Are the people of Senigallia really so devout?

The truth only dawns on me when, in the middle of the Latin mass, people begin to sob. Then the priest says something about 'our losses' and I understand: we are here to mourn the recently departed; we are here to pray for their souls. I close my eyes and kneel. I pray for the ghostchild that I lost today, and plead with God not to let its father die. 'If you will only let Leonardo live, Lord,' I whisper, 'I will devote myself entirely to your worship and will never ask anything of you again.'

When I open my eyes, the crucifix on the altar shines with a strange and dazzling light. A halo seems to hover above the silver Christ's head. I wonder if my prayer has been answered.

34

CESARE: The church bell tolls, a dozen times. The year has ended – in blood and triumph. *Annus mirabilis.* The year has ended – and I have won.

I dismiss my gentlemen. I tell them – go get drunk. I tell them – go fuck whores. They beg me to go with them, but I say no. I have work to do.

I am thinking ahead – always ahead. I send messengers to Rome, Florence, Venice, France. I send messengers to Mantua, Ferrara, Perugia, Bologna.

The messages say – the traitors are captured. The messages say – they planned to kill me. The messages say – DON'T FUCK WITH THE BORGIA.

I summon Machiavelli. I tell him the whole story. He congratulates me. 'It was artfully done, my lord,' he says. 'A most beautiful deception.'

'I told you I would show them, Niccolò – our enemies. Mine are captured, and yours confounded. And now the Signoria has seen how I treat my enemies . . . perhaps they will prefer to be my friends?'

When the envoy's gone, I move to the window. I stare out at the world – vast and invisible, waiting to be conquered.

I feel like a god. I feel like Caesar. I feel like I am standing on the peak of a mountain.

I go to the castle. Down to the dungeons. Paolo sees me. He rattles the bars. Screeches: 'You gave me your word!'

I stand close to his cell. Put a finger to my lips. Draw a finger across my throat. He shuts the fuck up.

I go to see Vitellozzo. Tearstreaks in the torchlight. He begs: 'Let me see the pope. Let your father grant me indulgence for my sins.'

I laugh. 'I never knew you were religious, Vitellozzo. Michelotto, did you know Vitellozzo was religious?'

Michelotto shakes his head. 'I knew he was a pussy though.'

He gets out his razor. He gets out his poker. He gets out his pliers and hammer and nails.

I say: 'Give me your list of names, Vitellozzo.'

He looks at me blankly.

'The names of the soon-to-be-dead. That you keep in your cloak pocket.'

He looks sad. He hands me the piece of paper.

I see Machiavelli's name. I see Soderini's name. I see my own name. I smile. I write – 'Vitellozzo Vitelli'. I cross it out. I hand him back the list.

'Read it,' I say.

He reads it.

'You're a lucky man, Vitellozzo. You've just done something very few men ever do. You've seen into the future.'

VITELLOZZO: 'Even in defeat you will still be victorious.' The words of my brother spoken in a dream come back to me now – in this grim dungeon that stinks of blood and piss and death. The world is grey and cold as it has been since Paolo's death but soon I will leave it and enter another world: a fairer and more beautiful world. I will be reunited with my brother once again and I will leave behind the Hell that this world has become.

I have not always been a good man – I have done evil things in my life. But I am a better man than he who will soon have me put to death. He seemed surprised that I did not scream or plead for mercy when his scarfaced torturer began slicing up my flesh. I doubt Borgia himself would have lasted two minutes of such pain. But in the end my courage will count for nothing.

He taunts me now: 'It doesn't matter how bravely you act, Vitellozzo – history is written by the victors. I'll tell them you were a coward and they'll believe me. I'll say you wept like a woman and begged my forgiveness. I'll have your wife and children killed of course and I'll take control of your town. Nothing will remain of you but your name which will be a mere footnote to my own story. Fool. Coward. Traitor. Loser. That's how you'll be remembered.'

I say nothing. There is nothing to be said.

Oliverotto is dragged into my cell and he immediately begins blaming me for his involvement in the conspiracy. He says it was all my idea – that he argued against it from the start. I shake my head and sigh. Doesn't he realise that this is what Borgia wants? For us to turn on each other and humiliate ourselves. 'For God's sake!' I say. 'Let's just get it over with.'

Borgia says: 'Yes – let's. I have much business to attend to. Michelotto? Dispatch the traitors, please.'

I am shoved onto a chair – back to back with Oliverotto. Michelotto ties us together then loops the ligature round both our necks. I can feel Oliverotto trembling. I can hear him weeping. But *I* do not tremble nor do I bloody weep. Tears come to my eyes when I think of my children who will soon be exterminated by this monster but I do not wish to give him the satisfaction of seeing my weakness so I think instead about my brother Paolo looking down at me from heaven. How proud he is and how noble! How colourful the sky and the clouds and the angels are up there! The leather strap tightens under my Adam's apple and the thug inserts the lynchpin. Oliverotto grunts with panic and jerks the chair up and down. I can feel his skin hot and slick with sweat at the back of my neck. I will be with you soon Paolo – with you in a land where there is justice at last and all the monsters have been slain and only the good survive. I can't breathe. The veins in my hands look like snakes. I am sorry I never revenged myself on your killers my brother but . . . 'It doesn't matter,' he whispers. 'Your victory is at hand.' I stare at the bloodstained wall. Then the wall fades and I see a glorious light shine in a thousand colours.

CESARE: Their faces turn black. Their tongues swell up. Their eyeballs pop and shitstink fouls the air. Michelotto slices open Vitellozzo's chest – rips out his beating heart and shows it to him. Spits in his eyes as the light of life dies. Now THAT's how to fucking kill somebody.

He unties the ligature. Throws the lumps of flesh to the floor. In Spanish I say: 'Burn the bodies. Display the heads.'

Michelotto nods. He sharpens his axe. 'And Orsini?'

'Save him for another day,' I say. 'You don't want to open all your presents in one go.' He grins and I leave the dungeon.

On the way I pass Donna Paolo. He looks up from his filth and his tears. Hope in his eyes. 'Cesare,' he whispers.

'Paolo,' I say – and smile. 'Your strategy was flawed. I think you'll find this is checkmate.'

He howls as I go upstairs to the palace.

Alone in blackness, happy in triumph, I fall asleep – and dream of Lucrezia.

In my dream we are together. Naked in bed. The bed is at the top of a mountain – above the clouds. Up there, no one disturbs us. We are King and Queen of the World. We kiss. We make love. In the dream this does not feel wrong.

I wake up, a bitter taste in my mouth. I open the shutters, look out the window. Sleet drives down. Everything's grey.

In my mind's eye, I see the dream mountain. The peak somewhere up in the clouds. You're not there yet, Cesare. Still a long way to go. Still much work to be done.

I go outside. I inspect my troops. I study maps, I give orders. At noon we march.

Five miles outside Senigallia, a messenger arrives. A man from Mantua, bearing gifts and a perfumed letter. I read the letter – from the marchioness. She says:

> We send you a hundred carnival masks because we believe that after the strains and fatigues which you have undergone in these your glorious undertakings, you should also find time to amuse yourself blah blah blah . . .

I smile – fancy words. I look at the messenger – a spy, no doubt. I examine the masks, one by one. White ceramic, each face different.

This one looks like bullnecked Vitellozzo, that one like ratfaced Oliverotto. I think of my victims – their dead eyeless faces in my hands.

I choose the blankest mask of all – and fasten it to my face. The mask of death. Its empty lips curled in a smile.

My face will be dead and eyeless too one day. My fate will be that of my victims. But first I must triumph, make myself immortal. I must reach the mountain peak – before death reaches me.

All around me, people bow and scrape. Envoys and poets – they sing my praises, kiss my feet. They say I am at the zenith of my power. They say I've triumphed, true glory is mine.

They don't have a fucking clue.

You think this is glory? You think this is triumph? This is NOTHING to what will happen in the future. This isn't the end – it's just the beginning.

I spur my horse forward. We march into driving sleet.

35

LEONARDO: The greater the darkness into which the pupil goes, the more its size increases, and this increase makes the darkness seem less. In the same way, our eyes adjust to evil – they grow used to it, they learn to see through it. But I am beginning to wish that I couldn't. For the first time in my life, I am beginning to wish that I were blind.

Today we march on a small hilltop town called Santa Quirica. It is a dry morning, the sky low and turbid. The countryside around is beautiful – or would be, were it not for the bleakness of the season and the clouds of smoke and the stench of death and the howls of mourning that this army leaves behind in its wake, ruining everything.

I have not seen the duke, except from a distance, for several days now. The last time was in Perugia, when he called me to his room in the palace and, after studying the maps I brought him, said that he had someone who wished to see me. Then he rang a bell and watched as Dorotea entered through the door at the room's far end and walked up to me, smiling and tearful. She held my hands, speechless.

an absolute invincible unconditional love, like that which a

'I am very glad to see you,' I murmured.

This was true, in a way. I felt relieved that she was still alive, but also guilty, confused, fearful, embarrassed. I glanced sideways at the duke, who bowed sarcastically and said, 'Well, I will leave you two lovebirds to each other for a moment.'

When he was gone, I began to stutter an apology, staring at the floor as I spoke. I wished to say how sorry I was that I had fled her room secretly that night, that I had not even once dared to ask where she had gone afterwards, but before I could express any of this, she put her finger to my lips and said 'Shhh . . . you do not have to say sorry for anything, Leonardo. You are alive – my prayers were answered. Nothing else matters.'

I looked at her face and was astonished by the way she smiled at me. As though she knew and forgave everything. As though (and this was a particularly strange, inexplicable thought on my part) she were already dead, and were speaking to me from the next world – through veils of mist, amid clouds of grace and wonder.

She did not say anything else. I held her – awkwardly at first, and then with relief and comfort. I stroked her hair. I kissed her forehead. I let the tears flow down my cheeks. Somehow I knew that I would never see her again.

'Thank you,' I whispered.

'For what?'

'For everything you have given me.'

'It was my pleasure,' she smiled. 'Truly.'

Soon, too soon, the door opened and the duke reappeared. He stood with his arms crossed, watching us mockingly. I tensed with anger, but Dorotea calmed me. 'He can't hurt us now, Leonardo.'

Still smiling, she let go of me and walked away – out of the room, out of my life.

When she was gone, I looked at the duke. 'You won't . . .'

'Have her killed?' He looked amused and bitter at the same time. 'No – there's no need. Where she is going, she can do me no harm.'

'Where is she going?'

'Donna Dorotea has decided to join a nunnery,' he said, with a sneer.

And that was the last time I spoke to the duke.

Santa Quirica, by the time I reach it, is already on fire. Most of the inhabitants, it would seem, fled long ago. The church bell is ringing so loudly that the few screams of agony are barely audible.

I ride, with Tommaso, to the church, and look up at the great bell which makes this sound. It is at least ten braccia in diameter. I open my notebook and sketch it, then make a note to myself to remember the way it moves and how its clapper is fastened. I say something about the bell to Tommaso, but he just looks away from me, silent. He has asked me several times now for permission to return to Florence. Each time I replied that I needed his assistance here. I regret this now – I should have let him go.

'Look!' Tommaso cries suddenly. 'Look what they are doing to that old woman!'

I glance over to where he is staring. I see an old peasant woman, her arms tied to a tree branch above her head, her bare feet hanging above a campfire that the soldiers are stoking with wood. The flames lick her soles. Her mouth is open. But I can't hear her scream – all I can hear is the sound of the great bell.

I look away. I look back at the church.

Tommaso urges his mule a few feet closer to where the woman is hanging. 'Oh my God – *look!*' he yells. 'They are pricking her feet so that the fat drips onto the fire!'

I close my eyes. 'I can't look,' I whisper.

'But master – this is your work now!' Tommaso taunts me. 'This is what you do! This is what you're paid for!'

'Please . . . stop, Tommaso. Stop torturing me.'

325

'I am not torturing you! *They* are torturing *her*! Can't you see the difference?'

I close my eyes tighter and listen to the bell. Then the bell stops ringing, and I can hear the woman's screaming.

After some time, the screaming stops.

pull away his mask and see the

'She's dead now,' Tommaso reports. 'They're cutting her down. They wanted to find some treasure, and they thought she might know where it was hidden. Apparently she didn't know anything. They tortured and killed her for nothing.'

horror beneath

I ride my horse away from the town square, away from Tommaso, past smouldering ruins, over rivers of spilt wine, through warm fogs of ash. I try to remember the precise curve of Dorotea's smile, but already it is fading from my memory. Eventually I hear the hoofbeats of Tommaso's mule. I turn to my friend and say, 'You have my permission. You may return to Florence tomorrow.'

He nods his thanks. 'And you, master?'

'I will try to find a way out of here.'

23 January, 1503

NICCOLÒ: Oh bliss! Another abandoned village to add to the duke's ever-growing list of conquests! Another night spent lying top to toe with some stinking poet in a freezing cold haybarn, never quite daring to fall asleep in case one of the roaming drunken soldiers sets fire to your new home! I am heartily sick of following Valentino's army around, so it is with great joy that I greet the arrival, today, of the Florentine ambassador, Jacopo Saltieri, who has come to replace me and thus allow me, tomorrow morning, to leave. He will

326

negotiate an alliance with the duke, while I return, at last, to my beloved hometown.

As soon as I have debriefed Saltieri, I go to see Leonardo. It is just past lunchtime when I set out, and evening when I eventually find him – alone, in a small, half-ruined farmhouse out in the fields about a mile from the village. He has lit a fire and is sitting on a bench close to it, squinting through the gloom and the woodsmoke in a brave attempt to read a book. By his own standards he is in a somewhat dishevelled state – ash smudges on his cuffs; his face darkened by two or three days without shaving – but compared to most of the dregs of humanity with whom we travel, he looks a strange and splendid creature in his violet tunic and emerald hose: like a peacock surrounded by mud-covered pigs.

A look of alarm crosses his face when he hears me enter the room, but then he sees who it is and smiles. 'Ah, Niccolò . . . I did not think anyone would find me in this isolated place. But I am very glad that, of all the people who might have found me, you were the one who did.'

I laugh, unsure whether this is really much of a compliment, and then tell Leonardo my good news. He embraces me and offers me wine, and the two of us sit together on the bench before the small fire. 'I am very happy for your sake, Niccolò. I know how glad you will be to get home. But I must confess, I will miss your presence here. There is really no one else with whom I feel able to talk.'

This reminds me of a worry that has been nagging at the back of my mind for some time now. 'Do you have any idea what's happened to Dorotea?'

'Ah . . . yes.' Bizarrely, Leonardo looks guilty. 'I saw her, briefly, about a week ago.'

'Oh. And is she all right?'

327

'She seemed fine. Very well, in fact. She has decided to enter the sisterhood.'

'What?' I laugh, and think of her thighs rubbing against mine. 'Dorotea? A *nun*! That's the most ridiculous thing I ever heard!'

'More ridiculous than a peace-loving artist working for a violent tyrant?' He looks at me for a second, and then his eyes flick away, distressed. 'I'm sorry if I've been distant recently, Niccolò. It was nothing personal, I assure you. Your friendship has been one of my few consolations in these last few months.'

'You've just got too close to the flame,' I say. 'The duke is the kind of man best admired from a distance.'

'I am afraid I would no longer admire him even from the other side of the ocean. Though it would certainly be a more bearable situation than remaining here in his orbit.'

I smile. Leonardo is a typical sensitive-artist type. He sees only the evil means, not the virtuous ends. 'Borgia is the greatest leader Italy has produced since Lorenzo the Magnificent,' I declare. It is the first time I have said this out loud; it sounds good, feels true.

'Well, I can't say I was particularly fond of Lorenzo either, but at least he wrote poetry and admired art and didn't go around burning old women to death.'

'Leonardo, I've told you before: these atrocities would happen whatever. They always have, they always will. Even under the most gentle and enlightened ruler. Soldiers are soldiers: sometimes they go crazy and act like wild beasts.'

'Wild beasts kill out of hunger or fear. It is unjust to compare them to human beings.' There is silence for a time, and then Leonardo sighs. 'Oh, I'm sure you are right, Niccolò. I'm just getting squeamish in my old age. But, still, I would very much like to follow you back to Florence.'

'Well . . . that could probably be arranged.'

He looks at me sharply. 'What do you mean?'

'I had a letter from the gonfalonier the other day about your plans for diverting the Arno. He has shown them to several influential people, all of whom approved the idea.'

'But the duke . . .'

'The duke wishes to make an alliance with Florence. The arrival of the ambassador – finally! – signals Florence's intention to negotiate with him. If the Signoria asked for your release as a gesture of goodwill on the duke's part, I doubt whether he would refuse.'

Leonardo stares into my eyes for what feels like a long time, then turns his gaze to the flames in the hearth. 'Niccolò, if you could truly arrange that, I would be . . . eternally grateful.'

'Consider it done,' I say. 'Now, let us both celebrate! More wine! Music! Women! Boys, even, if you prefer! Oh, and do you have anything to eat in this hovel of yours, Leonardo? I'm absolutely starving!'

27 January, 1503

CESARE: The evening lengthens. The sun sinks behind the hills. Messengers come and messengers go.

I sit down with the Florentine ambassador – Jacopo Saltieri. We're negotiating an alliance. It's like stabbing water.

I miss Machiavelli. He understood, he believed. He had the decency to be embarrassed when he fed me the Signoria's bullshit. But never mind – he's gone now.

I oil Saltieri. He makes a request – to 'prove my goodwill'.

I lean back in my chair. Goodwill, my arse. Those fucking Florentines – I'll burn their city to the ground one day.

'Go ahead,' I say. 'What's your request?'

They want me to release Leonardo. He is needed in his homeland. A project of great prestige and importance.

I think about the pros, I think about the cons. 'All right,' I say. 'I'll release Leonardo – but only if he wants to go.'

Thinking – he won't.

Thinking – he despises the Signoria.

Thinking – he admires me.

I dismiss Saltieri. I summon Leonardo.

In his eyes – weariness and worries. But still that pure flame. The flame that burns in my eyes too. The wish to work miracles.

I embrace him. We sit down. We drink and we talk. I tell him the Florentine request. I say the decision's his. I say I want him to stay – but I won't stand in his way.

He stammers, he looks away. Fuck. Now I know he wants to leave. But I don't know why.

Because his friends have gone? Because he's tired of sleeping in tents and castles? Because he hates war?

He tells me – it's all of these things. And one other – he wishes to paint again. His desire has been rekindled.

I sneer: 'PAINTING? How can you choose to make people's portraits over the chance to make history, to build an empire? You think your little canvases will last a thousand years?'

'Perhaps not.' He stares at the ground. 'But a small truth is better than a great lie.'

Cold fury. You dare call me a liar? I say nothing.

Finally he works up the courage to look in my eyes. 'My lord, it has been an honour to serve you. I am sorry that . . .'

'You have been a disappointment to me, Leonardo. I hoped we would achieve greatness together. But you have let me down.'

'I always did my best for you, my lord. If I . . .'

I say: 'You broke your promises. You stole my mistress. And now, at the first opportunity, you abandon me.'

I think – I wanted you to be my friend, Leonardo. I wanted you to love and admire me. I wanted you to immortalise me.

But I don't say this.

I grab a bag of ducats – drop it on the table. 'Here is the money you are owed. Take it and go.'

I turn my back on him. Stare out the window. See my own bitter smile, reflected. These principled geniuses – lose one, buy another.

I hear footsteps – and then silence. I turn around, a sneer on my lips.

The bag of gold still on the table.

28 January, 1503

Dawnlight and firesmoke. We march south – we march to Rome. I tell the soldiers – 'You're off the leash. Loot what you want. Rape who you will. Burn everything.'

I ride through the choking air. I ride across rivers of blood. I ride past towers of flame.

Ride to the top of a hill. Turn around and look north. I see fields on fire – orange flames, black crops. Clouds of smoke drifting. Leaves of ash floating.

Can't you feel it? *I* can fucking feel it.

I turn my horse to the south, dig my heels in its flanks – and ride FAST.

III

Where the Wind Blows
(Summer 1503–Autumn 1504)

36

CESARE: Sweat and swelter. Heat and horror. This summer's infernal – this city is Hell.

The shutters are closed – against mosquitoes. They come in whining clouds. From the western swamps. From the stinking Tiber. Carrying disease, carrying death.

My cousin Fatty Lanzol died yesterday. Remember him? He was there at Juan's last supper.

All over Rome, people dying – and none of them killed by me. Well, not many. A few corpses hang from the Ponte Sant'Angelo. Criminals, enemies, traitors. Their rotting eyeless faces scream – DON'T FUCK WITH THE BORGIA.

All night in my small dark room – I study maps, I make plans. I send messengers, I read reports. I squeeze envoys, I grease cardinals. I stare at the human chessboard and ponder my next move.

When dawnlight comes, I rub my eyes. I stretch my legs and open the shutters. Cool wind, silver sky.

I dismiss Agapito and call my gentlemen. We ride to the hills. We ride to the forests. We hunt with the leopards, then ride back to Rome – to sun-glare and bloodstink.

I visit my mistress. We fuck in her shuttered boudoir. We fuck and she sleeps. And I ride back here – to my small dark room.

Outside the noon bell tolls – it's too hot to move, too hot to think. So I lie alone in blackness and close my eyes.

And dream of a cool mountain peak.

5 August, 1503

Leather and velvet smell. We sit shaking. Through the carriage window, the city blurs. The sky is bloodcoloured.

'Open the window. It's too fucking hot in here.'

'No, Cesare!' my father squeals.

'Why not?'

'The mosquitoes.' He cringes. 'We must not take the risk.'

'I'd rather die of malaria than fucking suffocate in this rolling coffin.'

Hoofclatter slows. Through the window, the city comes into focus. The horses have begun to climb Monte Mario.

'Please, Cesare. Be patient. We'll be there soon. It's cooler, up in the hills.'

We are going to supper at a cardinal's villa. Adriano Corneto – one of my puppets. One of my pawns.

It's a farewell supper – in my honour. Tomorrow I ride to Romagna. There, I will wait. If the Spanish take Gaeta in the next few days, I invade Florence. If they don't, I join the French army – and ride south to crush the Spanish. Then Louis will make me a gift of Florence.

Heads I win, tails I win. Finally I stand on the cusp of greatness.

But still my father's nervous. 'What if I die?' he keeps asking.

'You're not going to die.'

'But what if I do? August is a fatal month for fat men. And for popes. Cesare, you have to think about this.'

'Everything is prepared.'

'But if you're in Romagna . . .'

336

'I've told you – I'm leaving five thousand troops behind in Rome. Michelotto's in charge of them. If you die, they'll seal the city. Michelotto will squeeze the cardinals. They'll elect a friendly pope – a puppet pope. My power will be secure.'

'What about Della Rovere?'

'He'll be taken care of.'

'Don't underestimate him, Cesare. He's a clever man. A dangerous man.'

'He's a dead man,' I say. 'Stop worrying.'

'I can't help worrying, Cesare.' A tender creak in his voice. I look in his eyes – hope and pride, teardrops and nostalgia. The sentimental old bastard.

'If you were to lose your power, my son, after all the work we've done to reach this point . . . after all our sacrifices . . .'

I look in his eyes. I see Juan's ghost. I look away – out of the carriage window. Crimson sky, sloping vines.

'We're here,' I say.

Finally I'll be able to breathe again . . .

Supper at the cardinal's vineyard. Overlooking city and sunset. Long treeshadows – warm and dark blue. The scent of ripe tomatoes.

I drink wine. I eat food. I listen to the whine of conversation. I listen to the whine of mosquitoes.

Someone says: 'Would you pass me the salt please, cardinal?'

I flash on Juan's face, across the table. At another supper, another vineyard – six summers ago. I flash on Juan's face, in the open bier. The wound in his throat sewn tight. I close my eyes – blink the memory away.

'Is everything all right, your magnificence?'

I open my eyes. 'Yes, everything's fine.'

'Is the food to your taste, Don Cesare?' the cardinal asks.

'Delicious,' I lie. The food tastes like shit. It tastes bitter, wrong. But I don't say this – the cardinal is my pawn. I must charm him. Keep him in my pocket.

And maybe it's me anyway. Maybe the bitterness is mine. I look around – everyone eating, drinking, laughing, talking. My father's nerves forgotten – a pretty young whore on his knee.

Yes – the bitterness is mine, not the food's. It's in my head – in my memories. Well, fuck my memories. Fuck the past. Fuck Juan's ghost. We must all make sacrifices for the family.

I wash the bitter taste down with cups of wine.

The sky darkens – turns black. The city disappears, the vineyard disappears. The stars above shine bright and cold.

I look up and see my fate, written in their constellations. Like Alexander – king of the world, dead at thirty-two.

Only four years left! I clench my fists. Wish it was tomorrow. Wish I was on the road now.

Calm. Wait. Soon.

I drink more wine. I listen to the whine of conversation. I listen to the whine of mosquitoes.

Needlesharp pain on my neck. I slap the bloodsucker dead. The stain on my hands – black in candlelight.

I wipe it on the tablecloth, forget about it. I've spilt so much blood already . . . what harm can a little more do?

37

LEONARDO: Liberty tastes sweet. The absence of fear is like the sensation of cool water on the tongue of a thirsty man. This is one of those rare periods in my life when I look up and see the mountain peaks of happiness nearly every day. There is harmony between Salai and myself . . . the project of diverting the Arno is, for the moment, progressing smoothly . . . Luca Pacioli teaches me more and more of the secrets of mathematics . . . and I have begun painting the portrait of a young Florentine lady, Lisa del Giocondo, which is giving me great pleasure.

I promised I would bring you back to life, and I

I am going to see Niccolò this evening. We are meeting for a drink in a tavern near his office because he wishes to discuss a major new commission with me. It is past seven o'clock, but when I open the street door of my studio the heat and brightness assail me, so I go back inside and retrieve, from a drawer in my room, the special dark glasses which I manufactured earlier this summer. I put them on and walk out into the street, the metalbright glare calmed to a smoky autumnal twilight. I had the idea, if you remember, last summer in Cesena. It occurred to me that I could use the stained glass of cathedral windows to replicate their cooling, dimming effect. I asked a glazier to produce a pair of slightly convex, amber-stained lenses, and Tommaso soldered the glass into a frame he had made. But amber seemed to accentuate rather than diminish the glare, so I experimented with different colours. Dark brown is the best, I think.

Of course my appearance attracts stares, remarks and laughter from the ignorant, but that is only to be expected. As Niccolò says, the mass of men are afraid of anything new – they prefer to hide in the shadows of the past rather than confront the dazzle of the future.

In the Piazza della Signoria, I see my friend sitting alone at a table outside in the shade. He smiles. His usual smile – warm in a cool way, ironic yet sincere. 'Has anyone told you that you have rather a sinister air, Leonardo, wearing those . . .' He fumbles for a word to describe my spectacles.

'I call them sun-glasses.'

'Not bad. I don't think they're going to catch on though.'

I shrug. 'They work for me.'

'Which is all that matters.' We embrace, and Niccolò orders wine, bread and olives. Then, typically, he gets straight to business. 'Leonardo, would you be willing to paint a fresco on one wall of the Great Hall?'

'I would be delighted – in principle. What is the subject? Has that been decided yet?'

'Not specifically, but it will undoubtedly be some heroic battle scene. Some glorious Florentine victory to inspire us. I know it's not really your thing, but when the topic came up your name was mentioned – and I know you need the work . . .'

'The *money*, Niccolò,' I smile. 'I have more than enough work to last me a lifetime – it is money that I need.'

Since I came back to Florence, I have withdrawn fifty ducats from my account at Santa Maria Nuova – and I have earned almost nothing. Sometimes I dream about the bag of gold ducats that I left on Valentino's table – I dream that

I took them, and wake up feeling joyful and relieved. Then I realise it was only a dream.

Niccolò looks embarrassed. 'It will pay quite well, I think – although this *is* the Signoria we're talking about, so . . .'

A vast painting of a battle on a wall of the Great Hall in the centre of Florentine government . . . yes, it's perfect. Such paintings always make war look picturesque, virtuous, divine. But I *know* what battle looks like, how it feels. If I could paint that ferocity, that fear . . . *the horror beneath.* And here is something that might truly last the centuries – not hidden away in a monks' refectory, but proudly displayed in the Palazzo della Signoria. I look up at that great building, which towers over us now – its battlements and arches, its tower and clockface, on which the minutes of my life are rapidly diminishing . . .

'Would I be allowed to paint the scene the way I wanted to, with no interference?'

'Of course – as long as you stick to the given subject. You're interested, then?' He sounds surprised.

'Yes, Niccolò. I'm interested.'

NICCOLÒ: Leonardo and I have another cup of wine and talk about the Arno project. It's going slowly, as these things always do in Florence. But, still, it is going: I am moderately hopeful that it might work out the way we planned. In the meantime, I am glad that Leonardo has agreed to paint the fresco in the Great Hall: it will give him an income, and it will also make me look good in the Signoria. Leonardo is the most eminent artist in Florence, after all. I've noticed that people always seem slightly awestruck when I tell them he's a friend of mine.

Around eight we finish our drinks and say goodbye, and I walk home. I whistle as I go: returning to the bosom of my family is no longer the torment it once was. Primerana has stopped teething or suffering from colic or hating her father or whatever it was that made her scream her head off for two hours every evening, and is now adorable. As for Marietta . . . well, she's pregnant again (yes, I know): her belly is large, her cheeks glow scarlet, and she's mostly docile, affectionate and content. It's been *months* since she threatened my life with a kitchen implement.

I step inside, and they both hug me: Marietta round my chest, and Primerana round the knees. I pick up my daughter, kiss my wife, and ask them about their day. Marietta recounts it for me – in mind-numbing detail. I listen for a while, then get bored and start thinking about work. When Marietta asks me about my day, the same thing happens in reverse. I tell her about Pisa and the Arno project; about Ser Antonio and the latest office politics; about Valentino and the pope and the war in Naples; she nods along – I can see her trying to focus on my words, to grasp their meaning, until finally the effort becomes too much and she just smiles – then drifts into the kitchen to supervise dinner.

When my two darlings are in bed, I go up to my study and work at my latest masterpiece for a few hours. It is only a short work – a kind of analytical history – and I don't suppose it will ever be published, but it gives me pleasure. It's called 'Description of the methods adopted by the Duke Valentino when murdering Vitellozzo Vitelli, Oliverotto da Fermo, and others'. Inspired, I wrote it in a single evening, and since then I've just been polishing sentences, reordering paragraphs, and altering (and altering back) bits of punctuation.

Before I go to bed, I read it through again. It's almost like a popular romance, with Cesare Borgia as its hero. I wonder if I should send him a copy?

near Rome

DOROTEA: The convent is situated on a hilltop outside the city, and the small courtyard is shaded by several old fig trees, but even so the heat is unbearable during the day. So I spend the hours between Prime and None in the cool of the chapel, mostly praying and cleaning, and work in the vegetable garden only in the mornings and evenings.

To my surprise, I enjoy gardening. I water and hoe and pick the vegetables – the tomatoes are particularly delicious at the moment – and carry them back to the kitchen in wooden crates. I have been assigned this task because I am one of the youngest sisters here.

Would you like to hear about my fellow nuns? Well, they are a curious band: some tyrannical, some officious; some devout, some selfish; some gay and some gloomy; some cruel and some kind; much like any other random group of people, I suppose, except that here there are only women. No men. No one to look at me as though I am a goddess or a piece of meat; no one to cause me ecstasy or agony.

Among other women, life is tranquil – and, yes, a little dull. No doubt Niccolò and Cesare imagine that I'm going crazy, so far from adventure and excitement, but this isn't true. I feel glad to have lived through the dark, rich madness of the last two years – and equally glad that I am no longer living through it. To be free to contemplate it, safely, from a distance.

As for Leonardo . . . he is in my heart, and always will be. Nothing else needs to be said.

38

CESARE: Sweat and swelter. Heat and horror. But the flames are INSIDE me now. It's night-time – dark and cool. But I'm on fire.

My father is sick too. The fever took him this morning – so I know what's coming. But still the violence of it shocks me.

My blood boils. I shiver hard. The teeth rattle in my skull. Bitter saliva dribbles down my beard. And then I retch.

Like I'm strapped to the rack. Like ten men jumping on my chest. Like a dozen swordblades shoved in my guts.

I puke all over my bed. I puke all over the floor. I puke all over the bedcurtains. I puke all over the walls. There's blood in the puke. My bile is black.

Afterwards I'm too weak to stand. They carry me to another bed – smother my shivering in blankets. They give me water, they give me pills. I drift into sleep.

I dream that I am dying.

The days blur. Waves of heat and waves of horror. I sweat all my strength in my sheets. I never piss. I never eat.

I dream of Lucrezia – me and my sister on our mountain peak. We fuck. Her on top. She says my name. Her eyes are closed.

She opens her eyes – and fucking SCREAMS. She's look-ing over my shoulders. She's looking past my head. She's screaming her fucking head off.

I slap her face. I yell. 'What's wrong? What's the matter?'

But Lucrezia only screams – and pulls herself off me. She crawls away. Her body naked. Her skin stained with blood.

I feel liquid on my back. Warm, oozing, thick. I feel fear. Disgust. I crawl out of bed and look where I lay –

Dead babies. Dead men. Their faces white and eyeless like carnival masks. Their mouths open in silent screams. Juan and Ramiro and Vitellozzo.

Blood leaks out the bed. I feel the earth tremble. Blood pours down the mountainside. I feel the earth shake.

The mountain collapses. The world turns black and I

Trembling cold. Shivering dying. Can't breathe I can't. Ribs cracking, heart shrivelling in the COLD.

All around me – doctors' faces. Their mouths mournful, their eyes sad.

'FUCKING SAVE ME!' I yell. 'I'm losing it all! I can't be sick now. I can't die now. Power was mine – but it's slipping through my fingers. Save me, save me, before it's too . . .'

But they can't hear a word. My voice a cracked whisper.

I'm dragged from the oil jar. I'm pulled from the ice-water. Feel myself floating – eyes near the ceiling. Drift into sleepless dreams again and I

The mountain smashed to bits. The mountain only rubble. Everything I strived for, all those years wasted.

I am alone. The world is dark. Smashed rocks and dead bodies. I am buried alive.

Rage inside me. I unsheath my great sword – and cut my way out. Cut through the rocks. Cut through the corpses. Hack an escape route – towards the light.

I cut and I hack. Heads fly, blood spurts. Legs and arms and hearts are shredded. Rocks turn to dust. Rocks turn to flame.

And then I see a head – rolling from my swordblade. Blood fresh on the metal. A new corpse. I go closer to the head – peer down at it. A jowly old man's face – I recognise him and

'. . . is dead, my lord.'

A voice I know. Open my eyes. Candlelight in darkness. The ceiling. A scarred face.

Michelotto.

I try to speak – hiss nothing. Who is dead?

'The pope has died, my lord. Your father is dead.'

The world collapses everything turns black and . . . NO!

I try to speak – hiss nothing.

'What shall we do? We await your orders, my lord.'

I must speak. Four years and then – king of the world. Can die then, not now. I won't . . . I must not fail. I . . . fucking SPEAK!

'Seal . . . off . . . the chamber . . .'

The ghost of life fluttering from my throat.

Michelotto puts his ear close to my mouth. 'I didn't hear you, my lord. I'm sorry. What did you say?'

'Seal off the chamber.'

The voice louder. Michelotto nods.

'Take all his treasure. Hidden. Search everywhere. Tell no one . . . he's dead . . . until the room's empty.'

346

near Pisa   *23 August, 1503*

LEONARDO: We reach Riglione, which is located by a bend of the Arno, about four miles from Pisa, and I climb out of the carriage and stretch my back and legs. Tommaso, Salai and Niccolò follow me out, and a certain Captain Guidicci (an upright, moustachioed fellow with a long, aquiline nose) greets us formally. He points east. 'On a clear day we would be able to see the enemy from here.'

I nod. I have no idea why he has told me this – perhaps it is just an attempt to make conversation? I decide to ignore the comment, and hand the captain the letter from the gonfalonier, which he reads, very slowly, then carefully folds and hands back to me. I can see doubt and suspicion hidden behind the courtesy in his expression – why, he is wondering, are the resources of the army being expended on some harebrained scheme hatched up by an artist and a pen-pusher? So I don my Haughty Genius mask and demand to inspect the fortifications and the course of the river.

This proves to be the right tactic. After his initial surprise has worn off, the captain responds warmly to my peremptory tone. Taking orders is something he can understand. We are shown the whole terrain, and I sketch most of what I see.

my fingerprints erasing God's – the glorious works of Nature being perfected

We eat lunch at a quiet, pleasant tavern in the village. After being told several times to stop addressing us as 'sir', the captain relaxes enough to voice his doubts about the project. These doubts are perfectly logical and reasonable, and I am happy to explain to him why they will ultimately prove irrelevant and why the diversion of the Arno at this

347

particular location will save Florentine troops from a futile and expensive war. By the end of the meal, the captain and I are on first-name terms, and he bids us farewell, promising to write to the gonfalonier of his satisfaction on the matter.

When he has gone, Salai breathes out with relief. 'What a stuffed shirt!' he mutters. Niccolò raises his glass and says, 'Bravo, Leonardo! You handled him brilliantly.'

'Thank you Niccolò, but it really wasn't difficult. The captain is an intelligent man.'

'But somewhat narrow-minded. You did a wonderful job of widening his mind.'

'Now we must do an equally good job of diverting the river. You are sure the Signoria will not alter my plans?'

He hesitates. 'One can never be absolutely sure of anything with the Signoria. But I *am* sure that the gonfalonier trusts your judgement.'

'Rivers are powerful creatures,' I say, hoping to make my friend see the necessity of following my plans exactly, rather than attempting to save money by cutting corners. 'They must be treated with the greatest care. We must *coax* the Arno from its present course – we must not treat it roughly or with violence.'

'Like a woman?' Niccolò says.

I laugh. 'I thought, in your opinion, women *should* be treated violently? I seem to remember you admiring Valentino's attitude towards Fortune on those grounds.'

'That's true,' Niccolò smiles. 'But, as you said at the time, if Fortune is a woman, then women are capricious – and capricious Fortune has betrayed poor Valentino in the most outrageous way.'

'Oh, you mean his illness?'

pull away his mask to reveal

'Not just his illness, but the timing of it. For his father to die when he himself is on the verge of death. Of course, the timing may not have been accidental.'

the horror

'You mean they were poisoned?'

'Possibly. Anyway, it seems that the duke is now over the worst of the fever, and will live. But he is still very weak, and prone to delirium. As a result, his enemies have taken advantage and have begun to attack all the towns he conquered in Romagna. Guidobaldo has already retaken Urbino; Gianpaolo Baglioni is marching on Perugia; and the Vitelli family are expected to be in Città di Castello by the end of the week.'

I mutter, 'The work of years undone in days.'

Niccolò gives me a sharp, amused look. 'I thought you had no sympathy for the duke?'

'I have no sympathy for his methods, but I admired the magnitude of his ambitions. It is always sad to see a man's dreams turn to dust.'

'I wouldn't write the duke off just yet,' Niccolò says. 'I think he may still have a few tricks up his sleeve.'

39

NICCOLÒ: It is dusk when I arrive in Rome, and the streets are like inkstained pages. I am excited to be here at last – in the centre of the most glorious empire ever to stretch across the globe – but when I tell the coachman that I would like to get out and walk the last mile to my inn, he looks at me as if I'm off my head. 'You'd be stripped, beggared, killed and butchered before you even got halfway, sir. Maybe raped too, if you were unlucky.' The city, he says, has been in a state of total anarchy ever since the death of Pope Alexander. 'People used to be scared of young Borgia and his spies. Now they're scared of all the villains who used to be scared of young Borgia and his spies.' I look down the same narrow sidestreets I looked down a minute before, and seem to perceive menacing shapes moving in the darkness; to hear cries of pain and savagery where before I heard only street vendors and laughter. I get back into the carriage and lock the door. 'And on top of all that,' the coachman shouts, as the mules move forward again, 'the bloody plague is back! No, if I was you, sir, I'd stay shut tight in my room all the time I was here.'

My room, however, is not the kind of place you would want to stay shut tight in. The inn is well located – close to the Vatican and the Castel Sant'Angelo, where the Duke Valentino is now living – but it is also a tiny, filthy, overpriced shithole. There are fleas in the bed and cockroaches on the walls; and, whenever I am still for more than a few seconds, I hear rats scurrying across the floor. Besides, I have too much work to do: people to see, places to go, information to gather.

I am here to observe and report on the papal election. Alexander's successor, Pope Pius III, lasted less than a month before going upstairs to meet his boss in person. Some say he was poisoned, of course, and it is not beyond the realms of possibility, but he *was* a very weak, old man, and was only elected in the first place as a way of giving the real candidates more time to prepare their election campaigns. The coming election is the one that matters; the event which will define the future of our country – and perhaps (who knows?) my own future too.

I begin by visiting Cardinal Soderini – my old friend Francesco – who gives me all the latest rumours and writes letters of introduction for me to Della Rovere, Riario and others. Later, I pay calls on Cardinal Amboise and Cardinal Ascanio Sforza. At ten I go back to my inn and try to make sense of all I've been told. The Duke Valentino, everyone agrees, is in a strong position: he is over the worst of his illness, and all the candidates need his support in order to be elected. Puzzlingly, however, the current favourite is Cardinal Della Rovere: the bookmakers are taking thirty percent of their bets on him. Yet surely these two facts are at odds with each other: if the next pope will need the support of the duke, then Della Rovere cannot be the next pope – because the duke would have to be insane to support his oldest and most dangerous enemy. I shake my head: it makes no sense at all.

Around midnight, I blow out the candle and lie awake in bed, feeling the fleas bite my ankles and listening to the rats' claws scratching and drumming over the rough wooden floorboards. I close my eyes and think of Marietta: she was sobbing when I left, inconsolable. Were I not so keen to see Rome, I might even have tried to get out of this trip. She is due to give birth to our second child within the next week or so. I pray to Fortune that it is a son, and that the child survives. Oh, and I pray that my wife survives too, of course.

I fall asleep, and dream of Valentino.

29 October, 1503

CESARE: A room in the Vatican. The fire smoking. The sound of rain. We sit round a table. Me and my cardinals – and my bitterest enemy.

Cardinal Della Rovere – the old bird of prey. White hair, hawk's eyes. He smiles at me. He's courteous, charming – and so am I. He's subtle, dangerous – but so am I.

Why are we here? Because we need each other. He needs my votes – these eleven cardinals. I need guarantees – from the next pope. And Della Rovere looks like being the next pope. Unless I stop him.

He's greased everyone – it must have cost him a fortune. He says to my cardinals: 'I will pay for your votes, gentlemen. Fifteen thousand ducats each.'

Their eyes pop. I do the math. There are thirty-seven cardinals in the college. Even my father didn't pay THAT much to be pope.

'That's very generous of you,' I say. 'But they won't vote for you unless I tell them to.'

My enemy smiles. My enemy nods. My enemy says: 'I am well aware of the power you hold, Cesare. Equally, you must be aware of the power I hold.'

I smile. I nod.

He says: 'Together we control the fate of Rome – of the Church. If we are enemies, there will be chaos. Destruction. Civil war. It will be good for the Venetians – not for you, not for me.'

I nod. What he says is true.

'So let us be friends. Let us put the past behind us. We are intelligent men, Cesare. We are not hotheads like Vitellozzo. What interests us is power, not vengeance.'

'I would not like to end up like Vitellozzo.'

My enemy smiles. 'Indeed. I must compliment you on that deception, by the way. It was cleverly done – a work of art.'

'What will you give me – if I agree to support your candidacy?'

'What do you want?'

'I want to be confirmed as Captain General of the Church.'

'Certainly. There is no better man for the job. In return, however, you must obey my commands. You will be the pope's warrior – not an independent power.'

'Of course.' I nod. I smile. 'I also want to keep my cities in Romagna.'

Silence. My enemy frowns. He nods – slowly. Then he says: 'Why not? As long as they obey the papal authority, you may rule them as you wish. You will, of course, be given the troops and money needed to win them back from your enemies.'

I breathe out. It's been easier than I dared hope. Too easy, perhaps. 'How do I know that you will keep your word?'

'My word is my bond. You may ask around, Cesare. I am nearly sixty years old, and I have never once broken a promise. The question is, really, how do I know YOU will keep YOUR word?'

I nod. What he says is true. The cardinal has a reputation for honesty. And I . . . I do not.

'What do you propose?'

'Swear to me, Cesare – on your sister's life.'

Lucrezia – the only person in the world I love. I nod. I make my face sombre. 'I swear on the life of my sister Lucrezia that I will keep my word.'

Behind my back, I cross my fingers. Such oaths mean nothing without God – and God does not exist.

My enemy nods. 'Very well. And you will give me your support in this election?'

'I will.'

The cardinals smile – fifteen thousand ducats each. Della Rovere smiles – he's the next pope. I smile too – my empire regained. Everyone's happy.

I leave the Vatican. I go back to the castle. In my small dark room, I ponder the human chessboard.

Yes – fucking YES. Before, I was losing. All I saw was defeat – my cities stolen, my power diminished. And now . . . I think I've just made the winning move.

31 October, 1503

NICCOLÒ: It's the middle of the night, but I'm wide awake. The college of cardinals meets tonight to decide the identity of the new pope. According to the bookmakers, it's a foregone conclusion, but . . . could the duke really support Della Rovere? It still seems incredible to me. I haven't seen Borgia yet: he has had no time to spare. But I saw Della Rovere yesterday, and he looked like a man who has just eaten a good meal – or fucked a beautiful woman. More likely the former, in his case.

I walk about my room – the sound of my footsteps keeps the rats at bay – and nibble salami as I think through all the permuations and possible consequences. Then I hear urgent knocking at the street door, and rush downstairs to answer it. My landlord gets there first and lets in the papal messenger. Outside in the street, twenty armed guards stand in the black drizzle.

'You brought a few friends, I see.'

The messenger smiles grimly. 'There were fourteen corpses dragged from the Tiber today. I didn't fancy joining them.'

I invite the messenger up to my room, serve him a cup of wine, and listen as he tells me the news. Nothing is official yet, but he has it on good authority that Cardinal Della Rovere will be named as the new pope tomorrow. 'The vote was practically unanimous. He will take the name Julius II.'

'How did he manage it?' I ask.

'He paid a lot of money and made a lot of promises. So many promises . . . I do not think he can possibly keep them all.'

6 November, 1503

CESARE: My apartment is grand – gold and velvet everywhere. So why does it feel like a cage? I pace its length. I stare out the windows – rain, grey skies. I wait. I brood.

The pope's been pope nearly a week – yet still he hasn't kept his promises. I am not Captain General. Romagna is not mine.

Did he lie? Was I deceived? No – it cannot be. The first consistory is on the ninth. The pope will make me Captain General then.

Calm. Wait. Soon.

Afterwards I will ride to Romagna. I will win back my cities. I will be Caesar once more.

355

Remember the fate of Il Moro – power is a state of mind. Never surrender – always believe.

Yes – I must believe.

But a persistent voice whispers doubt. Why does this room feel like a cage? Why does the Venetian envoy not come when I summon him? Why does the pope avoid me?

I pace the room. I stare out the windows. I growl at servants. I roar at envoys. I am a monster – caged in a zoo.

Agapito knocks. Agapito enters. He stares over my shoulder. He looks nervous, fidgety. 'The Florentine envoy to see you, my lord.'

In walks Machiavelli. He brings me news – bad news. The Venetians are closing on Faenza. The castellan of Imola has surrendered the fortress.

That thin smile as he speaks. Is he mocking me? Is he laughing at my fuck-up?

Machiavelli asks what I mean to do. The Florentine Signoria is worried, he says. The Venetians are their enemies. It's a dangerous situation blah blah blah.

I feel angry. I don't know why.

'You come here asking for favours?' I shout. 'You think I should help Florence? Fucking Florence – you have always been my enemies. I don't blame the Venetians – I blame YOU. With a hundred men, you could have secured those cities – but you couldn't be bothered.'

I look at his face – the smile wiped off. I look in his eyes – shock and fear.

I yell at him: 'So Imola is lost? Fuck it – I will raise no troops. I will risk nothing to recover what is lost. I will no longer be fooled by your weasel words. I'll give EVERYTHING to Venice. Let them take all my cities. I'll see your republic ruined! Then it will be MY turn to laugh!'

I look in the envoy's eyes – fear fading, something else growing. I peer closer – what is it? I see . . . boredom. I see . . . laughter.

You worshipped me once, Machiavelli. And now you come here and roll your fucking eyes? Now you come here and stifle your fucking yawns?

I will CRUSH you, little worm. I will DEVOUR you, little Florentine. I will rape your women and drink your river. I will smash your buildings and burn your fields.

'You hear me? You hear me? You fucking hear me?'

NICCOLÒ: Yes, your lordship, I can and do hear you. Unfortunately for us both.

It takes a great deal of effort to stop myself laughing in Borgia's face as he raves at me, and yet at the same time I can't help feeling sad; disillusioned. Is this truly the same man – the same magnificent prince – whose presence and subtlety and cool intelligence so impressed me in Urbino and Imola, in Cesena and Senigallia? What on earth has happened to him? He is unnaturally pale and thin – his face has a haggard, skull-like appearance – but it is not his physical condition that worries me. Before, the Duke Valentino never said what he was going to do; now, he says (loudly, repeatedly) that he is going to do what he is plainly incapable of doing. It is as though the old duke has been secretly killed and replaced by some bad actor.

In order not to spend longer than I have to in such dull and dispiriting company, and in order to avoid being punched in the face (which seems increasingly likely as time goes by), I decide to soothe the duke with gentle, reassuring words. Little by little, he calms down. When I finally escape from the interview, it seems to me to have lasted a thousand years.

Florence   *8 November, 1503*

LEONARDO: I wake early, to the sound of monks chanting. When I am washed and scented and dressed, I walk through the stilldark streets to the baker's. I pass the ugly shrine at the crossroads. I pass two prostitutes chatting in the gloom. I pass a drunkard vomiting in someone's doorway. Once again, I see my dream city arching over the narrow, winding, shadowy streets of this real city. But nowadays the thought does not bring despair or regret. I feel as though anything is possible – as though, by force of will, I might truly build the city I only sketched before.

the artist's mind transformed . . . into the mind of God

I give the dough to the baker and he puts it in the oven. I watch as it rises, hardens, turns the colour of gold, savouring the smell and my hunger . . . and then I carry it home, wrapped in a cloth so my hands don't burn. I eat breakfast in the great room, alone but for the cat, purring as it rubs against my ankles, and contemplate the shapes in my notebook. They are good – frightening and beautiful.

a spiral of fury a maelstrom of killing a vortex of

When I have finished breakfast, and washed and scented my hands again, I pick up my chalks and begin to draw. Hours pass in eyeblinks. I love the work, the absorption, but it is scary how fast the days flash past when I am lost in a picture, as now. In fact, I am lost in *two* pictures – the commission for the Great Hall of the palace, and . . .

her face fills my mind

I put down my chalks and walk back to the bedroom. The portrait is propped on an easel in the corner, near my bed. It is the last thing I see before I fall asleep at night, and the first thing I see when I wake the next morning. Her face. I stare, now, at those eyes, that mouth, the rivers and

358

chasms of remembered landscapes dark bluish and autumnal behind her, below her, smoky and blurred by the perspective of loss. One year ago, in Imola. Forty years ago, in Vinci. Thinking about the past gives me a kind of vertigo.

I take the flat mirror from my pocket and place it next to the canvas, then examine the painting in the mirror. This is always the best method for seeing one's own faults and weaknesses. Reflected, inverted, the painting looks like someone else's work. I stare at it, and I know that it is still not right. Not quite. Not yet.

to understand the mystery of that smile

Through the thick walls of the monastery, the voices on the street come to me as murmurs, breaths of wind. The air in the room smells of oil, turpentine, lavender. I mix my paint. I choose my brush. I enter the picture and lighten the sky . . . deepen the shadow . . . alter the line of her lips . . . When I am *in* the picture like this, it is as if I no longer exist, or as if I exist more truly – a soul unbound from its physical constraints . . . *set free.* The world beyond the limits of the frame melts away, with all its troubles, its fears and doubts, and I inhabit the stopped moment, the resurrected memory. I breathe her air, I smell her scent, I touch her skin, feel her warmth. She smiles at me.

I withdraw from the painting and am suddenly aware, again, of the flesh of my body, the pull of the earth, the sleeping cat on the bed, the spiderwebs glistening on the ceiling, the afternoon sunlight staining the wall reddish-orange. I breathe – come back to myself. To the 'real' world.

The client (the husband of Madonna Lisa, who is ostensibly the subject of my painting) found me here a few days ago. He brandished his contract, demanded his purchase. I calmed him down, made promises, then went to see Salai. My assistant is now charged with making a copy of

359

the painting – preferably one that looks a little more like the lady herself, and less like my memories, my haunted dreams. This one I will keep for myself. I do not think I will ever sell it.

I promised I would bring you back to life, and . . .

I walk to the other end of the room and close my eyes. I let the memories blur, merge, glow beneath my eyelids. Dorotea, when she said goodbye. My mother, when I was young. Love, goodness, the mystery of life.

. . . and I will

Then I open my eyes.

40

NICCOLÒ: 'A son, Francesco! I have a son! We will call him
Bernardo, after my father. I hope I can be as good a father
to Bernardo as Bernardo was to me. Would you . . . would
you consider becoming the child's godfather?'

To my surprise, the cardinal gives me a bearhug of
such intensity that for several moments I am unable to
breathe. He picks me up off the ground with a strength
I had never guessed at, and when he puts me down again
and lets me go, I see tears of joy in his eyes. Husky-voiced,
he declares: 'Niccolò, it would be a great honour. Godfather to your son . . . this is wonderful news! We must
celebrate.'

Over dinner we get through three bottles of the cardinal's finest Salerno wine, and talk of sons and fathers.
Eventually, inevitably, the conversation touches on politics,
and I tell Francesco of my latest meeting, yesterday, with
the Duke Valentino. To my astonishment, the duke actually apologised for his behaviour at the previous meeting.
He then went on to talk about how we must look to the
future, not the past, and outlined his plans for an alliance
between himself and Florence in order to drive the Venetians from Romagna. It was a plausible imitation of the
old duke, and yet I was not truly convinced. The old duke –
the *real* duke – had leopard's eyes, hungry and focused; this
man's eyes were more like a madman's, slipping between

softness and ferocity as easily and purposelessly as the sky above us changes from clear to overcast.

Francesco looks unsurprised by my description. 'He is no longer the same man we met in Urbino, Niccolò. He is irresolute, suspicious, unstable.'

'He says it is due to his lingering illness.'

'That may be so. Or it may simply be that, having been accustomed to the greatest good fortune, he is still stunned by the blows she has given him recently. To be perfectly honest, I am not at all sure the duke will ever again leave that apartment of his, never mind regain his Romagnan cities. It seems to me he is slipping, day by day, into his grave.'

When dinner is over, I bid farewell to Francesco and hire several soldiers to escort my carriage to a house in the centre of town. This is where Angelina lives. She is a sweet, naughty girl; I have been seeing her every few days lately – this damp weather makes the beans swell and the holes tighten, so to speak – and I would go every night if I could afford it. I sit in the dark carriage, the wheels bumping suggestively over cobbles, think happily of my newborn son, and dream of Angelina's white and nubile body.

Finally the carriage comes to a halt. I unbolt the door and jump down into the street. As my feet hit the ground, I hear one of the soldiers say, 'Crying shame.' In the silence beyond this, a child coughs and some distant music plays. I walk towards Angelina's door and then, seeing it in the torchlight, I freeze. A crude red cross has been painted on the plain wood.

'I'm sorry, sir,' someone says behind me.

Oh God.

I hammer on the door and shout, 'Angelina! Is she dead or alive?' But there is no answer.

Oh God, please no.

I remember kissing her, touching her, licking her, screwing her, only three nights ago. Was she infected then?

Oh God oh God oh God.

I am going to die. My life will never amount to anything. I will never find true love. I will never exercise true power. I will never write my name into the pages of history. I will never even see my son. I am going to die: an obscure, thirty-four-year-old envoy, lost in an ugly, faded city; that will be the end of me . . . of everything.

I get back in the carriage and bolt the door. I think of Angelina's soft white flesh, covered with oozing black buboes. My heart is pounding so fast, I feel I am about to vomit. As the mules pull the carriage deeper into Rome's foul darkness, I hold my head in my hands and weep.

Rome   *17 November, 1503*

CESARE: I open the shutters. Breathsteam in darkness. I stare out at the world – vast and invisible, still unconquered. I remember my childhood dreams – I wanted to be Caesar, I wanted to be Alexander.

And here I am, prowling a cage in Rome. Waiting and hoping and dying inside. Wasting my time. Wasting my genius. Wasting away.

The messenger comes from Florence. I listen – I hold my fucking breath. But their answer is no. Cold longwinded bullshit – but no safe-conduct, no alliance.

I punch the wall. I scream at the darkness. I send for my favourite envoy.

Machiavelli comes in, and I rage at him. I rage at Florence. I yell: 'You've let me down AGAIN. Well, you've let me down for the last time. I will ally myself with Venice. I will ally myself with the devil. I will do anything to bring your republic down.'

I rage and I snarl. I pace and I roar.

But when I look in his eyes – I see no fear. I don't even see boredom or laughter. I see pity. Fucking PITY!

Machiavelli is bright – I always knew it. But he's unbearably bright now. Seeing into all my darknesses. My hidden corners. My secret passageways. Seeing through the holes in the mask I wear.

Finally I stop yelling. Machiavelli answers me – cold long-winded bullshit. Playing for time. Stringing me along. Sliding the thin swords into my skin. Just like I did to all those noble, powerful, enraged bulls.

Am I bleeding, am I slowly dying? Is the great sword raised above my neck?

I dismiss Machiavelli. I summon Agapito. I tell him: 'We leave tomorrow. All of us. We go to Romagna.'

Agapito frowns. 'What is your plan, my lord?'

'I don't have a fucking plan. I don't know what I'm going to do. But I HAVE to get out of here. Don't you see, Agapito? It's driving me crazy. Now stop asking questions – and do what I fucking tell you.'

'I'm sorry, my lord.' Agapito sighs. He stares at the floor. 'I will give the orders, but I will not go with you. I no longer wish to serve your lordship.'

Et tu, Agapito? I say nothing. He bows. He goes.

I do not punch the wall. I do not scream at the darkness. I stare out at the vast invisible world – and know I will never conquer it. I will never be a Caesar. I will never be an Alexander.

All my dreams are dust.

NICCOLÒ: The morning gets off to the best of starts. It is a rare dry, bright day in Rome, and when I examine my naked body in the light that comes through the open window, I find not one black bubo. For the tenth consecutive day since I saw that red cross on Angelina's door, I am in the clear. I am healthy: I have survived.

I go to the Vatican and am greeted by the news that Cesare Borgia, who set off from Rome only a week ago, has been arrested by papal troops for the crime of refusing to surrender his Romagnan castles to the pope. After that, I hear various rumours: that he wept as they took him in chains to the boat; that the pope intends to have him beheaded in St Peter's Square.

Everyone in the court laughs and jokes about the duke's fate; I laugh along with them, but the laughter does not touch my soul. Valentino was my one great hope. Who else is strong enough to drive the foreigners out of Italy, to unite us as single nation? Who else is going to offer Niccolò Machiavelli the position of power that he so craves and deserves? The duke is a pale shadow of his former self, and nothing can save him now; but that does not mean I can't regret what might have been.

I work hard all morning, petitioning cardinals and writing reports to the Signoria, and in the afternoon Francesco suggests that we go for a walk. 'You've been here nearly a month, Niccolò, and you still haven't seen the city's ancient ruins. For a man who loves history as much as you do, that's scandalous.'

So we go to see the Colosseum and the Circus Maximus. We explore the Baths of Diocletian. We talk of Cicero and of Caesar, of Brutus and Augustus. After a while, Francesco goes back to the Vatican and leaves me alone in an overgrown patch of grass near the Forum, where I munch roasted chestnuts in the cold sunshine and watch men in togas play lutes and sing supposedly ancient songs. Yet even here, even touching the very stones that *their* fingers touched, even looking out over views that *their* eyes saw, I still can't truly connect to the past.

It doesn't feel real to me. *They* don't feel real. Rationally, I know they were people like we are, with the same passions and the same bodies and the same hopes and fears. I want to know how they felt, each one of them. I want to think the way they thought, but . . . all I feel is stones; all I see are fields and hills. All I think is: I'm here and I'm now, and the past doesn't really exist.

And yet . . . history is speaking to us. Always, it whispers: too quiet to hear; in a foreign tongue. If only we could understand what it were saying, something of the gravest importance might be revealed.

I stare at the ancient ruins of the Forum and hold my breath.

History, I am listening. Speak to me.

And still it whispers: urgent, insistent. And still I don't understand a damn word.

I finish my chestnuts, pick up my belongings, and walk back to my inn. Goodbye history – talk to you later.

5 December, 1503

CESARE: Chainrattle and shitstink. The guards tie my hands together. They take me from the Vatican to the castle. Through the dim walkway.

We stop by a window. They push my face to the opening. I think – they're going to throw me out. Drop me to my death in St Peter's Square.

366

But they don't throw me out – they just make me watch. 'His Holiness said you'd want to see this.'

I frown. I stare. A procession in the square. Cardinals and priests. Monks and masses. And at the centre of it all, the pope. Della Rovere – my enemy, my betrayer.

I close my eyes. I pull away from the window. The guard puts his swordblade to my throat. 'He wanted you to WATCH, hellspawn!'

I open my eyes. It's his fucking coronation. Pope Julius II. He's used me. He's duped me. He's fooled me and fucked me. Even his name mocks me. It says: 'I am the true Caesar, not you.'

I watch – a priest holds a golden staff. Tied to the staff – a tow of flax. The priest sets fire to it. The flax burns. It turns to ashes.

The priest intones: '*Pater sancte, sic transit gloria mundi.*'

Holy Father, thus passes the glory of the world.

The guards push me through the walkway. They shove me towards the screaming and the bloodstink. They throw me into a small dark cell. They lock the door. They spit on the ground and laugh. 'Look at you now – the great Cesare Borgia!'

I ponder the human chessboard – check fucking mate.

I think of my sister – I'll never see her again.

I think of my father – dead and rotting in the ground.

I think of my empire – the scavengers picking it apart.

I think of my dream mountain – smashed rocks and dead bodies.

I think of my enemy – the crown on his head.

I think of myself – a monster in a cage.

Thus passes the glory of the world.

41

DOROTEA: The beginning of my second year here. The sky is low and grey today, and a cold wind blows. A silk merchant came this morning and told us the news about the duke. Apparently he was strangled to death by Don Michelotto on the pope's orders, and his corpse thrown into the Tiber. Everyone here agrees that this is divine retribution – and, of course, I do not argue with them. My past is a secret which I prefer to keep. But deep in my heart, I have compassion for Cesare. I have not forgotten the things he did, to me and to others, but tonight I will say a prayer for his soul.

For the last three days it has rained so hard that we have not been able to set foot outside. Sister Roberta whispered to me this morning that she knows my secret. I said nothing, but she must have seen me blush. How can she know? Who could have told her? She is a sly, cruel woman and I fear the uses to which she might put her knowledge.

Some sunlight today, and I worked in the vegetable garden. It is good to use my muscles. It helps me forget my worries.
    The bishop visited us today, and one of his servants told our kitchen staff that the duke is not dead after all. Apparently he is locked up in Castel Sant'Angelo, but there are

suggestions that he may be released. I felt a fool, having prayed for his soul.

Sister Roberta stared at me during Vespers, and afterwards, in the courtyard, she hissed: 'You must be happy – knowing that your lover is alive!'

I feel a constriction in my chest whenever I think about this.

Finally, the first signs of spring: buds on the apple trees. And the air this evening is scented, almost warm.

A surprise visitor for me today! My friend Stefania came. We sat in my room and talked. It felt so good to see her and to embrace her. I had imagined I would never hear from her again. She is married to her soldier, and seems quite happy. Her face looks much older than I remembered it, although only a year and a half has passed since I last saw her. Have I aged so quickly as well? We chatted normally until, just before leaving, she told me she had a message for me. I must admit my heart leapt, thinking she meant Leonardo. But when I asked who it was from, she said: 'From your husband. He wishes you to go and live with him in Venice.'

I am shocked. I do not know how to feel.

Laughter and whispering in the corridors when I pass. Has Sister Roberta told the others? This is unbearable.

A letter from my husband today, delivered by one of his servants. It is a long letter, mostly quite formal, but it ends with these words: 'My dear Dorotea, I know that what happened to you at the hands of that monster must have been horrifying, and I understand that you do not wish to think or talk about it, but must you shut yourself away from the world for ever as a consequence? I fell in love with you the first time I saw you, and very much wish you to be my wife. You are still a young woman: I believe, as my wife, you could find great contentment. My friends say I should forget you and marry someone else, but that is not my preference. It is you I want. Please will you come to Venice, to be my companion and to bear my children? Fruitfulness is perhaps the sweetest balm for your old pain.'

Thinking of my husband. Or should I say 'my husband'? I have read his letter more than a dozen times now. Thinking about 'fruitfulness'.

I received an anonymous note today – it was pushed under my door. I burnt it, and do not remember what it said, but I saw the words 'BORGIA' and 'WHORE'. I feel sick whenever I think of it. Perhaps it is time I left this place.

It snowed today. Very strange, as only yesterday it was so warm. This evening I will write to my husband, I have decided. I will also write to the Doge in Venice, asking him to guarantee my safety. What if my husband's letter is a lie, and secretly he wishes to punish me for the crimes he imagines I committed with the duke?

He writes: 'No one here doubts your innocence, Dorotea, nor suspects you of anything worse than being abducted and cruelly treated by a vicious tyrant. If ever any of my staff insinuated otherwise, you have my word that they would lose their posts immediately. Dorotea, please come: this house is so lonely without you.'

I have made my decision, and have informed the Mother Superior: I will leave the convent next week, and go to join my husband. He will meet me in Faenza, and from there we will travel together to Venice. I am relieved: Sister Roberta can torture me no longer.

I am also very nervous.

The carriage arrived in Faenza this afternoon. To my astonishment, there was a crowd of people there, in the square, cheering. My husband came to greet me: I hardly recognised him. In my memory of his portrait, he was so old, but I suppose that is just because I was so young when I saw it. Now he seems to me quite a handsome and vigorous middle-aged gentleman. Above all, he seems kind.

As he held my hands in the square and told me how happy he was at last to see me again, my attention was taken by a face in the crowd: a man with long, silver-streaked hair and deep, wise eyes. My heart leapt. Was it *him*? Was it Leonardo? But my husband said something to me, and I must have turned to him in order to respond, and when I looked into the crowd again, the face had gone.

Florence   *13 July, 1504*

LEONARDO: I walk through the still, hot air – it pricks beads of sweat at my temples. I can smell the lavender that I dabbed there earlier, but it does not entirely mask the stench of blood from the slaughteryards down near the river. The only sounds are of the bells in the Duomo and, more distantly, Santa Croce, tolling the hour. Nothing moves in the piazza but flies. Summer afternoons in Florence have a beaten-down look. At sunset the people will come out again, to eat and drink and walk and talk, but for now the atmosphere is like that of a mortuary. *Oh father I am sorry that I*

I knock on Niccolò's door and he embraces me warmly. I pat his arm. His keen eyes fix mine – 'Leonardo, are you all right?'

I look over his shoulder into the dining-room, where several men sit, drinking and laughing. The only face I recognise is Niccolò's colleague, Agostino. Niccolò sees me look. 'Some friends of mine – I wanted to introduce you. Would you rather . . .'

'My father died,' I say – because these are the only words in my mouth. The only words in my head.

'Oh no! I'm so sorry. When? How?'

'Wednesday morning,' I say. 'No . . . Tuesday. Oh, I don't know – the days blur. With this heat, you know . . .'

'My father died four years ago,' Niccolò offers. 'He was my best friend, and I still miss him. People told me that the worst thing about a father's death was seeing your own mortality more clearly – because you're no longer shielded from it, you know? But the worst thing for me was just not being able to talk to him any more.'

There are tears in my eyes. I turn away, stare at the wall of the entrance hall. 'I envy you, Niccolò. I was never so close to my father. I was always . . . a disappointment to him, I suppose.' I clear my throat. 'I had hoped that one day I might . . . but it's too late now.'

He touches my arm. 'Come, let's go upstairs to my study. We can have a drink there, and talk in peace.'

'I don't want to spoil your dinner party. Perhaps I should . . .'

'Nonsense. Come with me, Leonardo. We'll have a drink – and then you can decide if you want to stay for dinner or not.'

We go to his study. I pretend to admire his collection of books. I see my own lost copy of Plutarch's *Lives* there, and remember my study at the castle in Imola – how long ago that seems.

'When is the funeral?' he asks, handing me a glass of clear liquid. I drink it down – the taste is bitter and harsh, but afterwards I feel a cloud of red warmth in my chest and throat, and a kind of dizzy, radiant sweetness in my mind. Niccolò refills my glass.

'The funeral was today,' I say. 'This morning.'

'Was everything . . .'

'My father did not mention me in his will. Not even in passing.'

Niccolò stares.

'I was illegitimate – I think I told you that, didn't I?'

'Yes.' He recovers himself. 'Yes, you told me – in Imola. Are you going to contest the will?'

I smile – a smile as bitter as the taste of Niccolò's alcohol. 'No, I don't think so.'

'You'd probably win. I've got a friend who's . . .'

'It would be a waste of time and money. And it wouldn't alter anything, really, would it? I didn't want his books or his land. Just his . . .'

sometimes I despair of you

To fill the new silence, I drink some more of the clear liquid. 'Does this have a name?'

'Water of life. My cousins make it. There's a distillery at our place in the country – Sant'Andrea in Percussina.'

The warm red cloud bursts and spreads through my body, loosening my muscles, unlocking my smile. I think of Vinci. 'You should be there now, Niccolò – escape this summer heat.'

'I've just come back. Marietta and the kids are staying there now, with my sister and her family. I can only take two or three days of country air, then I start going slightly mad. And the gonfalonier wanted to see me. Oh, that reminds me! I had some good news yesterday – Soderini has decided to definitely go ahead with your river project. The Signoria will vote on it next month, and he's confident we can win that vote. All being well, work will begin immediately.'

'That *is* good news,' I say. 'And they are following my recommendations regarding . . .'

His face darkens, his smile fades. 'Well, I think they decided the costs of the original proposal were prohibitive. The project could only get the go-ahead if they managed to bring the price down, you see.'

'So they're going to cut corners.'

'Only tiny little cuts, Leonardo. Here and there. Nothing major.'

'One can bleed to death of a thousand tiny little cuts.'

the black wave coming down the whole world drowned beneath

'Have another drink,' Niccolò urges.

'No.' I hold my hand over the glass. 'Thank you Niccolò, but I think it's better if I go home now. I would only dampen the spirits of your guests with my long face.'

At the door we embrace. 'I'm sorry for your loss, Leonardo.'

'Thank you, my friend.'

'And don't despair of the river project. I'm sure it'll work out fine in the end.'

'Yes, perhaps. You know what you said about a father's death . . . about it stripping away the veils that cover the end of your own life, so that you see your mortality more clearly?'

'Yes?'

374

'I feel that. But I also feel . . . Did anyone ever suggest to you that the death of a father can have a positive effect?'

'Liberating you from their shadow and all that?'

'Yes – something like that.'

'Yes, I heard the theory. As I've said though, I just miss my dad. I wish he were here now – tonight. He would add to the merriment. Why . . . do *you* feel liberated?'

'I think so, yes. At least, I think I might. One day soon.'

42

NICCOLÒ: I duck in out of the heavy rain and sit down with
Biagio in The Three Kings. We order ale and pickled walnuts, but tonight there is no joking around, no trip to the
brothel, no Agostino: we are here to talk business. We are
here to talk rivers.

Biagio is working as the liaison officer between myself –
representing the Ten of War – and Colombino, the chief
hydraulic engineer on the Arno project. Colombino sent
me a letter the other day detailing his progress (or lack of
it) and his plans, and I showed this to Leonardo yesterday
evening. Dear me, he was furious. He says that Colombino
is a clown, and that the project is doomed to failure if we
continue on our current path. I asked him to write down
what he thought was wrong with Colombino's figures, and
– with a visible effort – he did so in the normal way: that is
to say, left to right, so that it can be read without the aid
of a mirror. He wrote comments (some of them not ter-
ribly friendly or polite) all over Colombino's letter; and it
is this heavily graffitied document which I pass to Biagio,
who studies it under the candle flame, first frowning and
pursing his lips, and then shaking his head and laughing
bitterly.

'So what do you think?' I say. 'I trust Leonardo with the
numbers. The whole project was his idea in the first place,
and he's very thorough where such things are concerned.'

'I don't doubt it,' Biagio replies. 'But there's no way we can make all the changes he suggests.'

'But if you don't, he says it won't work.'

'Then it won't work.'

I stare at him. 'Biagio . . .'

'Niccolò, we've already sunk seven thousand ducats into this scheme of yours. I had a bad feeling about it all along, especially when the gonfalonier kept asking me to bring the price down. Your friend's comments just confirm all my worst fears.'

'But . . .' – panic rising – 'you're not saying we should just *abandon* the whole thing?'

He stares into his mug of beer as if trying to read his future in the dregs at its bottom. 'I don't know, Niccolò. That's not my decision to make. But I'm certain that Soderini will never put the money in to do what Leonardo's asking for here. He won't because he can't. The Signoria is flat broke. We can't even pay the labourers we've already hired, never mind another four or five hundred of them.'

'Another tax?' I suggest.

'You're joking! There'd be a rebellion. We'd be hanged.'

I sigh, knowing Biagio is right, and listen to the rain as it smashes down ever more loudly onto the tavern roof. Inside, people cough and complain: the fire isn't drawing; the smoke drifts in thick clouds through the room.

'This weather isn't going to help either,' Biagio adds, somewhat unhelpfully.

'But if the project fails . . .'

'Salviati will have our blood. Yes, I know.'

I put my thumbs to my temples. Alamanno Salviati has been waiting to get revenge on me ever since his plot to lure me into treachery was foiled in Imola; now he has the perfect opportunity. I watch my friend as he reads despairingly through Leonardo's notes. 'So what can we do?' I ask.

Biagio shrugs; lifts his palms; turns down the corners of his mouth: the Florentine dumbshow for 'fucked if I know'.

A huge crack of thunder shakes the tavern walls; God pisses contemptuously onto the square outside. Biagio gulps down his ale and puts his coat on. 'Well, I don't know about you, Niccolò, but I'm going to run home before Florence turns into Venice.'

Venice   *3 October, 1504*

DOROTEA: Rain patters softly at the window and I look out at the canal below; a single gondolier floating silently past, black against the lead-coloured water. 'Another hand, my dear?' my sister-in-law asks. 'Or are you feeling too tired?' I smile. It is six o'clock in the afternoon: even in my current state, I don't think I will be retiring to bed just yet. I sit down at the card table and stroke my swollen belly, and watch as a new hand is dealt to me. And, in that ordinary, banal, perfectly dull moment, it comes to me with a sudden startling force: how happy I am.

I remember when I was young – it was only three or four years ago, but it seems a lifetime away – swearing that the one thing I would never do with my life was waste it playing cards in beautifully furnished drawing-rooms. And yet this is more or less how my life has turned out, and I feel no disappointment at all.

I suppose what I failed to see, back then, was how quickly excitement can grow stale; how close disappointment can feel to relief. But, above all, I never imagined *this*: the gentle kick and roll of new life inside me. I have known about my pregnancy now for four months or more – the baby is due early in the new year – and yet every morning, without fail, I wake up amazed by the shape of my body, by the thought of what has happened to me and what will happen soon.

Stefania wrote to me last week, asking if I was afraid. She is expecting too, and reading between her beautifully calligraphed lines, I believe she is in a terror of the pain, the possibility of dying. Logically, I ought to feel the same, but I don't – not at all. I don't know why, really. I just have a feeling that all will be well.

It is astonishing, the love one can feel for a creature that does not, in a sense, even exist yet. Already, my love for this child is vast, it is oceanic; how great will it be when I can finally see and hold my baby; when it cries and smiles and speaks to me? No one who is loved like that can die, I think; no one who loves like that can die.

I pick up my cards, study and reorder them. I look around at the other faces at the table. I smell the sweet smoke of the smouldering cedar logs in the hearth. I listen to the rain at the window. I wait for my husband to return from work and kiss me lightly on the cheek. I think dimly of the past – of Leonardo and Niccolò and Cesare, of castles and armies and ballrooms – and I sigh with contentment.

My sister-in-law looks at me sharply. 'Good hand, my dear?'

Chinchilla, Spain

CESARE: Through the arrowslit, I watch falcons circle and swoop. Through the arrowslit – the grey plain below, the grey sky above.

I listen – only the wind. The sound of God breathing. Is He watching me?

379

HEY! Are You watching me? Well, fuck You. Fortune, fate, God or chance – You used to be my friend. Now You've betrayed me. You've destroyed me. You've left me here to rot, You bastard.

I pace my small dark cell. I sit in the only chair. I lie on the only bed. I stare through the only arrowslit. I am served by the only servant. Haunted by the only ghost.

My dead brother, Juan. All day and all night, he stands and stares. I am here to be tried for his murder.

I stare right back at him. Fuck you, Juan. I feel no regret, no remorse. He was in my way – so I removed him. We must all make sacrifices for the family.

A knock at the door. My servant enters. He says: 'One of your trunks has arrived, my lord.'

He drags the trunk into my cell. I wave my hand – he goes. I unlock the trunk, open the lid.

Inside – no gold. No cash or jewels. No papers or poisons, no swords or guns. Nothing of value.

Inside – only junk. Silk robes and fur capes. Two squashed hats. Velvet fucking bedcurtains. And a hundred carnival masks.

I remember – a gift from Isabella d'Este. The Marchioness of Mantua salutes Duke Valentino – on his glorious triumph in Senigallia. The first of January, 1503. Less than two years ago.

At the time, I thought it was nothing. I thought it was just the beginning. But now, looking back – that was the zenith. That was the peak of the mountain.

I take out the masks – spread them across the cold stone floor. A hundred white faces look back at me. Happy or sad, evil or good – all white, all dead.

I see Vitellozzo. I see Oliverotto. I see Donna Paolo. I see Ramiro. I see Juan.

I look through all the faces ... till I come to my own. There it is – my deathmask.

I put it to my face. Imagine being dead, imagine being forgotten. I hold my breath. Hear God breathing.

HE will always be among us. HE'll endure, while I rot and vanish.

How do I feel? Look in the mirror – into my own eyes. What do I see? Fear and disgust. Hatred and anger. DEFIANCE.

I rip the mask from my face – hurl it through the arrow-slit. Watch it fly, like a white falcon. Watch it fall, glimmer, vanish into the grey abyss.

Fuck you, ghosts. Fuck you, fate. Fuck you, Fortune. Fuck you, chance. And fuck You, God – I'm not dead yet.

Florence   *4 October, 1504*

LEONARDO: I cannot sleep. Rain thunders down onto the roof and lightning flashes through cracks in the shutters, illuminating my room (the foot of my bed, the shrouded easel, the empty birdcage and its open door) with a ghostly urgency. *This is what you are*, the storm seems to insist. *This is what your life is. Look at it – look at yourself.*

I am awake, but I feel like a man in a dream. Thunder rolls through the sky like barrels pushed down a staircase, and rivers of rainwater run down the insides of the walls. When the storm is over, I must ask the builder to repair the holes in the roof. The cat yowls, panic-stricken, from under the bed. I try to calm it – reach out my hand to stroke its head – but it only hisses and retreats further into the darkness.

I decide to get up and walk around. I light a lamp. I drink some water. I take the lamp through to the main room and, climbing onto the platform, I study small details of the cartoon on the wall. As far as I can tell, no water is leaking through here to damage the paper, to blur my sharp lines. I look at the central image of the battle – the men's grimacing faces, the horses' stamping hooves – and then I climb down off the platform. In my mind, the picture is already finished. I am supposed to complete the cartoon and then paint it on the wall of the Great Hall, so that it may last through the ages, inspiring the city's leaders with its example of Florentine glory. But that labour seems to me a pointless and dreary exercise, and I must scale a high wall of dread and boredom before I can even begin.

to reflect is noble, to realise is servile

I put on the fur cape that the Duke Valentino gave me, put out the lamp and let myself out of the street door. Opening it requires all of my strength, but it blows shut with a wild banging that almost takes my fingers off. I lock the door and catch my breath as I turn into the full fury of the storm. The wind blows me sideways – it roars in my ears, blocks up my throat, brings tears to my eyes. The rain soaks my clothes before I have even crossed the square. I walk in spurts, in zigzags – slow left and fast right. In this way I finally, somehow, make it through the black howling to the riverside.

There is no one else here – no prostitutes, no thieves, no Officers of the Night. The storm has cleansed the streets of all other dangers. Alone I stand, gripping a treetrunk, and stare at the Arno, which boils and seethes like the ocean itself. In fitful bursts of lightning I see the water lifted into the air in the shape of a great belltower. I see it crash down, roar up again. I can hardly breathe. This is the most terrible and beautiful thing I have ever seen. The battle I have drawn seems suddenly feeble, meaningless. This – *this* – is the fury of the prime mover. Nature, not mankind. This is what I must conquer, defy.

to uncloud the light beyond – to look God in the eyes

After some time, I zigzag back through the tempest and pull open the door of my lodgings. Rain and wind chase me home. I lock the storm out and breathe the still dry air in grateful gulps. Shivering, I undress and dry myself. I must be mad – what kind of a fool goes out on a night like this? But I feel more alive, more *awake*, than I have felt in many years.

It is nearly dawn, and the storm receding, before my heart finally stops racing and I fall asleep. For the first time since that winter in Imola, I dream that I am flying. Strange, how real it seems – I can feel the wind beneath my wings. I can see my shadow below me, moving over lakes and fields.

near Pisa   *5 October, 1504*

NICCOLÒ: It is nearly midday when our carriage reaches Riglione. We get out, and are greeted by Captain Guidicci. He is not as friendly as he was the last time we saw him – more than a year ago – after Leonardo sweet-talked him into agreeing to the Arno project. Now our scheme is in ruins: the captain must think us charlatans; he must blame us for all the chaos and destruction that lies below on the flooded plain. Stiffly, he points out the smashed weir, the collapsed ditches, the sunken farms. He does not need to mention the bloated, floating corpses or the grim-faced soldiers carrying them away on stretchers.

Leonardo is silent. He looks like he is still in a state of shock. He has not spoken since I told him – as we set off from Florence in the carriage this morning – about the eighty lives lost in the flood: the men had been on boats which were guarding the ditches from the Pisans.

I say to Captain Guidicci what I said to Leonardo on the carriage journey: that it is not our fault. We made clear and precise recommendations, and those recommendations were ignored. Captain Guidicci looks embarrassed; he does not reply. We walk down to the bend of the river, our boots and leggings soon saturated and stinking in the thick mud, and Leonardo mutters under his breath as he studies the remains of the ditches: 'Not even half the required depth! Perhaps the fool thought if he made two of them, he could just add the two depths together? Such an opinion cannot exist in a brain of much reason, but . . .'

By the time we finish our inspection, our limbs are weary and our hearts numb. Leonardo and I say a cold farewell to the captain and take shelter in the same tavern where we ate and drank so happily last summer. The innkeeper recognises us – and scowls. I begin to explain that what happened is not our fault, but then I realise I am wasting my breath. Our fault or not, we will take the blame. Or *I* will, anyway. The gonfalonier told me yesterday that someone must be sacrificed, and the look in his eyes and the tone of his voice told me that I was that someone.

Picking disconsolately at his bean salad, Leonardo quotes Aristotle: 'Man merits praise or blame solely in consideration of what it is in his power to do or not to do.'

'Unfortunately,' I say, 'the world is not as wise as that great philosopher.'

'You will lose your job, Niccolò?'

'Yes. For a few weeks at least. Until the storm, so to speak, has blown over.'

'What will you do?'

'Oh, go to our place in the countryside. Get plenty of fresh air, you know . . . spend time with Marietta and the kids. And possibly write a poem: my great epic of Florentine history.'

'A great epic – in a few weeks?'

'Well, when I say Florentine history, I just mean the last ten years. One shouldn't be too ambitious.'

'Shouldn't one?' He looks out of the window. 'No . . . perhaps one shouldn't. And yet . . .'

'I was speaking only for myself, Leonardo. What will you do?'

'Oh, I am . . . working on something at the moment.'

'Other than the fresco, you mean?'

'Yes. Do you promise not to tell anyone, Niccolò?'

'Of course.'

He stares down at his hands. 'I am going to fly.'

I laugh, and then realise he isn't joking. 'To fly?'

'Like a bird.'

'With . . . wings?'

'Yes. It is a problem I have been studying for many years, but I think, now, that I may have found the solution. You see – a bird is a machine working according to mathematical laws. It lies within the power of man to reproduce this machine with all its motions, but not with as much power. What such a manmade machine lacks is the *spirit* of the bird, and it is this spirit that must be counterfeited by man.'

I stare at him. 'Has any man flown before?'

'Not as far as I know. Many have tried though. Only last year, Giovanbattista Danti crashed onto a church roof in Perugia. But he was following too slavishly the design of the bird, I think. Because when I said I wish to fly "like a bird", that was only a half-truth. In fact, it will be more like the flight of a bat – the wings not feathered, but membraneous . . .'

Leonardo goes on and on in this vein, his morning's sadness and guilt forgotten in the rush of enthusiasm that overtakes him, and I watch him with incredulity. How did I ever become friends with such a being? He is extraordinary, unique. It's also possible that he's completely barking mad.

We finish our meal, pay the innkeeper, and walk back to our carriage. Suddenly something occurs to me: pricks me with anxiety and sadness. I wonder if this will be the last time I see my friend. I wonder if he is about to fly out of my life for ever. 'Leonardo, you *are* planning on finishing the fresco, aren't you?' The gonfalonier will never forgive me if my esteemed friend lets us down twice over.

He smiles: an odd, unreadable smile. 'This is my plan, yes. But as we both know, Niccolò, plans may very easily go astray. Two years ago, when you and I first met in Imola, who would have thought that we would end up here together? Who would have thought that Dorotea would be happily married to her Venetian captain, or that the duke with all his money and connections and ambition would lie powerless and forgotten in a Spanish jail?'

I nod: he has a point.

Leonardo looks up at the grey sky swirling menacingly, mysteriously above us. 'We make our plans. We follow our dreams. We battle our enemies. We love our friends. We burn with so much passion and desire. But in the end, we are like flakes of ash ... we go where the wind blows us, don't we?'

Fortune's Smile
(1505–1516)

43

LEONARDO: We leave the inn at Fiesole before dawn and ride slowly up Monte Ceceri. It is a warm, dry, silver-grey morning. I ride my horse beside Tommaso's mule and the two of us talk about wind directions, emergency landings. Ahead of us, Salai supervises the four servants who walk the mules that pull the machine.

the great bird

It is mounted on a wheeled platform and held in place by ropes. Gusts of wind move it from side to side so it seems to have a restless desire to be up, to be gone, to float free from its earthly shackles.

the great bird will take its first flight above the back of Swan Mountain, filling the universe with amazement, filling all the chronicles with its fame, and bringing eternal glory to the nest where it was born

Salai turns back towards us occasionally and cracks jokes. He asks me whether I have made my will, and how much money he will receive in the case of my death. 'I refuse to answer you,' I say. 'I don't want you slashing my wings just to get your hands on my ducats.' We all laugh.

By the time we reach the peak of Monte Ceceri, the silver land is shining green, the grey sky polished like a vast turquoise. We rest, and eat the modest picnic of tomatoes, bread and goat's cheese that we brought with us. Salai lies back in the long grass. Tommaso inspects the joints and wings and harness. And I stand alone on the edge of the hill, looking down over miles and miles of fields and woods – and the single great lake, where several servants wait in rowing-boats, in case I am forced to land in the water. Then I lift my eyes to the sky and watch the other birds, my fellow fliers – admiring their mechanics, envying their freedom, imagining how it will feel finally to be as they are.

I am fifty-three years old, but I feel like a child again.

to carve my name in air

Tommaso stands up next to me. He licks his fingertip and holds it to the wind. Gusts seem to swirl all around us, not to blow steadily from a single direction. I do not mention this, and neither does Tommaso. Better to concentrate on what we can control. I ask him about the machine and he replies that all is well – it wasn't damaged on the journey.

'Then everything's ready?'

'When you are, master.'

I close my eyes. I take a deep breath. I open my eyes again. I nod.

Tommaso straps me in. The silk cords are, by necessity, very tight around my chest. Strange, how one must be constricted in order to gain one's freedom. I wear my sun-glasses because the best place to begin the flight is to the south, where a long gentle slope leads down to a sudden, vertical drop. The morning sun glares at me, filtered into sepia by the stained lenses. Tommaso guides me into the starting position and I stare ahead at the cliff-edge, the abrupt nothingness. The cords around my chest seem to grip even tighter.

'Are you ready, master?'

Well . . . am I?

'Yes,' I gasp.

'Go!'

I run, with Tommaso and Salai holding a wing each and sprinting alongside. The grass blurs beneath my feet, and I adjust their fall to miss the small rocks that litter the ground in front of me. The wind is roaring in my ears now. My sun-glasses are steamed up – I can see almost nothing.

'Free now!' Tommaso yells. It is the signal that he and Salai can follow me no further – they must let go of their wings and save themselves from the fatal fall. I am on my own.

Only ten yards or so now. I run, I gasp-breathe. My legs are tired, but my wings are lifting, pulling me upwards and gently lowering me to earth again and

fear rises

the earth is gone beneath my feet. I pedal air. I scream, but no sound comes out. My sun-glasses are ripped from my face by the gusting wind and the dazzle attacks my vision. I squint, my eyes watering. Am I falling? Am I going to die?

But no, the wings pull me upward again, and for the most sublime of moments I am hanging, as if held there by the hand of God, high up in the air. Just as I hoped, just as I dreamed. Mathematics made flesh – flesh made divine. *A miracle.* I can't rub the tears from my eyes, but I can see, through the blurring, the sun and the bright sky – I can look into God's face, into His eyes.

uncloud the light beyond

I am flying! I try to yell with joy, but the wind chokes the words in my throat. I can feel the sun's heat on my face now, the sweat pouring beneath my clothing. I can hear the machine's leather joints creaking, the wind howling in my ears. My arms ache, my back aches. I feel as though I have balls of cotton in my ears.

I wish I could lean down to see more clearly the land far below me. I twist my neck to one side, hoping to gauge

where I am, and then the moment is over – God closes His
eyes – and all I feel is panic, fear, plunging, out of control,
the weight of the machine dragging me down fast towards
the ground. I see nothing, hear only howls, shrieks, roars –
and in the fury of the fall I think of storms, of battle. I think
of the half-painted fresco on the wall of the Great Hall and
know I will never finish it. And I know as the ground rears
invisibly closer, as I fight to stop the right wing tipping me
up and over, I know that I can never escape the failures of
the past – the flakes of paint on the ground, the clay Horse
destroyed by arrows, the bronze melted down to make
cannons, the notebooks unfinished, the questions unan-
swered, the tethers of money and law, the disappointments
of love, the witherings of age, the inevitability of death, and
the lack of time the lack of time the lack of and as the dark-
blue lake turns vast below and smashes into me and I

dark pain relief floating not falling drowning dying dark

The heavy wings are cut loose and I am dragged from the
water by unknown hands, and turned onto my side. Cool
water pours from my mouth. I gasp, cough, breathe again.
The solid flesh of the ground under my fingertips, the massive drag of it – our bodies like iron filings on a magnet,
held here by a desire we cannot escape.

I look up at the sky – at the silhouetted falcons hovering,
their miracle intact, and I know that I am for ever

what man lacks is the spirit of the bird

earthbound.

44

CESARE: There's the signal – two owl-like hoots. I stand at the arrowslit. A rope snakes down before me.

The servant goes first. I watch him slowly descend. I watch him stop – freeze and dangle.

I pull the rope hard. Fucking move, arsehole – time is running out. They might raise the alarm. They might catch me.

I pull the rope again. I hear a low scream. I see the servant gone. About fucking time.

I crawl through the arrowslit – slide down the rope. Then I stop.

FUCK.

Now I understand – why the servant froze and dangled. There's not enough rope. It runs out here . . . thirty feet above the ground. What now? Climb back up or risk the fall? Think fast . . .

Noises above. Lights above. The alarm's been raised. I look down. The ground swims. Forty feet maybe. I sweat and swallow – get ready to . . .

FALL.

The rope's been cut. Earth rushes up at me. I close my eyes – wait for death.

Thud. Fuck. Burning pain – in my legs, chest, back. Can't move. Can't see. Something's broken.

I hear voices in the dark. Feel hands lift me up. Men carry me. Blind and bonesmashed.

They put me on a horse. Hands hold me in place. Screaming burning fucking PAIN.

I hear breathing – horse and man. I hear yells, screams
above. I hear a musket shot behind – the guards have killed
the servant.

Hoofclatter and windrush. Then I hear a voice say: 'We're
out, my lord. You are free.'

Villalón – Pamplona   *27 November–3 December, 1506*

Drifting and dreaming. Shifting and screaming. Waves of
opium and waves of PAIN.

My bones heal – slowly. My bones heal – badly. My back's
fucked. I walk like a cripple. Look in the mirror – hurl it
against the wall. Smashed glass everywhere.

But fuck horror. Fuck pity. Fuck the ugly hunchback in
the mirror. I was the most handsome man in Italy – but
fuck regret.

I'm alive. I'm free. Free to wreak my revenge.

But first I must escape Spain. This country is my prison.
Here I'm a criminal – hunted everywhere. I must get to
Navarre, in the mountains. There, I will be safe.

As soon as I can walk round the garden, I say: 'Let's
go.' Me and two guides – Martin and Miguel. Good men,
simple men. They would die for me. They might have to.

We ride to the coast. We ride HARD. By the time we
reach Castres, the horses are fucked. We abandon them –
walk to Santander.

Lowgrey and wavestorms. We talk to boat owners. I say:
'We must leave tonight.' The owners say: 'Are you kidding?
Look at that sea!'

We sleep in the inn. Wake before dawn. Walk through
the dark – to the port. The waves are lower. I give the boat

owner a bag of gold. He says: 'I must be mad.' He takes us out.

But out of the port, the wind blows stronger. The waves get bigger. The boat owner gets nervous. He gives me back the money. Docks the boat at some fishing village – many miles from Bernico.

Two days pass before we find mules. We ride them HARD. The muleteer sobs in our dust: 'Don't ruin my beasts!' But fuck the muleteer. Fuck his beasts.

We ride through winding mountain paths. Snowcold and muscleshiver. We sleep in caves. Our toes go blue.

At night I see Death – smiling, friendly. 'Come with me, Cesare. Take my hand. All this shit – it's just not worth it.'

I tell Death: 'Soon, but not yet. I've got places to go, people to kill. Wait till I'm thirty-two. Give me another year.'

Next morning – the snow ends, the sun shines. We reach the border of Navarre. We ride down into the valley. Enter the gate. Go to the castle. See the king and lift my hood.

The king puts his hand to his chest. The king says: 'God's blood! It's Cesare Borgia – like the devil himself.'

Viana, Spain   *12 March, 1507*

Windhowl and raindrum. Voices calling: 'The enemy is here!' My eyes snap open. I get up – look out the window. An army marching in the halfdark.

I call my servants. I am dressed in full armour. Yes – fucking YES. Weeks I've been waiting – for the enemy to show. Weeks wasted in this shitty little war.

But now's my chance. I must defeat the enemy – then leave this kingdom. Build an army and march on Italy. Take my revenge.

But first I must deal with NOW. I go outside. I mount my horse. I hold aloft the double-headed lance – a gift from the King of Navarre. I yell to my men: 'Follow me!'

I ride HARD. I ride FAST. Rainspit in my eyes. Mudslips under hooves. I look ahead – three knights waiting for me. I look around – where are my men? I see them behind – a blur on the horizon.

Caught in an ambush. But fuck it – too late now. I won't back down. Only six months left anyway. *Aut Caesar aut nihil.*

I charge the knights. Wield the double lance. Slash and smash. One knight down – his head caved in. Two to go – come on, you fucks! Do you know who I am?

I raise my arm – the double lance high. My victim's eyes – filled with fear. And then . . . PAIN. I look down – a lance in my flesh. The blade deep inside me.

I fall from the horse. Lie in the mud. Blood on my armour, rain in my eyes. Death appears – watching, waiting.

I climb to my feet. Blink rain, breathe. Each second an hour. Pull the lance from my flesh – screaming pain, pouring blood.

I squint through the rain – a dozen of them now. Moving towards me, their swords raised.

Death smiles. He reaches out his hand.

45

NICCOLÒ: I come out to meet you at the gate. We embrace: it's been a long time. You admire the view: yes, those are my vines and my olive trees, and yes, technically, that is my stream at the bottom of the hill. Other properties? No: what you see is what you get here. After all those years walking through the corridors of power, this is my inheritance: a wretched little kingdom of horse manure and childhood memories, melancholy in the fast-fading autumn light.

You clap me on the shoulder in an attempt to keep the conversation cheerful. You ask about my lovelife here in the countryside. I crack a joke about goats: you laugh and say, Oh Niccolò, you haven't changed a bit! But I think we both know you're lying. It's true I don't have many wrinkles for a man of forty-four, and that my body is as skinny as ever. But look closer; look in my eyes. That light-hearted, mock-the-world glint is gone from them, can't you tell? I am weary now, and wary: you have the slightly uncomfortable feeling that I might start to weep at any moment.

So what have you missed? What's happened to me? Well, quite a lot. Let me see. The high point of my career – the proudest moment of my whole life – came in the summer of 1509, when I led the Florentine militia into Pisa, finally putting an end to that long and dreary war. There were bonfires in Florence for two days afterwards and my friends all sent me congratulatory letters. That was a time of hope and exultation – for me personally, and for Florence. Looking back now, we were guilty of complacency. My militia took Pisa so easily that people believed it was invincible, and the gonfalonier decided he didn't need to spend any more money on it. This is a very Florentine failing: we laugh in the summer and weep in the winter.

The winter finally arrived last year, when papal forces – a band of hardened, bloodthirsty Spanish mercenaries – massacred my poor militia at Prato. Soon after that, Piero Soderini, showing all his usual bravery and determination, fled the city, and the Medici took over. I lost my job. I wept that evening, I don't mind admitting. Agostino and Biagio were sacked the same day, and the three of us drowned our sorrows together in The Three Kings. All night we talked about the past – our shared, glorious, yearned-for past – because the present and the future looked so grey and uninviting. I thought it was the worst thing that could ever happen to me. How wrong I was.

At the beginning of this year, a conspiracy against the Medici was discovered. I had nothing to do with it, but that did not prevent me being arrested, imprisoned and questioned. In the dungeons of the Bargello, they tortured me: I endured six drops of the *strappado*, and never accused anyone. I was proud of myself for that. Afterwards they shut me up in a tiny, dark cell and left me to wonder what the others might have said about me; whether I was to be freed, locked up for years, or executed in the square below, where I saw the traitor Bernardo di Bandino Baroncelli hanged when I was a young boy.

I spent a lot of time thinking about the past while I was in prison, and a lot of time thinking about Fortune. I remembered something that Leonardo said to me once: that Fortune is like the eagle in Aesop's fable, who picks up a tortoise because the silly creature wishes to fly. The tortoise soars high above the earth – for a brief time he lives his dreams – and then he is dropped to the ground: his shell is smashed to pieces, and his flesh is devoured by the eagle's cruel beak. It seems a very apt metaphor to me.

I was released from prison two weeks later – not because I was judged innocent, but because Cardinal de' Medici was elected pope (he took the name Leo X) and a general amnesty was declared in Florence as a mark of celebration. I walked out into a city of bonfires and fireworks. Marietta and the children emerged from the crowds and smothered me with hugs and kisses. The smoke got in my eyes and made me weep. 'We thought you were going to be killed,' they cried. 'You weren't the only ones,' I replied.

I shiver. It's getting dark now, and cold: come inside. Yes, these are my kids. Four boys and a girl: we have been lucky in that respect, at least. Marietta gave birth to another girl in May, but the child died after three days. We were all sad, of course, but – in a guilty way – also relieved. You know how it is: one less mouth to feed. Ah, you hear that screaming? Marietta hasn't mellowed much with age. Let's go somewhere quieter and more private, shall we?

This is my study: my refuge and sanctuary. You mustn't think too badly of Marietta: she is a good mother and a capable housewife; I could have done much worse. And yes, of course I love my family, of course they are a source of comfort and happiness to me, and you must never tell anyone what I am about to say to you, but – in all honesty – if my wife and children were all I had in the world, I would slit my wrists now. Women can live entirely for their loved ones, but we men . . . we must always have more; we must always have our dreams, our battles. But anyway, sit down, have some wine. It's a bit rough, I'm afraid: I can't afford to buy the fine stuff any more. This is made from our own vines.

So what has happened since my release? Not much. I enjoy the residue of life, which seems like a dream. I have a pleasant enough routine: I get up before dawn, prepare some birdlime, and go out with a bundle of cages. In the woods, I catch a few thrushes, and take them back to the house, where Marietta cooks them. I go to a spring in the woods and read some Dante or Petrarch or Ovid: I read about their amorous passions, and remember my own – Cecilia, Dorotea, Angelina and a hundred others – and these reflections make me happy for a while. (Cecilia is a grandmother now: I see her around sometimes; she has a moustache.)

After lunch, I go to the inn for the rest of the day, to drink and lose at chess and argue about the world, and when evening comes I return home and enter this room: my study. On the threshold I take off my workday clothes, covered with mud and dirt, and put on the garments I used to wear when I was an envoy. Thus fitted out, I step inside the venerable courts of the ancients, where I nourish myself on that food which alone is mine and for which I was born: the subtle art of politics. And for four hours at a time, I feel no boredom, I forget all my troubles, I do not dread poverty, and I am not terrified by death. You see, it is only in this silence, in this exile, this sad solitude of mine, that I have been able to hear and understand what History has been whispering to me all these years.

I am working on two books. The first and greater is the *Discourses on the First Ten Books of Titus Livy*, which I am writing in the margins of my father's book: the one I picked up for him from the printer's when I was seventeen. This is the book that will make my name; which will, I hope, echo down the centuries; a book about how to build and maintain a republic. But, in addition to the *Discourses*, I have also composed a short study, which I call *The Prince*. It is a kind of handbook for a new ruler. It does not say what a prince *ought* to do, in an ideal and nonexistent universe, as do all the other books written in the past; it says how things are now, in reality. It may not surprise you too much to learn that the perfect exemplar I have chosen for a new prince is the Duke Valentino.

I have thought of him often recently: of that dark firelit room in Urbino, where he first impressed me with his leopard's eyes; of the castle in Imola, where he built his army; of the joy and triumph in his voice when he told me what he had done in Senigallia. I do not think of his decline and madness in Rome the following summer, but of what might have been, had Fortune dictated otherwise.

Not everyone will like my short book, and I do not expect its fame to last beyond my death; but for a prince I think it may prove invaluable. And, who knows, perhaps they will reward its humble author by appointing him in some kind of advisory capacity? How sweet it would be to walk once more through those corridors of power, to climb those broad shallow stairways . . .

It is of this I think as I get in bed with Marietta, who farts softly and turns over in her sleep. I close my eyes and drift into unconsciousness, and I dream of what might have been, and what might still be, perhaps, one day.

Florence   *31 August, 1516*

I stand before the familiar black façade of the Palazzo Medici. Holding the leather-bound, gold-lettered volume of *The Prince*, I present myself to the guard and am shown through into the main courtyard. I am here to see Lorenzo II (grandson of Lorenzo the Magnificent), the new ruler of Florence, in the hope that he will condescend to give me a job.

The guard leads me upstairs, along a corridor of mirrors, and into a large marbled gallery. In a throne at the far end lounges young Lorenzo, surrounded by laughing sycophants. I take one look at the haughty, stupid expression on the prince's face and my heart sinks. Still, it is too late to back out now. I present him with my book. I kneel down, kiss his feet, and watch as he turns to the first page. In my mind I see the words he is now reading: words addressed to him personally:

> Those who desire to win the favour of princes generally endeavour to do so by offering them those things which they themselves prize most, or such as they observe the prince to delight in most. Wishing now myself to offer to your Magnificence some proof of my devotion, I have found nothing amongst all I possess that I hold more dear or esteem more highly than the knowledge of the actions of great men, which I have acquired by long experience of modern affairs and a continued study of ancient history . . .

He is yawning before he has reached the bottom of the first page, and I am resigned to failure. But then suddenly Lorenzo's eyes light up. What's this? Has some sparkling phrase of mine caught the young prince's imagination?

Alas, no . . . his eyes are focused *above* the page. I turn to look as a guard brings two racing-dogs into the room: slender beasts, straining at their leashes. 'Magnificent,' the prince breathes, tossing aside the book and striding towards the dogs.

I bow, unseen, and back off silently into the shadows. Walking swiftly through the corridor, I catch sight of my face in one of the mirrors on the wall. A small, balding man smiles back at me. His smile is thin, bitter, sarcastic, but not entirely without mirth. I must laugh at the iniquities of the world, his smile says, because if I didn't, I would cry.

I walk downstairs, through the courtyard, into the street. It is sweltering, and the air stinks. The Via Larga swarms with the poor mass of humanity. I look at them and shake my head: why on earth did I ever expect justice or fairness from a world inhabited by this rabble? People are selfish, cowardly, greedy, gullible and stupid. For a brief and lucid moment I see into the future: the *Discourses* mouldering unread; *The Prince* burnt on pyres and consulted, secretly, by men in thrones; my name become a byword for sinister trickery.

I sigh, and look up into the sky. Fortune smirks down at me; she blows a raspberry in my face.

Afterword

This book is a fiction based on historical fact. Leonardo *did* work for Borgia in 1502–3; Machiavelli *was* in Imola, Cesena and Senigallia at the same time; and there is evidence that Machiavelli and Leonardo worked on the Arno project together. Even Dorotea was a real person, although all we know of her is that she was abducted by Borgia, that she disappeared for a couple of years, went to join a nunnery in 1503, and in the end settled in Venice with her husband. The relationships between the four of them are almost completely invented, although Machiavelli's infatuation with Borgia is well documented, not only in *The Prince* but in his dispatches to the Signoria while in Romagna and Rome.

I've tried to use historical facts and primary source material whenever I could, even in the most fictional chapters. For example, Machiavelli really did pick up the bound copy of Livy's *History of Rome* for his father when he was seventeen, and the price really was three bottles of wine and a bottle of vinegar. There are hundreds of authentic details such as this dotted throughout the text: to mention just a couple more, Borgia did make Leonardo a gift of a fur cape given him by the King of France, and Machiavelli did order a new mantle to be sent from Florence while he was in Imola, along with a case of fine wine.

Machiavelli's voice is based upon his books and poems, and above all on his letters, which are very frank and funny. (Several of Biagio Buonaccorsi's more colourful phrases are taken directly from these letters.) Leonardo's voice is based largely upon his notebooks, many phrases from which I've adapted and interpolated into the text. Borgia's voice is almost entirely imagined – since he left practically no written records at all. The line about 'the ground is burning' is a direct quotation taken verbatim from Machiavelli's dispatches, however, so that gives a flavour of Borgia's thinking and vocabulary. The rather bombastic-sounding message on Leonardo's passport is another example of Borgia's authentic voice.

I have contradicted history in a couple of sections: most notably, the Salviati plot with the stamp was invented. In reality, Machiavelli had no power to make an alliance with Borgia (although he certainly wanted to), but when I wrote this part of the story in a historically accurate way, it fell flat. I have also altered a few dates, usually only by a few days or weeks, in order to help the narrative flow.

For anyone interested in delving deeper into the novel's historical background, I would suggest the following books as being the most reliable and enjoyable on their respective subjects:

Leonardo da Vinci: The Flights of the Mind by Charles Nicholl
Cesare Borgia: His Life and Times by Sarah Bradford
The Life of Niccolò Machiavelli by Roberto Ridolfi

The only history in English about these three men's crossed destinies is *The Artist, the Philosopher and the Warrior* by Paul Strathern.

My thanks to Jennifer Custer at A. M. Heath and Walter Donohue at Faber, who made helpful contributions to the final revision of the book; to my editors Helen Francis and Lee Brackstone for all their advice and encouragement; and most particularly to my agent Victoria Hobbs, who read the book more often than anyone would want to, and was there for me from the beginning to the end.

I would also like to thank diplomacy expert Geoff Berridge, who kindly sent me his e-book edition of *Machiavelli's Legations*, which was otherwise unavailable and without which this novel would not have been the same.

S.B., Italy and France, September 2007–March 2010